EATING THE FORBIDDEN FRUIT

ROLAND SATO PAGE

DEDICATION

I dedicate this novel to my mother, Okaasan, who unfortunately isn't present to witness its completion. I know you're looking down and hope you are proud. Miss you something terrible. I also dedicate the completion to my wife, who encouraged me to finish what I started. I know I have been difficult at times, but now when in doubt, you can read how much I adore you. You are the last face I want to see when I depart this world. Everything I do is for you and my children.

-Roland Sato Page-

INTRODUCTION

Today is a bitter cold morning. Even though I'm inside, I can hear the frigid air against the tall windows; it is as if the glass is literally cracking. The room is so quiet, the loudest noise is the shuffling of papers by a courtroom clerk. Time seems to be moving slowly.

I motion to my wife pointing to my wrist. I whisper, "What time is it?"

She puts up her hands showing nine fingers. I rub my face thinking: *9 a.m.? Shit 9 o'clock seemed almost thirty minutes ago.* I attempt to adjust my sight to read the old clock on the wall, but it is too far away. I think to myself that it's the kind of clock that hung above the chalkboard back in elementary school. Then I wish the impossible.

What I wouldn't do to have a time machine to go back to elementary school. Shit was so easy then.

I gaze around the courtroom noticing every little thing I have overlooked before today. I had been in this courtroom before for my arraignment, but I was in and out. I look over at the District Attorney's table and I notice an older white man mean mugging me tough. He's looking at me as if he caught me pissing on the side of his house. The DEA or FBI, I assume. I hear the sniffles of my mother and wife so I look back and smile showing them I'm a champ, I can handle this. Deep down the reality is I'm scared. And then it suddenly hits me. *Where the FUCK is my lawyer?*

Speaking of my lawyer, he deserves his own story. If you look up the word *cocky* in the dictionary, it will have his picture with a big ass grin. Sean Rosenbaum, the Michael Jordan of attorneys. And I didn't make that up. If you've been indicted with a crime and you need God on your side, Sean Rosenbaum is the closest you can get. Retaining a defense attorney like him naturally didn't come cheap. I kid you not, Sean smelled like money. I knew he was worth every penny because I was federally fucked.

Want to hear some crazy shit? At my arraignment, the Judge asked me to stand then he looked me in the eyes and said, "Mr. Page, if it were up to me, I would give you twenty years. You're a disgrace to law enforcement."

You might think I'm joking, but I fainted. As I lay near the bench, I could see the public pretender looking at me like he was thinking, *Are you serious?* He motioned to the judge with one finger, gesturing *one second*, trying to help me up. I wasn't getting up because in my mind I felt this motherfucker had it out for me. So now you feel me. Mr. Rosenbaum was a necessity.

Oh yeah. I didn't make a mistake when I mentioned the Judge snapped, "You are a disgrace to law enforcement?"

Here I sit, Roland Sato Lee Page, in the U.S. District Court for Eastern Missouri accused of conspiracy of drug trafficking and the distribution of cocaine. A former St. Louis Metropolitan Police Officer who got caught up. Now I know what you're probably thinking: *You lousy fuck. You were shaking motherfuckers down.* But that is so far from the truth. See I was just a guy who couldn't let go a part of my life that I buried long ago. I'm one of those guys who got through life thinking: *just this one time then I'm going to stop.* And then that one time bit me in the ass.

In the middle of my thoughts, the huge court door swung open and here comes Sean. I think to myself; *this dude needs his own theme music.* Maybe *Call Me* by Blondie or *Stayin' Alive* by the Bee Gees.

He sits down smiling, then out the blue says, "Damn that's a nice fucking suit."

A confused look comes over my face. "Sean man, my suit is the last thing on my mind."

He retorts, "Remember no matter what, always look good. Things will come out better. Presentation is everything Ro."

You know what? Deep down I agreed with him. So many years I got by because I looked good, avoiding the bullet of fate. I thought things came so easy if you looked good. Women, money, and success were for the chosen few. And I was one of the chosen, so I thought.

Sean leans over and whispers, "You got your speech together?"

I reply, "Yeah I'm good." Yet am I?

I lean back in my chair and gaze at the ceiling. *Where did I go wrong? How in the fuck did I get myself in this predicament?* I got to figure this out. *Think Ro. Think. When did you take the wrong road?* I began to daydream about the good ole days.

CHAPTER ONE

THE YEAR WAS 1971. I was six years old. The most joyous times at that age were backyard bar-b-ques. I enjoyed watching my pops lighting up the grill and explaining to me, over and over, that the key to great barbeque was the fire. It's those little things when you're a kid that you never forget. I also remember watching my pops pour *Miller Highlife Beer* in the barbeque sauce, then winking at me.

He'd ask, "You wanna sip?"

I'd smile and nod yes, making sure my mom wasn't around. Pops would get a kick at the face I would make after tasting the beer. It was so bitter, but I accepted a sip every time he offered. I'd wipe my mouth, then look up at this towering, dark complexioned man as if he was a God. My pops was my hero and he was invincible. He was a former master sergeant in the Army. He displayed medals on his wall from ceiling to the floor. After thirty some years of service and fighting in three wars, he had the medals to prove his service, dedication and skill.

He would catch me staring at him in amazement as he turned the meat with his hands. Shit I couldn't even get too close to the pit without getting burned. I admired this man. He was the toughest man alive to me.

Staring at my father, I hesitated for a second hoping I wasn't asking a dumb question. "Daddy what am I?"

He looked confused. "What you mean, papi?"

I said, "I wish I were dark like you. What am I? At school they call me a honky, sometimes a spic, and sometimes a chink. I want to know what *am I*?"

He laughed closing the pit and wiped off his hands with an old rag. He picked me up until I was face-to-face with him. "You're a Negro, just like your old man." With a big smile he said, "Be proud, papi, of who you are."

My ethnicity was still always a mystery to me. Politically correct term for races was oblivious to me at age six. I knew my father was dark with straight hair. My brothers and sisters talked of Indian descent. It saddened me to wonder if my pops was not my actual father. I used to stare in the mirror noticing my straight black hair and my light complexion. I hated it. At school being different wasn't a good thing in the early '70s. It seemed as if everybody made fun of me because I looked different. That was something I took personally because I felt it was disrespectful to my mother and her Japanese heritage.

Fumi Karasawa, my mother, a native of Osaka, Japan, journeyed to this country with my pops. She spoke little English yet made things happen. This woman was my heartbeat. I adored her dearly 'cause she made everything okay. If I had a stomach ache, my mom would rub my tummy and it would go away. If I had a headache, she would rub my neck and it would go away. I had the flu bug once and literally couldn't move. I had a temperature of 103 degrees. My mom lifted me up and carried me to the bathroom. She gave me a cool bath while brushing my hair. My mom possessed what I thought was supernatural healing powers.

I enjoyed listening to her tell me about my family in Japan. How she endured the bombing of Hiroshima. Often speaking on the racism she experienced after marrying a black man. She educated me without a classroom without realizing she was my teacher. Living in the U.S., my siblings and I never really learned the Japanese culture. Every now and then we picked up a few things here and there. Say for instance, when my mom changed my t-shirt she would say *"banzai"* in Japanese -which is like hooray in the English language. I would raise my hands to the sky and she would lift my shirt right off. It always followed with a kiss. On the flip side, Japanese discipline was no joke. Our daily tasks included cleaning the house and doing yard work. We folded the clothes down to the socks. In the mornings after I made my bed, it was checked. Mom had the assigning of chores down to a science. I wasn't exempt from a spanking now and then either. I must admit I was quite a bad shit at times. I feared making her mad 'cause she had a look that reminded me that she could give a ninja style ass whooping if I messed up. Fumi wasn't raising a soft child. She pushed me to be tough-something one might think my military father would have taught me. My mom was the glue that held me together.

The first day of grade school-back in 1971-was memorable. You know how the teacher makes every student stand, say their name, and what they want to be when they grow up? Well it was my turn and I was excited to share my future occupation.

I stood up and proudly blurted, "My name is Roland Sato Lee Page and I wanna be a pimp just like my daddy." The look on the teacher's face was priceless. Looking back, I imagined she thought, *"Where in the hell did this little fucker learn what a pimp is?"* Needless to say, it didn't take long for my mom to learn about my aspiration.

When I got home from school, I tried to take a nap thinking my mom wouldn't wake me up. It didn't work. I got my ass whooped.

She asked me, "Where did you learn about being a pimp?"

I kept shrugging my shoulders as if saying, "I don't know."

She whooped me some more until she figured out I wasn't going to snitch on my father.

Now my father wasn't really guilty. He never taught me the definition of a pimp, but he didn't have to. He exposed me to the lifestyle. After pops retired from the Army, he pursued a career as an entrepreneur. With an eighth grade education, his skills were limited. But boy my pops knew how to make bank.

He opened a bodega and pool hall in a harsh part of town. I often heard the grown-ups refer it as the *Hoe Stroll.* I never uttered the term because I remembered the ass whooping for uttering pimp and I wasn't going through that again.

It was called *Bob's Pool Hall & Bodega.* Titled after my father's nickname for Robert Napola Page. I enjoyed going to work with my pops playing tunes on the juke box, sneaking candy bars from the counter, and playing billiards with old cats who would let me win *'cause I was Bob's son.* I loved the attention and the title as *Lil Bob.* It made me feel important.

The one thing that caught my eye many times was the women who wore almost nothing and hung around the bodega. My pops always told me to stay away from the *nasty women*" He always referred to them as *hoes* to his friends and *nasty women* to me. Personally, I felt the title was unjust because a few of them were pretty to me. All of them were nice to me, giving me money, offering me hard candy. I never really got the reason why they loved hard candy until years later. It was used to camouflage their breath after they gave men oral pleasure.

So one Saturday afternoon, I wandered a bit down the block. I saw a beautiful dark woman sporting a big red afro. I had to get a closer look 'cause she was wearing a very short skirt and her shirt was tied in a knot showing her belly. I got closer and closer watching her count her money. All I know is, it was a lot of money. She stopped counting and smiled at me. "What's your name, cutie?"

I mumbled, "Roland," blushing from cheek to cheek.

"You like money, Roland?"

I answered, "Yeah, a lot."

"Where did you get all that pretty hair?" She inquired.

I smiled, "I think my mama."

She could talk and chew gum at the same time, "Well sweetie I can tell you one thing. You're going be a fine pimp when you grow up." She then handed me a 10-dollar bill and rubbed her fingers through my hair. That blew my mind.

I suddenly heard my pops yell from down the street, "Bitch, get your hands out my son's hair."

She yelled back down the street, "I'm sorry, *daddy*, I didn't mean no harm."

I ran back down to the bodega, looking back at the woman switching away as her skirt shook from side to side.

My pops grabbed me by the arm, "Boy don't you ever let them hoes play in your hair." I shook my head *yes*, but at that moment, I knew things would come easy for me.

So you see, my pops never encouraged me to be a pimp. He exposed me unintentionally to the lifestyle. I witnessed the dice games in the back room, how my pops got money for running the house. I discovered what a crap game was at an early age. On a good night, my pops walked away with a stack of money in each pocket. He would always break off about twenty or thirty for me.

This hustler I knew as my father inspired me to be a better man than he. For that I respected him tenfold.

He'd say, "You see what I do to get money? Well you be better than me. Get your money the right way." He would rub my hair and ask, "Do you understand?"

I'd responded, "Yes."

As I got a bit older, I felt that life was going to be easy like I did that time the woman touched my hair. As a youngster I thought things got better as you get older. Money brings happiness was my belief. My mom continued to be the voice of reason, encouraging me to stay focused, go to school, and get a good job. I must admit, I had great surroundings besides the pool hall. My siblings were my mom's support unit and shared her same philosophy. *Work hard and achieve*. On the other hand, I wanted things to come easy.

Despite our differences we were a tight knit family. In no certain order I love all my brothers and sisters equally. I have fond memories of each and every one of them. They were all protective of me. I guess because I'm the youngest, yet I believe I am my father's child. *The fruit doesn't fall far from the tree* is so true. I was stubborn. A rebel without a cause.

My second oldest brother, Robert Page Jr., who is five years older than me, was more of a father figure to me than a sibling. He's an intellectual, a comedian, and the ultimate big brother. If anyone could have kept me cool, it would have been Robert or *"Goon-Goon,"* a nickname I gave him. Don't ask me why I named him that. It's not like he was ugly or something. I often gave people close to me the weirdest names. Goon-Goon was my educator from homework to the facts of life. I remember having a conversation about subtraction then he would suddenly switch to French kissing techniques.

All our conversations were entertaining even when he made up stories to scare me, like the *"Woman with the Half Head."* It was a story about a woman who had her head chopped in half for some apparent reason. At midnight her head would levitate roaming throughout the house, which was scary because our house wasn't big at all. Goon-Goon said that the only way to kill the woman was to put a silver spoon in her mouth. Now my family wasn't poor, but with six kids, genuine silverware was the last thing my mom was concerned with. I was so haunted by my brother's story that I stole a spoon from my neighbor's china cabinet. I never got the chance to kill the woman with the half head, and I don't think my brother really grasped that he sacred the shit out of me. Besides those irritating things big brothers do, his good intentions outweighed the bad. He and I shared a bedroom, so when I couldn't sleep, he would tell me good stories like Huckleberry Hound. *"Ole my darling, Ole my darling, ole my darling Clementine."* I recall the conversations that entertained me too. For example arguing who would win if Ultra Man and Johnny Sokko the Flying Robot fought. I enjoyed those nighttime talks.

Goon-Goon was also protective of me, making sure I was okay. Every winter the water at the back of the schoolyard would freeze over. For inner city kids like myself this was quite recreational-ice skating in the hood. During recess I was playing and someone pushed me from behind. I went straight through the ice. Talk about freezing cold, I felt like I had jumped into a pool of needles. My brother gave me a piggyback ride for several blocks in the bitter cold weather so I could change my clothes. For things like that, I will always value our bond. I never did find out who pushed me!

My sister Linda was the youngest girl of three and four years older than me, but the most mature out the bunch. She was my mother's eyes and ears during her absence. I wouldn't classify my sister as a snitch, because she never really told on us. Let's just say when she gave us advice, we wondered if we didn't listen would our mother find out what we did.

Say for instance-if I was doing something I had no business doing, Linda would say, "Now you know if mama finds out, she's going tear in your ass."

Usually I'd wait a second contemplating should I say, *"Go fuck yourself!"* or just listen? Most of the time I would just keep it moving and say, *"Okay."*.

Linda and Robert were close, I suppose because they were only a few years apart. They tried to involve me in most of their activities, but sometimes I felt left out. If we played superhero, Linda was Wonder Woman and Robert would be Superman. I would be like how about me?

"Oh yeah Roland, you're Robin."

Yep, the lamest character in the comics. Sometimes I would go along knowing I'm the little guy. Sometimes thinking I don't need this shit and find my own adventures.

One thing I appreciated about my sister is she wasn't selfish. Linda kept me in fashion when things got tight for my mom. You see pops made money, but pops had a gambling habit among other bad habits--extramarital relations for instance. I believe Linda always knew and just never said anything. I believe my mom possibly knew too but just spared my feelings.

My pops was hard on my sister and I never really knew why at that time. I would walk in on the middle of an argument between Linda and pops, and she would be ready to say something, then stop when she saw me. She was careful around me. She made it her duty to watch my mother's back. I admired her for that. I remember when my pops would try and make Linda forge my mom's signature on checks. When Linda refused. *Oh shit!* My pops would lose his mind. Linda would run out the house with no socks and shoes and wait down the block until my mom got home.

I would ask her, "Why don't you just sign the check, Linda?"

She would say, "Nope, that's part of mama's military money too." I would just shrug my shoulders.

My two oldest sisters Josie 12 years my senior and Patty 11 years my senior were never really around me because of our age difference. What I do remember, I sure enjoyed being around them because they spoiled the shit out of me. I knew what to do if things didn't go my way. If I felt left out of Robert and Linda's activities, I went to Josie with my bottom lip poked out. She would straight snap on both of them. If Goon-Goon was picking on me, I went to Patty, who happened to be a tomboy. No sweat, Patty put Goon-Goon in check.

Patty had those hands. Josie is the soft-hearted sister who didn't want to see me cry. I remembered when I accidentally set the kitchen closet on fire trying to roast mini marshmallows. I know it was equally fucked up as it sounds. I burned the entire closet, the crackers were toasted, and the canned goods were singed. Trying to go to sleep again, didn't work. My mom made me go in the yard to get my own switch. I grabbed the limp one it looked like it was ready to give. I was crying the entire time. I handed it to my mom; suddenly the damn switch seemed to gain life by getting thicker.

I thought *"What the hell?!"*

She tore my ass up. Josie grabbed the switch from my mom. I stopped crying for a moment only to start again, thinking, "Appreciate it, sis, but you're a damn fool for that."

Josie fell victim to my mom's ninja shoe skills.

Clunk.

There goes Josie.

All my sisters babied me to a certain extent. That's the effect I had when it came to the opposite sex.

Lastly there's my brother Ronnie, the oldest of all, 14 years older than me. I shared the baby spotlight with him, but I didn't mind because of the circumstances that surrounded him. At age 11, while crossing the street, Ronnie was struck by a drunk driver. The vehicle knocked him 15 feet into the air, landing him on his head.

Ronnie was in a coma for over a year, and when he did come out, he had to learn how to function all over again. The driver was an army captain who never received any punishment. My father was overseas at the time. When he came home, he got his revenge. My pops beat that captain within an inch of his life. Surprisingly, the captain didn't press charges, but my father was demoted to sergeant. It took years and his third war tour to regain his rank of Master Sergeant.

Thank God I wasn't around to witness any of it. It probably would have affected me for life. I loved my brother dearly, but for a long time, I was frightened of him-not that he would harm me. His demeanor and his physical handicap made me feel uneasy. Ronnie functioned quite normally, yet there was something I couldn't place my finger on.

My father upset me at times because he treated Ronnie somewhat harsh. I know he wanted to just toughen him up, but Ronnie had special needs. I watched my mom stomach the abuse Ronnie received. Sometimes she would knuckle up with my pops to stop it. Could you imagine this 4'9" Japanese woman standing up to a 6'4' towering man? So many times I wanted to scream, *"Stop it!"* to my pops but was just too afraid.

Yet, Ronnie had a heart of gold. I remember he used to use both his hands as puppets and play with me. For a while those two handed characters were my best friends. He collected baseball cards with the bubble gum inside and would always give me the gum. Everybody found him hilarious because at the dinner table. Ronnie would chew his food then say "seafood." Opening his mouth wide.

Josie would yell, "Ronnie stop that!"

I admire my oldest brother. He held down a government job, copped a new Ford Gremlin, and overcame the odds. I didn't mind sharing the spotlight with my brother. Sometimes I wanted mama to give him more. He deserved it. I watched my mom carry the guilt for what happened to Ronnie.

The only time I got upset with Ronnie was when he bought junk food. This dude would hide it in his room like a fucking treasure. If I beg for some, he would never refuse. He'll just give me three chips out of a whole bag.

That's the Page family. The crazy group of biracial kids. If you fought one, you had to fight us all. I had no complaints as a youngster. Getting older, I found to be a bit challenging. I wondered would I have to sacrifice the benefits of being the baby?

CHAPTER TWO

GETTING OLDER, I thought elementary school sucked. This was the time when I wished the school would burn down. Tell you what, I knew school wasn't for me then.

Thinking, "To hell with college, high school and middle school."

During middle school years, my brothers and sisters weren't around. I was by my lonesome. Now in the '70s being a biracial kid in a St. Louis, Missouri, inner-city school wasn't easy. Bullying was an understatement. No exaggeration. I had a fight every other day. Always feeling the odds were against me. Shit, the teachers weren't even on my side. I recall chilling in the schoolyard when a group of dudes whom I didn't even know decided to throw a water balloon at me. It was made from the plastic lunch wrap. Standing up for myself, I go and grab a wrap from the lunchroom trash bin. I fill it up with water, walk right back into the schoolyard, and throw it right in the ringleader's face. It felt GREAT! Right until a teacher snatched me up by the collar and carried me directly to the principal's office. A full-day suspension!

You would think winter in the schoolyard would be a merry time, right? Fuck no, not for me. Remember the story of the schoolyard ghetto ice rink? They attempted that shit every winter. Ice would accumulate near the sewer in the back of the schoolyard. During the cold season, someone would attempt to push me in *every time.* I was actually having a blast on that ice-until some dumb fuck always tried to push me.

One would think a school would have extra clothes by chance, knowing unexpected *incidents* happen among kids. Or maybe a teacher would have the heart and give me a ride home to change my clothes. They always ordered me to walk my shivering ass home in the cold and barked, "Don't be too long."

Not amused yet? Check this out. Middle school in the '70s-- no kid wants a haircut. I had straight hair down my back Cochise Indian warrior style. Remember how kids get naptime if they finish a test early? So I scoot down in my desk and lay my head back to catch some Zz's after finishing a test. I wake up and hear a female laughing behind me. I sit up, brush my hands through my hair and hit a snag. This bitch put

Bubbalicious in my hair. How do I know it was Bubbalicious? Because only that shit can hold like crazy glue. My mom had to cut it out of my hair. Motherfuckers were joking about it for a week. Every time they saw the chunk out the back of my head. I was the butt of the joke.

Oh I'm not done yet. Who would guess a middle school kid had stress? One spring day, the sun was shining. The birds were chirping. I thought to myself, *"Fuck it, I'm taking stress leave."* I decided to just walk out the schoolyard during recess. I walked to O'Fallon Park to watch the ducks. Yeah, they had ducks in the city parks back then. Man I was relaxed. A much needed break.

Suddenly I hear, "Hey, you, come here!" Now this part wasn't that bad because I got into my first police foot chase. It took those truancy officers at least 30 minutes to catch me. St. Louis city neighborhoods are perfect for getting away from the police. Street, street, cross street, alley, one way. They had to call back up to corner me. To be honest, I still could have gotten away, but seeing too many police cars.

I called it quits enough is enough. You want to know the outcome? Go back to Chapter One. You remember the dead limp tree branch and mom's magical power to make it come to life? The point is I couldn't catch a break.

I wondered what happen to the easy times just a few years back. Then women were calling me *papi*. Now girls were calling me *dusty*" Come on, in middle school nobody was thinking about girlfriend or boyfriends. I wasn't into fashion. Hell, I wore the same pants two days straight without my mom knowing.

One thing didn't change. My mom was still the person who always made my problems go away. Growing up with a mother from Japan had many benefits. I learned how to curse people out without them knowing. The word "*Baka*" comes in handy when you want to call someone a dumb ass without openly offending him. How about walking around in the hood with a homemade sushi roll. Huh? That's right in the '70s. Can you believe it? Everybody was like. "What the fuck is that?!" Many years later everybody is on the Sushi crave.

Would you believe my mom called me Baby until I was like six? I slept in her room until I was seven. I truly think I was an insomniac without my mom near by.

Through all the ass beatings, Fumi was and always will be the rock for me to lean on. I would kill, steal, and burn all my comics for this woman.

Yet she told me to ignore stupidity. "Loland, have tough skin." Japanese can't pronounce R's very well. So they tend to sound like an L

I would be down the street suddenly my mom would yell, "Loland, come eat!" All the kids would mock her when she walked away. Oh yeah, one thing I wouldn't play about was someone talking about Fumi.

Last day of 4th grade I was eagerly waiting on the bell to ring for summer break. I was in a good mood. After the bell, there would be no school for three months. *A blessing!*

I'm sitting there and this dickhead name Cal looks at me and says, "Tell your mom I will be over for a half order of fried rice with Dick sauce." I went from zero to ten in a split second. I grabbed my pencil from the desk and stabbed him right in the hand. The scream. It was so fulfilling because this dude had been a thorn in my side all year.

Needless to say, I got expelled on the last day of school. I can't forget the expression on my pop's face.

With this confused look he said, "How the fuck did you get kicked out on the last day?" That happens in modern day sports. You get multiple game suspensions the following season, but *middle school?* I got booted out for the upcoming year. I was fortunate they didn't hold me back. Anyway my grades were gravy. It was worth it to defend my mom.

Summer break during middle school was the best. Sun, fun, and adventures was my daily routine. It was a change for me because I wasn't under my family wings anymore. I spent more time trying to make friends. Of course I had many acquaintances, however my circle was small.

I had two best friends I ran the streets with, Don and Eric. Both lived down the block from my house. We hung together sun up to sun down. Don was like a brother to me, he was a year younger than me. I often took up for him as an older brother would. I use to get jealous of him because he was a bit more privileged, sometimes picking on him just for fun. But make no mistake, Don was my ace. Eric was one of the tough kids in the hood. I think sometimes I hung with him for the intimidation factor. My mom didn't care for Eric very much, thinking he was a bad influence on me. Little did she know, it was just the opposite. I was the mastermind.

Being a biracial kid in the '70s was stressful. The haters and bullies were abundant. Don and Eric had my back on many occasions; for that reason, I had love for both of them. You see even at an early age; loyalty was important to me. If my friends had beef, I had beef. That was the rule of the streets. We had so many good times. It was the simple things that I cherish. Jumping on box spring mattresses on vacant lots, riding our bikes down alleys so dogs can chase us, going swimming in Fairground Park pool even though everybody pissed in there.

One hot day we decided to go fishing at the park. My pops had just bought a pocket fisherman so I snuck it out from his tackle box. The pocket fisherman was one of the greatest inventions of the '70s. It was a full-length fishing pole that folded into a much shorter version, which made it much easier to carry around.

Don, Eric and I walked down to the Valley to dig up worms. The Valley was a wooded section of O'Fallon Park where kids dared to venture into. Drug addicts to stray dogs frequented the Valley. There were many urban myths about it from the *Booty Man-* that raped young boys or the *O'Fallon wild dogs* that were said to attack kids at night.

We venture deep into the Valley looking for a bush with moist soil to dig the worms up. I noticed a huge bush with dark dirt near the roots. I start to dig when I notice two bare feet sticking out from the other side. It startled the shit out of me. I called Don and Eric over. As we walked around, there lay a dead naked woman. We stood there in shock for five minutes. I felt guilty 'cause I gazed at her naked body. It was the first naked woman that I had seen in person. We always took sneak peeks at father's nude magazine collection but this was the *real deal*, and it bothered me that it was a dead woman. Needless to say we doubled time out there and informed an old man fishing in the park lake. He walked to someone's house and called the police. That memory still haunts me to this day. The next day I read in the newspaper the dead woman was a teacher and her boyfriend confessed to killing her. We stayed out the park for a while after that.

Our other pass time was walking the train tracks. We would walk for miles, often stopping at Wonder Bread bakery, whose warehouse faced the tracks. We would wait until the workers weren't looking so we could steal boxes of Twinkies. Thinking back, I believe the workers walked off so we could take a box or two.

One day we would walk far eastbound. The next day westbound searching for new adventures every day, sometimes running into kids from other neighborhoods, some friendly and others we had to toss those hands with. My posse was inseparable, but summer seemed to pass by so fast.

We all attended different schools so we wouldn't see each other that much. Summer was a time of adventure and being mischievous at times.

Time marched on and we got older. Mischievous behavior turned to delinquent behavior. I was uneasy because I had to start a new middle school, yet I figured it couldn't be any worse than Yeatman, a school filled with bullies.

CHAPTER THREE

EIGHTH GRADE ROLLED AROUND, changing my whole perspective of life. I went from throwing rocks at girls to finding myself getting a hardon in class. I remember years ago what the prostitute said, "You're going to make a fine pimp one day." That time was now. During my early years, girls didn't find me attractive. I was the dirty mixed boy on the block. Eighth grade was *so* different. I started to get attention at parties, the mall, and even by my pop's bodega. Girls loved the long hair and my swag was definitely on another level. Starched Levi's, Ralph Lauren Polo's, or Izod Polos were my daily wear. Besides I was getting social security checks from my pops since he retired from the military and dependents under 18 received benefits, so I stayed fresh. See my pops had me when he was in his 50's. He still had the juice!

Still a virgin, I was careful not to engage in sex. I heard the horror stories of being a young parent, thanks to my brother Rob. He had me petrified about having a baby. He made it sound like getting a girl knocked up was a crime. Nevertheless, my imagination was undoubtedly of a horny teen. I got a erections if the wind blew my way. Sometimes in class I couldn't stand in fear that I would get noticed. I would fake a cramp so my teacher wouldn't make me stand during reading.

Me switching from public to private school was not by choice. My mom enrolled me into St. Engelbert Catholic School. It was all good to me because Don went there and told me private school girls were off the chain. Good riddance, Yeatman!

I must admit I wasn't disappointed with the change. I even made better grades. The girls. Oh man! I think I had a different fantasy every damn class period. I didn't have a girlfriend because I was still trying to find my lane, besides I was a bit shy. You see, *liking* girls was easy. *Approaching* them wasn't as simple. The thought of getting shot down bothered me. I knew girls thought I was cute, but, still, being rejected by a girl whom you have to see daily didn't set well with me. So, I pursued girls outside the school.

Back in the hood girls were jocking me pretty tough. Some even offered me sex, however I wasn't up for a smash session (sex), *yet*. I kept it pushing. One time my temptation got the best of me. This girl name Brenda, who resided around the block, constantly flirted with me. She would walk by my house while I would sit on my porch. She would smile whispering to her friends as she passed by. I decided to let her have it one snowy winter day there was no school. She said her parents had *Preview*, which was yesteryear cable TV, so I went over to watch a flick. We started watching Jaws a all time favorite. She's started grabbing me on the shark attack scenes. That's all it took. I got hard and my Jimmy (penis) was standing at attention. She invited me to her room and we got naked. I looked around because it's the first time I'm in a female's room besides sneaking candy out of my sisters' room. Shit the only time I was allowed in my sisters' room was if they wanted me to kill a bug or needed a cup of water. Yeah, I had family members who would call me to change the TV channel or to bring them a glass of Kool-Aid… but back to Brenda. It was the first time I'm in a girl's room for intimacy.

We both got under the covers and started kissing. I climbed on top of her acting like I knew what I was doing. I started to feel down there grabbing my manhood to put it inside her. Nobody told me a virgin is tighter than a bank vault. I swore I fractured my penis, lol. I was so frustrated I came before anything happened. I told my brother, which maybe wasn't a bright idea. He called me Numb Nuts while laughing in my face. Well my missed opportunity really wasn't a big deal. I hoped my first time would be a little more romantic anyway. I chalked it up to inexperience

Fate works in funny ways. One day after school I decided to walk to C&K Bar B Que. I'd been craving a hot link sandwich for weeks. On this certain day something compelled me to walk a quarter mile to get that hot link sandwich. Once I got there, bought my sandwich, and walked out, I bumped into a girl. We made eye contact.

I'm thinking, "Wow, she's cute."

She smiled greeting me, "Hi Roland."

I responded, "What's up. Damn you look familiar. Where do I know you from?"

She reminded me, "Tracey. We were in fourth grade together, you don't remember throwing an orange peel at me in Yeatman's schoolyard?" She caught me off guard.

Lying my ass off, I chuckled "Naw, I don't remember that." We exchanged numbers. In that moment I knew Tracey and I would forever have some kind of connection. Even if I couldn't put my hand on it at that time.

Tracey and I stayed in contact. We often walked over to each other's house. I liked visiting her. She had all kinds of board games so it was never a dull moment. I would even let her win at times. That happens when you like someone. I was crushing on Tracey something terrible but I was only 14. Also, I was an arrogant asshole. After a few weeks, I stopped calling her moving on.

Another memorable experience of mine was getting high for the first time. *Herb, Mary Jane, Ganja, Grass, Reefer*. Or as my pops called it *Stinkweed*. Whatever you want to call it, I had a stash hidden in my father's old golf bag placed in the garage. After school Eric and I would meet in the alley and blaze up. He was a freshman so he would tell me how high school life was.

"Nigga the bitches are on a totally different level, most of them will *ask* you to fuck."

I would shake my head saying "No doubt? Can't wait."

He would always laugh joking, "Dude when you're high you look just like a China man."

I'd reply, "Nigga I'm Japanese there's a fuckin' difference. Plus everybody eyes slant when they're high idoit."

Eric had a job at Mickey D's -McDonalds-and I was fortunate to receive free checks courtesy of the government. We had a master plan to put some extra cash flow into our pockets. We went half on a quarter pound of weed. *Kush* was cheap back then.

We made an oath to always be our brother's keeper, to rise to the top together, and we did just that at age 15. We didn't want to corrupt Don so we left him out our enterprise. Don didn't need to hustle anyway. It took a certain type of person to hustle. A street hustler must be greedy, ruthless, and a risk taker. Don was the little brother we protected.

Money was good and things couldn't be better for two young cats from the North Side. Eric and I stayed fresh and ladies loved us. We even named our crew *The Thunder Cats*. Yeah, after the cartoon where each character was a big feline. We thought it was dope because in our analogy some of the characters were mostly black. When a nigga smoke weed, we become a philosopher thinking of weird shit like the Thunder Cats. Anyway my pockets were stacked and my gear was on point. Any risk was well worth it.

One evening I asked Eric if he was down for the mall.

He approved, "Fa-sho (for sure), but it's too late for catching the bus." He was right however it was Friday plus I had a party to attend Saturday. I needed something fresh to wear. It so happened that my parents were out with friends. Pops left the keys to his car on his bedroom dresser. I knew it was risky-- not because I wasn't licensed and only 15-- but the risk was being caught by my pops. His car was his prized possession. It was a 1978 Cadillac Fleetwood Brougham, canary yellow with vogue rims and a flying bitch ornament on the hood.

When I mentioned it, Eric looked more afraid than me. "Dude you really want to do that?"

I reacted, "Nigga I need something to wear. We'll be back before they will. I just got to make sure I park it in the exact same space."

Pops allowed me to drive the car around the block when I washed it for him but never farther than a few blocks. I waited until my brother went in the bathroom, then I rushed out Eric waiting on my porch. We hopped in the whip and drove off. Man it was a rush; I kid you not. I looked over at Eric and we started laughing.

He yelled, "Nigga you wild as a motherfucker!"

We took the scenic route to River Roads Mall making sure we drove by the bus stops so girls could see us. I got a kick out of it 'cause it would always be a group of females that would yell,

"Can I go with you?!"

At the mall, I copped my fit from Stix, Baer & Fuller. Everything was going smooth. We'd make it back just in the nick of time. Well maybe I spoke too soon. I got about four blocks from my house and noticed some red flashing lights approaching me from the rear.

Eric shouted, "Oh Fuck. It's the cops."

I said, "Stay calm!"

Even though my heart was in my throat, I hesitated for a minute, then at that moment, I made a choice that changed my life. I tried to outrun the cops. I hit an alley at which time Eric hopped out and ran through an open yard. That caused the cop car to slow down. It appeared he contemplated probably chasing Eric, thinking he had a gun. I turned two sharp corners getting away. St. Louis streets are so congested with some short cuts that it's literally like a maze. I parked the car in an alley and ran through some yards to the rear of my house. I waited about 30 minutes and returned to get the car. There was no cop in sight. What a close call, right?

Not so fast... the very next morning, the day of the party, I'm woken by my pops' voice.

"Roland! Get your ass down here! *Now*!"

I slowly walked down the steps into the living room rubbing my eyes. "What's wrong?"

Damn! There's the police officer standing there. This motherfucker knew my father.

He informed my dad, "I knew that was your car, Bob. I thought someone had stolen it until an hour later I saw it was parked back in front of your house."

My mom gave me a death stare like she was going to snatch my heart out like a ninja. Surprisingly,, I didn't get an ass whooping after miserably failing to outrun the police after all. I didn't get to go to the party, but that's okay. I lived to party another day. My mom blamed Eric, not knowing I had masterminded the entire fiasco. Again!

You want to hear something crazy? My pops allowed me to drive the very next day. I think he liked that I had a little bad boy in me like he did. *Weird!*

Summer was ending and I was preparing for high school. My parents sent me to a private high school in U City, a popular suburb in St. Louis County. U City was known for attractive females and hot parties. Plus, I had relatives there. This was the day I eagerly waited on. I couldn't sleep the night before my first day of high school.

CHAPTER FOUR

MY FIRST DAY OF HIGH SCHOOL, was amazing. I remember walking into class and seeing everybody checking each other's gear out. Some were even choosing up on one another. I sat down in my first class and heard a "Pssst Ro."

It was Tim, a dude from my neighborhood who had also attended Yeatman with me. I felt a bit relieved. Tim was a pure athlete who knew everybody in the school already. Back in the day he was a bully to some. Yet I never saw him like that because we were pretty tight. He normally beefed with the cats I had problems with so everything was copasetic.

While walking through the hall, I heard a group of girls call Tim over. I stopped to look at my schedule.

I heard one of the girls ask him, "Damn Tim, who is that?" I acted like I didn't hear it, but subconsciously I was high fiving myself. At that point I knew things were going to be all gravy for me.

I didn't see Eric as much unless we were re-upping on the weed. I slowed down on the weed business anyway. The last thing I could afford was messing up my first year of high school. I don't get this new era of drop outs. High school brings a whole new circle of friends. Really you have no choice; you connect with these people every day. However, I saw Don, my other best friend, because he lived down the street, and like I said, he was more like a brother than a friend. Tim and I hung pretty tough too. Then there was Rob, a laid back cat from the West Side. I could relate to Tim and Rob because they were from similar backgrounds-city boys at a private county school. The advantage of attending a county school was seeing all the girls from others schools waiting on the bus stops. I got more numbers coming home from school than *at* school. Regardless of being appealing to the females, I wasn't much of a player. I never ever officially had a girlfriend. I mean I talked to girls but never asked a girl to *keep it exclusive*.

That changed soon enough when I met Brenda. It was strange how I met her. She was actually attempting to hook me up with her friend.

She asked me, "Do you have a girlfriend? My friend thinks you're cute."

I stopped browsing through my locker, "No I don't. How about you? You got a boyfriend?"

I got her by surprise, "No- not really."

I leaned against the locker. "Shouldn't you be hooking us up then instead of your friend?"

I could tell by her smile she preferred my suggestion. It was chancy but the heart wants what's pleasing to the eyes. Brenda was a sophomore and *very popular*. I kind of thought I was out of my league. After a few interesting phone conversations, we connected simultaneously. Brenda became my first official girlfriend. She was a true beauty Nubian princess with a deep dark complexion and the whitest smile; she was an all-natural beauty. I would stay after school so we could duck off by the lockers and make out. Brenda came from a successful family. Her parents were solid and I admired the whole family. She was spoiled however, and that was challenging for me. I liked the feisty attitude she had. Honestly she was probably my first love, at least based on what I understood about love.

She would call me late night sometimes whispering. She's the first girl to tell me, "I love you." I had never told a female I loved her in a romantic way. Tell you what, it felt wonderful. Your female relatives can tell you they love you, but it's different when a love interest says it. It lights a fire deep in your soul.

My mom saw the change in me. Not sure if it was the glow or just mom's intuition. Her troubled son was happy. That's all that mattered. She was thrilled. I enjoyed school and was meeting new friends.

Mom always reiterated, "Stay focused, Loland; young men need an education to move ahead in life."

My mom asked me to describe Brenda and I did. She didn't say anything but dark complexion was her attraction also. My pops was a man with a dark, deep complexion with straight hair. He had an exotic appearance being of Native American descent. Therefore, she wasn't surprised when I told her my girlfriend was dark skinned too. Thinking back, all my siblings were attracted to dark skin. They say opposites attract. Growing up I hated being light skinned so I nurtured an admiration for dark skinned people.

Mom told me an old story about Japan, how the Japanese wanted all the white soldiers off the island but didn't mind if the black soldiers remained. She said after numerous allegations of sexual misconduct, the islanders were intimidated by white soldiers yet compassionate toward how black soldiers were discriminated against. I sympathized with what my parents had to endure, especially my pops.

Meanwhile back on the block, Eric, who was still hustling, wanted me to get more involved.

"Bro I need you to watch my back. You know we do better when we move as one."

I hesitated, "Eric, man it's not that easy for me. Bro, I got school and that's not an option. You know how my parents are."

He rebutted, "Yeah bro. I hear you but making money don't sleep."

After that conversation Eric and I stopped talking. I knew he felt some type of way. I felt bad too, after all, Eric was one of my best friends. We started as thick as thieves. I guess friends grow apart.

On the weekends I hung with pops at the bodega. He expanded by adding pinball machines, pool tables and a jukebox. I noticed younger people started frequenting the shop. Pops enjoyed my company. I told him many times once I got old enough, I wanted to go into business with him.

He would say, "That would be cool but finish school first, how 'bout that?"

I wanted to be the first member out of the family to carry on his legacy.

My brothers didn't share my pops' business ideology. Pops was a hustler. Rob was dedicated to being the first college graduate in the family. I was proud of him for that. Ronnie's physical disability prohibited him from pursing that path, but I'm sure if he could have he would have.

In pops' presence I was *Lil Bob*. I enjoyed the title; it made me feel like I was next in line to be the boss. The shady characters around the bodega knew not to fuck with *Lil Bob*. My pops' reputation as a war hero brought much respect in the hood. People around knew Bob would fuck shit up for the right reason. Hanging with pops was quite an eye opener in a good and bad way. Good: pops forced me to approach a problem like a man. Never turn your back from a problem, face it head on and don't try and out run it because it will eventually catch up with you.

Like mom he told me stories of racism. That's what older black men do to educate younger black men to appreciate what we have now. He told me stories like what he and mom encountered when they were coming to the States from Japan by ship. They had just gotten married, but since he was black, he had to travel in the lower deck compartments on their honeymoon. It just so happened that a young, white female deckhand snuck my mom to the lower deck to spend time with my dad. During my early years, I heard stories that at times made me skeptical toward white people. One story to this day stays with me.

When my dad was a young man. He witnessed his father's death at the hands of a white man. My pops told me during the early 1900s in Mississippi there were black people still doing slave duties. They were so called *Free,* yet they had nowhere to go or no means of income so they remained at plantations, now called farms, for slave wages. My grandmother was an attractive black Indian woman who was favored by the plantation owner, excuse me-farm owner's-son. He had sexually assaulted my grandmother. My grandfather somehow found out and stabbed the owner's son. Well, the owner didn't like the news of his rapist son being stabbed by a black man so he shot my grandfather dead.

My father said he was young and the specifics aren't clear. It was traumatic enough to make him run away from home at 15 and join the Army. The years in between he didn't discuss with me.

All he would say was, "Just be glad you weren't living back then." He did say the Army helped him realize not every white person is bad, just a lot of them were *back then*.

I scratched my head at times cause my mom wasn't black. She wasn't white either. I chalked it up to maybe pops was an international player. He would often ask me what type of girl caught my eye.

I would say with a big grin, "Black is beautiful pops. Black is beautiful."

He would slap my hand with a five and say, "You damn right."

I enjoyed spending time with my father. Yet to this day, I don't believe I knew everything I need to know about him.

Back at school it was a learning experience. It's funny how a young man's instinctive behavior came so natural. Brenda taught me a lot without out even trying. Does that make any sense? She unlocked desires in me I never knew I had. Say for instance, I never had sex but trust and believe I knew where to put it and how to move. Brenda was a good girl and I knew what lines *not* to cross. To tell the truth, I was scared myself. So it was a discussion that never happened between us. Homecoming rolled around and I was excited. This would be my first official date. Going to Homecoming with an upper classman was an honor. I remember my brother Rob taking me shopping for my fit. We talked during the drive to the mall.

"Dude you're going to be the freshest cat there! Don't act too desperate if you know what I mean."

I'm puzzled, "Not really. What do you mean?"

He lightly smacked me on the back of my head, "Look nigga, don't be chasing after your girl like your henpecked. Lay back and play real cool like, hard to get. You got it?"

I nodded, "Yeah, I guess."

So here I am at the Homecoming dance held at the gymnasium of the school. It's a private school so you guessed it, the lights were only dim. I walked in like John Travolta in *Saturday Night Fever*, one of the greatest films of all time. I had a white and maroon outfit on. Slowly walking through the crowd, I spotted Brenda, looking like a Solid Gold dancer. I straightened my outfit up and walked up to her. She told me I looked nice. Just when I was about to return the compliment, I heard my brother's voice;

"Playing hard to get will make them jock you harder." I paused for a moment. Then I replied to Brenda, "I know."

She looked at me like I was a complete stranger. She immediately turned and walked away. My inner conscious was kicking me in the ass. We barely even spoke the rest of the evening. Shit, we even took pictures with different people.

My brother picked me up on the way home and asked, "How was it?"

I looked out the side of my eyes and shook my head.

He said, "What? Don't get mad at me 'cause you fucked it up. It always worked for me."

I snapped back, "Good to know. I don't want to talk about it if that's okay with you." That was one of his official asshole moments.

Back at school after a whole lunch conversation, I patched it up with Brenda. From that point on I discovered every man has his own formula only he can follow. I realized I have my own gift of gab that works for me. I regretted not taking a picture with my girl. I knew one day in the future I couldn't look back and have something to remember my first Homecoming. Nonetheless my relationship was going pretty well. Having a girlfriend made school fun. When other girls hit on me, I ignored the subliminal passes. It happened quite often in class but I was head over heels for Brenda. Like clockwork we made out by my lockers after school. She had to feel my erection through my pants every time we kissed. I would catch her glancing down every once and awhile, but she never said anything. We ended with her wiping her lipstick from my lips

Summertime rolled up fast I had the assumption that my relationship would be affected. I cared about my girl but I knew it was beyond my control. My relationship wasn't my main priority anyway. You see I knew I was young with many more things to experience. I figured *Que sera-sera, whatever will be, will be.*

I spent the beginning of the summer at the mall or the park meeting girls. Staying out past curfew then sneaking on the phone whispering to different girls was a daily routine. I barely spoke to Brenda, I figured she was doing her own thing. We remained cool though. Hey, without transportation, what choice did I have? Catching the bus was a turn off during the summer.

About mid-summer, I hooked back up with Eric. By then he was in deep and as he promised he'd hold me down. He was older and already driving. He had his own whip, making it convenient for us to hang out. It opened the door for me to discreetly flip a few ounces of weed here and there. The money I was stacking merely stocked my wardrobe. I was Polo down from head to toe. I was still receiving my father's social security benefits so mom never clued in. Every blue moon I would buy my mom a small token to let her know I adored her--an Asian vase from the South Grand international grocer, a steak & baked potato dinner from Ruth Chris, sometimes a silk scarf from Famous Barr. She would tell me to save my money for a rainy day. She didn't know money made my days sunny and I wanted her to have a sunny day too.

On top of my weed hustle, pops was kicking me out some cash for late night lookout at the bodega. The underground gambling racket was profitable in the hood. Crap games yield a few thousand on any given night. On the ride home, pops would slide me a hundred or so.

He sound off, "Do as I say, never as I do. Shooting dice ain't for you. You hear?"

I would shake my head looking out the window thinking he would fuck me up if he knew I wanted to follow in his footsteps.

The summer was coming to an end and I had a change of heart. I talked my parents into allowing me to attend a city school. Mercy was cool, but I was tired of catching the bus all the way to U City. Pops suggested I stay with my aunt who lived out there, but we didn't vibe too well. She was a bit too strict and she constantly had something to say about light skin black men; it rubbed me all the way left. So it wasn't hard to convince my parents the commute wasted money. I could deal with a city school, just as easy as a county school. Besides I hadn't even spoken to Brenda so that chapter was closed. I had no reason to go back there.

I got to go to Cardinal Ritter High for my sophomore year. Cardinal Ritter, although a private school, was located smack dab in the hood, which wasn't an issue for me. It didn't make me any difference-- one school is the same as the next. It's what I made of it. The word got out that I was coming to Ritter anyway. I had friends there also. Plus, it was near my neighborhood so it became easy access to continue business with Eric, who was at Northwest, a public school just down the block. Ritter started off cool but things sort of changed. Before coming to Ritter, I had a few shaky experiences with a couple of chicks that didn't end too well. I must admit I had an ego, in my eyes I had standards. Once I got to know a female and we had nothing in common, I would kick her to the curb. So, my reputation followed me. Oh yeah, by the way, I was still a virgin just a conceited one. I wasn't ready for that, *yet*.

After a week or so in, I was still getting to know people. As I walked through the hall, I suddenly heard a familiar voice.

"Hey Roland. How you been?"

I turned and things got immediately better. There's Tracey, the cute girl from Yeatman, smiling.

I think to myself, *"Wow, a friendly face."* I asked her to help me out with getting to know my classes. She graciously became my chaperone for the next few weeks. Tracey and I were already cool so I figured we could be like Bonnie and Clyde. Besides attending the same school, we lived not that far from one another. So we spent a lot of time together. I even neglected my hustle game to rekindle our friendship. I would buy her a matching polo shirt like mine when I went to the mall. Yep, I felt if there was a female out there for me, Tracey was the one. We would spend the entire weekend together, playing connect four or catching a movie. I wasn't 16 yet but pops would give me the whip every blue moon. Tracey and I claimed to be boyfriend and girlfriend, but what I appreciated was our *friendship*. Maintaining our bond over a decade meant a lot to me. The only others I had that bond with were Eric and Don.

After a month or so at Ritter, some of Tracey's friends planted a seed of suspicion in her head, things such as rumors of me cheating, me being an arrogant asshole, and the notion she could do better. What's crazy was that some of the ones telling her bullshit tried to talk to me prior to us hooking up; I didn't bite on it though. The accusations began to play on my mind. Things were cool but all the questioning was making me weary. I cared for Tracey yet I was still young and temptation was still there. Deep down I had notions of curiosity so maybe her friends were right. They were probably protecting their friend from the inevitable.

Eric and I attended many high school parties typically hosted at local halls, high schools, or hotels. We might not talk as much but I could count on Eric picking me up for a party. Tracey's mom wouldn't let her attend parties as much. In my opinion that's all a high school student has to look forward to. Tracey would try and talk me out of going sometimes but it never worked. The next day word always got back to Tracey that I was posted up with another chick. At times it was true and at times it was BS. I would always smooth things over with her.

A few of Tracey friends swore I wasn't the right choice for her. I never spoke on it, I always let it roll off. My attitude was becoming bitter. I felt I might as well be what her friends are accusing me of.

One weekend I went to a party at Holy Rosary School. It was packed. Walking through the crowd, I felt a tap on my shoulder. I turned around and there was Tracey with a not so happy look on her face.

"Hey mami! What's up? I thought you couldn't go?"

She said, "I wanted to surprise you."

I whispered under my voice, "You surprised me alright."

She snapped, "What you say?"

"Nothing, Nothing I'm glad you here." As I grabbed her hand something told me to look over her shoulder. I saw her hating ass support group mean mugging me.

One said, "That bitch Debra was just in his face and he was eating that shit up girl." I shook my head trying to ignore their comments.

Then I heard, "You need to smack the shit out of him."

Now that got my attention. Look I'm a peaceful dude. I avoid confrontation unless I have to engage. These bitches got me all fucked up. I looked back at Eric and he started laughing. They even got a dude name Tee, who attended Ritter, to chime in. Now until this day I thought I was cool with this nigga until he let these chicks soup his head up.

I heard him say, "Fuck that nigga, Tracey."

Then I saw Eric walk up on him and whisper in Tee's ear. I guess he didn't see Eric. Let's just say Eric had a reputation of being a savage in the streets. He was always my savior in need.

Tee said, "Naw bro I didn't mean it like that." The music was loud but I almost read Eric lips saying, "Then step nigga before you get fucked up."

I told Tracey, "Your friends think I'm quiet Roland, the little mix dude, but these bitches about to find out the real me popping that shit off." Tracey pulled me away from the crowd.

We were cool but things never went back to the way they were in the beginning.

Months went by and Tracey and I hung in there. I must admit she put up with a lot of shit. I wasn't a complete asshole, just a part time one. My inconsistency in the relationship became a problem.

School was out for some reason one day. I went to Tracey's house because she asked me to stop by so we could talk. We started talking and she told me all the negative shit she was hearing was getting to her. She said all of it couldn't be a lie. I knew it was the end. She said she started talking to someone else but that wasn't the reason for the break up.

I thought to myself, *Bullshit*. I told her it wasn't my decision but I have no choice in the matter. That was the last time I talked to her for a while. The break up opened my eyes to relationships. Yeah, I had conversations with other women but that's it; for the most part I didn't cross the line. After that day I said, "Fuck it! I'm never going to allow any female to hurt me again." I wasn't oblivious that I contributed to the break up. Regardless, I vowed to do the hurting if it ever came down to it again.

By my senior year, I decided to switch schools. Ritter just wasn't my cup of tea after my break up with Tracey. I wasn't the most favorable guy there. Usually I got along well with the girls but it was the opposite at Ritter. The dudes there were mad cool, no drama. Still, I needed a fresh new start. New friends, new girls, new hangouts were my main priorities. With less than two months left in the summer, I still was undecided what school to enroll in. It was a tossup between Sumner or Soldan. The thought of dropping out entered my mind but my parents would definitely kick me out the house.

At times I spoke to pops about me becoming his business partner, he would only say, "Do time, papi. Be a better man than me. Your old man never graduated from high school. I went straight to the Army. I want better for you."

My mind was already made up. Someday I will be my own boss, a successful businessman working alongside his father taking the family business to another level. The future goal was set. Finish school and hustle a bit more to stack enough funds to improve the bodega. Regardless of what pops said, I would show him rather than tell him.

Things began to change physically for me. I cut my hair into a more mature hairstyle therefore my hair started to wave up. I grew a mustache and my body got more developed. I had a new car, a 1982 Lincoln Mark VI, champagne gold. Women appeared to be more attracted to the new me making them easy access. I got around freely and my circle of friends changed. I had a tight crew that was down for me. With a new outlook on life, I was uncertain what the future might hold for me.

All I knew was whatever I wanted; I would do just about anything to get it.

CHAPTER FIVE

THE LAST FEW MONTHS OF THE summer were a defining moment in my life. I had a new whip most guys my age didn't have. My look was different being biracial and not even the typical Mulatto. I had an exotic pedigree which the ladies loved. I had a killer instinct when it came to relationships, and sad as it may be, women loved the bad boy image. I was dating a wide spectrum of women. Black, White, Hispanic, even older women, however I still couldn't get into Asian women; they reminded me of my mom. Pops caught on to my playboy lifestyle. He never told me how he found out. He had eyes everywhere.

He warned me, "You gotta watch how you move. You are different and driving a new car. Niggas will hate on you."

"I got this, pops," I give him my assurance.

The summer brought new friends. Still hustling weed, I expanded my reach into the projects. I hung around Laclede Town. This expansion brought a new group of friends. Gino was that loose cannon of my click--the type of cat you don't dare to do some ignorant shit cause he's going to do it. Lavell was the thoroughbred of the bunch. He was the comedian who would roast anybody then dare whomever to do something about it. It's funny how I met them. White Castle restaurant was the hang out in the summer. Everybody parked on the lot. You would see a little of everybody from all parts of town.

One night I pulled up by myself. I parked up front and a group of girls started flirting with me. A group of guys who was trying to get on those girls flirting with me got a bit jealous, I guess. They started saying some sideways shit to me.

"Get your pretty ass off this lot before we take your whip." I laughed at them and wave them off.

That pissed them off even more. "Nigga, we not playing with your bitch ass."

At this point, with the girls watching, I can't nut up even with odds against me.

I said, "*Bitch?* Nigga, I don't see your mama around!"

They started to approach me. Suddenly here came Gino and Lavell with a group of rowdy project niggas.

"Bitch ass niggas, why you trippin with ole boy? He can't help if the chicks choosing up on him. Step before we whoop your ass up and down this lot."

The dudes walked away after they realized they were heavily outnumbered. From that point on, we were thick as thieves. I would load four or five dudes in my whip. We would travel the whole city. The summer was almost up and damn near everybody in the city knew who I was.

Being around my new found friends was exciting. They constantly amused me doing the dumbest shit. Gino would start shit with people for no reason. I witnessed this dude walk up to a dude for looking at him sideways. When the dude's girl tried to step in to help her man, this nigga knocked her out. In my mind at the time, I thought that was the most gangsta bossed up shit I ever saw. As I said before, I had a jacked up mentality. At this point in my life, I started to smoke quite a bit. My pops noticed my bad habits and used every opportunity he had to literature me.

"Boy you high every time I see you. What the fuck is going on?"

I would brush it off assuring him I wouldn't let it consume me. "Pops just a little weed. Don't worry."

He'd always reply, "It's not so much you. I'm concerned about these crazy muthafucka's in these streets."

From sun up to sun down I would spend my day smoking weed and cracking a 40oz of Ole English 800 Malt Liquor. My friends liked the attention of being around me and I liked the security they provided. Everyone knew if you fucked with me, you might get fucked up by my cats.

It appeared every day was a new adventure in my life. Half the time I was drunk or high, which made the situations even funnier. Some things stick out, just to name a few. We were out in the county and decided we wanted to comp some more liquor so we stop at a small grocery spot. Mind you, we were all minors. I hand Gino a $10 bill.

He waved me off, "Dude I don't need that. Sit tight I will be right back."

A few minutes rolled by. Here came Gino running out the store with three employees and an off-duty cop chasing him.

He yelled, "Start the car!" At this time cops could legally fire warning shots. I heard two cracks like firecrackers exploding. The liquor went flying in the air and Gino tripped and fell. By this time the cop was up on Gino with his gun pointed right at him while he lay on the ground. The cop yelled at us so I peeled off.

Lavell was in the car with me. "Ro, drive around the block a few times." I go around the block a few minutes. After about ten minutes, I saw Gino limping down the street. We pulled over to pick him up

"What the fuck happened man?"

He was breathing hard, "They peeped me out as soon as I went in."

We all bust out laughing. I asked, "Why they let you go?"

He shrugged, "The cop panicked when I fell. He thought I was hurt. He didn't want to get me medical attention. Lazy muthafucka's."

Lavell jokingly, "Dude check your drawers, I smell doo-doo."

Gino breathless, "Head back to the city. We'll get some drunk to comp us some liquor."

Want to hear another? We're chilling at a local burger spot. Can't say the name, that's snitching on myself. I'm sitting on my car talking to a group of girls. They were asking me what's my next destination.

Gino yells from the rear, "Ro, pop the trunk." I had an ice cooler with a couple of 40 oz. in it. I popped the trunk thinking nothing of it. I heard a loud boom like a cannon go off. Then the lighted sign above the burger joint came crashing down. Everybody started running like crazy. I looked back and there's Gino holding my father's shotgun. I forgot my pops left it in my trunk a week ago. I forgot to lock it up in the basement. We hopped in the car and quickly pulled off. I was pissed until I saw we had gotten away with it. We laughed for weeks every time we drove by the burger joint.

Every day with Gino and Lavell was a different story, a different adventure. I never thought anything I did was criminal. I chalked it up to being young and adventurous. We didn't go looking for trouble, it sometimes just fell into our lap. The times we kicked it were some of the best memories of my life thus far.

The summer before my senior year was ticking away so I was going to make the best out of the last few weeks. My daily routine was the same. Wake up. Shit, shower, and shave what little facial hair I had. Put on a fresh fit then go get the crew and stop at the corner liquor store to get some 40oz or a bottle of Mad Dog 20/20. Lavell lived the closest so I swooped him up first then we got to Laclede Town and grabbed Gino. We'd hang out at Gino's for a while. Laclede Town was near many hot spots where we'd hang-Saint Louis University, Harris Stowe State College, and Blumeyer Projects. Why housing projects you ask? They had blocks and blocks of girls. I liked my women a little ghetto you see. I never feared my safety because I was pretty well known in the city as well as accepted in the hood. I was *Lil Bob* from the bodega. Laclede Town and Blumeyer were just a spit away but you had to have a pass to wander on the blocks. From hanging out I met a cat name Kelly that lived in the Blumeyer with his cousin. We became pretty cool. Kelly hung around my pops bodega and reminded me of my pops. For some reason pops favored Kelly. I figured real recognize real. He reminded me of my father. Kelly was the type of dude that stood on anything he did but avoided trouble if possible. When it came to women, he definitely held his own. He was a needed addition to the crew. Let's not forget about Don. He came around every blue moon. He got along good with the crew as well. As I said before, Don was like my brother and not a road dog. Contact with Eric was strictly business, but we were still cool--always will be but unless it came to weed, we just didn't hang anymore. However, if I had drama, I knew he was a phone call away.

My new crew was click tight and I enjoyed the Boss status. Now I didn't throw orders around or instruct hits on people. I was being a Boss in my own right. I usually made the decision of what we did, I never had to get my hands dirty, and my crew was very protective of me. So in my eyes, I was a Boss. The best thing about having a crew is the family you inherit with them. Gino's mom was like a mom to me, Lavell's little sister called me big brother, and Kelly's mom called me son. It was really an embracing feeling. Your posse becomes like your family. That's just the way it is. They know your flaws, your bad habits, and your secrets. My crew became family.

Back at the home front, mom could see the change in me. She often asked me was I on drugs.

I gave her an offended look like "I can't believe you asked that." Mom knew something was different. She just didn't have the specifics right. Being a mama's boy, it wasn't hard to convince her that I couldn't do wrong.

"Ma, I'm just a normal teen doing what normal teens do. I don't even smoke weed. It makes me too sleepy. If I was smoking weed, I would get the munchies. I would be way bigger than what I am now."

She would look at me and say, "Make the right decision, papi. I get scared cause you act just like your daddy."

That would catch my attention. I never knew what to make of that statement, was that a good or bad thing? Mom just wanted the best for me; honestly, I felt like shit lying to her. Imagine me telling her the truth. It would break her heart. My mother's feelings were the only woman feelings that I gave a damn about. When I was around my mom, I felt deceitful. It was the only time that I felt like a disappointment. Maybe that's why I avoided home. I would sometimes spend the night at Kelly's house camping out on the floor. Sounds uncomfortable? Not at all. Kelly's mom had those old quilts made of all different fabrics. She would give me at least three of them. It made a cozy spot. And, Kelly's mom could throw down on some grub. Don't get me wrong, my mom could cook; she was probably one of the only Japanese women in the United States that could cook Chitterlings without clearing out the house. She also had that international cuisine down to a science. But Kelly's mom made me understand the meaning of *Soul Food*. Neck bones, tripe sandwiches, deep fried catfish, fried green tomatoes, to name a few of the things she cooked that I loved. Man, I looked forward to picking him up just to see what she whipped up in the kitchen. I never had to ask for a plate either.

She would say, "Baby I'm going to put some meat on your bones if it's the last thing I do."

Kelly's crib was my home away from home- no doubt about it. Even his sisters treated me like a little brother, especially Cassie, she was extremely protective of me. She would boot up with any chick that crossed me. One particular Sunday I was in Forest Park cruising the area. It was the place to be on weekends. The Lincoln was deep. Kelly always rode shotgun, Gino and Lavell like the back seats. They said it was roomy. So we pulled over and I'm sitting on my ride. Two females in a beat up car pulled up on me.

"Damn daddy! What's your name?"

I leaned down still sitting on the whip. I see that the one talking to me wasn't my type. My nice way of saying she was ugly as a muthafucka.

"Curtis" I replied, knowing that's not my name.

"Curtis, can I get your digits?" I look her dead in the eyes and calmly said "Nope." She swole up quick fast in a hurry.

She yelled, "That's why I don't fuck with light skin niggas. They think they're the shit."

I remained calm and smiled at her. "I never said I was the shit, baby girl. Maybe you think I'm the shit. Apparently so, you pulled up on me."

She threw her car in park and got out. Her friend tried to grab her arm. "Come on girl, we ain't got time for this shit."

But the girl still walked up to me. "Nigga, I will bust your window out."

Mind you, I'm still calm. The crew was laughing their asses off. I'm thinking to myself, "This bitch is blowing my high." I say the first thing that comes to mind.

"Baby girl, I never put my hands on a girl, but you'll be the first chick I choke the fuck out."

She went to swing and Kelly grabbed her and pushed her away.

She screamed, "You need your boys to fight your battle!"

I turned my back and said, "Bitch, that's what bosses do."

Now I tell you how fate works. Cassie came out of nowhere and clocked this chick right across the jaw. She fell in front of her car at which time her friend got out and picked her up.

Cassie looked at the friend and said, "What bitch? You can get it too!"

The friend quickly put the beat down girl in the passenger seat and drove off. By now a crowd had formed around us.

Cassie yelled, "Nobody going fuck with my little brother."

That's the type of people I considered family. The hood had its advantages and disadvantages. It could be rough but loyal at the same time.

School was about to start in two weeks and I had decided to go to Sumner. Gino and Lavell attended Sumner High so my mind was pretty much made up. Plus, it wasn't far from the bodega, making it easy to go help my pops out. Two weeks before school, I decided to detox my body so to speak. I wanted to slow down on smoking and drinking, after all this was my last year of school and I needed to focus. Gino and I tried to talk Kelly into coming to Sumner, however by district regulation, the Blumeyers bussed to McKinley on the south side. All the city kids wanted to get on the *Deseg Program*, especially if you could get a nice quiet county school. Me, myself, I wanted to be at a city school. The hood was good to me, I felt safe. This was Kelly's last year so it probably was senseless to leave his school. After all he'd been there since freshmen year. The crew agreed it made sense. Since I was driving anyway, I told him I would come swoop him up after school once I left Sumner.

Oh I forgot to mention-while I was enrolling at Sumner, my counselor told me by my attending private schools for three years, I had accumulated more credit hours than public school required. In simple terms, I only had to take three classes to graduate.

I know it seems as if my summer was spent hanging around my crew, but every once in a while, I went on dates. Usually I dated girls who had friends to hook my friends up with. That's just the way it was.

One day by chance I was driving past McDonalds. I saw three girls walking down Natural Bridge. Let's just say Natural Bridge isn't the place for three attractive girls to be walking. Something told me to pull over. I swerved to the right, catching Kelly off guard,

"Nigga what the fuck you doing?"

I point to the girls, "Let's pick these girls up; they need a ride."

I startled them the way I pulled over. "Excuse me would you like a ride somewhere?"

They looked hesitant at first.

One said, "We're okay. We stay up the street."

I was about to pull off, one of them caught my eye. At the same time, I caught her attention too. She had the cutest smile I've seen in a long time. I get a sense of innocence from her. This girl conducted herself properly.

She said, "I see you come by McDonalds all the time. I work up there."

I look and smiled. "I know. I saw you too. Hop in. I'm not going hurt you. *Promise*."

She smiled then told her friends to come on. She got in front with me and the rest piled in the back.

"What's your name?" she asked.

"Roland" I replied. Kelly looked over because I usually never give a strange girl my correct name.

"I'm Roland and you are?"

"Shelly" She said.

"Shelly, that's a nice name. Cute."

She corrected the way I pronounced it. "It's Shelly with a lee at the end."

Then she gave me a strange look. "Shelly? That's a simple name."

While giving me directions, our conversation kept getting interrupted. Before I know it, we were at her house."

I slowly pulled over. "That's your house, huh Shelly? I got to remember that when I come visit you."

She smiled, "Wouldn't you like to call first?"

"Of course," as I opened the glove compartment to grab a pen. I couldn't find a scrap piece of paper so I tore a piece off the owner's manual to write her number on. I'm thinking, *"No way I'm letting this pass me by."*

As I drove off, I vowed to myself that Shelly would be hearing from me.

So the next day came and I got up. I got a strange uneasy, feeling. I went to check the pockets of my jeans where I last placed Shelly's number. Nothing! I'm like "Shit. What the fuck I do with that number?" I even ran out and checked the car and came out empty handed. I thought to myself, *"Should I go back? Naw, that's too thirsty. I will catch her sooner or later. My loss."*

Well school started and I was excited to see how the school year would be. It's pretty familiar when you're from the city and go to a city school, you're bound to run into grade school and former classmates. The first few days were hectic. Trying to learn your classes, get books, and situate shit. After a week went by, things got real GOOD. Man I felt like Prince walking through the halls. The younger females were pointing at me. Some even asking can I feel your hair. I was in heaven. Oh, when I got in my car. Shit really went berserk. "Can I come with you?"

My ego couldn't have gotten any bigger. Life was spectacular. My friends were my wingmen. They hooked me up with more females than I hooked myself up with. Gino would tell me who was digging on me, Lavell would go pass a number off for me, and Kelly would occupy one female while I talked to another. What's crazy is with all this fame, I was still a 17-year-old *virgin*.

Not that I didn't have opportunities. I just wasn't ready, *yet*.

With fame also came haters. Now I could ignore most ignorant comments. My philosophy was you can say what you want, just don't touch me. One day that shit went out the window. During school I had early dismissal at 11:30 a.m. since I only had 3 courses. Gino and Lavell's last class was at 1:10 p.m. I'm walked through the hallway talking to one of the hottest girls at Sumner. We talked about the weekend, possibly hanging out. I noticed up ahead a group of guys staring hard. Straight mean mugging me. I could feel this about to go south. We walked and I'm thinking, *Okay maybe I'm paranoid.*

But, suddenly I heard, "That nigga cuter than the bitch."

They said it loud too. Now the whole group was twice as big as me, but regardless, a man's reputation is all he has.

I stopped, turned around and said, "So my nigga, you're a fag right?"

He grimaced, "Bitch, what you say?"

I spoke louder, "I said since you think I'm all cute and shit. You're a fag! That makes you the bitch, *Bitch*!"

I knew it was about to go down. I was wishing Gino and Lavell were around, but before I could put my books down, someone hit me from behind. I'm dazed for a moment. Then I'm curled up on the ground being stomped out. The only thing I remember was sitting in the nurse's office. Gino and Lavell ran in.

Gino yelled, "Fuck naw! We're going fuck them niggas up!"

Lavell looked concern, "You good, dog? Don't worry, pay back a muthafucka."

I slowly stand, "I'm good, just take me to my pop's place."

Arriving at the bodega, my pop was sitting outside. He noticed I'm red in the face and my clothes are kind of ripped.

He shook his head. "What happened, papi?"

I dropped my head. "It wasn't my fault. Some dudes jumped me for no reason."

Gino tried to butt in, "Mr. Page."

That's all he got out. Pops put up his hand. "I'm talking to my son."

My pops yelled down the street, "Hitman, come here!"

Now Hitman was an older cat that frequented the bodega. He had a reputation as being one of the most ruthless cats in that part of town. Nobody ever said his government name. He was only known as *Hitman*. He walked up to my pops and looked at me.

"Damn, *Lil Bob*! What happened?"

"Some hating ass niggas jumped me at school."

He looked at my father. "I got this Bob."

Now after the incident I laid low for a minute. I didn't even go back to school for over a week. My ego was crushed, besides I was embarrassed.

Once I got back, things were cool. People were comforting and concerned. After an investigation, the guys got kicked out, from what I heard. It wasn't their first incident like that. The shit even got back to the neighborhood so I was certain shit was going to get handled sooner or later. Gino and Lavell got suspended for trying to fight the guys after the incident. It happened the following day, but they were back about the time I returned.

I vowed to avoid trouble if all possible. At times it seemed difficult because I could control my actions, not other people's actions. A hater will be a hater.

On senior cut day, we decided to go up to U-City high school. I was excited to go because I had many friends there. They had a football game so a few students from Sumner decided to follow me up there. When we got there, I parked in front. I saw so many people I knew from my Mercy U City days. Of course there were the haters staring trying to figure out who I was. For the most part it was good catching up with my old friends. I was sitting on my car and a few girls walked up and started talking to me. We were having great conversation, but in the distance, I see a disturbance. People started gathering and it's apparent a commotion is going on. Suddenly I saw some dudes I know from Sumner running in my direction. I didn't even know all of them like that. I recognized two of them and they were merely schoolmates.

I said to myself, *"Why are they running directly to me?"* Urgency kicked in when one runs up and tried to get in my car. I lost my mind! In a spilt second I had about thirty U-City students tearing off my door trying to get him out.

I was trying to get them off my car. This dude got me into a fight I had nothing to do with. Of course it gave the haters reason now to react. Now there were 60 students beating the shit out of maybe twelve Sumner guys. The police came and ordered me to leave.

I was angry as hell and yelled, "Do you see my ride?"

The cop yelled back, "Leave or I will lock you up for trespassing!"

So I head straight to the bodega, more scared what my father is going do to me. The passenger door was hanging on by one lose screw. Pulling up, pops immediately honed in on the damage.

He dropped his head, "What the fuck!"

I began to explain, "Pops we got jumped at U-City. For real this time wasn't my fault."

He looked confused, "First of all, what are you doing at U-City?"

"It was senior cut day so we went up there to chill. I wasn't on any drama."

He exhaled, "You got the money to fix it. So fix it."

In amazement I say, "*Okay*." He never mentioned it again. For certain he was highly disappointed in me. He explained maybe it wasn't my fault, but I was guilty of not making wise choices in life.

I wondered what happened to the guy who jumped in my back seat. I can't recall if I ever saw him again. If I did, we probably would of whooped his ass. He turned a peaceful visit into a melee. The crew and I decided to stay in our lane. We only went to places where we knew we were good. I decided to hang with pops a few days to help out. Possibly make up for my fuck ups.

One day after school I went by the bodega. Pops asked me to go get him something to eat at Bing Lau Chop Suey. Sounded good. I could go for a shrimp St. Paul sandwich (Egg Foo Young). When I got there, I placed the order and went outside. It was packed inside so I knew it might be a minute before I got my order. Looking across the street I noticed a softball game going on. It looked like a lot of people there.

I thought, *"Fuck it, I might as well till my order is ready."* I walked over but the game has ended. I thought to myself, *"Shit I missed it. Oh well I'll go back."* I turned around and started walking back. I heard a familiar voice.

"You never called."

I turned around. There was Shelly with the gleaming smile. I remained cool.

"You know what, my clumsy ass misplaced your number. I'm sorry real irresponsible of me."

She poked her lips out and said, "Yeah- right."

"No for real. I beat myself over the head for losing it. I was going to stop by McDonalds but I didn't want to seem creepy. But here I am now."

She smiled again, "Yeah-here you are."

After that day things got so much better for me. I met someone with a great aura. This time I wasn't going to lose the number. I remembered it by heart.

I started seeing Shelly on a regular. We talked on the phone for hours. My brother would get mad.

"Nigga damn you always on the phone. Give somebody else a turn."

I would hang up and soon as the phone became available, I would call her right back. She would sneak on the phone late at night, whispering under the covers.

Sometimes her mom would pick up and say, "Shelly it's a school night."

When we would walk through the park, she would grab my hand or lean her head on my shoulder.

I would look at her and think to myself: *"I must be falling for her; it so easy showing affection."* Gestures like a kiss on the forehead came so natural. She would out the blue hug me from behind resting her head against my back. I never experienced this kind of interaction with a woman before.

Even the crew knew her and gave her due respect. Come to find out we had a lot in common. She attended Sumner but transferred to Kirkwood High to finish her senior year. Also come to find out I knew her brother Darren. He was cool and a great local wrestling standout. He was a year older than me. I believe he went to one of the community colleges in town.

Shelly came from a tight knit family like mine. I admired the bond she and her family had even though I felt they were a bit skeptical about me. Darren approached me at McDonalds one day. He basically told me, in a nutshell, he and I would remain cool as long as I treated his sister right. That wasn't a problem for me because Shelly had me wide open. Our chemistry was so right. I found myself addicted to her presence. Maybe because I was a bit more mature, I took our friendship more seriously.

After school I would always go by Shelly's house just to spend a little time with her. Sometimes I would take the crew with me. Gino liked Shelly's cousin Chrissie. Chrissie was really cool with me. She definitely supported Shelly and my friendship. I don't think Shelly realized how exclusive we were. Asking a girl to be your girlfriend was outdated and just down right corny. It never entered my mind if she was seeing anyone else, but this kid was spoiled. I wanted to make it perfectly clear I didn't like sharing. Shelly was an outgoing person; people who worked with her loved her. Everybody called her *Lil sis*.

One Saturday morning I met her at a McDonalds softball game. She wanted to catch an early movie. Once the game ended, a guy manager at McDonalds walked over and picked Shelly up to give her a hug goodbye.

Now I knew it was an innocent hug; the guy was older and maybe even married. Nonetheless I was still jealous, therefore I took the opportunity to do the corny thing of asking her to be my one and only.

"We've been talking for a minute. I think you know I'm really feeling you. I've never been interested in a woman like this before. So I wanted to know if you wanted to be my lady?"

She grabbed my hand as we walked, "You're asking me to be your girlfriend? That's so cute." She laughed.

I stopped and gave her a serious look, "Come on, mami. You got me feeling kind of corny. I'm serious."

She gave me a warm look, "Of course. I just want to make sure you're mine and mine only."

I winked and said "Deal."

That was the best decision I had made in a long time. I questioned at times was I worthy of a woman like Shelly who is every man's dream-- ambitious, devoted, and loving. I was in love and it was scary because I knew I was a fuck up. The odds were against me. My crew consisted of all single horny guys who encouraged me to be a whore like them. Just keeping it real. Being faithful wasn't a problem though. I think Shelly had her suspicions about my friends although she never said anything. I could tell she wanted me to spend time with her alone. I understood why. Most of the time when my boys were around, I was high or drunk. That wasn't Shelly's forte' but she never complained. I loved her for never judging me.

Trying to live up to my parent's expectation was a bit stressful. And this naturally beautiful girl I so adored made me feel like a king. She laughed at my jokes, would feed me popcorn at the movies, and rub my hair when we took a nap. She spoiled me more than my mom. My family embraced her also. It was the first time I brought a girl around since Tracey, besides at that time I was only 15.

Shelly calmed my storm. For that reason, my family appreciated her. Now her family on the other hand thought I was a playboy. It's hard to shake a reputation especially at age 17. They were always polite but I'm sure they told her move with caution. Now her mom was another story. I see where Shelly inherited her sweetness. Shelly's mom was the type of woman who saw the best out of anyone. Her voice was so soothing.

Shelly knew I was popular. Sometimes I was just cool with girls strictly as friends, nothing sexual. It still made her uncomfortable and rightfully so. To be honest I would have had a problem with it if the shoe were on the other foot. Men will never admit that we are hypocrites. Trust and believe I had no intentions on betraying her. I just liked conversation with the opposite sex at times. Listening to the fellas all the time would fuck a man's head up.

Could you imagine everything would be *"Fuck her!"* Sometimes I wanted a softer opinion.

I had one home girl name Kendra. She was more of a homie than the crew. Shelly wasn't crazy about the situation but she dealt with it. I never told her that Kendra was gay, it wasn't my place. It probably would've made things easier if I did. Darren didn't like it one bit. Kendra took me to White Castle one night. We were laughing walking out and guess who is there?

Darren! He was with his partners.

He said, "I'm going make sure I tell my sister I ran into you."

I said, "You do that."

He got angry and then said, "My sister's at home waiting on you to show up Muthafucka!"

I shook my head, "Darren I'm just up here trying to get something to eat. It's not what you think."

"Fuck that. It's exactly what I think!"

As we pull off the lot, I thought, "Oh shit. I know Shelly's going to trip especially with her brother in her ear." I call her as soon as I get home.

"Man, your brother."

She cut me off, "I heard. Just tell me it's innocent."

"Baby it is. You got nothing to worry about. I will have Kendra tell you."

She was quiet for a second, "That's not necessary but I have to be honest. I'm not too crazy about her. I think she likes you."

I sighed with relief. Darren and I were never cool after that. Deep down I knew he was right. Shit I would have done the same for my sisters.

I would tell Shelly, "Look I understand were your brother coming from. I don't owe him an explanation. I owe you. That's your brother it's up to you to handle that."

Her mom was always the peacemaker and I believe she was cheering for us to make it. She wanted happiness for her daughter. It was the respect for her more than Shelly why shit didn't get ugly. She kept Darren and I in check.

As time marched on, we got more serious about our relationship. The discussion of sex, my bad, making love, was brought up quite often. We had passionate chemistry but she got scared when it came time to going all the way. I was ready. I loved her so deeply in my mind making love would only bring us closer. I would stare at her sometimes and tell her how beautiful she was. She would say, "Stop" but I knew she liked the attention. If the crew knew some of the stuff I was saying they would drive the shit out of me. Being romantic came so natural when I was around her. Discussing our future plans came up often. One thing in agreement, we wanted to be together forever. At times I think she didn't trust me. She would often say, "Please don't disappoint me baby." When she said that it would penetrate my soul. I had no intentions on ever leaving this girl. After a few months in, our chemistry was burning hot. We knew it was time to consummate the relationship.

One night we stopped in the park in a secluded spot. I was excellent at finding the private duck off area. The mood was so right at that moment. We started kissing passionately. Man I barely took a breath, with every kiss I wanted to taste her. She allowed me to unbutton her shirt and unsnap her bra.

I thought, *"YES."*

Before she would stop me saying, "I want our first time to be perfect."

Now when you're 17 you don't have the luxury of access to a house or even a private room. At that moment, no other time was perfect than right fucking now. I could feel my manhood stretching to the point that it was hurting. The only relief was something wet and warm. What I expressed in words now, I whispered every word in Shelly's ear. I gently nibbled on her ear and kissed her neck. I paused a moment and looked her directly in the eyes. "Mami I want you so bad. I wish I had a private place to make you feel comfortable. But for me, here and now is right. We could be on a sinking ship and as long as I'm with you, it's *so* right."

That sealed it. She undressed in the back of my car and gave me an experience I never felt before. What I said wasn't a hustle either-that's what made it so erotic. There was no doubt in my mind this girl loved me deeply. The first time was painful but she endured it. Toward the height of making love, she put her fingernails into my back to give me an experience of pain. That physical contact made me erupt. After a minute or two, I gathered my senses. I was still on top of her. I kissed her on the nose and she kissed me on my shoulder. We gazed at each other for a few seconds. She whispered, "Did you cum in me?"

I closed my eyes and slightly dropped my head sighing. "I'm sorry baby. I did I got caught up in the hype. I can kick myself in the ass."

She hugged me. "Just don't leave me if something happens."

I hugged her back tighter and whispered, "Never."

We had so many erotic experiences and every last touch was romantic. That was the amazing thing about us. We were spontaneous if the moment was right. We would make love on a golf course, drive in theater, even in the parking lot of the movie theater. Yes, she deserved better, but you can't stop passion when it's burning. Sometimes it's uncontrollable. Shelly was my drug and I was addicted. Not just the sex either-this beautiful girl soothed my soul.

Things were going great with Shelly and the crew was fussing that I kicked them to the curb. They insisted that I get my priorities in place. In their mind neglecting them was neglecting the weed business. They didn't have the resources or finances that I brought to the table. Eric would front me work and allow me to get him on the back end. The crew didn't have it like that so their pockets got thin. Shelly didn't know my hustle. She thought maybe I was just spoiled and my parents gave me anything I wanted. I would bring her around the crew every so often. I wouldn't expose her to danger. It was truly the glory days.

Shelly got a kick out of the fellas. They enjoyed her company at times. They knew if they wanted me around, there was no choice. I was spending time away from home yet I still saw my mom during the day. We would catch up and talk about what was going on.

We would argue once in a while but no matter how upset I got; I wouldn't leave without telling her "I love you."

She was good with that. My pops on the other hand didn't get the respect I should have granted him. I barely saw or spoke with him. Two hustlers so much alike caught up in their own lives. I had an uneasy feeling I was neglecting the bodega. I would wake up with the intention of going to sit with pops, but I would get diverted and wrapped up in my own needs.

One night about 8 o'clock, I stopped by the house to grab some more money. I pulled up and noticed a police car parked in front of my crib. I immediately got paranoid but still hurried in. I told Shelly to wait outside.

I was thinking *"shit did they find my weed stash in the attic?"*

As I walked in I saw my mom panicking. She ran to me, "Thank God you're here. Your dad got shot!"

All the guilty emotions I have ever felt flooded my heart. I immediately thought it's all my fault. I should have been there like I intended to. I rushed my mom to Barnes ER. I don't believe the police even told us what hospital. I just knew Barnes is where trauma and shooting victims went.

We get to the hospital and I told the triage desk, "My father was shot. His name is Robert Napola."

She cut me off and said, "Room 11. He's on black out but you and your mother can go back."

I looked at Shelly and she said, "Go head baby. I'm here."

I thought "Damn, I'm lucky to have her."

I put my arms around my mom and rushed to the room. The curtains were closed but I could hear my father's voice from the hallway.

"I don't know who shot me. I keep telling you. What do you think in a few minutes God's going to come tell me his name?"

I felt relieved. My mom started cursing him out in Japanese. He started laughing saying, "Damn, I thought you'd be happy I'm not hurt."

I asked, "You, okay Pops?"

He looked at me and said, "If three wars didn't take me out, I'm not going to let some nigga off the street take me out."

He looked at me and then looked at the police. I ask the police, "Can we get a moment with my father, officer?"

The officer shook his head in frustration, "Sure we were just leaving If you hear something Mr. Page please don't hesitate."

They walked out. I peeked out to make sure they were gone.

I leaned over to hear my pops whisper, "Their going to keep me for the night. Drop your mom off. Go back to the bodega; the money is under the mattress. Grab my pistol under my car seat. Drew was the one who shot me." He sees the anger in my eyes and grabbed me by the arm to pull me closer. He looked me in the eyes. "Don't you do shit. You don't make a move. He shot me cause I was going to shoot him. That's *my* drama not *yours*."

I shook my head "No." I say, "Not acceptable pops. He gotta get touched." I knew Drew. He was a groupie that hung around the bodega. He was actually one of my pop's groupies but he was the type of cat I never trusted. Couldn't put my hand on it until now.

My pop's sits up and gets louder. Anyone could see the military authority my pops possessed. "Boy you will do what the fuck I tell you. Do you understand?"

I looked to the wall and shook my head "Yes."

He barked, "Look at me when I'm talking to you. Do you understand? Everything will get handled in due time."

I looked at him, "I understand pops." My mother and I hugged him.

I did my pops' wishes. I took mom home first, then Shelly. During the ride, I'm quiet. She pulled up the middle armrest in my car and scooted next to me rubbing the back of my head. Tears started rolling from my eyes. She wiped them away kissing me on the cheek.

"He's going be alright baby."

I replied, "I know, mami. That's not it. I should have been there. I've let him down. He would have never let me down."

We pulled up to her house and I parked. She scooted even closer, almost in my lap.

"He doesn't want that type of life for you. If you were there, it probably would have been worse. Plus, I need you. So like you promised him, promise me you won't do something stupid." She started crying hugging me tight. I pulled her closer smelling her hair.

The next day when I picked my pops up from the hospital, he got up from the wheelchair and walked to the car as if nothing happened.

He turned to the nurse, "I got more metal in me from the war. Three times this amount. This is nothing."

We went back to the bodega. Pulling up, he's greeted by a crowd smiling and praising him, "We're glad you alright Bob!"

I then heard something like, "Let's get a dice game going!"

He smiled, "Let's get to it." I watched him walk in the back without a limp.

He turned and looked at me smiling and then nodded his head. I leaned against the jukebox slowly looking around the bodega.

I thought to myself, *"I can never let this happen again."*
Week later pops was a diabetic so he wasn't healing like he should have. He started walking with a limp resulting in him to using crutches. I must confess the whole ordeal was extremely stressful. I was scared for pops' health. I was still in school and I had Shelly to think of. I knew sacrifices were going to be made that were not in my favor.

I started hanging around the bodega a little more often with the crew. It would always be at least two deep. Kelly always carried his pistol and if he couldn't be around, he left it with me. I would spend at least a few hours there. Majority of the time I was high. I would mask it with Polo cologne and Visine so pops wouldn't suspect me. Once I felt pops was surrounded by stand up guys, I would leave. Hitman came around when he could. He would pull me to the side assuring me pops was good.

"*Lil Bob* don't worry I got this. He raised his shirt showing the pistol tucked in his waistband.

Time at the bodega meant time away from Shelly. The absence of her only added to my heartache. When I would go visit or pick her up, I could tell something was bothering her. She never complained. Shit I could see the difference but I lived in denial. Most the time I would come around her drunk or high, tainting my whole perception on life. I loved Shelly more than life but at times I got caught up in my own woes.

I would tell her shit like, "Look if I don't make you happy, why don't you find someone who does?" She always comforted me, knowing what to say. Deep down I started to realize she was too good for me.

Thus far I had made mistakes but I never lost a grip on reasoning. The bodega was exposing me to temptations that were contradicting the morals I was taught. My pops at times fell under the weather so I would go run the business for him. Being a veteran, the VA would admit him to a rehab for days to weeks outside St. Louis. My pops hated me around the bodega but what choice did he have?

He constantly warned me, "Papi, always make the right choices in life. If something is brought to you and it doesn't sound right. Let me know."

I would assure him, "Don't worry pops I know how it's done." The harsh reality was. I was doing my own thing.

During my pops absence I saw other opportunities to increase the profit coming in. My presence at the bodega attracted younger females; it was the cherry on top for the crap games going on. Most of the patrons were older working men who had nothing better to do than gamble and trick their money off. The math was simple; more women more older guys showing off who had deeper pockets. The result was more money in the house. Also selling a dime bag here and there kept me from venturing off. The money stayed in house. Of course my pops would flip his top if he knew. However, bills needed to get paid and I was in charge. Hitman and the crew were there to watch my back. Hitman even had my crew shook.

Gino would say, "Nigga I'm wild but that Muthafucka on some other type shit. I'm not trying go to the penitentiary." Hitman made me feel like a true Boss.

"*Lil Bob*, you're a boss now. Pops wants me to hold you down and that's what I'm going to do," he'd tell me.

The extra-curricular activity I knew my pops wouldn't like so I kicked Hitman out to keep things on a low.

The business didn't skip a beat. I would take money to my pops every week. One particular time he looked weary and out the blue apologized to me.

"I really don't want this life for you, Papi. Pops will be back soon."

I rubbed his shoulder letting him know how much I appreciated him.

"Pops, I appreciate you believing in me. Don't worry. I'm good."

He then asked me if I was going to school. I looked down and said "Sometimes."

He rubbed his head with disgust, "If your mom knew she would blame this on me."

"It's not your fault, pops. I'm grown. It's just I can't concentrate on school right now. School's not paying the bills."

He would sit up from the bed and yell, "You're not grown! You're only 17. What the fuck have you done or seen yet? I want you to finish school. You want to spend the rest of your life in the fuckin bodega? Is that the life you want?"

I'd hold my head down and say, "No I want better but for now what choice do I have? For real I think I could double the revenue at the bodega."

He promised me if I finish high school we could discuss a partnership.

Word got out that I was hit and miss at school. It got to Shelly who was so disappointed. She wanted the best for me. Dating a high school drop-out only meant one thing in the '80s. Flat out loser. Frankly I didn't care what anybody else thought of me. The thought of disappointing Shelly bothered me, bad enough we wasn't spending much time together.

"Is it true you haven't been to school in weeks? You forget I know everybody at Sumner."

"You know why I haven't been. Who else is going keep the business afloat? Huh? My brother is away at college. My sisters are all married. Who else I got Shelly? Yeah, I want better for myself, mami, but what else can I do? Your dreams are yours. How you get there I applaud. My dream is mine. How I get there is my path. You never judged me before. Please don't start now when I need you."

She'd rub my chest with both hands, "I love you, Mr. Page."

I smiled then winked, "I love you too Mrs. Page."

This stellar woman never let me down. *Never let me down.*

Shelly wasn't having the neglect though so she came around the bodega to keep me company. I usually didn't want her around that type of atmosphere.

One day, she gave me a sad face, "I'm so hungry."

"You are? Let's see we're right by the west end. Come on I know where we can go."

We started walking down the street holding hands. It was a warm spring night. I pulled her closer and put my arm around her neck.

I whispered, "Thank you."

She looked and said, "What for?"

I lean my head against hers, "Holding me down."

As we walked a guy with a nappy Afro passed by stops then asked, "Which way is Delmar?"

I replied, "You walking the wrong way bro. It's back there."

He quickly turned around a full 360 degrees twice and walked away fast.

He yelled, "Thank you very much!"

I gave Shelly a strange look and start laughing. "He's special, what you think?"

She laughed back, "You think?"

We began to discuss what college she wanted to attend.

She said, "I been thinking about SIU Edwardsville. What do you think?"

I shrugged my shoulder and said, "That sounds cool. It's not too far right over the river. I been thinking about my future too, mami. Maybe I will enroll at the community college."

She gave me this big grin and said, "I thought about the nursing program there too."

As we were still walking, she wrapped both arms around me. I asked, "What if we move together?"

She grinned again, "I would like that."

I joked, "That's all-- like? Not love?"

Suddenly the same guy walked by real fast and almost bumped into me.

"Yo, excuse me! You didn't find Delmar."

That's all I got out. He turned around swung as if he was trying to knock my head off. He hit me on the chin knocking me back into some bushes. I was dazed for a quick moment but I snapped out after I heard Shelly scream loud.

I hopped up to see he's chasing Shelly punching her in the back. I ran after him yelling, "I'm going fuckin' kill you." He ran off and I gave chase.

Shelly screamed, "Roland come back!"

I stopped and ran back thinking she was hurt. "You Okay, mami? What's wrong?"

She started crying uncontrollably, "Oh baby." I looked down noticing my t-shirt was slowly turning red.

She said, "He stabbed you, baby." She began to scream for help. I awakened in the ambulance. She's still crying.

I comforted her, "Don't cry baby. I'll be alright nothing I can't handle." Déjà vu! Like father like son.

The incident made Shelly and I bond tighter but it brought a division between her and her family. They were concerned with her wellbeing. Word started to spread maybe it was a hit or retaliation from something I had previously done. The harder they pushed us apart, the harder we fought to stay together. Like her family, my mom thought maybe Shelly was a distraction for me. After all I had been an honor student at one point. She felt that I was too young to worry about a relationship. My mom never wanted to see the bad in me yet she knew there was bad in me. Does that make sense? I guess you know my father didn't take the news well. After discovering I was cool, he blamed me like I forced this dude to pick up the knife and cut me. He slid my collar to the side looking at the five-inch cut on my neck.

"What the fuck you do that would make him want to do that? Look at your neck. You do realize he was trying to slit your throat? Papi, muthafucka's don't do shit like that for no reason."

"Pops I swear to you. I have no idea why. Maybe he was cracked out his fuckin mind. He didn't try to rob me. He just did it and ran off."

I know it sounded like a broken record to pops. One can't always control the nature of people around him. I felt like my parents wanted me to live in a glass casing to protect me from outside forces. I couldn't live like that.

He asked, "Shelly okay?"

"Yeah I ran him off before he could hurt her."

He nodded, "That's good. That's good she wasn't hurt."

I scratched my head and say, "Now if I had a strap."

He immediately cut me off, "Boy you ain't no gangsta. You a little mix boy that went to private school and got into a few beefs. Now you ready to shoot someone? Throw that shit out your mind. I better never catch you with a gun!"

"Okay! Okay pops I got you. All I'm saying is that people carry guns now and I don't wanna be caught with my pants down."

He rebutted quickly, "Don't do shit that will make a person wanna pull a gun on you. How 'bout that?"

I acknowledged him nodding yes.

All the negative feedback from the incident started to play on my psyche. I questioned myself. Did I do something to somebody? I wondered maybe I should distance myself from Shelly. I never would forgive myself if something I did resulted in harm to her. Avoiding her wasn't easy. I loved her with all my heart. Crazed and confused, I started drinking, making all the wrong decisions. Hanging around the crew, they started to encourage me to see other girls. They liked Shelly but advised others if I wanted to get her off my mind. *Cheat*. I never thought I could cheat on Shelly until it happened. I can't even speak on it because it was meaningless. I can't remember her name. It happened so spontaneously. I barely knew her. She lived down the street from Kelly and invited me in her room one night. I felt like shit. I didn't call Shelly for a few days.

After a week of not talking to her, she called.

"Hey. Long time no see. Where you been?"

I spoke low, "Nowhere, mami. Just around helping my pops and shit like that."

"Did I do something to you Roland?"

I paused, "No not at all."

In a pleasant tone, "Can you come see me?"

"Sure." She invited me to her sister's house. Once I'm there, we talked. I told her how much I missed her and let her know she's too good for me. She suddenly undressed leading me into a bedroom. We began to make love. Her moans aroused me so I thought of different ways to keep her pleasured. I licked her toes while I was still inside of her. Then after I climaxed, I realize women can have multiple orgasms so I began to kiss her all the way down between her legs. She started to shake. I began licking and tasting her. I started to talk to her from between her legs. This came so natural.

I asked her, "Do you know how you make me feel?"

She whispered, "How?"

I drove my tongue deeper inside her responding, "Like that." I came up and licked her ear saying, "It's wet and warm. It feels so good to be inside you baby."

After that experience, we made love like two grown-ups. We were talkers letting each other know how delightful it was. She would always let me know when she was climaxing. That way I could thrust deeper, grabbing her from the lower back so she couldn't run. I never let a time go by where I was selfish. I made sure she got hers. And I used every tool I had to make sure--finger, tongue, lips, whatever it took to get the job done. We would get sore from making love two or three times a day. It was the most beautiful experience I ever had.

Still I couldn't get right. I started to have so many affairs. Some of the girls knew Shelly and just wanted to get with me for a fuck. I stooped to an all-time low. I slept with two sisters at the during the same time period causing them to fall out with each other. One time I was headed to a hotel party and I saw some guys who lived in the neighborhood. They pulled next to my whip. A girl in their back seat yelled out, "Hey Roland with your fine ass. Can I ride with you?"

I was drunk as a skunk. I said come on and let Gino drive. She and I got in the back seat and went at it all the way to the party. Gino actually parked on the street and I was so drunk we were still going at it.

To let you know how reckless I was, the crew and I went to Halls Ferry Movie arcade. We're leaving and a group of girls started following me.

The oldest out the click said, "Aren't you Roland?"

I said, "Yep, do I know you?" I noticed she was fine.

"No but everybody knows you up at Normandy."

I walked up to her and said, "You should come with me."

"I can't but you can take me home. My mom is working overnights."

Before I knew it, I'm in her room with her legs spread eagle. She said, "I shouldn't give it to you so quick but I like you. We're going to keep in touch?"

I whispered, "Of course," smiling while my face is pushed in her pillow.

I gestured my lips saying, "Yeah right."

Now during all this, I know you're saying, *"What the fuck I know about love?"* You're so right. This new person I become was plagued by drugs and alcohol. The old Roland was long gone, buried in his selfish woes. The Roland who cherished Shelly had gotten corrupted by his stupid street philosophy.

Shelly wasn't stupid by far; she'd heard things but didn't want to make waves. She was putting up with my shit. Sometimes my conscious would get the best of me. Speaking to me, *"You foul ass dude. You know damn well you don't deserve her."* We would always talk it out and make up.

She pleaded, "I don't want to break up. I want you to do right by me." I would reach deep down and get it together for a while only to fuck up again. Progress then regress. I know you're wondering if I wore protection. *Of course!*

School was almost out and I had to get it together. One day I was at school. Yeah, I was at school, you heard right. I told you it was a hit and miss. I was at school and had an epiphany. Unless you get it together Roland, you are going to lose everything good to you including your life. As I stood by my locker, the thought of me being homeless entered my mind. I slammed my locker and walked straight out the school.

On the way out, the security guard said, "Where you going? Class is in. Do you have permission to leave?'

With the most serious look on my face, I replied: "Yes sir. Not to worry I'm not coming back."

I left the school and went straight to the Army recruiter's office. Guess what? I never returned to school not even to clean out my locker.

The next day without studying, I passed my GED. I didn't have to take classes because my GPA was up to standard. I only needed three credits to graduate. The recruiter asked me, why didn't I just complete the school year or even go to summer school. I told him I had my reasons. I needed to go.

The news didn't go to well with Shelly. However, she was supportive. I told her I was doing it for us. I was in need of discipline. I was losing myself, the man she loved. We discussed marriage with her eventually coming with me. She said she would. I believed her. The ball was in my court, all was needed was for me to man up. My family excluding my father was all for it. They wanted me to get out the city before the city made me a statistic. Pops, a retired war veteran, was against the armed service. The remote possibility of war breaking out was his fear. He tried to talk me out of it but my mind was made up. I told him I would be back a better person like he wanted. We would put our future business plans in effect.

I booked the first available date out. I scored so high on the ASVAB test I pretty much could go when and where I wanted. I got my orders to go after literally a month and a half. I was ready to bounce.

The day I left, Shelly drove my father and me to the airport. They walked me to the gate. Surprisingly my father shed a few tears. It hurt me cause I never saw my pops cry. I shook his hand and hugged him.

"I will be back, pops."

I kissed Shelly as she started to cry. "Be back before you know it baby girl." Then I was gone.

CHAPTER SIX

ARMY BOOT CAMP WAS FUN. I met so many people of different cultures, religions, and political beliefs. I even came across a few racist soldiers. It's funny how the thought of war can psychologically unite a brotherhood. Not saying it erased racism completely however it did calm tensions down a bit. One thing in basic training that will always stick out is my drill sergeant. Mine was a brother from New York, Sgt. Rivera. In my opinion, he was the coolest NCO I have had the pleasure of knowing. Basic training introduced me to some of the nastiest people I ever met. Have you ever seen an individual blow his nose with his hand? Downright disgusting! Oh in the field I saw a soldier wash his ass then his face. It blew my mind. I couldn't believe he washed his ass first then out the same towel to his face like nobody was watching. I couldn't take it. I told him if he were an Indian his name would be *Ass before Face*. He didn't take the joke well. We banged it out in the mountains of Alabama.

My Bunkie became my hang out partner. Pvt. Long from Lubbock, Texas. Isn't it strange when you're in the military you identify people by rank and where they're from? Long was a country boy, truly if it wasn't for him, I would have folded at times. Dealing with the physical training was a breeze. After all I was a military brat myself. My pops was three wars deep Army hardcore. My expectations were high, I could handle this. I have strong DNA. The demanding training, the combat exercises, and classroom sessions distracted me from thinking about Shelly, but sometimes I would look up to the sky wondering what she was doing. Blue skies reminded me of her smile.

The separation from my family and friends were another thing. I missed my parents. I would call to talk to them once a week. I could have done it more but I I said before I didn't want distractions. Out of sight, out of mind. However I worried about my pops. I wondered if Hitman was keeping his promise protecting him. I was sure he was. He was a loyal dude. I didn't talk to my crew but I often wondered what my boys were up to. I would often think about the wild shit we've done, laughing to myself.

After boot camp, there was AIT. At this stage of training, we had so much more liberty. It was like being on the streets again except with a whole new family and restrictions. I needed the discipline if I was going to get my shit together. What I remember most are the weekends. I was stationed in none other than NYC and loving it. NYC during the '80s was the hottest era on the face of this Earth. Long and I would hit the clubs every weekend, two or three a night. We picked up a third leg to our posse. A native New Yorker by the name of Pringle; he was a reservist so he was familiar with all the live cubs in the city. Man, no dull moments for me. My routine consisted of training, drinking, partying, and PT.

Yeah it was fucked up because drinking was a problem for me back on the block. No worries though, the Army kept me in check.

The Fever and Roxy's were our favorite nightspots to frequent. Long and Pringle loved the Spanish women there; me myself, I couldn't get into the exotic females. Reminded me of my sisters so it was sort of creepy. Hey, I loved black women--the way their deep complexion blended by their feet to their naturally shapely curves. Not to mention their feisty attitude-- I found it challenging.

I loved the way a sister would say, "Boy bye, I hate you," only to fuck the shit out of you if your game was tight. However, I looked but didn't touch; after all, I was there for a mission. Getting my shit together.

Being in the Big Apple was wonderful especially since I was a Hip Hop junkie. The rap game was blue collared if you know what I mean. There wasn't too much fakeness and the message was dope. KRS-One, Rakim, Public Enemy were delivering the real. I watched Boogie Down production rock the hottest performance ever at a Fort Dix nightspot!

The schooling was easy; my MOS was Aviation Flight Operation basically a pencil pusher for air traffic control. As of yet I didn't have any diversions in the military so my grades were on point.

About one month in, I noticed one of my instructors started to flirt with me. Her name was Sgt. Desiree' Cruz, a black Puerto Rican from Miami. She was subtle with her flirtation. Fraternization was prohibited in the military, especially among the recruits. She was feeling me out to see where my head was. I would leave her a Reese's Peanut Butter cup every day on her desk. One particular day in class, something told me to look up and she winked at me. I had my reservations. Believing in karma I wanted to be on my best behavior, but I was lonely. Also not knowing what Shelly was doing at times bothered me. That phrase *"Jodie got your girl and gone."* is real. I sometimes would call Shelly to let her know if there was any doubt in our relationship, I would understand.

It would upset her, "Where is all this coming from? Have you met someone yourself? If that's the reason say it."

It was what I needed to hear, thinking I must be the luckiest cat alive. Regardless of Shelly's assurance, I was still skeptical. My paranoia got the best of me. I completed my course with Sgt.

Cruz. If it was going to happen, the time was now. I was moving on to another class therefore I wouldn't see her as much if any.

One lunch break I approached her, "Hey Sarge?"

She smiled, "Page, you can call me Desiree now if you like."

I nodded my head, "I'm just showing respect, mami."

She smiled, "So I'm your, mami? I like that."

That was all I had to hear.

She was about four years older than me. This woman played no games. We set up a date on a Saturday. It was convenient because she had her own apartment in Queens. I was nervous because things were moving fast. I would go stay with her on the weekends. We had sex on the first date. It was my first relationship with an older woman. Back home I talked to a few cougars here and there, nothing serious. Her sexual appetite was on a different level. I wasn't used to having another woman cuddle up on me. That was strictly for Shelly.

Foreplay was my specialty and Desiree demanded it. She was great for my ego. She would have orgasms at the drop of a dime. Sucking toes, clothes burning, fingering, and oral pleasure were mandatory in the bedroom. At night while she was asleep, I would stare at the ceiling feeling like shit.

I would say to myself, "*If Shelly leaves me, I deserve it.*" I had my suspicions about Shelly. What I didn't know couldn't hurt me.

My AIT was four months long. I was already 18. I hadn't returned home in months not even for the holidays. I wanted to save money plus Desiree had no family state side. She would throw a fit if I talked about going home.

She would say, "You always said you stayed in trouble back in St. Louis. If things are going good for you here, then why leave? You're a grown man now. I'm here. Isn't that enough?"

I was so conflicted. I started to see how demanding Desiree could be.

At times I would think, *"What the fuck did I get myself into?"* In a short time, she insisted we have a *relationship*. Well I did soup the situation up at the same time I felt we just had a thing for the time being. Desiree started to talk about me requesting permanent duty station in New York once my technical training was up. She insinuated how marriage would make the Army more acceptable of our situation. Things were getting out of hand. I went along with it for the moment. I had a little time to sort this out. I figured when the time came, I would handle it. I felt bad Desiree was good to me nevertheless my heart was with Shelly. Desiree's possessive ways began to annoy me.

During the weekdays, I got my break from Desiree so I returned to the barracks. Walking across my company one afternoon, my First Sergeant called me to his office. "PFC Page, when was the last time you called home?"

I waited a second, "It's been a while, First Sergeant."

He stopped fumbling through some paper and gave me a serious look, "I suggest you call home soldier."

Rushing to the pay phones, I immediately called home.

"Hello!" I heard my mom's voice and closed my eyes. Her voice sounded so pleasant. I almost start to cry.

"Hey mama. How's everything going?"

"Loland where have you been? We've been trying to get a hold of you. I called that girl Desiree. Didn't she tell you?"

A rage possessed me, "No, mama, she didn't. Are you Okay?"

"Your daddy is sick. His diabetes has affected his condition. The bullet in his leg has caught gangrene. They have to amputate his leg." She started crying.

My voice started to crackle. I tried to stay strong. I dropped the phone to my side. "FUCK!"

I heard her call my name, "Loland, you there?"

I pick it back up, "Yeah, mama, I'm here. Who's there with you?"

She really started to cry, "Only your brother, Ronnie."

I told her, "Mama don't worry. I will work things out. I'll be home soon." I can tell my assurance soothed her. "I love you mama. Tell pops I love him too. I'm coming home."

I hung up the phone then wiped the tears from my face. I picked the phone back up and slammed it back down.

I thought, "*I'll wait to confront this bitch face to face.*" How could a person be so fucking selfish not to say my mother had called?

Reporting to the chain of command, eventually my company commander advised me to take as much time as I needed. The command station was aware of my situation. Pops had deep connections with the military's brass. I was ready to go home the next day. I couldn't wait to see what excuse Desiree would have.

The next day I caught the IND subway to Desiree's apartment. Usually I changed into my civilian attire, but this day I was mentally off. I'm in my BDUs. I'm sitting alone staring off not aware of my environment.

Suddenly I'm alerted by a voice, "Wah gwaan wid yuh?" I looked up and notice three dread heads.

"Everything criss man?"

I looked confused saying, "What's up homie? What can I do for you?"

He sat across from me and pulled the butt of a pistol from his coat. He didn't point it at me but he made sure I saw it. I let out a deep sigh.

"What the fuck do you want man. I don't have anything for you to take. I got $15 to my name."

I shifted my legs outward in case I had to do something. I wasn't going make it easy for these muthafucka's to knock me. I noticed one of them light up the biggest cigarette I had ever seen. I smelled a familiar aroma. It's the most fire weed I ever smelled in my life.

He put his hand on my shoulder, "Dat fifteen do jus ire."

I shrugged his hand off my shoulder and gave him the money.

Pitifully shook my head from side to side, I mumbled, "Man this isn't my day."

He smiled, "Big up man ya luk stress. Hit dis." He passed the cigarette to me.

I give him a crazy look, "Dude look at my uniform. You know I can't hit that shit!"

He stopped smiling and flashed the gun again, "Dat's na a request Man."

I snatched the cigarette from him. As I pulled on it, I see the tip light up while the sparks make a popping noise. I immediately started to choke. They started laughing hysterically as they exited the train.

I didn't report the incident. Can you imagine, "Excuse me, officer, I was robbed of $15 by three Rastas, oh yeah they made me smoke some weed."

Now walking to Desiree's apartment, I was more heated. I knew this wasn't going to go well.

As I walked in she was lying curled up on the bed watching TV. I tossed my keys to her apartment on the bed as I started packing the little items I left there into a duffle bag.

"So when were you going to tell me my mom called?"

She immediately sat up looking surprised. "I'm sorry baby. It completely slipped my mind. I was so tired after work. Is everything alright?"

I was so pissed my hands started to shake. "Fuck naw! Everything's not okay! My father is sick. They're going to amputate his leg next week!"

She started to stutter, "I, I, I was going to tell you."

I cut her off, "Desiree, that was two days ago."

She noticed me packing my duffle bag, "Where you going?"

I saw her eyes tearing up as her voice crackled.

I threw my hands in the air, "Where you think I'm going, Desiree?"

"Okay, then I will go with you."

"Desiree, you can't go with me. I'm not sure when I'm coming back. Command center issued a hardship separation for me."

She hopped up hugging me tight, "Don't leave me, Roland. Not like this. It was a mistake. I simply forgot. I would never do some shit like that on purpose."

I hugged her back, "Let me go handle my family affairs, then you can come and see me."

She cried laying her head on my shoulder, "I'm not going see you again."

I rubbed her back, "Of course you will, baby." She was right though. I had no intentions of returning.

Going home, I was nervous. No one knew I was coming except my mom. Arriving at my home, I stood in front of the house for a few seconds and smiled. I knocked a few times.

I heard my mom. "Who is it?" the Japanese accent made me smile wider. She opened the door.

"Loland, you're back!" I hugged her for two minutes straight. I started crying.

"Mama, where's pops?"

She pointed to his room, "He's here until the operation."

I heard his voice, "Is that my baby boy!"

"Yeah pops. It's me" as I slowly walked in his room, he sat up from the bed. He looked me up and down noticing the air assault wings pinned on my chest.

"Papi, look at you." He smiled. "Soldier on, young man."

I replied, "Soldier on, Master Sergeant."

I fell in his arms and it reminded me when I was a young boy-the way my father hugged me to comfort me.

"Pops, you alright?" My voice saddens.

He gave me a look of reassurance, "I'm good. Don't you worry about me, this ole dog got a few good years." Hearing his voice relieved all the stress I was carrying.

A day went by without me calling Shelly. I wasn't sure how to deal with seeing her again. I was fearing the unknown. A few hours passed and I gave in. She deserved that respect.

I called her house and her mom picked up, always pleasant as usual. She told me that Shelly was at her sister's house. I wait an additional few minutes. Suddenly the phone rings.

I picked it up thinking, "Shit, I was about to call Shelly."

"Hello." There's a short silence.

"So when were you going to let me know you're back?" It was Shelly.

"Hey you. I just got back. Actually I was about to call you."

She told me her mom called her right after I hung up. She thought I would call immediately but as I said before I procrastinated. She asked me to hurry over.

Pulling up to Shelly's house I was nervous, excited, all of the above. I didn't know what to expect. I walked up to the door cool, calm and collected because maybe she was peeking out. Before I could even knock, she opened the door.

I walked in and she quickly closed the door behind me. She hugged me so passionately it caught me off guard. I hugged her back and started to smell her hair. From there we couldn't keep our hands off one another. She would keep stepping back looking at my chest. The military life does a body good. Everything was physical and emotional. We barely said anything. I was aroused from the moment I hit the door. It's the first time that she hurried to undress me. We made love for hours, falling asleep in each other arms. After a nap, we woke up and talked all night. She told me all the 411 in the city, the update on my friends and how they were protective of her in my absence. It was like I never left. I realized what true love was. No matter through time, space, or distance, a person's feelings would never change. That's love. The question now was, did I deserve her love?

I never mentioned my military life when we talked. I avoided the discussion. I could tell she was curious but didn't want to rock the boat. After a day or two, she told me something that ruffled my feathers. While I was washing my car she said, "I was going tell you something but don't over react. Okay?"

I stopped washing the car and looked at her, "I can't promise anything if I don't know what it's about."

She smiled, "You look good in that tank top with your muscles."

I shook the towel towards her splashing a little soapsuds in her direction, "Stop playing. Tell me."

She hesitated, "One of the guys that jumped you last year called me out by name."

I dropped the towel, "When and where?"

She explained as she was going into White Castle after a party. He recognized her saying, "That's the bitch that dated the nigga we jumped."

I started to pace back and forth. She walked over to me and hugged me. "Don't let that get to you. I just thought you should know in case you run across them. I don't want you to be caught off guard."

I wrapped my arms around her and gave her a kiss, "I'm cool baby. No worries."

I thought to myself, *"Pay back is a bitch."*

The day of my father's operation rolled around. I was there every step of the way. He was at Scott Air Force Base, about forty minutes outside St. Louis. That day will scorch my memory for the rest of my life. I walked in the recovery room and I saw my father look at me with tears in his eyes. I approached the bed and he suddenly pulls the cover back. The shock of his leg missing hit me like a ton of bricks.

I got light headed and quickly sit down.

"My God!" I started to cry. I caught myself. I had to be strong for him. I grabbed his hand.

"We got this, pops. We got this."

My mother helped my father in every way she possibly could. Emotionally, financially, and spiritually; I believe it was the first time I heard my mom pray to Christ. It threw me for a loop. She was Buddhist so the shift in faith baffled me. It wasn't hard to figure out regardless of your belief, Allah, Yahweh, we all call on a higher power.

Once my father came home, it was either my mom or me that dressed his bandages. I became his personal chauffeur until he got the swing of driving with a prosthetic leg. That took a while. My pops was an old strong proud individual. He didn't allow this physical disability to get the best of him.

Shelly was a great help also. She pushed me to put my life in order. I ignored the past infidelity. I vowed not to return to my old selfish ways. The first thing I needed to do was get a job. She was working at the mall so she brought me applications to some of the neighboring clothing stores. It didn't take long for me to land a job either. I started a full-time position at the Oak Tree men's clothing store. It was one of the freshest spots for men's clothing at the time. My closet was well stocked with all the current fashions. Besides work, she got me enrolled into Forest Park Community College.

The military granted me an Honorable Discharge due to my father's situation. They informed me if and when I wanted to return, it was a phone call away. I knew I had to manage my time to help my father at the bodega. Having a full schedule kept me busy. What was good was Shelly and I worked and attended school *together*. At work, we took lunch together; at school, it was the same. We were connected at the hip. She kept me focused. Shelly wasn't thrilled about me being at the bodega yet she never complained; she was the rock I so needed. Plus she saw the change in me.

One Friday night I went to get my mom some White Castle hamburgers. I pulled on the lot noticing a thick crowd of people hanging out. I thought about going to a different one but I say, "Fuck it. I'll run in and out."

Walking out, I checked my order. On busy nights they never get the order right.

From the distance I heard, "Roland! Hell naw! "I looked up. There's Kelly, Lavell, and Gino the entire crew. They run up and we do a group hug. After a minute of handshakes pounding each other up and more hugs slapping me on my back, they ask, "Nigga, where you been. We heard you was home."

Kelly, always considerate, said, "Bro I heard about pops. I go by there every once a while to make sure everything straight. I figured you would reach out when you were ready."

I must admit I was happy to see each and every one of them. Gino started pushing me to their car, "Nigga I know you want to take a swig of this Ole E."

I laughed, "Why not. What's going on? Where's everybody coming from?"

Gino said, "Skate King has the Hottest High school night."

I shook my head as I looked around to see any other familiar faces.

We caught up for about thirty minutes laughing and joking. Lavell cracked jokes about everyone, Kelly asked me how was New York. Already on the third forty of Ole E, I felt good. Something told me to scan the area again. I saw out the corner of my eye, one of the dudes who jumped me.

I ask Gino, "Is that the nigga that jumped me back in the day?

Gino turned around and said, "Yep that's the nigga. What you wanna do?"

I noticed he was drinking with a group of cats from Sumner whom I was actually cool with. I told the crew to go over and start conversation with them.

"This between me and him. Just make sure nobody jumps in."

They casually slid over there and I saw everything was friendly. I got short hair therefore no one recognized me. I popped the trunk of my car and grabbed a golf club that I had in there for years. It came in handy just for situations like this. I walked around the lot avoiding the crowd and using the golf club like a cane. Nobody even noticed that I was lurking.

I thought, *"I don't even know this muthafucka's name but he's about to know mine."* I saw him take a long chug from the forty of beer.

I crept up and said, "What's up bro. Long time no see!" I swung the hell out of my five iron.

CRACK!

He fell against a parked car. I saw he was leaking blood from his mouth. The forty spilled all over his face. It caught everybody by surprise. "Damn!"

Nobody reacted because they knew this was a foul dude. He was known for doing fucked up shit to people. Guess what? Karma came back and bit him in the ass.

As I walked away, one of the guys I knew said, "Ro that was fucked up. You didn't have to do him like that."

I looked over my shoulder, "Just like he didn't have to do me."

I suspected there would be some sort of retaliation about the incident but there never was. I heard sometime later that he got shot while on the riverfront after jumping an older dude with his girl. He was paralyzed from the waist down. Some people never learn.

I never told Shelly what happened. I knew she would have overreacted. She noticed the crew was back in the picture, not to her liking. I understood why. The crew brought out a wild side of me that was hard to control. Maybe it was due to the drinking or maybe it was birds of a feather flock together. The fellas knew the pressure I was committed to becoming a better man and wanting to secure my future at all costs. They agreed that's what we all needed to do.

My pops' health started to decline and he would have to take extended rest periods. One day, two days, sometimes a week. I had to pick up the slack. This threw a monkey wrench in my college schedule. Shelly would stay on me. I would snap on her although I knew she just wanted the best for me.

She would say, "You're changing again, baby. I'm scared."

I would sarcastically shout, "Shit is easy for you. Look I got a lot on my plate. Could you try and understand instead of riding my back?!"

One day at the bodega, Hitman approached me. "*Lil Bob* I got a business proposition for you. Have you ever did cocaine?"

I thought nothing of it, "Naw. Heard it's a hella of a high. Never have though. Why?"

He pulled out a small sandwich bag with chunks of white powder in it. He handed it to me.

"*Lil Bob* this shit here is the new thing. This can turn the bodega around." After that day my life went from bad to worse. I started selling grams of powder. Most of my clientele were young white females who had money, students from the universities. I still worked at the mall part time and I had some of the managers hooked. Some would even give me free clothes to pay off the debt. I didn't care, it wasn't my job on the line. My pops wasn't around much so I pretty much did as I pleased. I would close the bodega and go hang in the Central West End, a classy entertainment part of the city. It consisted of restaurants, nightclubs, and novelty shops. Oh yeah, it also had plenty of women with money. I became popular among the white top 40 clubs. They love to party. The difference from the urban clubs is white people want you to have as much fun as them. You don't have to buy drinks cause they will get you fucked up without your spending a dime. One evening, sitting in a VIP booth at TOP's nightclub, I meet this exotic looking female name Beth.

She walked up to me and asked, "Do you mind if I have a seat here?"

"Go ahead," I replied.

She scooted next to me, "What's your name? I'm Beth."

"Hey Beth. I'm Roland."

She smiled, "Roland. You're handsome, if you don't mind me saying. What's your nationality?"

The music was loud so I leaned over, "I'm Japanese, Black, and Indian, a mutt so to speak. How about you?"

She put her hand on my leg, "I'm American Irish and Vietnamese."

I looked her in the eyes, "*Nice*."

She whispered in my ear, "Do you like to party?"

"Party like what Beth?"

"I got some coke. Do you want some?"

I paused and looked around. I was thinking "*Is this bitch an undercover or what?*" I should of got up and walked away but I didn't.

"Sure." I then snorted my first line of coke from a straw and small envelope.

I soon saw why people call cocaine *White Girl*. It's the in thing, it can hook you, and give you the illusion you're on top of the world.

Beth and I started seeing more of each other. She was from a wealthy family; they lived in a huge mansion off Lindell Avenue. Their house was on some Scarface type shit. Her family members were liberals, the type that were friendly to Black people. Beth's family was welcoming to me. Shit, I thought they would be judgmental about Beth being around Black people. Not! They even accepted my crew. My friends loved her too.

"Dude you better lock her down. You'll never have to work again," my boys told me.

In a way, they were right. I stopped going to class and work. I got fired from Oak Tree; they suspected the entire store of stealing after an inventory audit. As far as college, I said fuck it and never went back. I started using coke on the regular. Beth had plenty of it as long as I was with her. The times that I wasn't, I would hit my savings account if I had to. I figured it was meant for us to meet; I was hustling a little here and there, but Beth kept the dope available.

Beth was generous to me. I wanted to use her car, she came through; I needed liquor, she would hit her father's wet bar; she shopped at Saks Fifth Avenue and always brought me back an outfit. She fueled my addiction.

Beth invited me to a party in Chesterfield for AG Edward's investment; her uncle was an executive consultant for the company. The party was hosted at a mansion built on the side of a cliff surrounded by a man-made lake. It was quite an experience. There was lots of coke, rich snobby people, and free alcohol everywhere. I sat on the patio with Beth and she asked me how I liked the party.

"It's great. Damn this house is nice. So this is your uncle's spot?"

"Yeah when he transferred from Jersey, they rented it to him."

I looked around in amazement, "Must be nice. Shit if I could afford this…" I paused, "I don't know what I'm saying I need a new car and can't even afford that right now." I laughed.

She leaned on my shoulder kissing me on the cheek, "What type of car do you want?"

I looked at her, "A Pontiac Fiero."

The next day she called me. "Hey, can you ride with me to look at some furniture?"

"Sure! You want me to come get you or what?"

She always seemed so happy, "No I will come get you."

She picked me up. We rode on Lindbergh and I asked, "What furniture store is out here?"

We pulled up to a Pontiac dealership and she said, "I will give you the down payment, you just might need a co-signer."

After three days and my older sister co-signing, I had my new black Pontiac Fiero.

By now you can see I started distancing myself from Shelly. I loved her to death but the drugs had me. She would always plead for me to save myself. She saw me spiraling out of control but I was in denial. In my eyes, I was just having fun. I took advantage of the one woman who loved me unconditionally. I became abusive to her physically and verbally.

So many times I would catch myself and say, "Baby when I start to trip, tell me so I can catch myself."

Easier said than done. I started to flip out more often. It wasn't that I desired Beth more than Shelly, not at all. It was the addiction that came along with being around Beth. I didn't even love Beth. There was no comparison between the two. Shelly was a queen and I'm not saying anything was wrong with Beth. It was just we were bad for each other. I knew I was losing Shelly. It was a matter of time when the break up would happen. The thought of her absence from my life petrified me. She made me better in every way, but if you don't treat a queen like she deserves to be treated, she will move on.

After a night of partying, I went to pick up Shelly. She had already told me that she wasn't happy but I wasn't hearing it. We were riding around in my new car.

She looked at me worried, "You're not the same man I fell in love with."

I gave her a crazy look, "What are you talking about? I could be with a bunch of other chicks, but I'm here with you! Why you act like I'm the one with the problem, maybe it's you."

She started to cry, "I can't go through this Roland. I love you but I wanna be happy."

I got in a rage, "So what the fuck are you saying? You want to see someone else?"

She grabbed my hand, "No, it's not about someone else, but I deserve someone who appreciates me."

I snapped, striking her in the face. At that point I knew I had lost this woman and there was no redemption that could possibly fix what I had done. We had confrontations before that she tolerated but this was beyond forgiveness. I saw the look of fear in her eyes. I drove to my house begging her to forgive me. I noticed her eyes started to swell.

"Oh mami, I'm sorry! Let me go get you some ice." I ran in the house thinking, *"You dumb fuck, you did it this time! You don't deserve her!"* When I got back to the car, Shelly was gone. I knew I would never see her again.

I sunk into a deep depression fueled by drugs, a lot of reckless sex, and partying. My crew sensed my heartache but they encouraged me to take advantage of my relationship with Beth. Beth was comforting and she had no clue about Shelly. She thought the stress from my pops' health was the main reason, when in fact it was a whole plethora of problems. She meant well but buying me things didn't make the problem disappear. From time to time I would think of Shelly, seeing landmarks that reminded me of her.

Beth's cocaine habit was getting out of hand. She would want me to indulge so she wouldn't feel bad. Money was more important to me than a fucking high. Beth usually agreed with anything I suggested. So I devised a plan for her to make money and support her nose candy habit too. It didn't take much persuading. She went for it hook, line, and sinker. Hitman connected with his dealer to purchase four ounces. Mostly my clientele snorted so the quality was pretty good. Never stepping on my product kept my people coming back. I stuck with the basics-only grams or eight balls. With Beth's parents out of town, it was the perfect opportunity to package it up. All the time I was packaging, she and her friends were doing lines. I finally told her that was enough. She had to slow down; it was defeating the purpose.

The magnificent part of our venture was I really didn't have to sell as much. Beth's friends, classmates, and co-workers brought nearly all of it. Like clockwork, every Friday they would page me for a hook up. Certain customers I would credit, knowing they would pay by week's end. What I loved about my clientele, I never had to flex or coerce them to pay. Shit they were working class people, students, and a few business owners. What amazed me was the number of teachers that used coke. So much for a mind is a terrible thing to waste.

Beth resided in a rear apartment at her parent's estate. It was very much updated and private. I would stay there day after day barely going home. I would check on my mom and pops but only for a few minutes, then I was on the go. We would stay up for hours partying late. Kelly would come help me move the product. Gino was locked up for an assault with a weapons charge; from the word on the street, he pistol whipped a man who owed him money. Lavell had a full-time job and moved in with his baby's mama. Kelly and I hung out damn near every day. Of course Beth would tag along. I enjoyed partying with her; it was really fun at times. She would rarely allow me to spend money. Yet deep down I knew I couldn't keep this lifestyle up. How long would it be before the partying would catch up to me?

I felt like I was losing control. I missed Shelly. The one person who told me what I *needed to hear*, not what *I wanted to hear*. Every now and then I would see her in passing. She completely ignored me. I never had the guts to approach her and apologize. What could I say? *"Sorry for fucking your life up."* Oh well life marches on. The fall semester for college was here. I decided to go visit my brother Rob at Central Missouri in Warrensburg. He was on his last year. I planned on taking some product up there to sell, of course without him knowing. A few female acquaintances knew I was coming so I had already arranged a kick back. I told Beth it could be dangerous traveling out the city. I asked her if we got caught, what would her father say. Again, she agreed and thanked me for being considerate.

Yeah right. I went home to make sure everything was in order. Pops was there. At this point he was confined to a wheelchair. He rolled to the living room while I was packing.

"Papi, do you think you can take me to get a rib tip sandwich? I want to get some fresh air."

I stopped what I was doing, "Yeah, pops, but should you be eating swine?"

He rolled to his room, "I'm 75 years old. I'm going to eat what I want to eat."

He often said those words and I never argued with him. Sometimes I wished I did. As we are riding, he gave me detours and I suspected he wanted to just talk.

"You're always on the go. What are you doing?"

I replied, "Nothing pops. Just working."

"Is that right.? Where you work?"

I paused a second, "Kelly got me a job at UPS."

He turned and looked at me, "UPS? When you started at UPS?"

"I've been there for a minute. Overnights that's where I been."

"You still dating that white girl. What's her name?"

"Beth" I quickly said.

"Yeah- Beth. You know you fucked up letting Shelly go."

I looked away, "Well pops, I had no say in the matter. She left me."

He shook his head from side to side, "Cause you were fuckin' up."

I sighed, "I can't do anything about it now."

"No you can't but you can make sure you're not still making the same mistakes. That would be a start. Look papi, I'm an old man. It's a blessing to live to be my age. I want you to be able to do the same. The route you're going, it might not happen. I'm not afraid of death but no man wants to bury his child before he buries himself."

I was silent for a few seconds, "Pops you're trippin' over nothing. I'm good. Don't worry I'm not doing anything to cause trouble. Tell you what when I get back from visiting Rob, I will come around more. How 'bout that?"

He smiled, "Boy you full of shit."

I laughed.

When I arrived in Warrensburg, my brother was waiting outside his dorm with his friends so I didn't get lost. Kelly was with me. "Hey there's Rob. Ain't the color of his frat Black and Gold, right?"

"Yeah he's an Alpha" I replied.

As I pulled up he threw his hands in the air. "Damn dog! What took you so long, it only takes me two hours to get here."

I get out the car, "Well Rob I'm not used to traveling for hours."

I smiled and gave him a hug. He put his arm around me almost choking me.

"Hey frat! This is my lil brother. Roland. He's the black sheep of the family." He started laughing.

He pointed to them, "Ro, this my frat brothers." He named about five of them but I was too high from the joint we lit up on the way down to remember.

I nodded, "What's up."

He gave Kelly a pound and hug also. "Go get your stuff and take it to my room."

I told him that we were staying with a girl name Denise.

He started to laugh, "Okay you just said fuck your big brother. I know the little girl Denise she's been talking about you for the longest; cool just don't get in any trouble."

I grabbed my gear, "Man you sound like pops."

Soon as I met up with Denise, I send Kelly on a food run. She and I got it in. We started on the bunk bed then I picked her up and laid her on a giant beanbag. "Can't do that bunk bed."

She giggled and palmed the back of my head as I pounded away. When Kelly came back, the both of us were exhausted.

He started cracking up, "I hope it was good nigga. You out of shape?"

We were laying on the beanbag with a blanket over us. I looked up, "It was Great!"

She took me on a tour around campus, introducing me to people.

Most of them said, "Isn't that Rob's lil brother."

"Girl I know Roland."

"Is that your man? He's fine."

I kick it with Denise for that day and we have sex all night. Saturday came and I went to have an early lunch with my brother.

He asked, "You been with that little girl all night? Tell me you didn't raw dog her?"

SATO-PAGE

"Mann what you think? Of course I had protection." I lied.

He patted me on the back. "Look the Alpha party is tonight; I want you to come. So stick around. Right now I gotta go prepare the hall."

Kelly and I looked at each other and gave pounds.

"Let's go to the mall in Columbia. I forget the name." Kelley suggested.

I agreed, "But, I need a fresh fit." We blazed up a joint and cracked a 40oz on the way there. It was about a 45-minute drive. We browsed the store and I saw an Adidas outfit in the biggest store there. I went to grab my wallet noticing my pockets were empty. My eyes get big and I turn to Kelly, "Bro I left my wallet at Rob's dorm!"

Kelly started to laugh. "Nigga I wasn't planning on paying for shit anyway, if you know what I mean."

I smiled, "You ain't said nothing but a word." We started to grab clothes real casual like, as if we were going to try them on. Kelly even asked a sales woman where was the dressing room. She smiled and pointed to the corner. We grabbed the merchandise playing it off like we were getting each other's opinion. I don't think we even had a cue to run. It was instinct; we took off to the exit where my car was parked. An older lady gave chase, but it was cut short by the cologne display. I heard a scream and the sound of bottles hitting the floor. The entire thing went down so quick that we were back on the highway headed back to

Central. We laughed all the way back to the campus.

For a moment I thought, *"Boy if pops only knew, he would kill me."*

When we arrived at the campus, the sun was going down. I pulled up to my brother's dorm lot. I saw him with a worried look on his face. He started to walk up to me fast. He grabbed me by the arms, "Man, where you been?" I think how the hell did he find out I was shoplifting?

He started to cry, "I've been looking for you all day." He dropped his head still crying. I grabbed him back, "Rob, what's wrong?"

He took a breath, "Pops had a heart attack. He's gone."

I stepped back and silence overwhelmed me. I looked at Kelly as he started to cry. In a daze, I fell to my knees. Rob picked me up and we embraced, both crying.

After about five minutes, he said, "You gotta call mama."

I almost stopped crying, "Mama shit!" I ran to the dorm entrance where the pay phones were located. I franticly pat my pockets looking for a quarter. Nothing. I started looking around to everyone.

Suddenly Denise ran up and hugged and kissed me. "Baby, I'm so sorry. What do you need?"

Panicking I said, "I need a quarter, mami." She immediately dropped one in the pay phone. I heard my mom's weeping voice, "Hello." I can't even hear her accent.

"Mama you Okay? I'm so sorry I wasn't there."

She said, "It's wasn't nothing we could have done. It was his time. Your pops knew his time was near."

"I know, but I thought I would be home. I thought I still had a little time with him. I never expected it like this."

She started to cry, "No one knows when."

CHAPTER SEVEN

ONCE ROB and I arrived home, the reality set in as soon as I saw pop's car parked in front of the house. I stood there for a minute trying to imagine him sitting behind the driver's seat. I reminisced about when I was five or six watching him pull up and seeing his hard smile. When he got out, he stood so tall over the roof of the car. I would look for his hands to see if he brought me something home. White Castle, McDonald's Fun Meal, or a box of Cracker Jack with the prize inside.

Rob held the front door, "Come on man."

I hurried to hug my mom. I held her tight as she rubbed my back, "Yeah, daddy's gone."

I walked into his room and sat on his bed. On the nightstand I saw his watch and his military ring. I was speechless. I thought to myself hoping some divine way he could hear me. "You tried to tell me pops. I didn't listen. I'm so sorry. If I would of known, I would have stayed. I'm so sorry, papi." I broke down and cried uncontrollably.

Two days later at the wake, Beth took me to view my father's body. I sat in the private room and just looked at his motionless body. Wouldn't it be a joyful miracle if he would just wake up? All kind of scenarios lingered through my mind except the apparent.

My father was never coming back. Beth put her arm around me and rested her head on my shoulder.

She whispered, "I never tell you how much I love you." I snapped out of it looking at my pager at 11:40 a.m. I kissed her on her forehead, "Love you more."

The next month or so was difficult times for me. The bodega shut down; the landlord was aware of my father's death. I found out my father never resigned the lease on the space. I tried to renew the lease but discovered the landlord had already leased it out to someone else. I felt that my whole life was collapsing. I looked for answers usually available when pops was here. I had to be a man, figure things out myself. I took things for granted when he was here in the flesh. This man I so adored was no more. I thought my father was invincible, but we are all only human. Nothing is guaranteed besides death.

I slumped into a dark abyss. I drank more, did more drugs, and had no regard for life. Every time

I made a decision to get my life together thinking about the promise I gave my pops, I would renege, promising to do it another day. I began to stay more at home to be that support for my mom. Much to Beth's disdain, she would cry like a spoiled brat that I was neglecting her. I didn't have the energy to even entertain her behavior. I would just walk out shaking my head with her slamming the door. This bitch must be crazy. I recently lost my father and she had the audacity to act like this.

One morning all alone, I was sitting in the living room of my house. My mother lit a candle by my father's picture above the mantle place. I had the TV on but I wasn't watching it. I was pondering about at what breaking point would I get my miserable life in order. I began to talk to myself, "Pops, I wish you were here to help me. I can't do this alone. Please let me know something. Anything. Are you listening, papi? Your baby boy needs your help. Do you even forgive me? Oh pops please!"

I began to cry. A few seconds elapsed and the candle flame dimmed to nothing and the TV turned off. I sat up quickly. Suddenly the candlewick lit up to a bright flame and the TV came back on.

I stood up and grinned from cheek to cheek. I said, "I hear you pop. I hear you loud and clear."

That evening I told Beth we shouldn't see each other anymore. I stood accountable for the decision.

"Mami, it's nothing you did. It's me. Sometimes two good people are bad together.

We're both on a road to destruction. I don't want this for you and definitely not for me."

She didn't take it well but Beth wasn't a confrontational person. She eventually accepted my decision. We remained friends for a few months until we just lost contact. I heard she enrolled into college somewhere on the West Coast.

Through the next year I straightened things up quite a bit. My mother praised the mature attitude I now possessed. I mean I cut out the hustling, slowed down on the drinking, and I enrolled back at the community college. I was taking Criminal Justice classes, it seemed to be the easiest route to a degree. I still dated a lot with no established commitment. I was doing me. I even reconnected with Brenda, my high school sweetheart, from time to time. She had a great head on her shoulders and often gave me the advice I needed. We maintained a genuine respect for one another.

The school career placement center really came through with the J-O-Bs. Let's see, I started as a developmental assistant for a state mental institution. That was quite an experience by law; you can't recite any of the residents names. Still I had fun working there. It was so hilarious at times watching these grown men interact with one another. People use the words crazy or retarded not knowing that many individuals with disabilities share emotions like anyone else. They can be sad, happy, and boy do they have a sense of humor. Never ever did it dawn on me that some actually get drunk from drinking water. No shit *Water*

Intoxication, look it up. One of the white residents called every black male worker *Willie.* He didn't act racist; actually he was really cool with the brothers. He just called us *Willie.* You know what's fucked up? We answered to it.

The state hospital job was good but my schooling demanded more career experience. So I transferred to the Missouri State Correctional Facility and that was short lived. Being a Correctional Officer wasn't for me. I was acquainted with too many people incarcerated there. Sooner or later, I would have been placed in a compromising situation. Either someone was asking me to bring contraband in, or someone recognized me from my former dealings. I didn't immediately resign, I remained there for at least eight months.

During my quest to pursue a gratifying career, I was bored. Yet my determination to make my father proud was a motivation I couldn't abandoned. In death, my pops' influence over me was inspirational

Social life was humdrum for this one-time loose cannon. I had no love life what so ever. Of course, I dated but that was usually capsized with me being turned off with the female. Look I wasn't being picky, I merely was searching for Mrs. Right. If she did exist, I had yet to meet her.

My life as a prison guard was everything but exciting. For one, my work schedule was so unpredictable, I was plagued with insomnia. The shifts rotated every month and my body could never get accustomed to a shift. I wasn't sure how long I could tolerate a tamed lifestyle. Trying to be what I believed my pops perceived as a responsible man was my goal. I stood true to my commitment regardless how it made life so fucking boring. I worked at a prison 45 minutes outside of St. Louis. My coworkers were mainly wanna-be cowboys and some of the most backwoods individuals who grew up only knowing one black person in their entire life people. You had many that were cool but there were of few that had a fucked up perception on life. In their minds, it was white inmates, wetback inmates, and nigger inmates. For real, like nigger was an actual ethnicity in their opinion and nothing was wrong with it.

After evaluating my prolonged future, I decided to quit the turnkey career and pursue life as a full-time student. There was one dilemma. No job meant no money. What a decision but glancing in the mirror at that ugly ass correctional officer uniform, my mind was made up. Being a junior G-man was the pits.

Leaving the prison felt liberating; as the convicts would say turnkeys are part-time convicts. As a full-time student, my social life improved a little bit. I dated on a regular but, not to seem disrespectful, they were random females. Some of the names or faces I recollected. I found that avoiding emotional attachment kept me more focused on my studies. In fact, emotional detachment was less strenuous on the wallet. On occasions a female would offer to pay for a movie date, lunch at Culpeppers, or called just for some good ole steamy sex. My financial status had taken a hit and I was conflicted on returning to a hustler's paradise. What's a player to do?

Certain things during a man's college life, he doesn't forget. One afternoon while sitting outside Biology Lab, I was organizing some notes from the previous class. Down the long hallway this jazzy looking girl was causing quite a ruckus. She was arguing with some dude who appeared not to take no for an answer. As she got closer I could make out some of the conversation and it was quite comical.

"Damn baby you fine. You look like Vanity 6. Let me take you to dinner or something."

She rolled her eyes, "Boy, do you understand what No means? I don't want to go out with you. Plus you making me late for class."

As they approached I slightly laughed and shook my head. I believe it caught her eye.

"I can't give you my number because I got a man," she said.

He looked confused scrunching up his face, "Stop lying, where is he?"

She looked me dead in my eyes, winked, and smiled. "There he is. Hey baby, sorry I'm late."

She then caught me off guard because she tongued kiss me for at least ten seconds.

I thought, "Where the fuck have you been all my life?"

Dude stopped and waved her off. I heard him mumble, "She like them pretty niggas."

She pulled back and wiped the lipstick from my lips, "Is he gone?"

I laughed, "Yeah, you're safe, mami."

As she pulled out a piece of gum, she paused, "Mami? Oh wow I got me a Latino man."

Chewing that gum, she had the sexiest chew. I wished I was that stick of Double Mint.

"Glad I could assist you. I'm Roland by the way. And you?"

She grabbed her books, "Tierra. I'm late for class. I will be back here when I get out. Will you wait?'

I slowly nodded yes, "Sure why not. Can I have a stick of gum?"

Her next action almost had me sprung. This chick leaned in, kissed me and then stuck her gum into my mouth.

Tierra and I became smashing buddies, so to speak. Every day after school, we would rush to her grandmother's house like two horny rabbits and get it on. She was like my best friend with fringe benefits. Her grandmother worked the midnight shift somewhere I never knew. She was gone all the time. We would lay up in her bed and just talk like two best friends. She would ask me to come swoop her up. When I got there, she would peek out the door with a robe waving me to come in. As I got upstairs, off came the robe. She shared the same commitment issues as me. Why mess up something good? Our arrangement worked out fine.

Sundays were our designated hang out day. We would go to the most unusual far out spots-places where black people don't typically go. We went to Lake Carlyle Beach, the only beach front lake in the area, only with dirty water. We would go to Busch Wildlife, walking the nature trail. Now it might seem romantic but we wanted to just get out the hood. I lived in the Penrose area and she was from the Ville. A tranquil moment was a peace of mind that any sane person needed.

Tierra was daring, humorous, and comforting all in one. She was my true Bff like no other. Many times she would defend me from haters trying to come between us, exposing the fake ones pretending to be cool with me. I wondered if she had an appetite for the same sex at all.

"Hey best friend, look to your right, a girl checking you out. You better go get those digits."

I would casually turn around, take a quick glance, "She kind of cute. Oh wow you jealous?"

Infamously she'd roll those eyes, "Jealous? Boy please I saw you looking at her when we walked in. Stop frontin' go over there and pull her so we can take her home."

She made similar comments too often that raised my curiosity. Can't lie, the idea was tempting.

My money stash got depleted to my last couple of hundred so I had to make a few moves. I went by Eric's house to see what he had going. I had heard through the grapevine bro was living his best life. I knocked and took a seat on his stoop. He came out and immediately opened his arms, "My nigga! Stand up and show me some love."

I stood giving him a hard, sideways hand slap, "Dude your number changed I see."

He slapped me on my back, "Yeah moms did it, said I was giving the number out too much. Hoes were calling my crib all late and shit. Crazy. How you been? What brings you my way bro?"

I took a second looking around the neighborhood, "Shit sure did change, E. As kids I never thought there were so many responsibilities with being an adult. When we were kids no worries, no bills, and no stress. Damn! I miss those days."

He canvassed the neighborhood with his eyes, "Yeah bro, I feel ya. That's life Ro. We all go through it."

He lit a cigarette, "So again what's up? You don't come see ya boy unless it's something serious."

I chuckled, "You know me huh? I need some work. Pockets getting thin so I figured you would..."

He cut me off, "Enough said. My brother's keeper right?"

I smiled, "No doubt."

Eric stepped inside for a minute. Sitting back down I pondered on the yesteryears he and I shared as homeboys. I could always count on him even when I wasn't the friend he was to me.

He came back out and handed me a brown paper bag. I glanced in the bag. There was two ounces of chucky white powder wrapped in sandwich bags. I folded the bag and placed it under my arm. "So you flipped the script. No more herb?"

He nodded, "Times a changing lil brother. You gotta change with them. Only herb I got is when I'm smoking it. The turnaround on *Girl* is way more profitable than herb. You good with that, right?"

I smacked the bag, "Oh, I'm *real* good."

He laughed, "Oh okay, cause I thought you was scared or something."

I replied laughing, "Never that."

He pounded me up again, "Dude I'm going to get back to watching the Thundercats. You know Panthro is a brother right?"

Walking down the steps I stopped and turned, "E, I know I don't come around enough that's because I know I can always count on you bro. I always know you're good. Definitely my brother's keeper."

The next few weeks I got my money up pretty quick. The Coke business was a different game than the weed business. You have to be on your Ps and Qs. There's no room for a lame in this business especially in the hood. In the weed business, the customers are laid back; after one night you probably won't see them for a day or two. Now the Coke game brings some grimy characters and you might have to get grimy with them. I stayed away from individuals who would try and pond shit to me. If they stole from somebody to get high, they'd do the same to me--maybe even try and set me up to get robbed. I call them Crackheads, and whenever possible, I tried not to deal with them. I wondered if I had to lay a motherfucka would it be worth it, facing that murder sentence. That way of thinking always kept me safe. Expect the unexpected, never let your guard down, and trust no one. You hear it all the time in gangsta rap. There's truth in some of those lyrics.

I started to treat myself again. I bought a used Kawasaki Ninja 500 motorcycle. It came in handy on the gas mileage, shaking any unwanted people like Five O or a stickup kid. I outran a cop or two who wanted to flag me; before they could even turn around, I was weaving in and out of traffic and then poof. Gone!

Tierra loved my new toy. She always had some reason for me to come by. "My granny needs milk for her Honeycomb cereal." Or "I'm on my period and I need some tampons." Later that night, she would ask for sex.

"I thought you were on your period."

She was caught off guard, "Oh I'm actually coming off."

Anything so we could cruise the streets on my bike. It was apparent that Tierra's feelings were getting stronger. I could tell. After sex she would look me in the eyes and rub the side of my hair. She waited to see if I would say those words. It never happened.

The second semester rolled around; my schedule was really light that year. I only took two classes, so I could focus on getting my money up. I also got a part time gig at California Shirt Works inside River Roads Mall. I was lucky to land the job as an airbrush artist. I had the pleasure of painting T-shirts, Sweatshirts, even jeans. Airbrushing was popular in New York during my military stint when I was stationed there. I was amazed with the natural talent of graffiti artists. This was more of a hobby plus I gained more working clientele. It's crazy how many young women snorted coke. I mean some of the finest females one might not think would indulge. You never would know she enjoyed the nose candy.

School wasn't the same; Tierra couldn't enroll that year because of financial problems. She got a job at another mall. We sort of lost contact; if she did call, I was never at home to know. My mom often complained about too many females calling.

"Loland, why do you give this number out if you have no intentions on calling these girls?"

I asked, "Mama do they leave a name?"

"No and I don't ask. Just stop giving my number out."

I replied, "Okay ma. I'll stop giving this number out. Next time try and get a name please so I can tell them."

The older mom got the meaner she was. She could be rude to strangers.

I did have a pager but mom said, "That's not my duty to give your pager number out. I'm not your secretary."

The opportunity to meet more females at the mall got out of hand. I was literally talking to at least four different women. Mary was an older woman who worked at JCPenney. Her husband was away in the Marines. We hooked up from time to time even in the mall parking lot. Sue worked at Jeans West. She was more of a challenge; she threw airs like she had more than what she claimed. I hate a chick that constantly brags. I took her home and smashed this snobby bitch on the first night.

She told me, "I rarely do this, I hope you don't think bad of me." Of course, I went with the program.

No not at all. It's the chemistry between us, mami. It's funny how you don't have to know a woman long to realize you have chemistry with her. Me and you were meant to be." Like I said first night; 45 minutes after walking through her door, I was in her. I made up an excuse afterwards, trying my best to avoid her at work.

"Oh man I just took my break. Wish you'd told me earlier. Maybe tomorrow."

She got the point eventually. She would just roll her eyes when I walked by.

Then there was Sandy, a freak out of this world. I had to use a rubber on her even though she told me she was on the pill. This chick was kinky with a badass body. Hooking up with her was a bet with one of my fellow airbrush artists. Sandy was the assistant manager at Casual Corner. She made the ass of her Jordache jeans look like two scoops of chocolate ice cream. Yummy! We went at it in her dressing room during the store's audit. Sandy was the first woman to ask me to eat her ass out. I ate pussy on many occasions but not the ass. Yuck! Yeah I cut her off after a few weeks. Not just because the ass thing, it was an accumulation of things. Like one day she told me she brought me lunch. It was a fried Bologna sandwich. Don't get me wrong, I grew up on fried bologna with the slit to take out the bubble, but for lunch?

Then one time we had sex and her feet smelled musty. There you go, three worthy reasons for me to tell her to keep it pushing.

Mary was the first married woman I had relations with.

She would say, "It's completely innocent, just physical. I have no intention of leaving my husband. But a woman needs affection. Do you understand?"

I would comfort her the best way I knew, "I understand, Mary. I don't want you to leave your husband. You're honest. I admire that but there's nothing innocent about this, mami. I feel like a piece of shit; your man is away serving our country. I've been in that position before so I understand how you and how he feels."

She wrapped her arms around my neck and kissed me. "So you want to stop seeing me?"

I put my hands on her ass, "Hell no, but we have to be careful. It's a sin what we doing."

One day while I was cutting my mother's yard, Mary stopped by with a female friend. She doubled parked and ran up to me, "Hey handsome! How you doing?"

"Good and you? Who's your friend she's looking at me weird."

She looked down, "Oh that's my husband's cousin. She's cool. She understands my situation and won't say a word."

I turned off the mower, "Mary you are trippin! That's your husband's family. Don't think for one minute she won't tell on you. You're being messy."

She tried to kiss me, however I pulled back. "Call me later." I went back to cutting the grass. As she pulled off that passenger watched me until she was out of sight. I had the most uncomfortable feeling about this situation.

When karma taps you on the shoulder, heed the word of God. Out of the Ten Commandments, God addressed cheating multiple times.

The rainy spring season was making it hard to maintain a well-manicured lawn. After only two weeks mom, asked me to cut the lawn again.

"I know it's been only two weeks. Could you cut the grass, Loland?"

I mumbled so she couldn't hear, "Shit." But answered, "Sure mama."

It was hot for a spring day. The sun was shining bright so I was squinting. As I was cutting the grass, I noticed a silver newer model car pull up fast. We lived right off the highway so I was thinking it may be a lost driver again. A burly dark guy exited the car and walked up to me with no emotion.

I turned off the mower. "Can I help you?"

Suddenly he decked me right in my face. Before I knew it, my mom was tapping me on the face.

"Loland, get up! Why that man punched you like that?"

I shook my head rubbing it at the same time. "Fuck mom, your guess is better than mine."

She stood up over me, "Don't curse when you talk to me. You know why he punched you like that."

A few days went by and I hadn't seen Mary, not even at work. One night after leaving work I was walking to my car. I noticed the same silver newer model car parked three spots over from mine. When I got closer, I saw the high beams from the car flash. I was thinking, I hope that muthafucka's not going to try this shit again. Problem was my strap was in the car under my seat. I started walking faster to my vehicle grabbing my keys so I could hurry and open my car door.

I thought, "Get the strap. Get the strap."

The window of the parked car came down. "Roland, it's me."

I ignored it and grabbed my strap, tucking it in my waistband.

The voice said louder, "Roland it's me. Come here!" I recognized the voice.

"Mary?" She got out and leaned against her car. I slowly approached.

She folded her arms and started crying. "I'm so sorry."

I looked away, "So what happened?"

"Like you said. His cousin asked me to loan her some money; when I told her no, she told him."

I scratched my head, "When did he get home?"

"A week ago." She replied.

"Man, fuck! I told you. I got my ass whooped for you being messy."

She cried harder, "You're not the only one."

I looked at her, then leaned against her car. "Shit sorry, mami. I told you karma is a bitch. You know I want to fuck your husband up but I can't cause it's my fault. I knew what I was getting into. I just got to let this slide."

She stopped crying and gave me a puppy dog look. "I'm going to miss you. Thanks for making me feel wanted. I hope you don't hate me."

I exhaled, "Naw Mary, I could never hate you."

She smiled and kissed me on the cheek and whispered in my ear, "Good, because I love you Mr. Page."

I never saw her again. I wondered if she's okay.

School became too overwhelming. Even though I was only taking two classes, it was inconvenient for my goal. I had a plan to stack my money and eventually reopen my family business. I ended up withdrawing from school, which would allow me to return next semester without paying tuition again. Now working full time at the mall, my savings grew. I wasn't involved in a relationship therefore my expenses were pretty thin. I didn't go out much; if I did, it was with Kelly who was hustling along side of me. We took care of ourselves.

I enjoyed airbrushing and I expanded my fan base. Many appreciated my talents, identifying me as an artist. I loved that title because growing up all I ever wanted to do was draw. And now I was getting paid for it. Being the 80s, most of my artwork consisted of Greek fraternity logos, graffiti lettering, and painting the polo man onto Levi jeans. As my fan base grew, my ego grew bigger. At California Shirt Works, I was stationed in the front window for all the spectators to see my skills. Needless to say, most of the spectators were girls. The money wasn't great; the majority of money came from the sales staff throughout the mall. But Coke was a party drug. The more you did, the more you wanted. As I said before, one had to choose his customers wisely. My customers kicked it 24/7 nor were they cheap with their high. Every Friday like clockwork, they would go cash their checks at the bank, stop by my spot or meet me at the mall's game room. Quarter grams, teenagers -16th of a gram, and eight balls were popular. Months passed by and my bank account was growing thicker. I was content on how my life was progressing, but as they say: all good things must come to an end.

Unexpectedly California Works closed. I'm not sure why, the owner never gave any indication or explanation. I was truly crushed, but life moved on so I readjusted my game plan. I posted up in the U-City loop and worked strictly off my beeper. This made things so much simpler. All my clientele either came to me or I met them in a neutral location.

Being jobless wasn't so much a concern anymore. With more social time on my hand, my boy Kelly started coming around more. I needed his muscle and crazy antics to secure my back. Kelly purchased a 1979 Cadillac Seville aka Short

Dog; man, it was a thing of beauty. Cruising around the city, we had great times in that car. Even though it was older, it caught many of eyes. Plus, Kelly being mobile eased up my workload in the dope game. It was more than enough to go around, supply and demand.

The Loop consisted of the loyal customers who were never short on their paper -money, referred their friends, and weren't shysters. That went a long way with me. Shit most of them were college students who lived nearby. I would always get invited to the campus parties. I was the token black drug dealer whom everybody loved. Just think some of these people would be future doctors, lawyers, and politicians.

Everything was all gravy. Life couldn't be any better. Yet somehow I felt something was missing in my life. All the random women who were running through, I'm surprised I never got any of them pregnant. Sometimes I would raw dog it just for the hell of it. Tons of sex always ended up with me getting tired of the females quickly. I would smash on the first date at times and never call them back. At times I couldn't remember their names. Kelly ended up getting married. That was definitely a curve ball in my direction. I didn't even know his wife. You would think that I would know my best friend's girlfriend that turned out to be his wife. Nonetheless I supported my boy's decision and union.

Amy was an older woman and I guessed Kelly needed the security. She was a teacher and owned a townhouse in the Soulard area. Amy knew of my activities and wanted Kelly to distance himself from me. I didn't get upset or nothing. That was her job to keep him straight. I envied the idea of my friend having a good woman. A true friend shouldn't hold his boy back anyway. *Right*?

My bank account was right so I did the most responsible thing at that time. I went and copped me a new whip and boy was she a thing of beauty. I bought a black 1988 Ford Mustang GT convertible with red leather interior. A new car can do wonders for a person's ego.

My mom started to get suspicious of how I was getting expensive things. She was under the impression that I still had a part time job. I never told her that I was actually jobless. Needless to say, she knew a part time job couldn't make me afford a new drop top Mustang. I told her I got it on the first time buyer plan financing it for 60 months, a new thing at the time. She listened to the explanation but I knew she didn't fully believe it. She offered to help me get my license plates. I accepted the help because if I turned it down, she would have suspected something fishy. I spent more time in my car than in the house. During the chilly days, I still dropped the top. I loved the attention. It's true: A beautiful car can get you all the ass one can desire. I knew guys who had a nice car but were broke as fuck. However, I had a nice ride and money in my pocket. I was living the high rollers life.

One night I was under the weather so I decided to stay in. My mom kept trying to get me to eat Campbell's chicken noodle soup. I told her

I was good; I just needed some rest. Running the streets was catching up to me. I was laying in my bed reading a Right On magazine when the telephone rings. I picked it up and heard a familiar voice.

"Hey... How you been?" A pleasant voice said.

I smiled, "Hey Shelly. What's up stranger?"

"Nothing, I was thinking about you and thought I would give you a call." I hesitated for a second, "It's good to hear from you. I thought I would never hear from you again. Rightfully so, I owe you the biggest apology. I was in a fucked up place at the time."

She told me she forgave me long ago. Those words healed my heart immediately. Our conversation went good. I could tell that she missed me and if I pursued her, I probably could rekindle something. I didn't though. I was content that she forgave me. Deep down I felt Shelly was too good for me. I was living a trifling lifestyle. If you truly love someone, you don't hurt him or her any more than you already have. What Shelly and I had was in the past. I currently wasn't in the right frame of mind. From that day forward, we talked from time to time. I now believed we were friends.

The weather started to get a little warmer so I pulled the ole motorcycle out. It sure saved me quite a bit on gas. It was relaxing at times just to ride for long hours. I would take small trips to Lake Carlyle in Illinois just to clear my head. I would climb the hill by the dam, then watch the eagles roost among the trees. As strange as it sounds, this city boy was a nature freak. I always was fascinated by wildlife. Growing up, I looked forward to the new issues of National Geographic or watching Mutual of Omaha Wild Kingdom. Don't ask me why I found that stuff so entertaining. The outdoors was peaceful; I often wondered what it would be like to live out there. Then reality kicked in, Black people and nature just not compatible. My other preferential hang out was Forest Park where all the other bikers gathered. There were a lot of biker's clubs but I was a loner. I didn't fancy the idea of allying myself with any groups. Not my style. I did enjoy giving a girl a ride every now and then. Girls loved motorcycles so it was definitely an eye turner piece of machinery. The Ninja, my motorcycle, put a couple of notches on my belt. Having sex on a bike was a bucket list goal that I conquered early.

Men, we do the craziest things like try and remember everyone we ever slept with. While showering I would subconsciously count how many sex partners I had. At age 20, there were about 40-50 women that I could recollect. No lie! I would shake my head at times realizing how fucked up I was. I couldn't even remember some of the women's names. Hey at age 20, who gives a fuck? When I got horny, I would call Tierra for a sure booty call. Otherwise, I would go to a nightclub in Illinois called the Wiz. Never failed, I would leave with something hot.

One particular Friday night I met an interesting female by the name of Cynthia. Cynthia was one of the most exotic looking females I ever laid eyes on. Just by appearance, you couldn't guess her nationality, but she was Black and Sicilian. I didn't give a fuck what she was, I was getting up on that. We made eye contact as I was coming out the men's room and she out the women's restroom area. I was walked out waving my hands to dry them. You know how nightclubs never put paper towels in the restrooms--nasty ass.

She was doing the same. She smiled. "It's a shame isn't it?"

I smiled back, "You would think how much they make every night that they put some in there."

She felt my hands, "Exactly! Your hands are dry now. And they're soft, you must not do hard work huh?"

I pulled my hands away, "I might not do hard labor mami, but I work hard at what I do."

"Mami? I like that. You want me to be your mami?" She put her hands on her curvy hips.

"Baby girl, you can be whatever you want to be. I'm Roland."

She laughed, "So rude. I'm Cynthia, and tonight I want to be your friend if that's okay with you?"

"Miss Cynthia, that's just fine with me."

As she straightened out my shirt worn down from the sweat inside the hot club, she said, "That's not the alcohol talking is it?"

I chuckled. "Maybe, but regardless I'm not too drunk to know I like what I see."

An hour later we were in her basement room going at it just as sweaty as we were at the club.

If Cynthia and I had met any other place besides a nightclub resulting in first night sex, I would have pursued somewhat of a more stable relationship. However, if you smashed me the first night, I wondered whom else would you do. Don't get me wrong, we kept in touch and even went out a few times. She had crazy terrific sex. I even told her what she wanted to hear. "I love you, mami." She told me the same and that I was the only one she was with at the time. I doubted it. Our soirees carried on for about two months until Cynthia moved out of town to attend college. That was that.

Things got a little lonely for me. I was striking out with relationships and there was no shame that it was totally my fault. The streets and playboy lifestyle were getting old. Street life can be overwhelming; it's not like you have a routine schedule. Day by day may be a different story. Whatever life throws at you, you got to be prepared. Strike, foul ball, hopefully a homerun, nothing is certain.

A Sunday afternoon my mom asked me to run to the grocery store to buy some rice. She was making Sukiyaki -my favorite. I had a craving for it so I rushed to the store on the Ninja. Shopping for mom when she was cooking Japanese cuisine, you had to be on point. You brought the wrong ingredient; she would go ballistic. Bringing home minute rice for Sukiyaki might get me slapped in the mouth. Really! Oriental people take pride in their rice cooking skills, no cheating if you understand what I mean. I got the rice and decided to drive through Penrose Park just to be nosy. I got to the intersection to enter the park. The light turned red so I stop. Got to be careful cause Five O is usually posted off in the cut -hiding. I took off my helmet for a second to wipe the sweat from my head. The car next to me blew its horn and rolled the window down.

"How are you, Mr. Page?" The voice sounded so familiar. I flipped up my helmet's visor bending down. Oh snap it was Tracey! What a sight for sore eyes. The light turned green and I was at a loss for words. Behind us cars started to blow their horns.

I quickly said, "Pull over in the park."

She smiled and said, "Okay let me cut in front of you."

Usually women don't make me nervous but Tracey had that effect on me. All sorts of questions popped in my mind en route to the park. Word around was she got married and moved to Michigan. I hadn't seen her in years, but what I saw *Wow!* We parked, I got off my bike taking off my helmet. She exited the car and my heart dropped.

Subconsciously I was talking to myself. *"God damn, Ro! She's finer than a motherfucker. Keep your fingers crossed she's single."*

She walked up to me with the prettiest smile and hugged me for a while. The hug amazingly told me everything I needed to know. She missed me and I felt the same. It was like my pops was sending me a message from Heaven,

"Boy don't mess this one up."

We pulled apart and I said, "Hey you. Man where you been? Are you home or what?"

She straddled my bike and said, "I moved home after separating from my ex."

"So your divorced? What happened?"

She looked down "That's a long story but I'm in the process of getting a divorce. You'll get a chance to hear it, don't worry." She smiled.

We exchanged numbers and made plans to see each other the next day. I watched her pull off and I hopped on my bike.

Before I put on my helmet, I looked up to Heaven and said, "Thanks pops. Don't worry I won't."

CHAPTER EIGHT

A FEW DAYS WENT BY before Tracey finally called me. She asked me to ride with her to JCPenney to pick up a few things for her kids. I didn't act surprised; I had heard that she had a girl and boy by her ex-husband. On the ride to the store, the conversation was everything but boring. We caught up on what was going on in her past and current life. She couldn't wait to tell me the stories she heard about me and ask if they were true. I kept it truthful admitting to some and denying others. Off the bat the chemistry was hot and heavy. This time around I moved with caution, not to give off a thirsty or desperate vibe. I heard the best things happen for those who wait and that's the path I was taking. Time was moving slow with no complaints from me.

In our short trip to the store, we covered a lot of ground-- at least enough to know things happen for a reason. Tracey pulling next to me on a busy street and me taking off my helmet to wipe sweat from my head was not a coincidence. What divine power made that happen within those few seconds on that particular day? I felt my father from the heavens made that happen. Not to be too fucked up at times, I didn't know whether to look up or down when spiritually addressing my pops. He was a good father but not a totally righteous man. Maybe he brought someone back into my life to make me a better man than he.

Tracey came around every day after work to visit me. My mom remembered her from elementary and high school. Amazingly, mom was nice to her. For once I believed my mom was rooting for Tracey to win me over. She would stay for a while then go take care of her responsibilities. I respected that about her. Many of the young mothers I met would put me first thinking I liked that dumb shit. Nope, not the kid; it was the opposite. I had a strong mother and if I was to be with a woman, she would have to be as dedicated as my mother. Tracey administered just the right amount of time to her family and to me.

On the weekends, I would give her some money to pay a babysitter, normally her grandma Sissy. Sissy was one of the old ladies who was so pleasant to talk to. She always had a smile on her face and wore bifocals that made her eyes appear far back in her head. She had this thing about offering everyone cookies. Now I'm not fussing, those damn cookies must have had cocaine in them because they were like crack. I couldn't get enough. She made chocolate chip, sugar, and my favorite oatmeal raisin. It was convenient for her because Sissy lived downstairs from Tracey. You would think with me meeting Sissy, I would have met Tracey's kids. Not the case. Tracey was understandably careful on introducing me to her children. To be honest, I wasn't too eager to meet them either. It didn't bother me that she had kids. It was more how they would feel about me.

One day while giving Tracey a ride on my bike, she asked, "Can we take some food to the kids? Do you mind?

"Not at all. What you want me to get?" We grabbed two kid's meals from Mickey D's. I pulled up to her flat. She got off and I pulled the McDonald's bag from my inner jacket.

"Here, I will wait for you."

She took off her helmet and reached for my hand, "Nope, I want you to come with me."

I hesitated, "Mannnn, are you sure?"

She snapped, "You don't want to meet my kids?"

"No, it's not that. I do. Let's go." I thought, *"No time like the present."*

Entering Sissy's house I heard, "Mommy!' followed by running footsteps. Around the corner came two little kids hugging their mother. She introduced me as her friend. She told them to introduce themselves.

"Hi mister, my name is Ashley!" The girl said.

"Hello Ashley, I'm Roland."

Tracey's son stepped behind her peeking from behind so I said, "Hey big guy. What's your name

He looked at me and quietly said, "Ricky." He actually gave me a look like *"Who the fuck are you?"* But that was okay; I was a new male face.

Ashley and I hit it off immediately. She was adorable. When she talked, at times she would look straight up in the air and not at the person she was talking to. I would sometimes look up like what is she looking at. Due to Adenoids, she would talk through her nose giving her the cutest animated voice. It sounded like a stopped up Tweety bird. When I came over she would ask me nearly a hundred questions. Ricky would walk up from time to time and just stare like he wanted to say something. I thought to myself *"This kid is giving me the creeps."*

When he did try to say something, Ashley would step in front of him and push him away to continue her questions. I would think to myself, *"This little girl is a champ."* I got a kick out of them when I visited. It was like watching the *Little Rascals*. You know kids get into it so they would play fight. I wouldn't break them up at times just to see where it was going. Ashley and Ricky would play rough.

When Ricky would get the best of Ashley, she would say, "Okay Ricky, okay time out." He would stop. Then she would say, "Ricky calm down, put your hands to your side." He would comply.

Now I'm watching curiously to see what's going to happen next. Wham! She would smack fire from his face.

Tracey would run in to the sound of Ricky crying. "You both better sit down now!"

Every time I came over I would play with them, especially Ashley. She was truly a tomboy. Time after time they would get into it while fighting for attention. When Ricky would start to get the best of Ashley. She would call time out.

I wouldn't break it up too quickly thinking, *"I know this dude not going to fall for the time out routine again?"*

"Ricky, time out. Put your hands down." Yep, he did it every time. Finally, I couldn't take it anymore and I called time out before she would get one off. Tracey would tell me not to get them riled up. I would say, "I don't have to. Their already on 10."

Tracey started bringing them around on weekends. I admit it was strange sometimes cause being around kids was new to me. I didn't mind though. I knew I had to be their friend if I wanted a relationship with Tracey.

A month went by and we were having the time of our lives. Tracey finally asked me why I hadn't been intimate with her. I told her I was trying to be respectful and waiting for the right moment. She told me the moment was right. We would often get a hotel and she would cook. Our chemistry in the bedroom was like fireworks, never disappointing. I fiend for our rendezvous; we couldn't stay away sometimes, making love in garages, parks, even my back porch.

Tracey brought out the best in me. I would even make Japanese food for her, something I picked up on just watching my mom. I was always a quick learner. She loved Japanese food and I had the privilege of educating her on the difference between Japanese and Chinese food. I even turned her on to sushi. She returned the favor one evening, inviting me over. Now remember, Tracey's family owned a flat so Sissy, Tracey's mother, and Tracey all had separate units. She cooked for a romantic evening and I felt real special. I was comfortable at her house by now. I went in the kitchen to see what she was making. I opened the pot and it was a large piece of meat just boiling in water. I took a double take to see if I was tripping. It was a plain chunk of meat, no seasoning, no vegetables, just meat boiling. Wait, I'm sorry, she did make some peas on the side. She told me it was her mom's recipe.

I thought to myself, *"Well that's the most easy fucking recipe in the world. A chunk of meat."* Hey, I gave her an A for effort. I ate it and complimented her on the bland meal-except I didn't say bland, I said delicious.

Christmas was rolling around and I noticed something was bothering Tracey. She was down. It took a while for her to tell me the truth. She said her ex hadn't helped with anything since the breakup. As a single parent with only one income, it was hard on her. It saddened me to see her upset. I told her it was my obligation as a friend to help.

I went and bought the kids Christmas presents as well as Tracey. When I gave it to her, I saw the look on her face; she wasn't used to a man going all out for her. I loved to see her smile.

My days were pretty much free so that's when I was out making my money. I believed Tracey knew at the time what I was doing but never asked.

When she did hint around the subject of how I got my money, I changed the subject saying, "It's not your concern and that's the safest way to keep it right now."

Our relationship was prospering just in the nick of time. I needed stability in my life. When I was grounded, better things happened for me. I was really exhausted from the rollercoaster ride my life was traveling. Evolving into manhood required that I make better decisions so I started soul searching. I wanted to confide in Tracey but I thought if I revealed my true profession, she would cut ties with me. She was a working girl who believed in a working family foundation. She would often make comments about how her previous relationships consisted of lazy men with no inspiration. She explained how she was the breadwinner the majority of the times. All these signs made me reluctant to speak on turning my current career to a professional career. However, I had to start sometime soon because my entrepreneur spirit was manifesting. There was an urgency for me to get my shit together.

Fate soon reared its head one afternoon. The dilemma was solved; I had no choice but to let Tracey in on my secret. I never favored doing business in my hood because of the haters and schemers. My name was being tossed around too much. That's how it goes, someone gets caught and volunteers your name. That's how the snitching game is played. The rule is never do business with someone you don't know and never be thirsty for money. Follow those two rules, you might stay free for a while. I was standing on my front yard waiting for Tracey to pull up. I was in a good mood so I wasn't thinking anything unexpected. Suddenly I see a burgundy car approaching slowly. As it creeps up, it pulls over near the curb in front of my house. I back up and slightly bend down seeing who was driving. I glanced around and positioned myself in case I have to run from harm's way. The passenger side window slowly retracted down.

I walk over and lean down, "What's up homie? You lost?"

"Naw guy. I'm not lost. I'm looking for a hook up." I immediately stepped back, "A hook up? I guess you are lost because ain't no hook up here."

This was clearly an attempted set up and I wasn't buying it. The driver was a black dude with a cornball ass haircut. He sounded like a Harvard motherfucka trying to be street. Everything this cat did was a dead giveaway. On top of that, his persistence was a red flag.

"Come on man. I know you know where the crack rock is."

I laughed in his face. "Crack rock? My man you got me all fucked up. Look I tell you what, go around the corner and see if you see a jack ass around there." I walked off using all kind of profanities that I can't remember. I might have made some new ones up combining a few. He pulled off. A few seconds later Tracey pulled up double parking in the street.

Hey, " You ready?"

I look around paranoid as fuck. I started to stutter. "Uh-huh, yeah give me a m- minute."

She gave me a confused look., "Baby what's the matter."

I looked concerned, "Mami, I will tell you everything; right now I need you to leave."

Just as I stood up I see the burgundy car about three blocks down approaching. I notice a second vehicle appearing to be a dick-detective- car.

"Oh shit. I'm fucked."

Tracey looked in her rear view mirror. She quickly said, "Give it to me."

The questionable look on my face said it all, "What?"

"Hurry boy! Give it to me."

I reached in my waistband and gave her a paper bag in the shape of a baseball. She quickly drove off and gets on the highway right by my house.

At that moment the burgundy car sped up without parking, coming to a screeching stop. The second vehicle slowed down but the driver, evidently a cop, waved him to go after Tracey. He pulled off and entered the highway too. I threw my hands up and backed up. I thought how lucky I was my mother wasn't home.

"What's up? Why all the ruckus, bro?"

He walked up to me pushing me against the car. He started to search me, grabbing my crotch. I jumped. "Damn bro, watch the nuts!"

He yelled, "Shut your fucking mouth! I know what you're doing."

I smiled shaking my head from side to side, "You must be misinformed bro. You definitely got the wrong one."

After a few minutes of interrogation, he walked around my house kicking over bricks or anything he felt could conceal dope. He came up with nothing. The second vehicle came back around and I sighed in relief. A white guy with a crew cut exited the car; he had on some Farmer John ass attire.

He asked, "Did you find anything?"

The black dick said, "I take it she got away?"

He responded, "She wasn't in sight when I hit the highway. She could have exited off Florissant or keep straight down I-70."

I chuckled, which irritated the dick. "You see something funny? I don't see a damn thing funny."

I gave him a serious glance, "Look I know you're doing your job. I don't take this personally one bit. Like I said, you were misinformed, that's it."

He looked down for a second and they walked away without saying anything.

I sat on my porch for a few seconds processing what just happened. I looked up to the sky thinking could God be on my side, when it comes to selling dope. I shook it off standing up. At that moment, it hit me. If it were not for Tracey, I would be up shit creek without a paddle.

I hopped on the ninja just in case they were still around I could easily lose them. During my travel to her house, I was amazed. She actually knew what the deal was and she still had my back.

I began to talk to my pops, "Papi, she's the one huh? As fucked up as I am, she never judged me and was my Bonnie. Thanks pops for bringing her back."

I rushed to Tracey and we discussed the entire event. She gave me an earful with no rebuttal from me. After all she saved me from a tight spot. When it was all said and done, she gave me an ultimatum: get my shit together quick, fast and in a hurry, or she would be out of the equation. I had every intention on complying. I have found my ride or die. Tracey motivated me to pursue a respectable path and she helped me every step of the way.

Over the next few weeks, we would sit and discuss things that would improve our situation. Such as me enrolling back in college, her going to cosmetology school after I finished my schooling, and what money I did stack, invest it properly.

As we discussed things, I had an old notebook that I kept for years. I would keep memos of important things I didn't want to forget. It also had drawings that I did when I was bored. Tracey happened to look through it one evening while chilling over at my house. She was impressed.

"Man, this is good. I see you still can draw."

I snatched the notebook, "Give me that. Stop pulling my leg. That's just me fooling around."

She replied, "No serious baby. They're good. As much as you like to draw, why don't you follow your dream of airbrushing?"

I opened the notebook and breezed through the pages, "Airbrushing is a trend, that's too iffy."

She thought for a second, "How about tattooing? You'll be good. You fit that bad boy image and you're popular enough to pull it off."

I'm silent for a while, "You know that might not be a bad idea? Got to look further into it."

She told me, "I'll get on it right away."

Tracey and I discussed our future plans quite often. She would write things down in detail: time frame, capital needed, and profit projections. I was honored to have her as my number one supporter. She was more excited about the vision than I was.

I started summer classes at the community college. I wasn't sure of my field of study so I took the safest route by taking an EMT course. I thought if all fails, everybody needs some type of medical attention. The medical field was always in demand. Tracey was also sending my resume to different employment leads. Most of them she wouldn't even tell me she was simply applying for them. I didn't mind, I felt comfort in it. She was investing her time into me. She must of seen something in me.

Because it was summer, we spent our weekends doing all sorts of fun stuff. She even took me on a picnic and made one of my favorite tuna salad sandwiches with sliced hot pickles. It was the little things she did that made me realize I loved this woman-it wasn't a schoolboy crush but a grown man type of love. Occasionally we did family outings with her kids. I bought a season pass to Six Flags so we did that often. I took her to the boathouse renting a foot paddleboat. We took a snack and a bottle of wine out, making it romantic. Big mistake, we got so tipsy that paddling that damn boat back was a task. The attendant wondered why we were so exhausted. We downed a whole bottle of red wine, not to mention we paddled to the other side of the park.

Never again!

Tuesday and Thursday I had no classes so I would take her lunch. She loved Chinese food so I would go to the Rice House and order her favorite, beef 'n noodles with extra red pepper. St. Louis had the best hood Chinese food in the world. Not the restaurant cuisine, I mean the kind in the white box with red designs and greasy. We would go sit in the park by her job. The conversation was always pleasant, sometimes we lost track of time making her late. No relationship was perfect, but ours was damn close. I finally knew what it felt like to be in a serious commitment. When you're grown, you don't have to assume the obvious like if she wants exclusivity. Natural love says it all without being said. Know what I mean? What's crazy, you don't need to know a person long to realize that you yearn for their attention. Hell, people have spent years together finally getting married just to discover they were being deceived. You got married men living the life on the down low and its only revealed when the significant other tests HIV positive. I knew Tracey was mine the first time I laid eyes on her.

Without her knowledge, I still hustled a little now and then. My savings was getting low so what choice did I have? Of course, I wanted a job but a *rewarding* job. I wasn't prepared to flip burgers or bus dishes for minimum wage. Tracey wasn't the materialistic type of woman so I was able to live a modest lifestyle. She would take care of the tab the majority of the time we went out eat. She gave me the comfort I desired. At times I felt guilty because I knew she had kids and was spending a lot of time with me. I was never judged even if I was doing badly.

I hadn't seen Kelly in a minute so we decided to kick it one Thursday evening. Kelly was happy that Tracey came back in my life. He saw the change in me. Plus, me being in a relationship made it easier for a married guy like Kelly to be around me. We decided to go to the Brass Rail Thursday Ladies Night. It was packed wall to wall, it seemed like everybody we haven't seen in centuries was in the building. We were drunker than a skunk, I didn't know what to expect because usually Kelly, liquor, and I were an equation for disaster. I felt kind of guilty without Tracey around. I wasn't doing anything either. Yeah .I got approached a few times but a brother wasn't taking the bait.

Kelly chimed in saying, "Damn nigga, you must be in love. You turned down that fat ass with the quickness."

I laughed, "Well I learned from the best. Shit is contagious."

The night was winding down and a bartender who I used to serve back in the day recognized me. This guy was a straight dope fiend.

"Ro, what's happening, my brother!"

I hate when white guys change their lingo to sound black. He extended his hands to give me some pound. I looked away and left him hanging.

He smiled, "Oh it's like that? Well, I know you got something good for me."

I never gave him eye contact, "Naw, I don't indulge anymore."

He stepped back, "You don't *indulge*? Now come on man. Don't be like that. I know you got a little something, something for me."

I gave him a fucked up look, "I don't have shit for you. How about you just give me a Corona?" I could see he's visibly pissed but he slides me a beer. I tossed him $5. "Keep the change."

I began to tell Kelly as he was driving on the way home that I felt funny.

Kelly looked over, "You just drank too much. Sleep it off, you'll be okay."

I shook my head no and started rubbing my head, "Naw dude this ain't a drunk high. It's something else. I think that fucking bartender slipped me a mickey."

He glanced at me, "For real? Stop fucking around. I'll fuck that bitch up!"

I told him to take me to the Howard Johnson hotel by my house. Kelly, my boy, he made sure I'm straight before he left. He called Tracey and informed her of what happened. It was morning and I still felt like shit. Suddenly, I heard a knock on the door. I thought it was housekeeping, "I'm good! Go away!"

"Roland baby, it's me. Open the door!" Suddenly I knew I was going to be fine. Tracey's voice had that effect on me. I almost collapsed in her arms. She helped me into the tub and got in with me as I leaned back against her breasts.

"Hey, shouldn't you be at work?"

She rubbed my head, wetting it with the washcloth. "I took off to take care of you. I couldn't leave you alone, without you getting into some type of trouble." I fell asleep in her arms. Rest was easy, my queen was here.

After that day, I didn't want to see any type of drugs. A fucked up situation can play on one's psyche as it did that night. Tracey was happy about my new oath she said it was God showing me the wrath of drugs. I'm so appreciative for having her in my life, I worked on becoming the man she deserved.

Tracey's diligent employment quest paid off. I got a job offer at St. Charbel County Correctional facility as a civilian correctional member. My skepticism about working in the town almost got the best of me. You heard stories about people of color not being welcomed in that region. Yet ,I took the job. *Why not?* I needed to show Tracey and myself that I could be a law-abiding citizen. The benefit of having parents from another country allowed me to play the race card. Employers had to practice equal opportunity. I pimped that shit as much as I could. Hey whatever works, right? I was truly *Black and Proud*, but a nigga needed to use every possible resource he had. I had to play the international role until I decided to claim my conscious preference to be Black.

Training was easy. It didn't take a rocket scientist to learn the detention policy and procedure. Being a Correctional Officer does require a substantial level of common sense. I must admit the majority of the staff was cool. I had the perception that there would be a bunch of tobacco spitting hillbillies with cowboy hats. To my surprise it was the opposite. Most of them were young educated men and women however they were conservatives. Working there, I would hear discussions of politics, social issues, and sports. Talk like that was enough for me to get a feel of whom I would be cool with and whom I wouldn't be cool with. At times they would ask my opinion and I would try and deflect from answering. Sometimes I would give my opinion, which was usually the opposite of theirs. There were only a few black employees. We all got along quite well. I would do my eight hours then clock out and bounce. Any gripes I had, Tracey would lend her ear, being my stress reliever.

Working at the jail was similar to the military lifestyle. People who worked there were either former military or individuals who wanted to be in the military but couldn't make the cut. I kept to myself and observed my surroundings. Everybody was pleasant yet I still had an uneasy feeling. I really got upset when a recently made sergeant asked me to cut my hair. I had the ponytail thing going on, you know like Andy Garcia had in the movie *8 Millions Way to Die?* Dude crushed my ego making me cut my hair. Tracey consoled me telling me how good and professional I looked.

I thought *"Yeah she would want anything thing that took attention from me."* Yet, I understood after thinking about it. I seemed more of an inmate than staff. Matter of fact, I probably got along better with some of the inmates than staff.

Inmates got 24 hours to analyze you and they will. If you're having a bad day, if you come in rough looking, if you're on the phone talking to a significant other. These motherfuckers will sit and watch you and read you like a book. They knew I came from the streets from my lingo and the way I handled myself. Also St. Charbel had a contract to house federal detainees. Shit, I knew most of them from St. Louis. I knew it raised eyebrows to some of my fellow employees. Out of curiosity, they often inquired *how* I knew them.

I would reply, "St. Louis is small; over that bridge is a totally different world." I was referring to the bridge that separated St. Louis from St. Charbel.

Back at home, Tracey and I were doing super good. I stayed at her spot more than I did mine. I could tell my mom was missing me. She never said anything because at least I wasn't running the streets. She often said there would come a time that I had to spread my wings. Tracey would make dinner for me every now and then. Other times she would just grab something quick like a burger or a box of fried rice. I started to feel like a family man.

I looked forward to the weekends with my mami. We made the simple things so priceless. Going to the clubs was cool; we stood out in the crowd. A lot of people would say we looked like brother and sister.

I would give them a clueless look. "Stupid ass, would I be hugged up or walking hand and hand with my sister?" Once in a while we needed alone time, like being cuddled up watching bootleg movies on VHS. You know the ones from the flea market that were 3 for $10. We enjoyed watching throwback movies like *Uptown Saturday Night, Cotton Comes to Harlem,* or *Superfly*. Tracey demanded we watch old love story movies; her favorites were *Mahogany, About Last Night*, and *Dirty Dancing*. For the kids we popped in the *Goonies, The Jungle Book*, and *Gremlin*s. *Gremlins* was a hard one to sell; Ashley was initially scared until midway through. Then she couldn't get enough of it. She would pop in the movie herself. I got a kick out of Ashley; she was so entertaining. She would watch movies like the *Wiz* and actually act out damn near the whole movie. My favorite movie was *Scarface*. Brian De Palma deserved the G.O.A.T award for making such an iconic film. I wondered did he know Tony Montana inspired many drug dealers? *Scarface* is one of the movies you can watch over and over again. In my opinion *The Godfather* was gangster but *Scarface* made Al Pacino a hood hero.

Most brothers would say, "If there were brothers in the crew, Tony would still be alive. No way we would have allowed that shit to go down like that." Tracey didn't want me to watch it so much; she thought it was a bad influence on me.

She would say, "Don't get no crazy ideas. Leave that shit for the movies."

I'd respond, "No worries baby."

Upon the end of my days off, I had an urgency to get back to work merely to welcome my days off again. Being well-rested to start a new week was a routine that I got accustomed to. After nearly working at the jail for over six months, things became more relaxed. My relationship with my coworkers was more cordial than before. Don't get me wrong, there were a few good ole boys there but I didn't fuck with them. One of the administrators by the name of Captain Border stood out among the rest because he went out his way to make sure I was good. Capt. was good people. He appeared to be a person who believed in treating people how they should be treated. It was always a pleasure to see him. He always told me if I had any problems then let him know. I believed him. Captain Border was the reason I remained at the jail. Right out the gate I had reservations about working there. Tracey was my motivation. It's difficult for a kid who had things come so easy for him to adjust to working a nine to five. So many years I cheated my way through life, but now it was time to be a man. Pops told me days like this would come. I wished he were still around so I could tell him I understand.

Life continued on and I finally officially moved out my mom's house. It was one of the hardest things I've done in a long time. My mom was cool with it. She was a little teary eyed but she was happy that I was moving like a man should. Mom gave me her blessing by asking me to paint the house before I left. I felt honored. *Yeah right*!

My next weekend off I started working on my mom's wishes. Tracey helped me every step of the way. I was a natural at painting. This cat didn't have to tape shit off to keep paint from smearing. My art skills came in handy. Tracey did the lower areas and I did the higher jobs like the upstairs windows. Mom sure made it difficult at times critiquing my work.

"Loland, are you sure you don't have to tape off the window?"

"Ma, I'm good look for yourself. I'm cutting down on time. It's how you cut the brush."

Mom would mumble something in Japanese. Tracey would keep painting until mom left, then burst out laughing.

"Oh that shit funny?"

"What did she say?"

"Fuck if I know, whatever she said wasn't nice."

We were on the last day of painting. I was doing the finishing touches on the front siding. Tracey was done and just holding the ladder. I was focusing on my job so I could get my ass off that ladder, but a distraction startled me.

"Nigga don't fall off that ladder and bust your ass!"

I looked down the street and here came Eric. I told Tracey I was coming down.

Eric walked up. "What's up my dude? How you been?"

"You walking E? What's wrong, your Benz getting an oil change? Good to see you homie."

Eric pointed at Tracey, "Who's your better half?"

"My bad. This is Tracey."

I put my arm around her shoulder. "Tracey this is my boy Eric. My brother from way back. I can't express how many times this cat had my back."

Tracey shook his hand. "Good to finally meet you, Eric. I've heard of you. I vaguely remember you from Yeatman."

Eric shook his head, "Good to meet you, Tracey. I heard you been holding my boy down. He needs that."

She smiled, "I'm trying."

Eric turned to me, "I drove by earlier and saw you out here. That's why I'm here. I gotta talk to you bro."

I motioned with my head for us to take a walk. Tracey got the hint and went to sit on the porch.

"This is different for a change. Usually I'm coming to you. What's up?" I asked Eric.

He dropped his head and sighed. "Man, I got myself into some shit. You remember Barry? Ole boy we ran with for a minute back in the day."

I nodded yes. "For sure. We all went to Yeatman. I holla at him every now and then."

Eric gave me a serious look that concerned me. "I think dude out to knock me."

I chuckled, "Wait a minute, you joking right? We go way back with Barry man." He gave me a stare and I stopped chuckling.

"My nigga, money can change people for real. We got caught up on a case together. Long story short, I got caught up in a bad way. He lawyered up and got a recog bond. The feds didn't even charge me, but they want me to roll over on Barry."

I hop up off the car, "Snitch?"

"Damn bro, don't say it like that. Yeah basically."

"You not going to do it, right? I mean bro we all know the risk of what we do or did. We make our own bed to lie in."

"I know, I know. They confiscated all my money so I have to get a public defender. They're going to railroad me. Look Ro, I took all the risk and that nigga ain't returning my phone calls. I need some cash to lawyer up too. The public defender claims that Barry swearing it's all mine."

I lean back against my car. "Really that's what he supposed to do. As far as you needing money, I can understand that but he can't have any contact with you. The feds got eyes and ears. Where you get he has a hit on you?"

"The streets talk. You know that. That's why I'm here. I can't talk to him but you can. Bro, we were ride or die partners for a long time. Stealing bikes from IGA back in the day. Barry will rap to you."

I rubbed my face, "E- man. I don't know."

Eric stood in front of me, "I had your back whenever you called me. Nigga you kicked me to the curb to run with your private school cats. Did I trip? No. The only time you reached out to me was when you wanted something. I knew that but I was still there. Did I ever tell you no?'

I looked him in the eyes, "Say no more. I'm my brother's keeper."

Eric smiled, "My nigga. I knew I could count on you."

After the conversation, I was literally in a trance. Tracey knew it was something serious. "Baby I know that look. Please tell me you're not going to do something stupid?' I stared at the sky for a few seconds. Tracey yelled, "Baby! Did you hear me?"

I snapped out of it. "No worries mami," I climbed back up the ladder.

The next few days weighed heavy on my mind. I didn't know how to approach Barry about the situation. This thing could go well as planned or real shitty for even me. With the information I knew, Barry could see me as an obstacle. Maybe I was just paranoid.

One day after work. I went to the apartments where Barry hung out at. Pulling up I saw a crowd of guys playing what appeared to be craps. I didn't exit the car until I saw Barry. I saw him kneeling.

Before getting out I sighed, "Eric, Eric man." I tucked my pistol in my waist band.

I walked up slow, "Barry my man. Homie!"

Barry looked up, "Oh shit! My dude- Roland! What the fuck?"

While giving me a fucked up look, I heard one of his boys say something under their breath.

Barry snapped, "Nigga- this my boy. Shut the fuck up! Matter of fact all you niggas hold the dice until I get back." Barry walked over and gave me a hug as we locked hands. "Ro, it's good to see you. How you been? I heard you like a married man and shit. I said get the fuck outta here not Mr. Rico Suave." He laughed.

"Naw B, not married yet. Let's just say I'm happy with the one I'm with."

He smacked me on the back, "Nothing wrong with that fam. All these hoes out here trying to lock a nigga down or get a nigga locked up. Child support tearing niggas up."

I laughed, "Show you right. Barry you know why I'm here homie, *right*?"

He stopped smiling. "Yeah I do. Ro, you know you my guy; if you were anybody else, I would have those cats pat you down or even stomp the shit out of you. But it's you. The same stand up nigga I grew up with sharing Now&Laters or a quarter bird of dope. What I say I'm only going say once… Stay out of it bro. This ain't your situation. You got good vibes in your life. Don't let two no nothing niggas like me and E pull you in some shit." I stepped back looking at the ground. Barry extended his hand for a pound. "You understand?"

I looked him in the eyes and grinned slightly, "Understood homie."

As I'm walking away Barry yelled out, "But for what it's worth. I'm not going turn a punk ass dope charge to murder."

I smiled, "My dude!"

I couldn't get a hold of Eric despite trying for over three days. I asked around and the word was he left town. I was worried because I didn't know how the feds would come at him for running. I tried, but what more could I do?

Moving in with Tracey was an easy transition; I knew that, that's why most of my stuff was over there already. I left a few fits at mom's in case I wanted to step out. The apartment was a two bedroom, but it would suffice for the time being. We took the back bedroom and the kids had the front bedroom. There's always a question moving rather your new place would feel like a home. Fortunately, wherever Tracey laid her head was home to me. I had to tell Tracey to relax for the first few weeks. She was stressing trying to make dinner and be the perfect girlfriend.

"Mami, this isn't the 70s where a family has to strive for a white picket fence and a home cooked meal every day. That's a thing of the past, at least for me. A Big Mac meal is cheaper than a home cooked meal." She was relieved to hear that.

Our sexual life was thriving. Therefore, we weren't using protection. With that being said, you can guess what came next. Yep, Tracey was pregnant. Four weeks to be exact. I had mixed feelings about this. Was *I ready to be a father? Could we even afford another child?*

I hinted around about an abortion and Tracey stopped talking to me for two days. I made things right. I explained that I was nervous and just thinking about our financial well-being. In all actuality, I was happy that we would share a living creation between us.

She agreed, "This pregnancy is making me emotional. I just want to make sure you don't run out on me like my ex."

I assured her, "Time won't repeat itself, baby."

The pregnancy was a new experience for me. I was just as emotional as she was. The mood swings, the morning sickness, not to mention the late night food cravings. Tracey would have the weirdest appetite for Vienna sausages and pickles. *What the fuck?* Getting up running to the 24-hour market was tiresome, but not too tiresome for my mami. I would rub her back when she threw up. I would rub her feet at night. Sometimes I had to be that voice of reason when she would exceed her diet-in other words, *pig out.* I would catch her around three in the morning raiding the fridge,

"What are you doing in there?"

She would quietly say, "Nothing just getting a drink of water."

"Why do I hear a jar opening!"

She'd pause and sounding like a little girl would reply, "I'm so hungry baby. Can you go get me some White Castles?"

"Yeah," I always gave in. I would hop on the Ninja and take that short ride. Lucky White Castle was 24 hours.

She would sit up in the bed and smile. "I love you baby. I will take some tums for the gas."

White Castle gave her gas out of this world. It smelled horrible. I would ask her, "Are you half zombie?"

She would roll her eyes. "Real funny Ha, Ha. Just for that I'm going to fart right on you." Then she would laugh, "Nigga you like to smell my farts because you love me."

"No the hell I don't; your farts are toxic but I do love you. Why you think I'm up at 4 in the fucking morning?"

Tell you the truth those early morning talks made me love her even more. However, every day can't be sunny, life brings rainy days sometimes.

It was a Saturday morning. Tracey woke me up. I jumped up. "Am I'm late for work?"

"Baby your mom is on the phone. It sounds important."

I hurried to the phone. "What's wrong, mama?"

"Eric's sister Keisha stop by looking for you. It appeared to be important. She left her number. You want it?"

I sighed in relief. I thought it was concerning her. "Naw mama. I have her number already." I immediately called her as Tracey watched. "Hello Keisha? This Roland, what's up?"

After a few seconds I dropped the phone and sat on the floor.

Tracey screamed, "Roland what happen?" I covered my face and started to cry. Tracey hugged me tight and started to cry too. "Baby what's wrong? Please tell me?"

I wiped my tears and just looked down. "Eric was killed last night."

She hugged me, "Oh my God. I'm so sorry."

Eric was killed while leaving some girl's house. The particulars never came out. I guess the police were mum due to possible retaliation. So many possibilities went through my mind. Of course, Barry's situation was at the top of the list. Barry gave me his word and that's not like him to go back on his word. Without any concrete leads, I didn't know whom to blame. The dope game is wicked. It could have come from anywhere. I didn't know the girl he was seeing but Keisha assured me she had nothing to do with it. Tracey was my reasoning. She comforted me and talked me down from doing some stupid shit.

"Baby, Eric had his life and made his choices. You have to live your life. The baby and I need you. Eric said he was happy to see you happy. He wouldn't want you to waste your life in prison for some bullshit!"

"Bullshit to you. A brother's code to me, we promised to be our brother's keeper."

Tracey grabbed my face, "Okay nigga, then tell me this. Who you owe more? Your child or Eric?"

A silence consumed me, I hugged her tightly as I wept for my lost brother.

My mental state was everything but stable. I was no good at work or at home. Captain Border allowed me to use some comp time to get my head right. Dude was such blessing to work with. Most employers wouldn't understand. The day of the wake, I laid in bed all day. Tracey tried to get me up but all attempts failed.

"Baby you need to snap out of it. You know the wake is today."

I sat up, "Yeah, I know. I don't think I'm going to go. I don't like funeral homes."

"Nobody does, but if you're not going to the funeral at least go say goodbye to your friend."

I exhaled, "Never goodbye, mami. It's till I see you again."

I was conflicted whether to go, and before you know it, the wake passed me by. Suddenly a harmful feeling ignited in me. I reminisced about the times when Eric, Don, and I would ride our bikes around the city, stealing cupcakes from Wonder Bread, and jumping rooftops.

"Tracey, run me to the funeral home. I'm getting dressed."

We rushed to the funeral home getting there in minutes. I ran to the door as a custodial worker was locking up. He turned to walk away as I banged on the door.

He pointed to his watch, "We're closed." I held up a $20 bill, he opened the door.

"Please sir, I missed my brother's wake. Can you give me two minutes to say my peace?"

He grabbed the money, "Come on in, young man."

I told him who I was looking for and he directed me to the room. As I entered the doorway I saw Eric lying there so peacefully. Baby, I'll wait in the hallway. I approached slowly as if Eric might pop up and start talking. Man, he looked like he was sleeping.

Placing my hand on his, I started to talk to him saying, "Better late than never, right bro? Eric, I'm sorry for losing touch with you for all those years. Shit got crazy for me... Thanks for being there when I needed you. Stay up homie, till we meet again." I walked out of the funeral home realizing I would never speak with my friend again-- at least not in this lifetime.

Eric's death impacted my perception on life greatly; I despised the street life. I regretted the moment that he and I sold our soul for greed. I wondered was it man's nature to eat from the poisonous apple tree to constantly make mistakes without learning? I swore never to sell out again.

The homestead was strong; life with Tracey was rewarding in every manner. Sex was great while she was pregnant--maybe because I was so careful. When you can't engage like you want, it is a psychological enticement. Only complaint I had was her snoring. She needed her sleep so I couldn't wake her. I would stuff damp toilet paper in my ears. That barely helped, but it had to do. Even if I did try and wake her, I couldn't. Tracey could sleep through a tornado with no problem. I would sometimes just open her eyes laughing to myself. She looked like a dead fish on shore.

Sleeping on the couch was not an option. Tracey enjoyed sleeping with her butt against my leg and my absence would wake her. Ain't that a bitch?

I bought Tracey a messaging Motorola pager so she could have constant communication with me. With the pregnancy, it was mandatory she be able to reach me at any time. Man did she take advantage of the service. All types of weird shit came across my feed like;

SOS White Castle plz. Vess pineapple soda ASAP, and how about this one: *Back rub NOW*!

One evening after leaving work, I stopped by mom's house. My brother Rob was in town and I hadn't seen him in nearly a year. He and I caught up for over an hour, then I got to sit with my mom for a few.

Before I realized it, two hours passed. I grabbed my jacket to check my pager. Oh shit, I had five *911* pages from Tracey. I go to the phone discovering my brother talking to his fiancée. Rob said he'd only be a few more minutes. I said, no worry, there's a pay phone less than a half a block away at the gas station. I walked to call her.

"What's wrong? You okay?"

She was angry. "No I'm not okay. I've been paging you nigga! Why haven't you called me?"

I was relieved. "Shit, I thought something was wrong. I'm sorry, baby. Rob called me at work. He's at mom's house. I'm on my way."

"Bring me a blue raspberry Vess soda. Oh yeah 911 means emergency. You failed the test."

"Yeah, I know." I noticed a car with four dudes pull up slowly. The cat-riding shotgun passenger side got out. He had on a black hoodie. He picked up the phone next to me. My gut told me something was not right so I tried to bounce out quickly. I tried to talk to Tracey in code, but she was not catching on.

"Oh yeah, when did she do that?"

Clueless, Tracey asked, "What do you mean? Do what?"

I noticed that the guy hadn't put any change in the pay phone and he was pushing numbers like crazy. Unless he was dialing an international number, shit wasn't adding up right, besides this nigga didn't meet the international profile. I had to think fast.

"Hold on Tracey while I grab a pen and paper from the car." I dropped the phone and walked toward a parked car while patting my pockets.

The guy said, "Hey bro!"

I broke for it, up the street the opposite way from my house. My military instinct kicked in so I started running in a weaving pattern. I heard two gun shots noticing the sound of the bullets hitting a car and tree leaves. By the time he got off the rounds, I was well up the street. I know he was thinking *that motherfucker can run fast*. I back tracked through the alley to my car and got my strap.

My mother and brother were on the porch screaming, "You okay?"

"I'm good mom, get back inside." I racked my gun and walked up to the gas station. As I got closer, I noticed the car wasn't there anymore. I stood there looking at the pay phones thinking, "I'm one lucky man."

I rushed home to a hysterical Tracey. "What the fuck happened? All I heard was gun shots!"

I calmed her down despite feeling twisted inside.

She was crying, "You should have called me back. I called the police not knowing what happened."

I explained to her what happened instructing her to cancel the police call. I counted my blessings wondering how many more God would grant me.

With the recent chain of tragic events, I started to wonder what could I be doing wrong? I questioned my relationship with Tracey, whether the stars were in our favor or against us. I shook it off to paranoia, imaging what life would be like without her. The reality was she's the best thing that ever happened to me.

I started airbrushing t-shirts again for a hobby. I needed some sort of activity to relieve some stress. Tracey found it entertaining, too. She would give me an idea and then be amazed at how I illustrated it on the shirt. She would literally watch from start to finish. The kids found it more amusing; they would bring me t-shirts to paint. They had no plain tees anymore. I did everything from Minnie Mouse, and Michael Jordan, to the Gateway Arch.

My side hobby proved to be an excellent supplemental income. Tracey would sell the T-shirts at a local flea market. She took orders from churches, fraternal organizations, and reluctantly gang members.

I said, *hey fuck it, they're going to get it somewhere anyway. Why not from me?* A couple of my co-workers ordered a few t-shirts. All in all, most of them were good people supporting my endeavor; they wanted pictures such as deer, a 57 Chevy, and a family portrait. Airbrushing a diversity of designs kept my skills sharp. Staying busy was therapeutic plus I welcomed the challenge.

With my baby on the way, my career path was becoming clearer. I was pleased. I was pretty sure that whatever the future held for me; art was going to be a major part.

Only six weeks pregnant, of course, Tracey was still working. I didn't want her to, but realistically we needed both incomes. I was noticing the pregnancy was taking its toll on her. She was so exhausted, not like her pregnancies before. Concerned, I took her to the doctor's office. He instructed us to keep close observation for abdominal pain and blood spotting. I was a nervous wreck, the only thing I could do was pamper her and hope she wouldn't stress so much. Basically it was a waiting game. I tried not to expect the worse, but with the way things were playing out for me... I felt God had a grudge against me. I wasn't mad or anything cause blaming him would only make matters worse.

Confused and clueless, I wondered what I could do to improve my life. I questioned if my intent was pure. What I mean by intent: if I was truly committed to the relationship or was I merely appeasing my father's wishes for me to be a good man. Maybe I just don't deserve to be happy for the fucked up shit I did in the past. However

Tracey was innocent in this tragic story and only guilty of believing in me. Damn, I loved her dirty drawers. You get the hint?

A few days went by with no bad signs. It was the start of my weekend off so I made plans to take her to Red Lobster, her favorite. Tracey could eat a dozen cheddar biscuits for a meal. She would literally go through three baskets.

I would tell her, "Damn, leave room for the meal." That night she curled up and slept next to me. I was awakened by moans; Tracey was crying in agonizing pain.

I pulled the covers back seeing a pool of blood. I screamed, "Oh shit. Baby you okay?"

I got both of us dressed faster than ever before and rushed her to the Emergency Room. Upon arrival, they immediately took her back asking me to give her info to triage. By the time I went back to her room, she was crying up a storm. My heart dropped as I began to cry.

I hugged her tight as she repeatedly told me, "I'm so sorry baby. I know how bad you wanted this. I couldn't give you your first child. I'm so sorry."

I rubbed her back, "Baby most of all I want you. We can try again. Everything is going be alright."

"Promise you won't leave me because of this. I don't want you to think I can't have children. I don't know what I did wrong."

I wiped her tears with my hand. "You did nothing wrong. It's just the way things are. What type of man would I be if I walked out on you? We got this."

Actually I was crushed beyond explanation. Maybe I cursed us. Fuck I don't know. I pondered what was next for me.

I tried something I hadn't done in a while. *I prayed.* I didn't pray for wealth, I just prayed for a better relationship with God. I talked to Tracey about it and she approved 100%. She would ask me why I never referred to God as HIM.

I replied, "I don't believe there's a gender because God is forgiving like a woman." She looked confused. I explained, "You notice men aren't as forgiving as a woman. A man can cheat on his wife and call her a hoe or trifling bitch? A man will cheat and swear it won't happen again. He might even flip the script and blame it on the lack of attention. A woman will give in and forgive him. Think about it. God has the forgiveness of a woman."

Surprisingly, things calmed down. I had inner peace within my heart. From that day forward, I would quietly say a prayer in the shower.

Tracey was an emotional wreck. She was convinced that I was going to leave her. I assured her otherwise, but she didn't believe me. I could only imagine what she was going through. What could I do? Praying in the shower, that inner voice gave me the answer. Getting out of the shower, I walked into the bedroom. She was in bed watching the Young and the Restless.

"How you feel baby?"

She replied so slow I almost couldn't make out what she said. "I'm okay. You need me to make you something to eat?"

"No, I'm good. You need me to make *you* something to eat?"

"I'm okay."

I sat by her on the bed, "Tracey, you and I have endured a lot these past few months. All the shit we been through made me realize that if you weren't with me, I would have collapsed. In the past I ran from problems. I would just say fuck it and not think of the people involved. It's different with you. We're a team. You by my side, I no longer run from problems. I want to solve them with you. Solve them for you. You scratch my soul, mami, like no other. Would you marry me?"

She jumped up crying and hugged me. "Yes, I will marry you if you're serious."

I laughed, "No for play. Popping the question is nothing to joke about. I don't have a ring yet but we'll go pick one out." The magic of matrimony can repair one's heart.

That Monday we privately tied the knot at the courthouse. Don was my witness and one of her high school classmates stood as hers. She didn't tell her mom for a few weeks. I couldn't wait to tell my mom. Expecting her to jump for joy, she was reading a book at the kitchen table.

"Mama, I got something to tell you."

"Oh yeah what's wrong you need some money?"

I gasped, "No ma! I don't need any money! Tracey and I got married!"

Without looking up nonchalantly she said, "Loland, that's nice. I'm happy for you."

I stared at her for a while, "Okay mama I just wanted you to know."

I walked away slowly scratching my head. She stopped me. "Hey! Don't fuck this one up. You hear!"

I smiled, "I won't." For my mom, that was a stamp of approval.

CHAPTER NINE

BEING A MARRIED MAN WAS EXCITING. When we went out, I would introduce Tracey as my wife even to people who already knew we were together. Tracey would reintroduce herself as Mrs. Page. Word spread like a wildfire. My friends couldn't believe I was married.

"I take my hat off to her. She actually got your ass to jump the broom!" Some would say.

Tracey would make sure people saw the ring I bought her. I got a great deal at Anchors. In the club, she would drape her hand over my shoulder so the girls could see. In public she'd rub the front of my shirt with her fingers extended.

Some of my ex-female friends found out. The feedback was mixed. Some of them hated. Shelly contacted me in amazement. She said she had to hear it directly from me. I can honestly say there was no jealousy involved with her. I think it was the disbelief that I committed to someone. She wished me good luck. I knew she was sincere.

Remember, I was only a fresh 22 years of age. Typically, men my age were living in the prime of their lives. Sowing their oats. But this kid took an oath to be faithful to one vagina for the rest of his life. Honestly, I was content. I never felt this way about a female. I always felt the girl was the lucky one. She better be on her best behavior or I would drop her like a bad habit. Tracey didn't fall in that category. I felt fortunate to have her. I wanted to be on my best behavior.

As young newlyweds we tried to live the perfect life. No arguing. We walked on eggshells. Normally I let her have her way to avoid commotion. She would pout and I would give in like a sucker. A man isn't entitled to be petty anyway. Being accustomed to getting my way hadn't worked out so well for me in the past so I wanted to pursue a different path. Yet hearing the title Mr. & Mrs. Page was quite an honor. So everything leveled out anyway.

Our dedication was already in place before the vows. Now that it was official we could start planning for the future. We opened an official savings account under Mr. and Mrs. Page. This was our initiative to save for a house and establish a business that could fuel my legacy. Something we as a couple would take pride in and hand down to our family. My goal was to keep my promise to my father to become a better man than he was.

At my gig as a police officer they allowed me all the overtime I could handle. During the winter season, it was a great opportunity to stack some more funds for the holidays. I took care of Tracey and the kids. And they took care of me.

Growing up as a military brat on top of having a Japanese mom with a stern discipline belief, my upbringing wasn't harsh however it wasn't a cakewalk. Of course my beliefs were that of my parents and I wanted to pass on the same values. Coming into an already made family wasn't easy. I knew I couldn't force my philosophy onto Tracey.

Understandably, Tracey's mother and grandmother didn't believe in discipline of any sort. They wanted to buffer things seeing as the kids didn't have their biological father present when I was coming around. If the kids didn't want to follow Tracey's rules, then they would make her feel guilty because they were acting out. I didn't make waves but I questioned many things that happened. At times I put my foot down respectfully telling them that under my household, there were just some things I wouldn't allow. Say for instance, I didn't care how much a boy toddler cried because he wanted to play with a doll, I wasn't letting that shit happen. I could be wrong but the law of nature is that Barbies are for girls. I didn't give a fuck even if it was a Ken doll. I encountered situations like that, or like the time at Six Flags I witnessed another toddler playing with the kids. This baby could have even been smaller. The stranger toddler accidentally bumped into the kids and I saw Tracey's elders kick the kid on the sly.

I shook my head like *"What the fuck?"* What's crazy is that when I met her grandfather, he looked me in my eye with a serious tone and asked, "Do you know what you got yourself into? Do you even know what you're up against?" I looked confused and saw Tracey shrug her shoulders. Tracey said she told me she lived a sheltered life. She was rarely disciplined and that's why she was so accustomed to getting her way. We discussed the matter a few times.

I told her, "I understand sometimes parents want to compensate for things they feel they couldn't provide for you but baby, without no discipline or constructive criticism, how can you raise a child to be productive in society? How can you teach a child how to cope with life's trials and tribulations? That's the duties of being a parent. Haven't you heard of tough love?"

She would sometimes agree with me but argue how could she do something she wasn't used to. I would tell her, "I tell you what, if I stink, then tell me I stink. Fuck my feelings. It's a way you can communicate the fact to me so I can understand. I'd rather hear it from you than get embarrassed by a damn stranger."

We agreed to disagree sometimes but I rolled with it for her. I bumped heads with her family at times, but I cared for them. I would have to tell them. "Look me and my mom get into it all the time, but make no mistake, I love her. I know she sincerely wants the best for me. You can disagree with someone and still care for them."

Sometimes they listened and other times I could see they were thinking: *"This motherfucker thinks he knows everything."*

I would laugh to myself, thinking: *"No not everything, just how shit is going to roll up in here."*

Hey that's what family goes through, it's not always peachy keen. Tracey knew that I compromised on the simple things such as the curtains color, what we ate for dinner, or what movie we should go see. No problem, let my baby pick those things. Quickly she realized when it came to the future of the family, I was the alpha male.

I told her, "Mami, of course in a relationship we have to compromise, but when it comes to certain things, we're *not* equal." I continued, "Tracey, if a person breaks in the crib, do I expect you to protect me? No! It's my duty to protect you and the kids. So if it comes to making decisions for the family's welfare, I need you to respect that cause I will give my life for you if need be."

She agreed. "I know you got my back."

"Good, cause I do. I promise you this. I might fall but without any question, I will bounce back. I will always have a plan 'B' for the family. That's my promise to you."

Transitioning into a family loving husband was easy. Pops must be proud of me. My wild lifestyle was gone, the selfish Roland of yesteryear was no longer. I went to work every day without missing a day in over a year.

Reporting to work, my friends would ask, "How's your wife?"

I would pause and think, "Did they say my wife?"

Usually the person would repeat it laughing, "How's your wife? *Tracey?*"

I would laugh too, "She's good."

The people I worked with at the county jail were cool as a fan. I enjoyed some of their conversations; it was like being in the military again. The ones who hunted a lot would bring me deer sausage to take home. I remember the first time I did. I got home late and put it in the frig and Tracey ate some for a midnight snack. She told me how good it was the next day.

When I told her that it wasn't Summer Sausage but deer meat, she screamed, "Ewww, I ate Bambi!"

She made me taste it, "Not bad. I prefer jerky though."

I was always open to socializing with people of diverse cultures, beliefs, and religions. What choice did I have? Both my parents were from different ethnicities. Shit, my mom was a Buddhist so who am I to judge? Want to hear something crazy? Growing up on military bases, you are exposed to people from so many separate backgrounds. When my pops retired and we moved to St. Louis in the '60s, it was a nightmare for me in the beginning. Even though I identified myself as black, I wasn't accepted by my own. I was subjected to prejudices for being a different type of black person. Kids have no filter so you can guess the ridicule was vicious. Regardless, I remained loyal to my culture. My parents made sure of that.

Being content at the jail, I took the initiative to advance. I enrolled into the Midwest Police Academy sponsored by St. Charbel.

Figuring that law enforcement might be my career path I said, "Why not, it's free?." Content but not quite satisfied, deep down I often pondered what the future might hold. Tracey encouraged me to grasp the opportunities yet still pursue better ones. She continued to submit applications everywhere she could think of. We talked about our goals for the future. Being rich, having a son that would be famous, and traveling the world, Tracey talked of wanting to see Japan. I envied the thought also. Conflicted if I was thinking realistically or following a pipe dream, I often felt like an under achiever. Never speaking to Tracey about the desire to hustle and hit a lick, I buried the thought deep inside hoping the old me wouldn't emerge.

The academy was fairly simple; the physical part was a cinch. After the military the skinny mixed kid was no more. My body was built for the conditioning the academy required. The academy only enhanced my physique. I would often wash my car with no shirt on and females would drive by eyeing or honking.

Tracey would get pissed. "Okay nigga don't get some bitch ass beat. Why don't you put on a shirt anyway?"

"I don't want to get my shirt wet. Why you tripping anyway? I'm not studying anybody else."

She would roll her eyes, "I'm just saying if I did that shit, you would have a fit."

I'd laugh, "If you did it, you'd get your ass locked up… that's the difference. Genius."

"Fuck you, boy!"

I would give her that look, "Okay wait till I'm done."

Of course, we'd send the kids downstairs to their grandmother's apartment. As a married couple, our sex life was incredible. We would make love in the morning, noon, and at night. The shower was always a great place for a quickie. Early morning wood was the best--when a man is at his hardest and can go a long time. I enjoyed watching Tracey try and be quiet especially when she came. I would cover her mouth with my hand. I would sometimes think about the sexual escapades I had with my exes wondering if Tracey did the same. I'm sure she did. That's life. Certain that I wouldn't act on the past, I simply left it at that. It never would be a conversation on my part.

Time passed and the family was headed in a good direction. Then the unexpected brought us a blessing from above. Tracey was pregnant once again! Emotionally we were thrilled but the anxiety of the unknown outcome made the journey like a rollercoaster. After the last miscarriage, I was devastated. Tracey already had children so I questioned was *I* the reason?

She would build my confidence, "Think positively baby. God is going to deliver this time."

I smiled, "Yeah. I think so too."

She hugged me, "What you want-- a boy or girl?"

"At this point, mami, just a healthy baby."

Obviously, I wanted a boy. That's a given.

How my pops always said, "Be a better father than I was to you." That stuck with me forever. I was committed to leaving a legacy for my seeds. Whether it would be in law enforcement or any other venture, I had time to figure it out. But first thing first, I would pray that God delivered us a healthy child. On pins and needles, I made sure I didn't stress Tracey one bit.

About six months into the pregnancy, everything was going as well as expected. Our prayers were answered. Guess what? It's a boy! This point right here was the most joyful moment in my life and each day that went by, it got better.

Tracey got huge; I mean it was like she swallowed a volleyball. I was there to make certain she didn't want for anything. I would rub coco butter on her stomach, rub her feet, and talk to the baby every day. Placing my mouth against her belly every day, I would tell my shorty I couldn't wait to see him and about all the adventures we would have once he was here. Most importantly, I promised to raise him to be a better man than me.

Here's the funniest part of a pregnancy-choosing the name. My mami made it easy insisting we name him Roland Lee Page Jr. I was down for that. It was important that I carry on my father's name. My brothers Ronnie and Robert had girls so the responsibility was on my shoulders. The next exciting thing about the pregnancy was speculating how the baby was going to look. One thing for certain, we knew the baby would be loved regardless.

I would joke, "All babies are cute. Yeah right!" So many people thought Tracey and I were brother and sister. I guess it was the fair complexion and the grade of hair. Tracey was black and Irish decent so Lil Ro would be somewhat of a mutt.

Our family would look at the ultrasound read outs and say, "Oh wow, he has your eyes Tracey... Roland he has your mouth."

People already assumed how he would look. I would tell Tracey, "You're a bad motherfucker if you can look at that ultrasound printout and see all that shit their talking about. It looks like an image of the Earth from space. I'm not listening to all that noise.

CHAPTER TEN

THE COUNTY JAIL STARTED TO HOUSE Federal inmates. I noticed more and more brothers being housed there. With that being said, I noticed more and more people I *knew*.

Walking through the housing units I would hear, "Roland, what's up my dude?"

I would down play it hoping the other correctional staff wouldn't notice the familiarity.

Some would even whisper, "Damn dog, I would never guess you with a job like this."

It became concerning for all the right reasons. A federal inmate from my neighborhood arrived. Immediately I knew there were going to be problems; not because we didn't get along, we did get along. I knew this cat and he knew my past. I hoped he would respect my situation and would not cross the line, running his mouth. I only had two weeks left in the academy and two months for Lil Ro to arrive. I didn't worry Tracey with it; maybe I was just paranoid.

Unfortunately, my paranoia was my sixth sense telling me my past would bite me in the ass. Federal inmate phone calls are often monitored especially in an ongoing investigation.

The inmate dropped my name a few times in his phone calls--even jokingly that he might ask me to bring some weed in. Now he didn't mean any harm but joking like that is all-bad in a jail environment. I got called in by Captain Bording who was accompanied by I guess a few Federal Marshals. These motherfuckers interrogated me like I was an inmate. I was confused and angry. I requested to take a polygraph test. Captain Bording appeared to be on my side, but what could he do with the feds breathing down his neck too.

The investigation was over a span of two weeks. Tracey could tell something was bothering me. I kept quiet. Praying that I would get through this.

I kicked myself thinking, *"Why would you take a job like this knowing your past? It's my fault."* Reality was, I had to deal with it. I remained on duty despite the investigation. My fellow employees were supportive of what little they knew. I was instructed to keep quiet. From what I was told, the inmate stood on his word that I never did anything unethical. Even with the recorded phone conversations, he denied knowing me besides from the jail.

The day I took the polygraph test was my first brush with the law. What was scary, I worked for the law. Sure I ran from the police back in the day but it was for mischievous shit not criminal stuff. They never told me what exactly I was accused of doing. During the polygraph test, I was asked if I ever engaged in drug activity.

I answered "No." I was asked if I would bring contraband into the jail. I answered "No."

"Have you ever discussed committing drug transactions with inmates?" I answered, "Hell No!"

"Simply No is sufficient Mr. Page."

"Okay, no then."

"Just no, Mr. Page."

"Okay, no."

He got agitated, "No, Mr. Page."

I thought let's not make the dude mad, "No, sir."

After about 30 minutes of questioning, it was over. The feds remained straight faced and emotionless.

"You can return to your duties, Mr. Page. We will contact you at the appropriate time."

Was I nervous? Fuck yeah! I continued to work with my stomach in knots. Two days passed and finally Captain Bording came to my housing unit.

He walked in, smiled, shook my hand, and said, "Sorry for putting you through that." He winked and walked out.

Remaining calm, I was doing triple flips in my mind. "Yes, thank you God!"

At home I could go back and enjoy my soon to be blessings. It was on a Monday that my son arrived. What a wonderful feeling watching your child being born. I was warned about how gross the birth was. Not for me. It was the most amazing thing I'd ever witnessed in my life. I cried like a baby. I was able to spend the night with Tracey. For an hour, we both stared at him. This 7-pound baby captured both our hearts.

Mom visited the next day. She was excited saying, "Oh my Loland, he looks just like you." My heart dropped when my mom showed a baby picture of me. She then said, "He looks like a 'Sato,' an enlightenment, one who stands on a pedestal."

Tracey's face lit up. "That's it baby. Roland Sato Lee Page Jr."

Taking a deep breath, I smiled, kissing my baby boy on his head.

After we argued with the nurse who said he couldn't be a junior because my name wasn't Sato, a doctor came in sternly telling the nurse, "Who are you to tell them what their child's name is? Write down junior for God's sake."

I gave the nurse a look like, *"You heard him bitch. Write down junior."*

Tracey had to remain at the hospital for an extra day to make sure she was able to sustain her normal vitals. I was upset because I graduated that next day from the academy. Now titled Officer Page it appeared my life was shining oh so bright. After the graduation ceremony, I rushed back to the hospital, but not after my classmates took a shot of tequila with me in the parking lot.

They then yelled, "Go handle your business, Daddy."

Tracey came home with Lil Ro and the apartment seemed so heavenly. This little dude brightened the whole house up; I would stare talking to him.

"Man I can't wait for you to be one. No better yet five. How about ten."

I'd catch myself, "Roland, just savor the moment and enjoy every day, month, year. Yeah, sounds good."

The beauty of being a new father was unexplainable. The pain of being a husband to a mother who recently gave birth was another thing. Why didn't anybody warn me about the hardening of the breast during nursing? She couldn't take the breastfeeding so the milk dried up quickly and from what I could tell, it was extremely painful. Tracey was moodier. Thank God, a man can't get pregnant. Then it's the no sex rule for weeks. We failed that miserably. *Don't judge me.*

Lil Ro was the heir to my legacy. He was my first born who was the splitting image of both of his parents. Understanding that we had other kids, we had to mesh the family together. As any big sister should be, Ashley was happy. She literally would sit next to the baby and talk to him. Since his eyes started to open, he would look and smile at her. It was a little more difficult for Ricky. We understood he was used to being the baby of the family. I could tell the way Ricky felt bothered

Tracey's mom. Don't get me wrong, she was happy for us but she paid more attention to Ricky so he wouldn't feel neglected. I was cool with that. It bothered Tracey, but I told her to let it go. Sissy was the greatest babysitter once Tracey's maternity leave lapsed. I felt comfortable knowing my son was safe with her.

At times I felt guilty having my own son. I didn't forget we had two more kids. One really has to watch what they say around kids not to isolate them. However, the glow that radiated from me when Lil Ro was in my presence, I couldn't hide. Even the kids saw the difference. I really tried not to show a difference but I'm only human. Damn, how can you contain such a wonderful feeling? Was I bad for feeling this way? The reality was that there was a difference. At times there was conflict between Tracey's family and me.

It ended with me saying, "I love you guys and respect you. You guys may have a greater influence over Ashley and Ricky than I do. I wouldn't expect anything different, but this little guy here is all me. It's my responsibility to raise him the way I feel suited. I respect your input. However, make no mistake, Tracey and I have the last say. Point blank period." We made things work.

Dramatically Tracey's ex came back into the picture after years of being absent. I often wondered if certain individuals behind the scenes contacted him trying to stir the pot. Tracey was done with him--that wasn't the problem. It was the fact he tried to come at her, scolding her on how to raise the kids. As a man and a father, it confused the fuck out of me. That's lame as fuck to have the audacity to pop up and try and lecture her on parenting.

What made it worse was this dude's father tried to go in on Tracey, not even placing blame on his punk ass son. Now my pops raised me to know that a man doesn't run from his responsibility and he admits to his mistakes. What kind of man would place blame on a woman raising her kids without any help? To say the least, I snapped. I told him if we ever crossed paths, somebody was going to get fucked up. Either him or me regardless.

"Nigga swing when you see me."

Tracey's mom tried to keep the peace setting up a meeting with his dad. Oh yeah, check this out, her ex's new wife attended the meeting. But her ex didn't even show up. In my mind, we can never be cool. The new wife had more balls than him. His old ass father tried to stick out his chest, but I brushed it off like, *"Old ass dude you can get it too."* I was raised not to be fake. I don't have to be rude but no way I'm going to smile and joke like everything is gravy. Tracey stayed cordial like she should for the kids' sake. The new wife attempted to give advice to Tracey, but she wasn't having it.

Tracey told her, "You can't comprehend cause my ex left me high and dry for you. He took my car to visit you. Crashed it and never came back. I'm not blaming you, but you haven't earned the right to give me any advice." And guess what? Fast forward in the future. Dude leaves the new wife for another woman.

KARMA!

Tracey agreed to allow the kids to go to Michigan to visit their father. I was 100 percent in favor of that. This would only open a door for another story to be told another time.

Since this is my story, I'm compelled to speak the truth. Besides Sissy, I felt Tracey's family treated Lil Ro differently from the other kids. I know they loved him but my intuition told me they wanted to balance things out for the attention I showed Lil Ro. Tracey's aunt would always give her the JCPenney catalog to pick out some holiday gifts. When it came to me picking something out for Lil Ro, it was a problem. She had to dictate what I wanted my son to wear. It had to be bow ties and polka dots. I finally had to just tell her to save her money after she told me she just wouldn't buy him anything. I started to feel like a villain on raising my own son. Tracey would tell me not to take it personally, "My family is not used to a dominant male speaking his mind and enforcing it."

I acknowledged, "I understand, really I do."

Tracey was on point juggling being a mom and wife. I could tell her first marriage was superficial, merely a marriage on paper. He apparently didn't show her what a husband's duty was. The man leads the family to prosperity. With certainty I performed my husbandly duties. Every day she saw our bond getting stronger and stronger.

With a bigger family, we needed a house so we purchased a three-level home in my old neighborhood--not too far from my mom's house. It was so spacious that everybody had a bedroom. Lil Ro was growing fast. Tracey had separation issues so he slept with us. Late at night, she would sneak him into bed with us. I would have to get on her head at times.

"Baby let me know when you do that shit. I don't want to roll over on my boy. That's dangerous."

Eventually I would sleep at the foot of the bed, leaving enough space between us. Like her at times, I would wake up and kiss him in his sleep. He would smile as if he was having a pleasant dream.

Having a house was great. With that being said, doing all that's required for the upkeep is a headache. Mowing the lawn, cleaning all three floors, vacuuming, cleaning the blinds. Man, building this bitch was probably easier.

Our house overlooked O'Fallon Park, the same park that I fished in as a boy and infamously discovered a female's dead body. We would sit on the loveseat in the second floor den in the dark. Tracey would rock Lil Ro to sleep while I told her stories from when I was a kid. She loved to listen to my childhood stories. The kids weren't so crazy about the house. It was huge and I must admit it was sort of spooky. At the height of the VHS craze, the kids accidently played a movie titled *Candy Man*. The title seemed catchy to a child, but it wasn't about *candy*. It was actually an urban horror classic. Ashley couldn't sleep for over a month.

Ashley was so helpful with the baby. I would tell Tracey, "She really likes to help. Let's hope she doesn't get any ideas at an early age."

The neighborhood was quiet for the most part. The majority of my neighbors were older people. There weren't any problems until Tracey and I returned from Chicago one Sunday. Luckily the kids were at Sissy's house. Pulling up to the house, I noticed the light on the third level turn off. I asked Tracey if she saw it.

She said, "Yeah somebody is up there."

I parked past the house quickly instructing Tracey what to do. "Go to the neighbor's house and call the police. No matter what you hear, don't come down until you hear from me."

She frantically screamed, "What are you about to do?"

"I'm going in. What do you think?"

She grabbed me by the arm before I exited the car, "No just wait till I call and they show up."

"Tracey, let me go and do what I said. Now!"

I reached in my backpack grabbing my pistol. She ran to the neighbor's house banging on the door. I quietly opened the front door and entered. I hear footsteps on the second level. As I walked deeper into the house, I noticed the kitchen light on. I heard noises,

Tap. Clink.

I slowly entered the kitchen finding two young teens eating cereal at my kitchen table. I put my pistol to one of their heads, putting my finger to my mouth gesturing to hush. Suddenly someone jumped down a flight of stairs behind me. I let off a round hitting the person in the butt. He ran out of the house screaming. I heard Tracey scream so I ran outside to check on her.

"You Okay? What's wrong?"

"I heard the scream so I screamed."

I threw my hands up, "That was him, not me. I think I got him in the ass."

I turned and rushed back in. The two sitting at the table were trying to open my back door but couldn't. The weather made the wood swell, making it difficult to open.

"Sit the fuck down."

"Yes, Sir"

"How the fuck did you know I was out of town? Somebody had to tell you."

"Nobody, sir. We just noticed nobody was here. We were hungry."

I recognized one of them. "You stay around the corner I know your grandma. Oh you hungry, huh? Sit your ass down and finish that Capt'n Crunch until the police come."

Come to find out, they were only 14 years of age. Some loyal little fuckers too; they never gave up their friend. From the outside trail of blood, the police believe I may have wounded him. Never heard anything more about it. Except the one I recognized had to cut my grass free for the whole summer. His grandmother insisted since I didn't press charges. What sense would that have made? They were juveniles. I told her I would give him a pass since he was young; hopefully, he would change his ways.

Tracey started to realize what I was saying about the roles of a man and a woman.

She said, "I finally understand what you meant about men should be the dominant protector." We rarely spoke about the event again.

Upon graduating from the Police Academy, I immediately stepped into the role as an officer. I still remained in the jail but I was able to transport and book individuals in. I was feeling good because I knew I could use my certification to apply for other departments. The plan was to stay at St. Charbel and wait for my opportunity to transition onto the road. Road officers are the slang term for police officers. The usual protocol was you begin your career as a civilian employee; once you put your time in, you're given the privilege of attending the Academy. You graduate then become a Detention Officer with more money and responsibilities. After that, when a vacancy occurred, you got promoted to the road. It may sound a bit overwhelming, but it's a great opportunity for an ambitious person. Thinking I would advance with St. Charbel since there wasn't many black officers there was Plan A. Plan B was to take my training to another municipality. Either way, I had my future pretty much plotted out. I even enrolled into IHM Paramedic Institute to become an EMT.

My family was my motivating drive. The thought of being a great husband and father kept me focused. Tracey frequently complimented me on my appearance, mannerism, and determination.

I'm sure it was a peep tactic to prevent me from relapsing.

I would think to myself, *"Quit stroking me. I'm not going to fuck up."*

Two years passed at the jail. St. Charbel County community was becoming a diverse melting pot. It was apparent by the inmates coming in, and just driving through the area you could see a large array of races. Diversity requires a change in hiring practices. I noticed a few more blacks being hired to my pleasing. It felt good to see people in common among you. I'm not saying I didn't enjoy my white coworkers. The majority of them were cool and you had a hand full that were shaky. Those were the ones that stayed away from me and I avoided them. Typically, I meshed well with everybody. I noticed a few of the new black staff didn't mesh so well. With that being said I noticed that the scales weren't equal when it came to the treatment of black staff. The beginning was smooth; I was the young token black at the jail. Of course there were a few more but they were older or black on the outside and white on the inside, if you know what I mean. The brothers working now were from similar backgrounds as me. Not in a negative context, but they were young, educated and outspoken. I loved it. This made some of the white people uncomfortable. During social conversations, there was more than one black opinion. We were still outnumbered but there were more thoughts from a black point of view. Especially during election season, that's when people show their true colors. The diversity triggered more debates. Debates created more division. Division established clicks. It even placed me in situations between my old friends. They would often ask me my point of view. As a man, I would state my opinion seeing that it would leave some white employees surprised.

"Roland I never knew you felt that way."

I would calmly say, "The conversation never came up. But look man, I can disagree with a person and still have respect for him. It's a problem when a person can't respect another person's point of view. We're all grown and can't force our beliefs on one another. Both sides can be right to a certain extent. No one should think they're better than the other. Shit like that I can't rock with."

I could feel the tension in the jail. Captain Bording called me in one afternoon to discuss it. He seemed genuinely concerned but our conversation went nowhere. I told him that I believed that the black employees were treated unfairly. Regardless of the fact that I was treated well, it didn't excuse how others were treated.

He didn't agree, saying "Everybody was treated equally."

Agree to disagree. However, after that he never treated me different; dude was solid as they came.

I spoke with Tracey about the tension among my friends on both sides. She asked how did it make me feel.

"It's extremely uncomfortable. The department treats me great, but I still see how some of the blacks are treated differently--not malicious but unfair. Say for instance if a black employee and a white one get into it, the administration sides with the white employee. That makes me feel some type of way, baby. It's not fun anymore."

Supportive of my feelings, she'd say: "Well, I know you wanted to stay there but maybe it's time to move on. What you got in mind?"

"A lot of cats I went to school with work for the city. I can put a few calls in."

Her eyes widened, "St. Louis City?" She got quite. "Are you sure you want to go that route? Baby, you got a lot of haters out there. I'd hate to see you get caught up in some bullshit."

Hey, "You gotta have faith in me. The past is dead and buried. This is who I am now. My gut feeling is telling me it's time to move on."

She rubbed my back and kissed me on top of my head, "You got this. It's whatever."

My next day off I went to the St. Louis City administration office. Of course, I contacted a few of my friends from school who were city officers. They briefed me on the hiring process, the pros and cons, some gifting me to use them as a reference. Working in St. Charbel, I was educated on law enforcement hiring process. I filled out the application, submitted all credentials, and met my recruiter Lt. Ronald Williamson. I was lucky to get appointed to an older brother with wisdom and knowledge. He was helpful, sometimes going out of his way to assist me. Now it was a waiting game.

I didn't tell the jail of my intentions, not out of fear of retaliation. I just wanted to be private, not counting my chickens before they hatch.

My pursing better employment inspired Tracey to do the same. We brainstormed on career choices that might suit her. We talked about cosmetology, nursing, and medical coding. The dilemma was finding a job that wouldn't conflict with raising our children. Being young, especially Lil Ro, they needed quality time.

I asked her, "What about Corrections? What I do. It's easy; you can handle that. They pay better than where you are now."

She replied, "Do you think I can do it?"

"Hell yeah! You just have to know how to talk to people. Remember most people in jail haven't been convicted yet. Some might be even innocent and some just made a bad decision. Do your job, nothing extra and it will be all good."

She nodded, "Where should I start? Where you work now?"

I think for a minute, "No not St. Charbel. St. Louis County is always hiring and their pay is better than where I am. If I leave St. Charbel, I don't want you caught in any confusion; plus, it's far."

She laughed, "You just don't want to work with me."

I laughed, "That too."

Tracey applied at St. Louis County. We got a good feel because the hiring practice is very equal opportunity. The testing process is much simpler than the St. Louis City Police Department. She passed everything with ease. Now it was a waiting game for her also.

With fingers crossed, we marched on with our lives. Lil Ro got bigger. It's amazing how fast children grow. I noticed every little thing about my son. The way he smiled when I walked in the room. The foods that he loved and the face he made when he tasted something nasty. The little noises he made. I'm wondered if he was trying to say something. You know what's the most memorable moment? When he said, "Da-Da." The proudest moment of my life was when my mini me called my name.

Tracey was slightly jealous, "My little snuggles would call your name before mine." I would spend hours playing with him allowing him to touch my face, bite my nose, and crawl all over me.

Sometimes I would take a nap and Ro would crawl on me. Life was good.

CHAPTER ELEVEN

GETTING SETTLED IN A HOME can take time. Therefore, I took my time doing touch up improvements to our castle. On our days off, Tracey and I painted or did yard work together. It was happy times. Besides the burglary, the neighborhood was quiet. Thank God I didn't experience any further bad incidents.

My mom started spending time with Lil Ro. Apparently he reminded her of me. She would pull out baby pictures of me comparing us. Ro was attached to her also. She's his grandma and boy did she spoil him. Mom bragged on his strong Japanese genes.

"Oh Loland, he looks like a Japanese baby. Look at his hair."

Lil Ro had a head full of hair from birth. Lil man loved getting his hair brushed. It would put him right to sleep. Mom would always give us parenting advice, repeating herself over and over. Honestly mom was such a great mother that all her nurturing skills rubbed off on me. When Lil Ro caught a cold and had a stuffy nose, I'd blow in his mouth dislodging the mucous from his nose.

Tracey would say, "Ewww!"

Only thing I hated the most was cleaning poop. Baby poop smells just as bad as grown up shit. I heard a myth that wiping your face with baby piss clears your skin. Tell you what, you're a hell of a person to wipe your face with a pissy diaper. You'd never catch this kid doing some shit like that. Don't get me wrong, I changed many diapers. I just didn't like it.

Blessings were multiplied when Tracey and I both got the calls we had been waiting for. St. Louis Metropolitan Police Department contacted me offering me a position as a Police Officer. I would have to reenter their academy. St. Charbel certification wasn't accredited through the city. No worries, I had no problem doing that. I would have done it twice to get away from St. Charbel. Without hesitation, I accepted the job. Thus, I was a cadet in the St. Louis City Class of 91.

I respectfully resigned from St. Charbel-after all they gave me the opportunity to achieve what I had accomplished. Captain Bording gave me a great farewell. Honestly, I'd miss him and some of my friends. Goodbye! Gotta go, gotta go! The kid was headed to St. Louis City with no down time.

The academy wasn't an obstacle mentally or physically. I eased through the classes without effort. I didn't study. I didn't train. Not being cocky, I had already went through similar training which made it easy for me. My fellow recruits were cool, but I didn't make any close friends 'cause I knew I was there to do a job. Anyway, most of us would be dispersed to different districts. I wasn't anti-social; I just didn't get too caught up on being buddy-buddy. Again, I was presented with the dilemma of what ethnicity I associated myself with. Many thought I was 100% Hispanic; however, I made it clear I was Black in casual conversations. It didn't make a difference to anyone. The City had people of color in power so it wasn't like St. Charbel, but I still got the feeling it wasn't quite equal.

The instructors in the academy were major cool. I had no problems with any of them. Every now and then you come across an instructor who gave the persona that they were tough or from the street. A real street cat can see through shit like that. The ones like that, I read like a book. Straight cornballs. Be yourself. Save the tough act for somebody who's buying that shit. I'm not.

The City Academy was harder than the one I attended before. Despite not studying, I did fine. The daily routine, 5 days a week, was: PT-Physical Training, law classes, and lastly a guest speaker. Besides being boring the anticipation for hitting the streets was unbearable. I was anxious, not to lock people up just to mingle with the public.

About four weeks after I started the academy, Tracey started her classes for St. Louis County Detention. She expressed how easy it was. I gave her much advice on the operations of corrections. She acknowledged our discussions helped immensely.

With both of us doing well and on our way to better jobs, the weekends were ours. Normally Sunday was family day and Saturday was party night. Thanks to Sissy, Tracey and I had our alone time.

You may wonder about my friends. Well, I did too. I found out that Kelly was doing hard time in Australia for beating the shit out of his wife's brother. Gino was released from prison but after six months went back on a parole violation. I heard through the grapevine he got caught with a strap. Fortunately, I kept up with Don and Lavell. They would randomly swing by the crib checking on me.

Things were going good for the family especially with more income being generated. We started to save. My goal was to fix up our house. One of the requirements to work for the city was being a resident of the city. So I thought I might as well make the best out of our home. A nine to five was rewarding. Truthfully, I wasn't completely satisfied. I felt I wasn't reaching my potential. At times I pondered whether I should go back to hustling. Wouldn't be nothing major:, jump in, jump out. Coming to my senses, I realized how crazy it sounded.

What's crazier, the following week we had the course for ethical conduct. The instructor touched on the basis of moral and immoral behavior and how crossing the line would be dangerous territory for a commissioned police officer. He stressed the term fruit of the poisonous tree a term for tainted evidence. For some strange reason, that metaphor stuck with me. I wondered was this class a divine message to keep my eye on the prize: *Success*.

Immediately after ethics training came sensitivity training. This was an interesting topic. I thought back to St. Charbel, thinking this would be an excellent course for that department. Thus far everybody had gotten along keeping their beliefs and opinions to themselves, but this class… Man, the three-hour class damn near kicked off a riot. I was quite amused the entire time. The white recruits stated their thoughts on how slavery was years ago and they shouldn't be held accountable. The blacks talked of witnessing years of police harassment, motivating them to make a difference. I was proud on how my brothers and sisters handled the debate. Many wanted to know my opinion.

I hesitated, "You wanna know my opinion? Everybody has prejudices and anyone who will deny it is a liar. The only way to understand other cultures is to be open to debate and dialogue. Since I've been here, I've noticed the way we interact. I listen to some of the white cadets as they talk. You guys greet each other. How are you? Good morning. Good afternoon. You shake each other hands. When I walk up or a black cadet does, it's.

'What's up, my brotha?' Then you give me a high five. Look, we were both born in this country and we all speak English. Ebonics *isn't* a fucking language for black people. By the way, no you didn't indulge in slavery but some of your grandparents have and some of them are still living. So don't act like it was in the prehistoric era. I treat people accordingly. So next time you greet me, greet me the way you would do anybody else, if you don't mind."

I had stayed to myself most of the time. After that discussion, my fellow black recruits hung around me more. I wasn't a leader but I was well respected. One time in the locker room, I heard two people arguing. I walked over to see the commotion and saw two brothers about to fight. None of the other black cadets were willing to break it up. The white recruits appeared to be amused by the conflict. I rushed over and wedged myself between them.

I spoke loudly, "We're not going to do this fam. They probably want us to fight each other so we will get put out, but not today!"

I angrily gazed around looking at the ones who were looking on. They all turned, acting as if nothing happened. I shook my head.

With about three weeks left in the academy, a black female got expelled from our class. It wasn't discussed why, but before she left she said years ago she was present when her brother's house got kicked in. She didn't get arrested but her name was run for warrants and she was then released. The initial background investigation didn't reveal this.

It just so happened one of the drug class instructors recognized her. I thought shit like that could have happened to anyone of us. Who doesn't have a criminal in the family? I thought it was some bullshit. Ole girl was actually one of the outstanding black recruits. Almost a week after I was approached by my recruiter who hired me, advising me that the Assistant Chief of Police was curious about why there were periods of unemployment in my past. He wanted me to write a letter explaining the time I was without a job.

Startled by the inquiry, I rushed to find an explanation. I wondered if they knew something I didn't know. The thought went through my mind that maybe I was getting set up. I explained that some of my employment history had gaps because I had some jobs for short periods of time so I didn't report them. Also during my quest to find my career path, I was enrolled at the community college and pursued the entrepreneurial way of generating income. I submitted the letter hoping for the best. I was honest in my narrative. Of course, I left out my juvenile past, that part of my life was dead and buried. Fate excused me from ever being punished for my sins and maybe I was destined to be a productive citizen. After a few days, I was informed the assistant chief was pleased with my explanation. I was thankful.

Tracey was pleased with her new career. She boasted how easy the duties were compared to her previous job. She did patients accounts at Barnes-Jewish hospital and the daily routine was redundant at best. I told her now everyday might be a new experience, some good and some bad.

"Remember to never wear your emotions on your shoulder. Let them roll off. Some inmates will try and push your buttons. They enjoy that shit. Do your job regardless of your feelings. There's going to be times when you want to smack a motherfucker or tell them to kiss your ass. You can't do it. Just brush it off; once they realize their shenanigans aren't working, they will back off. Watch and see."

She told me my advice helped her understand a lot of things. With job satisfaction going both our ways, we were pleased.

The academy training was almost done. I couldn't wait. My classes started with approximately 30 recruits, 13 blacks; with one week left there were 23 remaining, 10 blacks left. We were issued our district assignments; some were happy and some not so happy. As far as this kid, I was ecstatic. I was going to the fourth district, the downtown area consisting of predominately corporate businesses. It was rumored that the elite cadets were assigned to the fourth district. Everyone in my class who was assigned the fourth district with me eventually went on to have a great career-one even became Chief of Police.

Graduation day was finally here. My entire family attended the ceremony. They were so proud of their little brother. It seemed like the one-time black sheep finally got his shit together. Tracey's family came too; they we excited. My achievement was beneficial for the entire family so everybody was rooting for me. Hell, I was proud of myself. At the graduation, I walked by a glass display case seeing my reflection in full uniform. I stopped staring in amazement.

"Damn, I did it pops. I'm walking the right path like you wanted. Thanks pops, it feels good."

CHAPTER TWELVE

ONCE IN THE DISTRICT, I was classified a Probe, a probationary police officer, a title I would have to wear for a year. Having been through the academy, my probe training was easy. It lasted a few months, and to be honest, I can't remember much about it. I had to ride with a training officer for that time period and I was happy once it was over. I'll leave it at that.

Enjoying the freedom, I was finally on my own. My supervisor was Sgt. Patterson, an Irish descendant dude with a tough exterior. He reminded me of an old school cop from Hell's Kitchen. I liked him off the bat because he gave me the feeling that as long as I do my job and don't put his career at risk, he'd have my back to the end.

I had every intention of doing my job and keeping my nose clean.

Fortunately, I was classified as a 41- a one-man vehicle, therefore I was by myself. The only down side was I did a lot of accident/crime reports, event details, and community policing. Nothing about the following was exciting except the community policing. I made it my priority to establish relationships with the downtown business district. I visited the local businesses, addressing any concerns, suggestions, or complaints. I also asked questions for my knowledge about the businesses, such as how they started. The associate(s) would go into the entire operation and the history of the company. It was just down my alley 'cause I adsorbed every bit of information I could. I was gaming myself up to learn the formula on a successful business, not only that, I gained influential alliances that would possibly prove to be effective for my future.

Vehicular accidents were a pain in the ass, especially on the highway and bridges over the Missouri River. Imagine on a cold dark night getting a report for the accident on the Popular Street Bridge-the bridge connecting Missouri and Illinois. Pure nightmare! The wind from the passing cars plus the breeze would literally shake the police vehicle. I would stay away from the edge overlooking the lake. We were instructed to view the scene then expeditiously escort those involved to a safe area to take the report.

Sometimes the drivers would insist on remaining on the bridge or highways.

"Officer I was told not to move the car so you can see who's at fault."

I was always professional, "I understand that; I already assessed the scene. I see your vehicle's position. My concern now is our safety so let's get to a safer area. How about that?"

Now in my mind I would be saying, *"Bitch it's cold as fuck up here. Do you see all these fucking cars driving by like they don't give a fuck if they hit us? I see your raggedy ass car so let's get the fuck off this cold dangerous ass bridge!"*

Did you know it was a policy that if the vehicle damage appeared to be under $500, it was the officer's discretion to refuse to write a report? We would write an accident referral form allowing the drivers to exchange information. Some officers were lazy and took this route. But I would simply write the report. What if that was my vehicle or maybe my family member's? I would want a report. I learned that many people would admit guilt in causing the accident but if you don't have a report they will deny it to their insurance. So I extended the courtesy of writing a report to all accident drivers I encountered.

When possible, I made visits to the neighborhoods and surrounding housing projects. I wasn't harassing people; I was just trying to show love. I passed out baseball cards on the regular. For the most part, the kids were more interested in my police vehicle and my on-duty weapon. I recall one particular time a kid told me all his family business.

"Can I see your gun?"

I would reply, "No little man, that's not a toy. You shouldn't ever play with one either."

Well, "My daddy got one. My brother got one too."

I shook my head, "They do? I hope they put it up so you can't touch it."

He wiped his noise, "My brother pulls it out all the time. He shot at some man yesterday. It was loud."

I just stared in amazement, whispering to myself, *"What the fuck?"*

Visiting the projects brought back memories of me kicking it with my partners back in the day. Walking through them, I saw families barbequing off their back porches, little kids running between the buildings, and older residents chilling under a shade tree. It entertained me to see a peaceful vibe in an area most police considered savage. Don't get me wrong some shit would pop off causing chaos, but it wasn't all the time.

Some of the other police would ask me, "It doesn't bother you to go down there?"

Without hesitation, I'd say, "Of course not. That's our job to protect and serve the community. Those people down there are a part of our community. I don't feel threatened one bit."

I understood some officer's skepticism about going down there, especially the white officers. At times I encountered harsh looks and unwanted vibes from certain people. For the most part I was treated with respect because I gave respect until otherwise. When the otherwise occasions happened, I would let them know real quick,

"Look bro, I didn't say anything out of pocket to you. I'm no threat to you. I'm here to tell you you're not a threat to me because if I felt you were, it would be handled real quick. I'm human just like you. You don't like to be threatened neither do I. I'm not going to allow anybody to prevent me from going home to my family without a war on their hands. So save all that animosity for your enemies. I'm not your enemy. I'm a cop trying to show my people some love. That's it."

I used that phrase a few times and each time it ended with the opposing side dapping me up-shaking my hand.

The women always showed love. They would flirt saying, "Come lock me up."

I would smile, "Never that. You're too pretty for jail."

I would give a compliment back knowing Tracey would kick my ass if she heard that. Truly it was innocent, I had no intentions on trying to get with anyone. I was just breaking the ice. I must admit though, I always loved a little hood in my women. Tracey could definitely get a little ghetto at times. Maybe that's why I loved her so.

What else could I tell you about a police officer's life? Oh yeah, the obvious: We ate for free. Before I started, I wondered why some of the officers were so out of shape. Shit, you eat for free whenever and wherever. Now really we're not supposed to abuse the privilege, but honestly if a cop said he didn't take advantage of the perk, he's *lying through his teeth.*

I heard stories of how some officers would get off duty and go to a restaurant like KFC and try to get a 6-piece meal. The manager would complain to the district commander. We would be briefed on abusing the privilege. After a few weeks, we would be right back chowing down. The only spots that didn't play that shit were the Chinese restaurants, which was a shame because most of the black cops like myself loved Chinese food. It was hilarious. When you got to the register, they would give you a mean look. "Tin Dolla."-Ten dollars.

I would smile thinking about how their accents and attitudes reminded me of my mom. They don't give a fuck. *"Pay me!"*

All the Asian business owners were isolated people, never rude but not too hospitable. My district housed many wholesale stores so when I paid a friendly visit they seemed very paranoid. Maybe it was due to the loads of bootleg and knock off merchandise they hid behind the counters. I never gave on that I knew it was behind the counter. I was there merely for a courtesy visit. Vice handled the fraudulent merchandise cases so I didn't bother.

My experiences with the fourth district were never boring. I encountered incidents each week that stained my memory forever.

One morning right out of roll call, I got a call for a possible burglary. I was assigned the call with a back-up unit. At a huge creepy warehouse out of Tim Burton's dream, a female employee greeted us. She was shook up and couldn't explain what she had seen.

Unable to understand her, I said, "Ma'am just show me."

We came upon a large room with overhead skylight windows. I noticed one was shattered. The area was shielded by furniture stacked up high. She stopped pointing to the area where I assumed the glass had fallen. As I walked around the furniture, I saw that a man had fallen from the skylight about 30 feet down. What took my breath away was he landed on a table turned upside down and the table's leg was impaled straight through his chest. He bled out what looked like almost every drop of blood he had. He was a man of dark complexion but the loss of blood turned his skin light. The blood had thickened inside the center of the table. I assumed he had been there for maybe a day. In cases like this, *Accidental Death* nothing suspicious, we'd call the supervisor and the coroner's office. Then it would be coded. Coding a call was a series of numbers used by police officers when a report wasn't required, the general activity of the officer, or informing the dispatcher the exact location of the officer. Like 10-20 referred to location, 10-22 meant disregard, and there was a whole list of others we had to remember.

A new officer had to earn his trust. The elder officers were always cautious on what they would say around the probes. Coming fresh out of the academy, you're instructed to report anything unethical or immoral but the veteran cops were reserved on opening completely up. All of them however were helpful. The veterans wanted to do their last few years in peace doing the bare minimum. The younger seasoned officers wanted to do aggressive policing. In other words- looking for guns, dope, and felonies. I wasn't sure what category I would be listed in. I got into a few foot pursuits and car chases with those mainly on the Hot Sheet-Stolen Vehicle List. However, I felt my calling would eventually be community or business liaison. I was certain I would be a white shirt someday. I had no desire to work in Narcotics reason being I didn't think I could be effective. The streets knew me; it would be difficult for me to infiltrate the activities. Plus, I didn't want any skeletons coming out of the closet so how about staying safely in the fourth and flourishing quietly.

Treading safely, I did my job to the T. I avoided cutting corners to assure I would complete my probationary status without incident. Many of my fellow officers started opening up to me. What a great feeling the trust must be growing.

Tracey enjoyed hearing my stories finding them either gory or comical. At home when the uniform came off, I wasn't Officer Page anymore, I was Roland. Sometimes I wouldn't even carry my weapon. I feared it might create more problems for me. I don't care who you are, guns escalate a person's judgment of self-defense. For instance, if you're walking down a street, a suspicious person might be approaching you. Normally you would cross the street to avoid any unexpected confrontation. With a strap on your side, most people would have it ready, some hoping it might escalate. Off duty cops pull guns more than street gangstas. *Real talk.*

My rec-off -days, were all about the *Fam*. We did something different ever week. The zoo, mini golf, skating at Skate King, or dinner at Union Station, we enjoyed every moment. Plans were as simple as a movie night with Tracey making hot and spicy wings. Lil Ro was there, always calm and obedient. He was such a good baby. He didn't cry much at all and had a smile on his face practically all day. How precious could it get, he even smiled in his sleep.

At work my family stayed on my mind. While driving I'd see little kids playing, bringing a warm feeling to me inside. I'd say to myself, *"Can't wait till Lil Ro hits that age."*

Out on patrol, I came in contact with many attractive women, some who tried to hook up with me. As tempting as it was, I remained loyal- not because I was disciplined, it was because I was that much in love with my wife.

The department had many internal love affairs for advancement reasons, extramarital reasons, or just for the hell of it. I witnessed married officers leave their spouses for a fellow officer or even their partner. It smelled like a cesspool. In fairness, there were good officers with strong morals who respected their vows. I had no intentions of pursing any type of relationship with a female in the department. The idea wasn't appealing to me one bit. One thing, I must admit, a majority of the female officers I knew were more professional than the men. Of course you had the ones who acted more masculine than the men, but for the most part they communicated better with the public. They definitely took more pride in their appearance. If you could see the condition of some officers' uniforms, you would wonder if they had a washer or iron. Food stains. Some of their brass looked brown. Now my shit was flawless. The way I dressed in my civilian attire reflected the way I carried myself in uniform. Now the detectives were on point, even the white dicks knew how to dress. Granted you might see one or two who needed salvation. Their necktie hung only half way from the neck because their belly was too big. Their sport coats were outdated and looked like something from Barney Miller. I made myself a promise when and if I made detective, my threads would be straight from GQ magazine.

We had a few officers that favored aggressive policing. Whatever floats your boat-- they enjoyed chasing young dudes through the projects up and down the high rise. Now don't get me wrong, I had my share of foot pursuits but half the cats we chased did it for kicks. They knew the maze of the buildings. Some of them didn't even carry dope on them, hiding it under a nearby brick or trashcan. I wasn't about to place a fellow officer or myself at risk for some thrill-seeking game.

Point taken, one rainy day a probationary officer right out the academy got in a foot pursuit with a suspect who allegedly brandished a pistol. He chased the suspect through the projects, shooting him after the suspect allegedly pointed a gun at him. It was broad daylight and residents were out. The suspect died at the scene. Many witnesses came forward stating the suspect never had a gun and that they saw the officer retrieve something from his vehicle, placing it by the suspect. The suspect, a young brother, who resided in the area was known for the running game. He even tried to bait me to chase. He would take off stopping when he saw me just looking at him from my vehicle.

"Damn Page, you not going to chase me huh? You not no fun dog."

I would grin, shaking my head as I pulled off.

The local community was outraged to say the least. I made no comment about the incident to fellow officers who were split about who was at fault. Of course it came down to race. The brothers didn't bash the officer but they had their suspicion on what actually happened. I never witnessed it, but I heard talk of planting evidence. I overheard a veteran officer say if I know in my heart that the dope or gun belongs to the *perp* -perpetrator, I'm giving it to him. I don't have to find it on him. I immediately walked away from that discussion. I didn't want to know or hear any of that.

Back to the shooting, the white officers felt it was a justified shooting. I knew the involved officer and he was cool with me. Actually he favored me a lot. He was Hispanic. Here's the tricky part. Some of the family members and local residents confused him for me. I was advised by Sgt. Patterson to be careful for retaliation. Now back to my statement.

"I was careful not to place my fellow officers or myself in danger." Hey if it's not a hot pursuit, wait to catch him another day. You'll run into him another time guaranteed. The odds will be in your favor. "Just my opinion."

Fortunately for me, the locals informed me they knew the difference between us. The uncle of the young man who died assured me there would be no retaliation.

He said, "Page, I just want justice for my nephew man. My nephew wasn't an angel but he didn't deserve to be gunned down like that. The neighbors saw your fellow officer get a gun from his book bag in the patrol car."

I looked him in the eyes, "Condolences to your family. I see the pain in your eyes. However, I can't respond because I wasn't there. I hate that it happened. I hate when anybody loses a life and there are no answers. I'm sorry for your loss." I shook his hand waved at his family in the background. Some returned a wave and others gave me a death stare.

Incidents like this deteriorate the trust of the community. It's hard to grasp that some incidents or arrests are justified, yet as history has shown some suspects can be victims. A suspect is a derivative of suspicion, to assume someone is guilty or involved in unfavorable activity. Police are human and with that being said, we are capable of error. I'll leave it at that.

The young man's death was saturated with media and protest. The community was visibly angered. It took months for it to simmer down.

Time passed and I would see the young man's mother from time to time. I felt for her. It was a loss time couldn't fix.

I was in the station one day and a group of officers were in the report room. I was sitting at a desk with my back to them, writing an accident report. I heard them talking about the incident.

"I have no sympathy for his mother. If she was doing her job her son might still be alive. She probably was out smoking crack"

Look, I knew I was a probe but I couldn't stay silent. I slammed my pen on the table and turned around. "I don't mean to interrupt, but since you guys are talking fucking loud interrupting my peace, let me ask you something. Are you a father? Do you have a child?"

He sarcastically responded, "What's it your business if I do?"

I grabbed my report and walked out, "I thought so. You couldn't be with a fucked up mentality like that."

What amazed me was there was a black officer among them. I mean mugged him the entire way out. Yeah, he and I never got along after that.

Let me be clear St. Louis City PD has plenty of good white officers. It would be safe to say a majority are good people. It's the few corrupt ones that cast the dark cloud on the department. Then you have some who are good but too loyal to the fucked up ones to say something. When I say corrupt, it may not be in reference to criminally. It may be morally that they became an officer to fuck with people. They hustled their way through the psychological test. Impossible? Shit I did.

I had many acquaintances in the department but nobody I was close to. Then one evening I was in the booking holdover, the area where suspects are booked before they're transported to the City Jail. I was in booking, searching a suspect, assisting a fellow officer. An officer from another district was giving a prisoner a hard time.

"You have no rights, asshole. I don't have to give you a phone call now. You can use the phone when you get to City Jail."

The suspect calmly stated, "It's only traffic tickets and I paid them. If you will allow me a phone call, my mother can bring proof. Look man, I just started a job. Look, I'm in uniform, at least let me call my job."

The officer responded, "You don't have to prove shit to me. Show it to the judge. Tell your mom to catch the bus to the court house." He smiled and quickly walked out.

The suspect snapped, "Fuck you asshole! That's why I hate all you motherfuckers! I'm going to lose my job for some tickets I already paid."

He then asked the lady who was in charge of the booking area if he could use the phone.

She politely informed him, "Can't let you out until I clear this lobby, sir, but I will let you use it."

He was agitated. "Fuck you, too. You're probably on his side. Ya'll don't care if a nigga lose his job. This some bullshit!"

I walked over to him. "Tell you what, bro. Let me finish what I'm doing and I will let you use it."

He looked at me, "Naw, you probably want to pull me to the back so ya'll can kick my ass."

I looked him in the eye. "Bro, I'm no threat to you and I definitely want you to keep your job. You didn't do anything that would make me put my hands on you nor would I allow it."

He smiled, "Nigga, I like your style. What are you? One of those Rico Suave niggas? You talk like a brother."

I kept my promise and allowed him to call his mom and employer. As I was walking out, the lady in booking called me over.

"What's your name young man? I appreciate how you handled that situation. You got some officer's that get them riled up, then leave them with me. I have to deal with the backlash."

"I'm Officer Page and it's no problem. Whatever I can do."

"I'm Beatrice. If you have any questions, just let me know."

Beatrice became my friend and big sister of the department. We would talk all the time. She gave the 411 on whom to stay clear of and gamed me up on doing things correctly. I even met her husband Jimmie and son Quincy. I admired her family, especially her husband who was a hard working businessman. He had a new Corvette and a Prowler.

One day I was walking through the station and Beatrice said, "Roland, Jimmie is outside; he wants to speak to you."

I went outside. He was sitting in the Prowler with the top down.

I greeted him. "What's up, big bro. Damn I wanna be like you when I grow up."

He laughed, "You not letting the job get to you? I appreciate you looking out for my wife."

"I appreciate her looking out for me."

Jimmie told me to come closer. "This car is just a material thing, little brother. You can get this if you want. Pursue your dream even if you gotta use this job to get there. Don't be stuck in a mediocre career. You hear me?"

I dapped him up. "For sure, big bro."

New days brought new experiences. I was learning more and more each day and not completely about crime. I learned how to communicate better with the public as well as how to read people's behavior. I always treated others according to how they treated me.

In law enforcement, you got to have thick skin. You have to allow things to roll off your shoulder. I believe every officer has had a person tell them, *"Take that badge off and I'll whoop your ass."* I would just laugh and wave them off. I had a talent to talk people down. Even hostile individuals who were turned up, I would calm them down. Every blue moon, I would encounter an asshole I had to put in check.

Sometimes I had to let a motherfucker know. "It's beneficial that you deal with me in uniform because if I was off duty and you were popping off at the mouth, it would be different. You see me out and ever threaten me or try and do something to harm my family, I will peel your cap back with no hesitation."

When you look a person in the eye, I mean *really* look them deep in the eyes revealing your inner soul, they know who to fuck with and who not to fuck with. For the most part, my time on the streets was pretty cool. In my district I became popular in the community and the business district. Many of the businesses offered me side security opportunities. Some would try and give me free shit all the time. Food, discount on clothes, free carwashes. I didn't pay to get in football or baseball games. At times I felt guilty, maybe I was abusing my authority. I didn't cross certain lines like taking free merchandise. That would be considered theft. Some officers would take whatever they could get free. I wasn't that thirsty.

I enjoyed working second shift 3:00 pm-10:30 pm. I got shift differential pay, plus I wasn't a morning person. Evenings in the fourth were cool. Most parts of the business district closed down by 7:00 pm anyway. The attractions in the fourth were amazing-Union Station, Laclede Landing, the Arch, St. Louis Center Shopping mall, and literally hundreds of restaurants. The fourth could be unpredictable-housing projects surrounded the downtown area. Once in a while a shooting would come across the radio. Usually the entire district would rush to the call wanting to see some action.

The older officers stayed clear often saying, "I'm close to retirement. I've seen enough action for a life time."

Going into the projects you had to use caution especially at the high rises. A few times people dropped large appliances onto the squad car. Pretty scary huh? Imagine a microwave smashing on a vehicle from 10 stories. It would blow all the windows out.

I got a call for a burglary alarm sounding at a Chinese restaurant one late evening. I met my assisting officer in the rear of the establishment. We noticed the back door had been pried open. We drew our weapons.

I asked him, "You got your mag light?"

He grabbed it, handing it to me. "It's all yours, lead on."

We slowly entered the business announcing our presence.

I yelled, "Police! If you're in here, announce your presence." I announced ourselves one more time adding, "This is my last warning."

We canvassed through the building till we located the lights. Turning them on, we walked through again.

I heard my partner, "Come on down. NOW"

I rushed to the back and saw an older black guy climbing down from the top of the walk-in freezer.

I asked, "You been up there all this time?"

He politely responded, "Yes, Sir."

I laughed a bit because the suspect looked like Grady from Sanford and Son.

My partner asked, "What's funny, Ro?"

"Nothing I'll tell you later.'

I cuffed the suspect and started to escort him out when he suddenly stopped. "Officer, can I show you something before we leave?"

I asked, "Sure. What?"

"Go open that freezer and look at the bottom shelf."

I walked over, pulling him with me. I opened the door and flicked the light on.

"Right there, the bottom shelf."

I looked, "What the hell is that?"

He said, "Look closer."

My partner pushed the suspect in as we walked in.

We noticed two clear plastic bags with skinned carcasses inside. One bag had what appeared to be turtles in it and the other we couldn't make it out what was inside. We got closer.

"What the fuck is that?

The suspect said, "Look closer, it's either cats or small dogs."

My partner and I looked closer and then looked at each other.

My partner smiled, "Damn he's right. I guess I won't be eating here again."

We took the suspect in, booking him for 2nd degree burglary. Sgt. Patterson contacted the Health Department about the frozen cats.

After a few weeks I noticed the restaurant was shut down. *Permanently*.

You hear the urban myths about cats and Chinese restaurants, but I saw it for myself.

Being out on patrol left me with so many stories to tell. I would share them with Tracey sometimes. She was amused by the way I narrated the experiences.

"You should write a book. You got so much to say. It's quite entertaining."

I gave her the side eye, "Yeah, right. I should write a book telling my adventures and my dark secrets. That's like dry snitching on myself."

She rubbed my back, "You can confess your love for me and how marrying me was the best decision of your life."

I laughed, "Okay true. Can I tell them your farts smell worse than mine?"

She punched me in the arm.

The best part of the day was returning home from work. When my keys jingled to open the door, I could faintly hear, "Daddy home! Daddy home!"

This happened every day. I'd step in. "Where's my baby boy!"

He would come down the stairs, "I'm coming! I'm coming!"

I would pick him up and hug him for a long time. This little dude made my life complete. I would stare in the mirror at my image talking to myself.

"You do what you gotta do to make sure you come home to your family."

One day I was driving through the newly built apartment complex in my district. I was checking out the scene thinking how nice they looked.

I said, "Hope they stay nice and quiet."

As I turned a corner, I heard from a parked car, "Hey Roland."

I stopped and backed up. The door opened, "How you been. It's Joy, I went to school with your niece Aiko. Do you remember me?"

"Yeah it's been a while, but I do. How you been?"

She walked over to my patrol vehicle and leaned down. "I'm good. I just moved down here."

"Okay, they're nice. If you have any problems just let me know. This is my district."

She smiled, "I will do that. You know I had the biggest crush on you back in the day. I was a little girl but now I'm a grown woman."

She stood up showing her shapely body as if to say look at me. I thought to myself, *"Oh Lord Roland, drive the fuck off before you get in trouble."*

She told me what apartment she was in, inviting me to come by any time. I played it off saying, "Sure." Then kept it pushing.

An image of my family popped in my head. I've been on my best behavior so let's keep it that way.

Then the summer was here. With that being said, a hot summer in St. Louis can be explosive. The district was jumping-busy-especially on second shift. The calls consisted of a variety of incidents like accidents, robberies, domestic calls, and shootings.

As a cop there will always be certain incidents that stand out more than others.

One time I was walking into Police Headquarters when a speeding car pulled up to a hard squealing stop.

A white guy screamed, "Officer, please help, my friend's been shot!"

I rushed down to his car with an officer who was standing outside smoking a cigarette. We looked into the car and what I saw will always haunt my mind. It was a white female slumped over in the seat. I didn't see her until I looked in because she was bent all the way over. I heard her slight moan.

Opening the car door, I pulled her up and asked, "Ma'am, can you talk?" I jumped back.

Her face was completely missing. The only thing recognizable was one eyeball that was hanging down. Where her nose should have been mucous bubbles were dripping from her nasal passage.

The other officer said, "God damn!"

I told him to call EMS. I asked the driver what happened.

"We were down the street when a guy walked up to the car and shot her with a sawed off shotgun."

I said, "Down where?"

He continued, "We went to the Peabody's to buy some dope, and when she handed the guy the money, he gave her the package. He just turned around threw the money back and pulled the gun out and *Boom*!"

I got a description of the suspect and sent it out over the air. The Homicide unit came out of Headquarters taking over the incident.

I looked into the car seeing the balled up money the suspect threw back in. It looked strange. Opening it up, I discovered it was fake money; turning the paper over, I just shook my head in pity. It *read "Gotcha!"*

It's shit like that I will never forget. Want to hear more?

I get a call for an accident on Interstate 70 eastbound. It's an NHL Blues game going on; we're playing the Red Wings, an infamous rival. The traffic is crazy. I have to run code driving off the roadway to get to my destination. Upon arrival I see a woman in distress walking back and forth behind a semi-truck. I pull around a vehicle stopped a distance behind the semi. A fucking car is pinned under the semi. Evidently the semi stopped and the car slammed into the back of the truck being pinned underneath it.

I immediately called EMS as I exited my car. I asked if there was anyone hurt or if there were any witnesses. Looking into the pinned car sent a shock through my body. The driver's head was missing. I dropped my head rubbing my hand over my face. The hysterical female witness looked at me,

"Now you see why?"

"Yes ma'am I do."

The driver of the semi is in a panic.

He explained, "These damn drivers drive crazy when these games are going on. Shit man I was stopped when I felt the impact. It was fierce too."

Once the Fire Department and Accident Reconstruction arrived, we managed to get the car from under the semi. They pried the doors open. Searching through the car, I find the driver's head on the floor of the back seat. The bystanders in the distance gasp. The female witness started to cry. I comforted her. This world has good people who just care about life even that of a complete stranger.

One more and that's it. I get a call for a welfare check at a retirement building. The caller, an older woman, informed me she hasn't heard from her sister in weeks and she won't answer the phone. She went on to say the manager wasn't on site so we were her only option. Once I get there I knock numerous times with no answer. I have the dispatcher contact the Fire Department to assist me in gaining entry. Waiting on the Fire Department, the sister's conversation saddens me.

"Baby, when you get a certain age like mine. You have to come to grips that you're going to lose love ones. My sister is all I have, but standing here, I know I'm going to be by myself. I went to Knoxville to see my daughter for a couple of weeks. When I stopped hearing from my sister, I got sick to my stomach. *I knew. I knew.*" She started to cry.

The Fire Department arrived getting the door open. As soon as I stepped in, the odor of death rushed into my nostrils. The sister called out with no answer. I drew my weapon telling everybody to remain outside the door. Attempting to turn on the lights, I discovered the electricity is off. I searched the hot apartment finally coming to the bathroom. I opened the door and I heard the sound of flies buzzing around. I turned on my flashlight and almost gagged. The lady was lying in the tub and the water was completely brown with slime surrounding the edges. I called the fire department in. They had the same reaction. The sister walked to the bathroom door then burst out crying walking away. I looked closer at the body; her organs had imploded from her abdomen. I had never seen anything like that before; it could have been a prop from a horror movie. My heart was heavy for a while; I have a soft spot for the elderly.

Even with all of these memories, I have to say I loved being a cop. Once I was off probationary status, there was nothing to even celebrate. I had already gained the trust of my fellow officers and Sgt. Patterson was really cool. I knew the district well and the district knew me. Everything was gravy. I could see myself doing this type of job for a lifetime.

On the home front things were A1 also. The kids were blending well. Tracey was doing great at her newfound career.

Want to know the best part of being off probation? The overtime and I could work secondary employment. Some officers were making $15 per hour. I could really stack some paper.

CHAPTER THIRTEEN

WORKING SECONDARY JOBS TOOK up quite a bit of my time. I think my part-time checks were bigger than my department paychecks. I preferred that Tracey not do overtime because of the kids. But I had a few secondary jobs: the library, Plaza Square apartments, and my favorite, the Rams Stadium. St. Louis had just acquired the NFL Rams so that meant free games, at least when I wasn't working.

When I was in the district, I got overtime pay for warrant applications and court appearances. Fortunately, we had numerous opportunities to save extra income. The money came in handy especially with fixing up the house.

Every Sunday during the summer, my neighborhood was chaotic due to young people cruising in and out the park. Since my house was directly across from O'Fallon Park, I couldn't find anywhere to park. It was so congested that by the time I was off, I had to park two or three blocks away. One day I parked in the alley behind my house. I positioned my vehicle so cars could get by. I then placed my Department ID tag on the rear view mirror. I went in the house until a parking spot became available in front of my house. As soon as one did, I went to pull my car around and I noticed a parking violation on my window written by an Officer McGirt.

I said, "What the fuck? Maybe he didn't see the tag."

I walked through the park until I could see a group of motorcycle officers. Walking up, I could sense it was going be a problem even though we were fellow employees. They had the most disdained look on their faces, watching the young black people walking and driving through the park.

I walked up, "Hello officers. Are any of you Officer McGirt?"

Of course, the bitterest one said, "I am"

I took a second look thinking, *"This motherfucker got a Wyatt Earp mustache."*

"Officer McGirt, you wrote me a parking violation for parking my vehicle in the back of my house. As you can see, there's nowhere to park. I live across from the park; I just got off myself. Could you help me out and take care of it? I would appreciate it."

I showed him the ticket. He didn't even look at it.

"No I can't."

No explanation why he couldn't. He could have said, "My supervisor instructed us no exceptions."

I stood there a few seconds then I gave him the most unfriendly stare I could muster.

I walked back to my house slamming the door. Tracey jumped, "What's wrong baby?"

"That Klan ass cop looked at me like I was speaking a foreign language. He might as well have called me a nigga. He looked at me like I was cruising through the goddamn park making his job hard. Racist bitch!"

She tried to calm me down, "It's okay; just pay the ticket. It's no big deal. It's a shame cause you're an officer too."

I was shaking mad, "I work on Laclede's Landing every day; whenever an officer asked me to take care of a ticket, I never questioned it. Sure, no problem. All the brothers extended that curiosity, but when it came to some of the white officers to return the favor, they acted like we were asking them to commit a motherfucking crime. Not all of them, but those hillbilly dickheads always gave us problems." I decided *"I'm going to run this to the North Patrol."*

Grabbing my keys, I headed straight to North Patrol, not far from my home.

I took the ticket to Area One North Patrol, where McGirt was assigned. I walked in and saw a black Lieutenant. I explained the situation. He politely said, "I will take care of it. Some officers don't believe in professional curiosity or even understanding you live over there."

I shook the Lieutenant's hand. "Thanks sir, I appreciate it. I just got home doing the same job as him. He didn't even give me the respect to look at me."

After the situation I told Sgt. Patterson, who is white, what occurred. He blew up mad. He contacted the officer, yelling and asking him what type of cop he was. Sgt. Patterson even called him a redneck prick. Sgt. Patterson was good people.

Working secondary in conjunction with my rotating departmental shift, I was exhausted. On top of that I had insomnia. I couldn't get to sleep sometimes until 2 a.m. and I had to be at work at 6 a.m. I was functioning on 3 to 4 hours of sleep. Once I got off, I had to be at secondary employment for about 3 hours. I tried sleeping aids but they only made it difficult for me to get up. Looking for an answer for the insomnia, I started drinking beer to help me fall asleep. It worked like a charm. I felt like shit drinking again, however it was so good to be able to sleep.

Knowing that Tracey would get on my head if she knew I was drinking every day, I would drink two or three beers before I got off work. Yeah, I drank on duty. Figuring I needed a rested night I would drink early camouflaging it with mint Listerine and spearmint gum. Sadly, the drinking made my job easier to cope with. During the day shift, I would drink in sub stations out of sight from the public. On the evening shift, I would park behind a school or down on the riverfront among the old abandoned factories. I knew what companies had security cameras and the ones who were just completely closed. Months went by and I was dependent on alcohol once again.

It didn't take long for the drinking to bring the demons out in me. Evil thoughts and temptation surfaced. I knew a few females who lived in the projects so I had duck off spots to chill. The district commanders thought I was socially interacting with the community. In a way I was except it was with the chosen female who was on my tip that night. I kept my dick in my pants but I knew I was still guilty sitting up with another female. Some of them would cook for me and others would have me over and sit up watching TV wearing booty shorts and a t-shirt. I kept my composure. I knew I was wrong yet I never crossed that line of sleeping with them.

Tracey started complaining about me not spending quality time with her so I started searching for a place to tattoo and airbrush out of, figuring I could control my hours plus triple my profit. I looked for beauty shops because they already had female clientele. After a few weeks, I found a perfect spot on a busy street right in the heart of the city. Perfection Salon was a popular full service cosmetology shop owned by a husband and wife. Marvin and Tanya Royal were a successful team. I admired their partnership. I spoke with Marvin on the phone and asked if he would be interested in having me work at their salon part time. He showed interest and I felt a good vibe from him. Dude was mad cool. He and his wife worked hard to build Perfection Salon and I wanted to be a part of the operation. I went to meet them in person on my day off. I introduced myself to Tanya and she told me Marvin would be there shortly. She told me the story of how they established their business. My respect for both of them was immense. Finally meeting them both, we agreed I would start in two weeks.

The next day I pulled my tattoo equipment out of storage and tuned it up. I ordered the needed supplies from TATTOO magazine, anticipating it would take two weeks to arrive. Tracey wasn't too thrilled about me tattooing. I asked her why but she had little explanation. Surely it was the female factor that had her in conflict. To ease her suspicion, I took her to meet Marvin and Tanya. She admitted meeting them helped. They appeared to be level-headed people. On the way home from their meeting, Tracey was quiet.

"You okay? What do you think?'

Looking out the window she responded, "They seem real cool. Tanya is attractive huh?"

I looked confused, "She's cool. Why you ask that?'

"The truth is I feel threatened when you get around attractive women, Roland."

I grabbed her hand, "Have you looked in the mirror? Why would I mess around when I have someone like you?"

She replied, "I don't know why men do it but they do. They'll have a good thing going and jeopardize it for some mediocre type shit."

"True shit. Not with us. Okay?"

She looked at me, "I'm trusting you Roland."

Tanya was a very attractive woman, I must admit. However, Tracey was beyond beautiful and the glue that held my family together. She gifted me with my heir.

Initially the tattoo industry was slow. I even contemplated throwing in the towel. I halted all the secondary jobs therefore I was hoping something would give. The salon had a strong clientele so word caught on. Suddenly I had customers out the wazoo. My clientele was deep and all females. They would come just to flirt with me. They would bring their friends to get tatted just to talk with me. I would subtly flirt with their friends so they would bring other friends. I would sometimes have more customers than the stylist.

Tracey would visit on weekends giving me the side eye if I was tatting a woman's breast. Her facial expressions showed her discontent in my new career.

She'd whisper, "You love your job huh?"

"I love the money not the job, mami. Don't confuse the two."

The truth was I did love my job, but not for the women. I loved it for the love of art. I found my calling.

Money was rolling in like the dope game, and like the dope game, I was meeting some cats heavy in the streets. That was part of the street scene. People were getting their clicks, sets, and themes tatted on them. Many got straight to the point. Women would put anything from *I got that wet-*

wet to *Good Pussy*. The guys would get *Money Over Bitches,* and *Trust No One*. I saw it all and did it all.

Working in a salon you witness a lot of drama. It could be quite entertaining as well as discouraging. I tried to avoid any type of conflict.

After hours in the shop it would just be Marvin, Tanya, and me. They would argue quite a bit saying some heavy shit to one another. I would just act invisible. Marvin would leave out. Tanya would ask me my opinion at times.

I would just reply, "No relationship is perfect and I can't judge your husband because I'm not perfect, mami."

She started to confide in me. I sympathized with her and occasionally felt guilty, wondering if I should be lending her my ear. Marvin was super cool so I really didn't want to get in the mix.

Back in the district I was making a name for myself. Many of the commanders acknowledged I was an outstanding community officer. When I pulled up on many of the scenes, especially in the hoods, the majority of the people preferred to talk to me. I could tell some of the other officers didn't like it. Truthfully I didn't give a fuck. Perhaps there were a few officers who wanted to do some conniving shit. But, not around me.

Sgt. Patterson assigned me many plush assignments. I conducted school visitations, business courtesy checks, and personal security details. I was pleased with the connections I was making politically and in the hood. I was trusted.

As much as my career choices were progressing, my marriage was a bit bruised. Tracey was insecure about everything I did. She didn't want me to tatt but she enjoyed the extra money. As much as she felt neglected, I felt taken advantage of. We argued often and made up in the bed. I would be hurt at times when she stared at me. I knew she was emotionally tender but I had to chase my dream.

One night we got in a crazy argument for some trivial shit. I got dressed and stormed out the house. I stopped at the liquor store to grab a beer. I just drove around the city until I came up on a club. Club Mercedes was the hottest nightspot in the city plus I was cool with the owners. I went in and posted up at the bar. The owner spotted me.

"Ro, what's up homie?"

I gave him a pound. "I'm good fam. How 'bout you?"

"Glad to have one of St. Louis' finest-term for St. Louis police- in the building."

"No doubt. This is my joint."

He signaled to the bartender, "Give him what he wants."

The bartender was a healthy dark chocolate female with her shirt almost completely unbuttoned.

"Hey you. What can I get you?"

I looked at the liquor selections, "Tell you what. Surprise me."

As she pouring all types of shit into a glass, I wondered, *"What the fuck is she making?. That's a lot of liquor."*

She kept looking at me. I asked, "What's up?"

"Don't you do tattoos at Perfection?"

"Yes ma'am."

She handed me the drink in a tall glass, "Enjoy. Before you leave, can I get your number. I want a tattoo."

I said, "Sure."

When I took a sip of the concoction, I said "Damn mami. You trying to get me fucked up huh?"

She laughed, "Next one's on me."

By the end of the night, I was lit. The club was emptying out but the owners asked me to stick around. I did until they counted down. Walking out, I checked my mobile phone seeing multiple missed calls from home.

I grabbed my keys and I heard, "Hey Roland."

It was Joy, my niece's friend.

"Joy, how are you?"

"I'm pissed; I think my friends left me."

I scratched my head, "You need a ride?" knowing I was too drunk to be giving anybody a damn ride.

"Sure, if you don't mind."

So I was driving drunk as fuck and feeling all kinds of guilty.

She smiled, "You know I had the biggest crush on you back in the day."

I rubbed my head as I grew uncomfortable, "You did? I had no idea."

She laughed, "Boy stop acting scared. I'm not going to bite you. You know you like what you see."

I looked over noticing she barely had anything on.

As I pulled up to her apartment I said, "Here you go."

She replied, "Come on in and sober up."

"Naw, I'm good."

She snatched my key out the ignition, "Your niece will kill me if I let something happen to you."

I was drunk as a skunk. So we go in and after a short conversation, we were going at it on her couch.

I caught myself and pulled out. "Wait I don't have protection."

She pulled me back in, "I'm on the pill."

The liquor had me all out of character, however it was no excuse because I was feeling like shit.

Afterwards I do a hoe bath, get dressed and leave. felt bad, not just for Tracey but for Joy. I hoped she was not misled, but before I left she said, "Am I'm going she you again?"

I turned to her, "Of course."

When I got home, I snuck in and found Tracey asleep. I carefully crawled in bed scooting next to Lil Ro. I looked at him and thought, *"Son be a better man than me."*

The next day Tracey woke me up and asked if we could talk. We discussed the distance we were experiencing and what we could do to make it better. We came to an agreement but deep down I knew we both were stuck in our ways.

The next couple of days, I was consumed with guilt. My sergeant noticed my distance and pulled me aside.

"I've seen many young officers come and go. This job can advance you. On the other hand, it can corrupt you just as fast. Don't let it infect the good things in life, Ro."

I got back to the salon and I was silent all day. Tanya looked concerned. She asked me, "Are you okay?"

I said, "I'll be okay. I got no choice."

She smiled, "I know the feeling."

I smiled back, "If only you knew."

Walking by she stopped me and smelled my neck.

"What's that cologne you're wearing?"

I said, "Armani."

She straightened out my shirt and rubbed my chest, "Let's go have a drink. I can use it and I know you can."

After work we went to the Riverfront and I confide in her as she does the same. We told each other how we respected and admired each other's grind. She said we would be a wonderful team.

I agreed, "Yeah I hear you. In another time and life, we would make a great team."

We stared at each other realizing we had already crossed the line with one another.

For the next few days I tried to keep my distance from Tanya. But then one day, I went to wash my hands in the bathroom and she entered and washed her hands the same time I was washing mine. She grabbed my hand. Suddenly we start to kiss passionately.

She whispered, "I want you."

I said, "We got to be careful, mami. People can get hurt if we pursue this."

She said, "I know. I'm not worried about the grownups. It's the little ones it can effect."

We know the ramifications but the passion, or should I say lust, is too powerful.

She got a motel room and we spent the night together. Tracey thought I was doing overtime in the district.

Tanya and I carried on for a while with no one having a clue. I was so discreet that people would never expect anything. I must admit, I felt extremely bad. Marvin was such a solid dude.

Tanya would say, "He's a good father but the heart wants what the heart wants."

I would say, "You are so right."

One day Marvin greeted me, "Ro, my brother how are you?"

I replied, "Good bro. How about you?"

He exhaled, "Man, stressing about my marriage, bro. Do you have the same problems?"

It caught me by surprise but I answered, "All couples do, Marvin. We're men so we handle the problems."

He shook my hand. "You're so right."

I asked Tanya later, "Does he have a clue what's going on?"

She said, "He always accuses me. What's new?"

I told her, "He's right though. Does he suspect me?"

"No, he doesn't."

I looked at her concerned, "He's going be crushed it's me."

Our sexual appetite was so spontaneous. We had sex on top of the car, in the bathtub of motels, and even in the park. Both feeling guilty, we consoled each other blaming it on our significant others.

Tracey started getting suspicious but never suspected I was having an affair with Tanya.

Tanya and I masked the relationship while in the salon. However, some of her friends started to figure out that something was brewing. Our affair was addictive. The more I was around her, the more she realized her marriage was on the rocks. As for me I was just making bad choices. I must admit that I questioned if Tracey was my soul mate. When I was at home, I would watch her play with Lil Ro while he sat on her lap. My heart started to physically hurt. I felt so horrible. Seeing the two of them, I knew I couldn't leave her. Yet I did care for Tanya and I wanted her to be happy too.

My cheating was accompanied with more drinking. Looking in the mirror, I hated my reflection.

I would talk to my pops, "Pops you told me to be a better man than you. I bet you would be so disappointed now."

Things were getting messy. Tanya would sneak in the restroom while I was in there. I bet her employees were saying *"What the fuck?"* We would go out in public leaving together. She was just as popular as I was. It was a matter of time before people would find out. I contemplated on cutting it off only to postpone that decision over and over. I promised myself I would do it the next available time. What was I getting myself into?

Tanya would go out her way to please me. Shit was getting serious and deep down I knew I was digging myself into a hole. She eventually left Marvin, leasing her own apartment in South County. She asked me how I felt about it.

"What do you think about me moving out?"

"I'm not sure what to think. Are you sure that's what you want to do?"

She replied, "It's not about you and me. We had problems long before you came around. I'm tired of the fighting. I do admit you make me feel loved again. I care for you deeply and I know it's foul how we hooked up, but the heart wants what it wants."

"That's what life is about. Happiness. You're a special woman you don't need a man to make you feel that way. I'm a bad person, not the type of guy you need."

"Roland, if you want to make it work with Tracey, do it. I'm telling you eventually you have to make a choice. No woman wants to share."

I shook my head yes. "You're right. The biggest obstacle for me and you is we have kids."

She cut me off, "Don't use the kids as an excuse. Families go through divorce all the time and the kids are okay."

"I understand that. That's other people. My son needs me and I need him. I may be a bad husband but I will never be a bad father. I put my needs second to his."

She agreed, "You're right. Marvin is a great husband and father. Sometimes two good people are just bad together."

We had deep conversations declaring to be each other's best friend. Tanya did make me feel special, often praising the ideas and the talent I brought to the table.

Sometimes females would come to the shop just to visit me. No one I ever invited, just random females trying to see what I was about. Tattooing was bringing in loot like the dope game. I could tell Tanya would get jealous.

"You better be careful with these young chicken heads. They'll get you caught up. Tracey will show up and choke one of those bitches and I will help her."

I laughed it off, "I'm hip. Don't think I'm stupid. I'm perfectly aware of what they want."

One day a young girl began to describe what type of tattoo she wanted and the placement. She pulled up her skirt showing me her thigh. I saw Tanya in the background fuming. Later that day we were preparing to close and she walked by my desk and put down a key. It caught me by surprise. I was thinking, *"Oh boy. Big mistake Ro."*

Tracey couldn't track my schedule because I would use the overtime alibi. However, she was no dummy.

"I'm not sure what's gotten into you but you're not the same. Is there anything you want to tell me?"

"No. I'm good. Is there something you want to say to me?"

"There is. If you're not happy with me, then you can tell me. I won't be happy about it but at least we can work on it. Don't make me look like a fool Roland."

"Tracey there's nothing going on, maybe a little job stress but that's it.

"Are you sure? Because you know I love you dearly."

"I'm positive. Love you too."

I thought to myself, *"Ro, you better cut it off now before someone gets hurt."*

Feeling like the scum of the earth I rehearsed what I was going to say to Tanya. Playing it over and over I wondered how the scenario would go. There were no good end results in the mess I made. One night after work I met up with Tanya to discuss some things. It was a local speakeasy in Midtown. She felt a bit uneasy about our meeting and I did too. I ordered us a drink to loosen up.

I tried to avoid eye contact, "How are you, mami?"

"I'm okay, Mr. Page. What about yourself?"

"Tanya, I'm not good at all." I took a sip of my drink.

"What's the matter? I'm a big girl say what you have to say."

"I gave thought about us and it's all wrong what we are doing. I'm trying to be a good father and I can't be that doing what I'm doing."

"That's an excuse Roland, but hey I don't want to be with someone who doesn't want to be with me."

I sighed, "I'm glad you understand."

She slammed her drink down, "I didn't say I understand. I said I'm not going to chase no man but the more I sit here the more I'm getting pissed off. You misled me to believe we had a chance. Roland playing with people's feelings is a dangerous thing."

"Tanya, I wasn't trying to play with your feelings. I honestly care for you but the fact is I have a complete family that needs me as much as I need them. I have to do what's best."

She yelled, "So fuck me?"

I looked at her, "Never that. I take full responsibility in this whole fucked up situation. But the truth is who am I willing to hurt, you or Tracey. The final decision is my son is not going to grow up without his dad in his household."

She threw the drink in my face, got up and walked out. I slowly rose, wiping the drink from my face. Luckily there wasn't a crowd to witness it.

I called out to her, "Tanya I'm truly sorry."

Without looking back she replied, "Yeah you are."

I began walking to my car. Suddenly she sped up pulling next to me almost hitting me.

I shouted, "What the fuck is your problem!"

She yelled back, "You know my problem. You got the wrong one. Tell you what, when you get home, I'll be at your house telling Tracey the truth."

I paused for a moment, "You know what. I don't give a fuck, do what you gotta do." She drove off as the front of her car clipped my side, pushing me into my car. I yelled, *"Bitch!"*

Pulling my service gun from my waist, a couple walking to the speakeasy retreated behind a parked car. I caught myself putting my gun away. I thought, *"Get a grip. But that crazy ass actually hit me. She was lucky I got restraint."* Going home, I wondered, *"Did this bitch actually go to my house?"* Pulling up, my stomach dropped. Tanya's car was parked right in front of my house. I parked staring at her every step of the way. She got out and gave me an evil look.

"After you, Mr. Page."

I swallowed my spit, "Fuck it, come on. I'm tired of this shit."

We got to the front door and I opened it slowly yelling for Tracey.

"Tracey come down; I have to tell you something!"

She walked down the steps looking puzzled and scared, "What's wrong?" Her voice crackled. Tanya stood in the doorway with her hands folded.

"I've been lying to you. I'm so sorry. Tanya and I had an affair. She's here to tell you."

Tanya butted in, "Tracey, I'm sorry also. Roland led me to believe he was going to leave you."

Tracey looked at me. I turned to Tanya, "I'm not leaving my wife."

Rage flooded Tracey's face. She smacked me across my face. For a minute there I could have sworn I saw sparks. I thought, *"I get hit by a fucking car now I get the shit smacked out of me."* Deep down I knew I deserved it.

Tracey looked at Tanya "You said your peace, now get the fuck out my house."

Slamming the door, she turned to me, "The kids are asleep. We'll discuss this in the morning after they leave for school. Enjoy the couch."

To avoid any more drama, I obliged.

That morning the kids were off to school. Lil Ro was dropped off at Sissy's house. Tracey walked in the bedroom while I was dressing.

"You no good motherfucker. While I'm here being a good wife, you out here trying to be mister playboy. What you thought you could have two households?"

I calmly said "I made a terrible mistake. I apologize. That's why I wanted to bring it out so I didn't have this dark cloud over my head."

She picked up the phone and threw it at me. "How could you do this to your family?"

I walked over to her to hug her; she stepped away. "Roland, it can't be you just kiss me and we make up. You *cheated* on me."

I said, "I'm only human. We are all human capable of making mistakes. I never intended on leaving you. I was selfish and I was going to eventually have to answer to God for that.

However, I hope you forgive me cause I forgave you."

She stomped her foot, "Forgave me? Nigga I've been faithful to you while you been out here having your cake and eating it too!"

Buttoning my uniform shirt, I looked at her, "Well who's Ronald?"

She looked at me in surprise.

I continued, "Oh wipe that shit look off your face. You didn't think I knew you were talking to a motherfucker? Telling all my business. Saying what a no good nigga I was. Huh? You didn't think I knew?"

She paused and toned down her voice, "It's not what you think. I wasn't trying to have a relationship. I was lonely and hurt, the distance you put between us. It was a shoulder to cry on. That's it."

I shook my head in agreement, "Okay I hear you. Regardless, it wasn't right. What I did wasn't right. So where do we go from here? Do you want to make it work or what?"

She sat on the bed, "Why didn't you say something?"

I walked over to her, "What could I say? Be a hypocrite and come down on you when I was doing some fucked up shit? I just kept it to myself."

She grabbed my hand, "How did you find out? He didn't mean anything to me."

"I don't want to discuss it. Just stop talking to the nigga before I have to fuck him up something terrible. As far as how I found out, I'm a cop, *Tracey*. I can find out anything."

It took a while for us to rebound from the trauma I caused. I did what I had to as a man.

Occasionally we would argue wondering if each other was wandering outside the marriage. I would agree with her that my actions triggered the problems. She didn't hold it over my head though.

I was concerned about Tanya. I called Marvin to apologize.

"Hey, Marvin, I wanted to say it was fucked up what I did. You allowed me into your business and I took advantage of it. I take full responsibility. Again I'm sorry."

"Roland, there's no sorry. You were *fucking* my wife. That's the most disrespectful thing a man can do. Any man would get fucked up over a situation like that."

After a minute of him yelling at me I got agitated. "Look I apologized and I understand you don't want it. Cool but me getting fucked up ain't going to happen. Whoever tries some shit like that might find themselves getting fucked up."

We left it like that.

CHAPTER FOURTEEN

WITHOUT MY TATTOO BUSINESS, I went back to doing secondary for extra income. It was truly missed. Tracey voiced her opposition for me tattooing. She felt it was the cause of our problems. I understood but I had no plans on giving it up totally.

While in the district I would look for ideal places to set up a tattoo spot. Nothing caught my attention. I knew it had to be a location Tracey would be comfortable with. She told me if the conditions were right, she would agree even helping me establish the business.

I waited patiently till the right opportunity presented itself.

My police career was becoming a routine. I was getting bored, after all I discovered my one true purpose career wise. Art was always my passion. I soldiered on in the district doing my job to my best ability. One thing I loved about police work was dealing with the public. My business alliances got wider and the love for my community got stronger. I would visit the most deprived areas of the district mingling with the people. A majority of the inner city didn't care for police officers; it was more of a distrust towards them Many young black brothers would approach me.

"Page, you hella cool but your fellow officers… Man, I can't stand them. Especially the white ones."

I would listen asking questions, "Why?"

"They free case niggas all the damn time. They'll pull us over talking real grimy to us. They'll even call us niggas if nobody is around. Page, they'll pull up, take our money out putting it into their pockets, then ask us how much it is. If we say it's $300 but it's really $450. They will keep the $150. That's real talk."

I advised them, "Why don't you go to Internal Affairs, they will investigate it."

They looked at me side eyed, "Page, they don't listen. Some of us tried only to get harassed more. Internal Affairs goes and tells them who put the complaint out."

I said, "Next time if you see a brother in uniform, say something."

"Man, some of the brothers look more intimidated than us to say something. They're disillusioned like it's us against them. You got a few brothers like yourself that's good people."

I replied, "Yeah I hear you some just don't want to make waves. The academy taught us to serve and protect all. We are actually peace officers. When some get on the streets, they get influenced by others to do their way of policing. Some may think whatever it takes to clean the streets, not realizing they're corrupting their oath. Kind of like do a crime to catch crime."

"Look Page, if you catch me in the act, I might not admit it, but it's all good. A nigga dirty so you caught me with my pants down. But to put a gun or some dope on a nigga cause you think I'm dirty, that's flat out fucked up. The police breaking the rules is why you got a lot of the ignorant motherfuckers beating their cases. I may hustle but you think I want to walk around with a strap to kill another black man? Page, sometimes you got Vice that will have partners out for each other's head because they told each of them the other snitched. That's real talk, bro."

I listened seeing the passion in their eyes as they took turns voicing their disgust.

"You got cops free casing and railroading cats. You got some cops that will tell us go get a job. Page, would you go work at McDonalds for minimum wage? That's cool for a student but not for a person who got 3 or 4 mouths to feed. They drive through here mean mugging us. I'm a grown man. If you show you don't like me, then I'm going show I don't like you. They hear the myth of the angry black man so they come out here with a chip on their shoulder. They get out the car already on ten. Tell them why don't they just check up on us to see if we having a nice day. Why is it only to see if we're up to no good? You can sit on the police lot and drink with your friends but we can't sit in front of our own damn house and have a beer? Page, you are rare bro."

I was amazed when these young brothers educated me. I was disappointed in myself; how could I forget the experiences I had with bad cops when I was young? Shit, I experienced situations now that some cops think different of black cops. They think we got the job because of affirmative action not because I worked my ass off to achieve everything I got.

I looked around shaking all of my brother's hands.

"It's a fucked up world we live in, but be happy to see black men in uniforms, young brother. Could you imagine a department *without* black officers? Tell you what, you got some good white cops out there. It's more good ones than bad ones. The bad ones just show their true colors, tormenting people they don't like."

As I drove throughout the district, I noticed fellow officers always writing tickets in the neighborhoods where they know people don't have much. But, in the business district, I would see a police let a driver who ran a red light go because he was wearing a suit. Yet the black janitor didn't deserve the courtesy. I started to see how the scales of justice were unequally balanced.

I started drinking more and expressing my growing dislike of the department.

I missed tattooing. You ever found something that you do so well it's like you were birthed to do it? Every time I put on the police uniform, I thought *how long will I be stuck doing this?* Don't get me wrong, it wasn't not a bad job. It was just not for me. I knew a lot of people who left the department and prospered. They used it as a steppingstone.

When I told this to Tracey, she told me it was the alcohol talking. Our previous experience made the tattoo business a complete turn off for her. The enthusiasm I had for body art grew more and more the longer I was away from it. Nothing or nobody was going to stop my dream, but how could I get Tracey on board?

I didn't drink at home much; however I didn't slow down. I would go duck off during the end of shift hoping I didn't get a serious call. I would respond to some calls under the influence, tainting my judgment. I would have conversations with females from every walk of life who worked in the downtown area. One would be a lawyer, the other a hostess for Hooters, or maybe a merchandiser for a fashion manufacture. They all were crushing on me. I used it to my advantage to get free stuff. This time I kept it real about my marriage. I explained I wasn't looking to get emotionally involved. I was just looking for a good time. They liked my honesty, the uniform, and the hint of bad boy in my nature. Crazy as it might seem, I didn't have sex with any of them.

I did security for a nice hotel in the downtown area. Working the late shift, I had access to free rooms all the time. I would allow a female to come keep me company every now and then.

The front desk attendants would shake their head, "Ro, are you really married?"

"Yeah I am. Quit thinking the worst, can't a man just have a conversation with a woman?'

One older woman at the desk said, "Would you care if your wife had conversations with other men?"

I smiled, "Point taken. She might be for all I know. I'm a fucked up individual, what can I say? But if you must know, I love my wife as my partner in life and mother of my child. Trust and believe no woman will take her place. Also, yes, she deserves better."

What other benefit did the hotel have? I would tattoo late at night on the weekends. Shit I was tatting while I was working sometimes. The hotel never had any problems.

One night at the hotel, I was sitting at the lobby bar. I was sneaking a few shots of Patron with Chris the lobby bartender.

Whispering "*Salud*," one after the next. Before I knew it, I had one too many. I noticed a group of people congregating at the desk so I quit.

"Chris I'm done man. You got me trippin. I'm on duty."

He laughed, "Go on you pussy."

I walked toward the front as the group dispersed so I stepped to the side. I noticed an older dark complexion woman eyeing me. I smiled, "How you doing, ma'am?"

"I'm doing great now. Are you here to lock me up?"

I laughed, "Nope now why should I do that?"

She came closer, "Do you want to lock me up?"

"What have you done for me to lock you up?"

She handed me her suitcase, "Walk me to my room and I will tell you."

One hour later I returned to the lobby straightening my uniform.

Chris shook his head, "Dude you're too much. Was it good?"

I looked confused, "What are you talking about?'

He replied, "For real."

I whispered to him, "Chris never snitch on yourself."

Riding through the district I noticed a fairly new beauty shop called TJ's that opened on the outskirts of the downtown area. I decided to pay it a visit. Once I entered, I saw a room full of familiar faces and one of them greeted me.

"Ro, what's up? Did somebody call you?"

"No, I was actually just stopping by. I passed by here a few times and wanted to show some curiosity."

I walked over and pounded a dude's hand, "Damn bro, I remember you from somewhere."

He said, "Charles from Laclede Town."

I remembered, "Yeah you stayed by Gino in Laclede Town. Who's the owner here?"

He told me. "His name is Tez but he's not in yet. What you have in mind?"

I replied, "I'm looking for a place to tatt out of."

He got excited, "No shit? That will pop in here. I'll give you his number. Tell him I referred you."

I called but got no answer so I left a message. A few days went by and I finally got a call from Tez.

"Roland, how you doing man? Charles told me about you. He said you're a good brother. Explain to me a little bit more on what you want to do."

I ran down my entire vision and expectations. He was just as hyped about it as me. We discussed a rental fee. Tez even built out my tattoo booth in a day. Dude appeared to be a humble cat. Tracey and I met his family, which included his wife and brother. Within a week I was up and going. Then I moved into the promoting stage. Tracey helped me pass out flyers I made. We went to Saints Skating Rink, all the popular malls, and anywhere people socialized. Shit, I even passed out flyers when I was on duty. I left no place untouched. Sometimes when I was out with my family Lil Ro, now 4, tried to help me pass them out. It worked especially with the women.

They would say, "Oh she is so cute."

I would inform them that he was a boy. They'd be embarrassed, "Oops I'm sorry he has all that long hair."

Tracey would pull Lil Ro's hair back into a ponytail like my mom did for me way back when. I put in some hard grassroots marketing with the assistance of my family. It didn't take long for the word to get out. I had a little of everybody come check me out, more women than men. I would get off from the department and head straight to the shop. It was so convenient because TJ's was in my district. I stopped by on my lunch break sometimes.

I was back with a vengeance. I had the local competitors in their feelings, mad because a black tattoo artist was locking down the industry. Only served them right. They overcharge customers and are some of the most unfriendly people. Some shops would upcharge black people just because of the color of their skin. They would even send spies to check out my operation.

I came in contact with a few black people who accompanied my customers saying, "I go to Ink King for my tattoos; they say you use fake ink."

I would laugh, "They say I use fake ink? So you mean to tell me people are making real and fake tattoo ink?"

They would think about it, "Well that's what they said."

I would politely say, "So because their white tattooist they're right? Is that what you're saying?"

After their friends would laugh at them, they'd feel embarrassed walking out the tattoo booth. I'd think to myself, *"Tap dance your ass down to Ink King."*

My tattooing business was going great. Tracey would come down and help me after she got off work. She would help the customers and prepare the stencils for me.

One day she showed up with Lil Ro. I saw her walk in the office so I took a break.

"There's my baby boy!"

He ran and jumped in my arms so I could hug him. "Daddy! Mama went to the doctor."

I looked at her strange, "You went to the doctor? What's wrong?"

She smiled, "I got some good news. Well, I hope it is."

I leaned against my desk, "Tell me! I need to hear some good news."

She walked up kissing Lil Ro and me. "Lil Ro is going to have a brother."

I was overjoyed with the news. We closed the shop to celebrate the addition to the Page legacy. The concerns Tracey had were the babysitter, her career, and how the pregnancy might affect her this time. I assured her I'd be there every step of the way.

Unfortunately, the fear Tracey had of the toll the pregnancy would have on her body was correct. She blew up like a balloon. I rubbed her feet and tried to manage her diet or should I say make sure she wouldn't pig out. We pulled together as a family. Ashley was an enormous help making sure Lil Ro was okay. She was a preteen conducting herself as a little woman.

Time flew by and we were soon meeting the new addition to the family. My prayer was answered, it was a boy! We named him early Robert Jiro Page. Robert was a title after my father and Jiro was my mother's idea. The odds were in my favor; I felt invincible. I was so pleased.

Tracey and I were in for the long haul. I felt no matter what I did, Tracey would stay by my side. Who would want a woman with four kids? Not happening. I kept that thought to myself realizing I was such a sexist bastard.

At home we argued from time to time over past situations, never coming to a resolution. Sometimes I would get stressed and leave for hours, driving around the city stopping here or there for a drink. Heading home late I'd think, *"Every relationship has problems, just hang in there. It's going to get better. I have to make it better."*

At work I would daydream. Imaging my life without Tracey. Snapping into reality, there was no way I could exist without this woman in my life. The thought of her absence frightened me because I knew it would affect my kids. I didn't think she would keep me from my kids, but I worried about the emotional strain children suffered from not having a consistent father to nurture them. It takes a village to raise a child.

TJ's Tattoos was the talk of the city when it came to body art. The cash was rolling in. Literally the lobby was like a nightclub. I'd start tattooing around 3:00pm and continue until about midnight. I opened seven days a week. After relief from the department, I headed straight to the clubs explaining to Tracey it was necessary for me to network.

Feeling guilty I called her, "You know I couldn't do none of this without you. Thank you mami for always having my back. You and I are forever. I love to the moon and back."

She returned the love, "We're in this together. Love you too."

One Wednesday, I had just arrived at the station. I was in roll call when Beatrice called me to the front desk.

"Hey sis, you called me?"

She was excited, "Where's your phone boy? Tracey trying to call you; her water broke!"

I ran to Sgt. Patterson, "Tracey's having the baby."

He smiled, "Go ahead! Take the department's vehicle but don't run code."-sirens or lights.

I called her screaming, "I'm on my way! Barnes Hospital right?"

She was calm, "Just hurry knucklehead."

Unlike the previous pregnancy, Tracey was in labor for over six hours. I sat right by her side.

"Why you think it's taking so long this time?"

She snapped, "How should I know. You don't think I planned this shit? I wish this little fucker would come on."

Right then, she screams, "He's coming! He's coming!"

I said, "How can you tell?"

She said, " I feel like I got to take a shit. Look between my legs!

I peeked, "Oh fuck! I see his head!"

She yelled, "Go get the God damn doctor!"

I ran out calling for the doctor. The nurse hurried preparing for the delivery. She realized there was no time left.

"Sweetheart, the baby is coming. I want you to listen to my instructions. Everything will be okay."

I was worried, "Where's the doctor?"

She was positioning Tracey's legs, "No time. You're going have to help me, Sir."

I stepped back, "Shit!"

I looked at Tracey; she was in pain "Whatever you need."

She instructed me to comfort my wife.

Suddenly the nurse blurted out, "Hand me the Medline clothes Mr. Page."

I grabbed the stack of clothes walking them around to her. I saw the full view of Tracey giving birth. It's like the nurse planned me being there. Handing her those clothes was perhaps a coincidence, but I walked in on my son squirming; his way out.

Unlike before, I witnessed this birth. Not by choice the nurse set me up. I was amazed when he was handed to me. This time was emotionally intense. I observed the start of a duo legacy. I thanked the nurse for the experience.

Oh yeah, the doctor came in after Jiro's birth.

"You missed it, Doc. The nurse held it down by herself."

Tracey remained at the hospital for one day before we were allowed to bring baby Jiro home. When we did, Lil Ro was more excited than we were. The thought of not being the youngest but an older brother overwhelmed him. I was happy that he was happy. Walking in my bedroom, I saw Lil Ro carefully lying beside Jiro talking to him.

"Jiro, I'm your big brotha and I'm going to watch you."

A tear came from my eye. Suddenly I realized I had to be the best I could be. No time to be selfish, it was about the family.

After a few days of rest, it was back to business. Same routine: district, then the shop. No play all work. By this time the shop was off the chain. My clientele had not doubled but tripled. Word had spread throughout the city. Also the quality of those who patronized the shop brought benefits. A few of the NFL Rams heard word of a black-owned tattoo shop. They were more than happy to contribute to my success. On top of that, all the nightlife business knew of a cop who was also a tattooist. Walking into any club, VIP status was frequent; of course with that came a handful of women interested in hooking up. This shop overshadowed the previous tattoo shop times ten.

So the tattoo game was growing; with that being said, my ego was growing too. The police department had become more of my secondary income. Saving money was on a regular; my bedroom dresser drawer looked like a bank deposit box. I was legally living the lifestyle of a hustler, not to mention a hefty portion of my customers were dope dealers, strippers, and hustlers. Therefore, my street cred was back.

CHAPTER FIFTEEN

THE MORE MONEY I MADE opened the door for more problems. Arrogance got the best of me. At home I gave the kids all the attention, neglecting a recovering wife. Tracey experienced post pregnancy issues was on an emotional rollercoaster, and I made the ride oh so difficult.

Let's get this clear, I love Tracey with all my heart. I had no intentions on seeking a better situation. But I was definitely a selfish prick. I felt as if I delivered more to the table and I was disillusioned. This behavior went on longer than it should have.

In uniform I was extremely moody, snapping on coworkers, sometimes the public. I avoided extra conversation with my fellow officers. The department had haters plus I just didn't want them in my fucking business. I thought it was bad enough some of them didn't have aspiration to achieve independence; they were comfortable with elevating in the ranks and hitting the glass ceiling. The Chief of Police made the most in the department. I wanted my checks to look like that. Fuck that, I wanted *more*.

On my days off, I would come in the station to complete unfinished reports. In civilian attire sometimes my tattoos were exposed. The white shirts would look at me like I was breaking the law. You know when you get that feeling somebody is judging you. Smirking, I would blow it off. Yet at times a few of the veteran officers would tell me aim higher. One in particular was Sgt. Patterson.

"Ro, if you get the opportunity to make a better life for your family, do it. Don't get caught up in the rattrap of the department's politics. This career can taint your judgment. Married officers fucking other married officers. They call themselves law-biding people. You're a young guy, go make it happen."

Here was Patterson, an older white guy, telling a young black officer to pursue his dream. I learned the department had genuine people of all walks of life. The words of wisdom Sgt Patterson bestowed upon me, I valued. I knew it to be true. So many former cops went on to become lawyers, consultants, and business owners. I had every intention of being inducted to that list of names.

Word got back to me that a few officers questioned my ethnicity. They felt I acted too black to compensate for not being all black. Yeah, you can imagine

I shook my head and told the messenger, "You can tell them go fuck themselves with a horse dick."

As I got more disenchanted with the uniform, I kept to myself. Being who I was regardless of my discontent, I still did the job to the best of my ability. However, it wasn't a mystery I was in pursuit of a fortune.

I tried so hard to suppress my disdain. Once, I got a call for a motor vehicle accident on the Popular Bridge overlooking the Missouri River. I was to inform the dispatcher when I arrived and whether there was a Department of Transportation vehicle in the vicinity. No officer is pleased with a call on the bridge during high traffic.

Soon as I exited my vehicle, I observed the position of each vehicle to determine who was at fault. The drivers quickly approached me arguing who was at fault. I informed them to re-enter their vehicle and drive to the first Illinois exit.

"Sir I already surveyed the position of your car; I understand you were hit from the rear, but it's dangerous up here so to prevent any further harm, let's get to somewhere safe."

This guy started mouthing but complied. Walking to my vehicle, cars were flying by at 70 mph one after another. Suddenly a piece of shit car stopped while other drivers blew their horns and swerved to avoid crashing into the back of the stopped car. In that stopped car, two old ladies rolled down their window and asked me, "Is everybody okay, officer?"

I was flabbergasted. "No ma'am everything is not alright because you're going to get somebody killed including yourself fucking stopping like this."

These ladies had to be every bit of 70 or 80 years old. The passenger frowned and flicked the middle finger at me. I stepped back. The driver yelled, "Fuck you asshole!"

Laughing I shook my head, "I guess I deserve that."

The old Ro would have been patient with a carload of old ladies. Clearly I needed to get things in check.

It was therapeutic for me at the shop. Art was my relief and making money was my addiction. A tattooist life is untamable, we know no boundaries. Whatever the customer wants, within reason, we will do and the cost is always negotiable. I had females offer $60 of food stamps for a simple name. If I knew them, I would take the trade. Some offered sex. I drew the line there. If you would fuck for a tattoo, you're a messed up individual. I wouldn't touch you with a 40-foot pole. Besides being a trick was not in my vocabulary.

I recall times walking into my private booth after hours and a woman would be fully naked. It would surprise some, but I'd maintained my composure. It was nothing I hadn't seen before. My encounters made me skeptical about the loyalty of a woman. When a guy brought his girl to get his name on her breast, I applauded their love.

"Man it's good to see black love. Most the time I'm doing cover ups. Nice to see you guys doing the couple thing."

I'd see that that made the guy comfortable with me. I started the tattoo and unexpectedly she gets light headed. She demanded a Sprite, "Baby please go get me a Sprite."

He'd be frustrated, "Come on girl. You only got a few minutes left."

She snapped, "I won't get this motherfucker if you don't get me a soda."

I looked at him, "I'm cool with it homie. I will wait. Shit happens."

As we waited, she kept looking at me.

"What's wrong, mami? You alright?"

She'd reply in a sexy voice, "You sexy as fuck. You got a woman?"

I'd be caught off guard as I stuttered, "Uh, uh. Well I'm actually married. If I'm not mistaken, you are committed too."

She'd smile, "He's just my baby daddy. It's not like that."

Confused, I'd say: "Like you're getting his name on your chest. If it's not, why are you doing it?"

She'd touch my leg, "He does him and I do me."

I scooted away, "You're beautiful, baby girl; under different circumstance *maybe*. But your man is putting food on my table."

She exhaled, "Shame, but I respect that. I'll be back anyway without him."

Situations like that made me feel like bitches ain't shit.

So many untold stories go on in the booth. Imagine some of the most attractive women coming to get sexy tramp stamps (lower back tattoo) only to fart in my face. That needle can make a nun use profanity. I witnessed on many occasions a parent bringing their teen child to get a tattoo. It could have been the most respectful polite young lady, but let the needle touch them and they scream:

"Oh FUCK! This shit hurts!"

"Smack!" Mom slapped her across the back of the head.

Mom would yell, "Sit your ass still! You wanted it. You going to get this motherfucker; I paid my money!"

Planting hidden cameras in the booth would create an interesting story line. What a great idea to present to a network one day!

Not pleased with the title TJ's Tattoos, I searched for a new name with the blessing of Tez. After all TJ was the title for the barbershop. I needed something to reflect the artistic service of the shop--something rare and priceless. I went through hundreds of names. Sitting in the bed with Tracey one night, we were casually talking. I noticed she was looking through one of my old National Geographic magazines.

"What are you reading, mami?"

"Oh nothing much, just rare jewels more valuable than diamonds."

"You trying to give me a hint?"

She laughed, "Well... Just kidding. I'm reading on a black pearl ring that's worth millions. It's a rare mutation; it's so rare that one black pearl is equivalent to multiple diamonds."

I sat up, "Black Pearl, that's it baby!"

So there you go, the birth of Black Pearl Tattoo Gallery courtesy of my wife.

Customers seem to favor the new brand of Black Pearl. All concluded the name was extremely catchy and asked who thought of it. Of course, I claimed the glory.

Tracey would look out the corner of her eyes and utter, "Yeah right."

Waiting till we were alone, I would jokingly say, "What's yours is mine, *right*?"

Tattoos are a distinctive method of identifying people namely suspects. Police would log specific markings into a worldwide database so law enforcement could identify them by name. Thus me being a tattooist I literally contributed to a high percentile of tattoos especially in the hood.

With that being said when my customers would get flagged by the police, they would say, "Why you stressing me about my tattoos. One of your own did it."

My name would get tossed around the city. I don't believe they attempted to implicate me in a negative way. It's just typical to name drop to avoid getting interrogated. Just so happened a cop/tattooist name was getting dropped. A few officers with good intentions warned me a few shady characters were saying I was their friend. In a way I was; they were my loyal customers so we were cool. I wasn't there to judge; I offered a service. It's not like we discussed dope deals while I was tattooing them... Until one particular day.

It was a Saturday afternoon I arrived at the shop late. There was a lobby full of customers. Tracey assisted the customers with what they wanted. She walked in my booth.

"Baby look out in the lobby. See that Hispanic looking guy in the first row? He said he knows you."

I peeked out to see the gentlemen she was referring to. He was an older dude, maybe in his 40's. He looked like a character from Scarface. I asked her what was he getting?

"He wants a Puerto Rican flag."

He finally got in my booth. "How you doing? My wife says you know me."

His heavy accent stood out, "Que pasa papi? My name is Manuel. You probably don't remember me. We met many years ago in the central west end. Bob was your pop's right?"

I was suspicious but I continued to tatt him. "Yeah he's my dad. I don't remember you."

He chuckled, "Let's just say I remember you when you weren't a cop. I'm surprised you became one."

I stopped tattooing, "So where you going with this conversation bro? You making me real uncomfortable."

He waved his hand no, "Oh hermano, I'm sorry. I don't mean any harm whatsoever. Forgive me please. I needed a tattoo and wanted to keep it in the family."

I replied, "*Family*?"

He continued, "Your pops was an OG to me. He knew my father in the military. We met at Scott Air Force base years ago. I was a bag boy at the commissary."

I sat up and thought for a minute. It hit me, "Damn you're right fam. I do remember you. Shit that was way back when."

We catch up talking for over an hour. He was dropping money on tattoos like it was candy.

For the next few weeks Manuel became regular, spending hundreds of dollars on tattoos. I never questioned where and how he got his money, but it was evident he was getting paid. He would just come and sit with me at times. I don't believe he meant any ill will to me. I got a sincere feeling from Manuel. I believe he was feeling me out. He had something he wanted to get off his chest but didn't know how.

Months went by and this friendly guy who knew quite a bit about my family formed a bond with me. After hours on a Wednesday, he brought a cold 6 pack of Corona.

"Papi, my father passed before yours. Your pops was like a father to me. I promised him I would look out for you from a distance. Do you remember Hitman?"

I was confused, "Of course. He was solid. Bro he came through for me and pops on many occasions. Have you seen him?"

"Not really. Last I heard he caught a body. Locked up behind the Walls-Jefferson City Penitentiary."

I took a swig of beer, "Fuck! I'm not surprised."

He leaned forward with a serious look, "Do you remember him fronting you that? Especially when your pops needed the extra income?"

I stopped and thought, "That was you bro? You were the connect?"

He smiled, "I was his and your pops connect. Not *yours*. We wanted to keep you clean. That was his fucking idea to involve you."

It all made sense now, "What made you look me up now? Man if my job knew."

"Don't worry that's long behind. Plus, you never got your hands dirty enough to get federally fucked, and you will keep it that way. I had to do a 10-year bid. Now I'm out and you're the closest family I got. Can't go back to Puerto Rico until my papers up."

Suddenly things became so clear. None of my family knew my pops' extracurricular activity. That's the way he wanted it. I see what he meant, be a better man than he. I was scared because I was a chip off the old block. I had something bad manifesting deep down. Brewing up. Just hoped I could contain it.

Manuel would only come visit me at the shop. I tried to get him to hang out yet he wouldn't. Dude reminded me of Eric. I would wonder if he was a figment of my imagination. When he came in the shop people got an uneasy feeling. They were intimidated by his appearance and his gang affiliated tattoos. He was a King no doubt.

"I can't hang out with you, hermano. It would put your job at jeopardy and my papers. Me here is strictly business. But if you need my help, just holla."

Manuel never discussed any illegal business with me. It didn't take a rocket scientist to guess what he did, however he never involved me. He would just come in and get tattoos. I knew he was doing a big brother thing; for instance, he would have me retrace his prison tats and pay me a stack and then tip me $200.

"Dude, you don't have to drop that much."

He would pull out a wad of hundred dollar bills,

"Familia takes care of familia. Don't worry, nothing's illegal about my money. I'm a business man just like you."

Come to find out he invested into three or four gas stations in the Illinois vicinity. He was a smart dude. His appearance contrasted with the knowledge he carried. He drove a custom painted pearl 1995 S Class Mercedes to match his Versace threads. He only showed up at the shop at night.

I asked, "Big bro, if I asked back then would you have plugged me?"

He crossed his leg sitting back, "Probably not. You did good for yourself. That's the hustler in you. Papi, some of the most successful businessmen are true hustlers. Some of them even did time. You'll be surprise who you will meet in the joint. People think I'm some Chicano gangsta but I graduated from Cornell University, upstate New York baby. He laughs.

He continued, "My lifestyle you don't want to know. That's why you don't know. Let's keep it that way Lil brother. Bien"

I dap him up, "Bien."

Manuel got a travel visa and told me he was visiting a sick relative in San Juan. "Papi, I have to go home for a minute, but if you need anything, I'm just a phone call away. Be back in a few months."

Like that, he was gone. He was a man of his word so I knew our paths would cross again.

Sgt. Patterson detached me to the detective bureau for a special assignment with an officer named Will. I didn't really want the task, but Patterson explained, "Ro, I need a balance for this assignment. You and Will know how to conduct yourselves professionally out there. Plus, you're a flashy guy. You can wear all your fancy duds."

I took the assignment reluctantly not knowing if it would disrupt my tattoo business. Come to find out it was quite the contrary. Handling the district assignments opened doors for me. Liaison visits to the Washington garment district expanded my suit wardrobe, visits to the Landing entertainment venues connected me with the top promoters in the city. I could walk backstage at any time. They would even ask me to do security for some R&B acts for the annual Majic Radio

Anniversary Parties. I got tight with the Diamond Group Entertainment Booking Agency; a well-connected promoter nicknamed D.O. always gave me the plushiest jobs. They paid extremely well-- $500 for an hour's worth of work usually consisted of driving them to and from the venue to their hotel. I could stay and watch the performance if I wish. Tracey enjoyed the privilege; she would bring her friends sitting VIP or backstage.

Black Pearl emerged as a brand. Many would ask if we were a gang with me clarifying Black Pearl was simply a business. With the tattoo shop popping, more beauticians and barbers came to work at TJ's. So there it was a perfect combination: TJ's barber shop in front and Black Pearl Tattoo Studio in the rear located smack dab in the middle of downtown St. Louis baby.

I continued to give my all to the department. It wasn't my character to half ass anything. The reality was the harder I worked for the badge; the money was still mediocre. The easiest duties of tattooing generated boo coo money. Black Pearl was in my district therefore many officers knew of my newfound venture. That being said, a handful of officers were happy for me and several handful of officers or haters were skeptical of how I was getting the money. The more side eyes I got, the more I flexed my arrogance. On my days off, I would go to other tattoo shops and get tattoos, using the opportunity to see how their operation was. I absorb all the knowledge I could. My chest and arms were hit up by now. The civilian attire the bureau allowed me to wear revealed my tats.

Walking through the station, a V-neck tee exposed my arms and chest. The white shirts would look in disgust. Eventually my lieutenant advised me it made some of the fellow staff uncomfortable.

I must admit the bureau was pretty cool. No constant supervision and the liberty to investigate cases was challenging. Oh so often I would get a fucked up assignment, for instance watching Laclede Landing public parking lots for would-be car burglars. How about walking around the St. Louis Center Mall trying to pinpoint truants cutting school. Boring!

Canvassing the fourth district I gained new customers all the time. I even came in contact with some of Black Pearl customers. The fact that I was a stand up dude prevented any unfriendly encounters. Many complimented me on how I conducted myself. One particular conversation stood out. While driving through the projects, I got flagged down by a group of young brothers.

I pulled over, put down my window, "What's up young brothers?"

They gathered by my window, "Aren't you the Five O that got the tattoo shop on Olive?"

"Yeah Black Pearl. Come check me out."

One dabbed me up, "I hear you hella cool bro. Why can't the other cops be like you?"

I laughed, "You'll be surprised young brother, a lot of them are cool. It's a random few that taint the reputation."

They all tried to respond but one controlled the conversation, "I can't tell. They get out the squad car with attitude. We could be chillin and they'd ask if we got a problem."

I shook my head, "I hear you, but tell me the truth, do you mean mug them?"

They quickly answered, "Damn right! I'm a grown man, dog. My balls swing just like theirs."

I said, "It's the cycle fam. They mean mug you and you do the same. Somebody has to just give a little."

"Page, you right but aren't you guys paid to do a professional job? You suppose to let certain things roll off your shoulder. Me looking at you wondering why you watching me is no justification to harass a nigga."

"I agree with you. We're paid to do a job but we're human too. The bottom line is we want to go home to our families."

He got excited, "I hear you! That's my point, we do too. We out here dealing with niggas around the way trying to knock us off, the last thing we should have to do is watch our back from the police. Page we just want to go home too."

Looking that young man in his eyes, I could feel his pain. He was actually scared—just so many brothers, not knowing if this day would be your last. The guys you grew up with are gunning for you because you live four blocks away on an opposing block. When you see the police instead of feeling relieved, you got the same knot in your gut when you encounter an enemy. The realities of the streets are you have nowhere to go, nowhere to turn, and no one to trust.

What a fucking life!

Weekends at Black Pearl were unbelievable. I had appointments booked for at least two weeks in advance. I would pray to the one above that my blessings remained consistent, sometimes feeling guilty that I asked for more tattoo customers. Was that Okay? You hear how marking your body is against the Bible yet our ancestors in Africa wore permanent markings to distinguish warriors from holy men. Piercings were a feature of adornment in civilizations before the bible. Why was this art form frowned upon? Would God be upset if someone got the Lord's Prayer tatted? Only God can judge me.

As I said earlier, the crazy thing about being a tattooist is the wild situations I would face time to time. Women would get the most ratchet shit on them, for instance *bootylicious*, *slippery when wet, and drop it like it's hot.* Hey I don't judge. When I did try and give constructive criticism, I was called a hater. So I'd leave it be. The late night sessions were extremely risky. The female clients would wear little to nothing. Women would wear no underwear knowing they wanted a tat on their thigh. A thirsty horny guy might find it arousing, but money was what gave me an erection. Fuck the pussy. Anyway some of the women had an odor, which made it so unpleasant I almost refunded the money and stopped my work. You'd think one would bathe before getting a tat but nope.

I had females say, "I'm getting a tat on my feet, but I'm warning you I had shoes on all day."

"Duh bitch why didn't you wash your damn feet then?"

They would put their foot on my pants, and kid you not, an hour later my pants leg would still smell like Cheetos.

The most entertaining were the strippers that would shake their ass while I was tatting them. Don't ask me why, they just did it. I wouldn't complain, I'm human. The strippers were excellent tippers; they understand the meaning of a cheap motherfucker. After tatting them, they would invite me to their club. I paid it forward, sometimes it was only right support those who supported me.

My lifestyle naturally infected my morals therefore homestead was spiraling out of control. I was shitting my marriage away, but the success of the business distorted my rationalization. Arrogantly, I told Tracey she should be glad I was generating more income from the family.

"You should be happy I found something I'm good at. Hell naw! You want to hold me back. I would support you at any endeavor you pursued. Don't make me chose between my wife and my future."

She would cry, "Your family is your future. Fuck the money. I don't give a damn about the money if I'm not happy Roland."

A man's pride is a motherfucker. I knew damn well I was wrong but wouldn't admit it. The chauvinistic belief that I brought more to the table consumed my judgment. Sometimes I would just agree with her to smooth things over. Now don't get it twisted, I didn't want to leave my marriage nor replace my wife. She was irreplaceable.

Lil Ro and Jiro were growing fast. The boys were a reality check. Every time I looked at them, I would hear my father's voice, *"Be a better father than I was."* The total package made me appreciate Tracey even though I didn't show it. While she slept, I would kiss her forehead looking at her for minutes.

"Thank you for blessing me with this family. You guys are my better half."

One afternoon, I happened to be in the station and Beatrice paged me to the front desk.

"Roland, there's a young man in the lobby wishing to speak with you."

I tried to look out and see who it was. "Did he say what he wanted?"

She shrugged her shoulders, "Nope he said it was personal."

She buzzed me out.

"How can I help you?"

He stood up shaking my hand. "Officer Page, my name is Jessie. I live in the JVLs and I just graduated from barber school. I was wondering if I could come work with you at Black Pearl?"

I grinned, "Well Jessie, the Pearl is the tattoo shop. TJ's is the barber shop."

He said, "I understand but I really want to work with you. I think you can keep me on the right path. Big bro, I'm trying to get my life together and I need solid people around me."

I saw the passion in his eyes. "Tell you what, meet me at the shop tomorrow and I will see what I can do. Bring your state license young brother."

He smiled, "I won't let you down."

I laughed, "Can't promise you anything but I'm always open to helping a young brother get his life in order."

Walking back in, Beatrice was smiling at me. "What?"

She replied, "Ro you got a gift when it comes to talking with people. They love you. Even some prisoners speak on how genuine you are. Don't lose that gift."

Working late nights at the shop then adapting to a morning shift at the department took its toll on my body. I started drinking pretty heavily, usually it was beer now it was Jose Cuervo Silver. Depending on liquor as a stress relief only made things worse. I was so moody; Tracey avoided any conflict with me; only thing that could calm the wild beast was the kids. The presence of my seeds extinguished the fire that was building inside me. I felt like the world owed me something. What was it? I didn't know myself. I was angry for no reason. Liquor eased my frustration.

On duty I would park in the rear of the nightclubs entering through the back. The club owners knew me on and off duty. They would slip me a beer concealed in a Styrofoam cup. I was a regular and the owners like the police presence. All the clubs had their favorites.

One night I decide to stop at Rivers Nightclub. I entered through the back. I sat by the bar with the owner and we were just speaking on random shit. A bouncer ran up requesting the owner and me to come outside. I heard a commotion as we walked out.

"Ro! Ro! Come here dog! These assholes giving me hell!"

I saw one of the St. Louis Rams players and two police officers yelling back and forth at one another. I walked over and asked the officers what did he do.

One snapped at me, "We got this. Nobody called you over here."

I looked amazed, then turn to the Rams players who happened to be my tattoo client at the shop.

"What's going on?"

He yelled, "Man this mother." I quickly cut him off.

"Calm down man so I can see what's going on. You yelling going to make matters worse."

He exhaled, "My bad. The promoter of the club asked a few players to roll through. He said we would be good to park in front so if some shit pop off we can exit quick, fast, in a hurry. I come out and these two cops telling me they're going to tow my ride. The owner even told them I was good. They said they don't give a fuck."

I instructed him to remain calm till I get back. The owner of the club called me over.

"Ro, those cops work for the club next door. We have been feuding for the past month. Their mad cause their crowd comes here so the cops try and write tickets by saying that's their property."

I quickly investigated the area noticing it was public parking with no specific ownership.

I calmly walked over to the cops.

"I was just trying to help the situation fellas but since you want to be dicks about it. You're working secondary and I'm on duty. If you tow his car, I'm going to tow everybody's car in front of the club you're working at. So I can't tell you not to tow the Rams player's car, but we're going to go tit for tat."

They looked at each other, then one grabbed the other by the arm. "Fuck him. Come on."

As they walked away I said, "What, you don't like the music of this club?"

One of them gave me the finger. I laughed out loud.

I told the club owner, "You know it's going be some shit about this. They're going to say it's a black against white thing."

He smiled, "How is that and I'm white, Ro?"

I replied, "You're a white club owner that welcomes black people into your club. It's not over."

Jessie the barber was working out magnificently. I was glad Twan decided to welcome him. He turned out to be a tremendous help to Black Pearl also. If I missed customers, he would get their number; if people tried to trespass into the rear, he would stop them; and he would refer his customers to me. I did the same. Customers would go get a cut while they waited on a tat, even the women would go to the only beautician up front. Jessie looked at me as a big brother. He would come and sit with me asking me the key to a good relationship, my story of my life, and how I achieved what I have. I met his mother who happened to know my sister Patty. They attended Northwest High School together. In my opinion Jessie was cool people.

I came to work on a Friday evening and Jessie called me over.

"Ro, your brother is back from Puerto Rico. He was here looking for you. I think his name is Mani."

"Manuel?"

He laughed, "Yeah that's it. He reminds me of Mani from Scarface. Ro is that nigga cartel?"

I turned, "Naw, just family."

I called and checked on Manuel later that night. He got back a little early that's all. He told me everything went well with his family.

The next day I walked in the shop noticing Manuel getting a haircut from Jessie. I thought nothing of it continuing to the back. Manuel came to the back.

"That barber up front is cold with the clippers, Papi. He ever cut your hair?"

No but I might give him a try one day.

We caught up on all the latest happenings. It was good to see my brother back safe. I never can put my hand on exactly what he did. I worried though because he would never tell me, probably for the best.

I kept telling myself that I had everything under control however deep inside, I was fighting demons. There was a battle brewing within me, good against evil, and what's scary was I didn't know who was going to win. I was not happy with what I saw in the mirror for some odd reason.

Couldn't put my finger on it, just a blank on the direction in life. Wish I could fast forward to witness what was in store in the future, but something was telling me it was not good. I would quit the department if it weren't for my family. I kept it pushing like there was no tomorrow.

The summer has arrived, and with that comes teen cruising in the fourth district. You know young kids hanging out showing off their cars. You can run them off one end of the downtown area to have them gather on the other end. The district major would have us detour them out the area--an almost impossible task. Kids didn't have anywhere to go, so fuck it, they cruised the downtown Riverfront or South Broadway street.

One late evening several officers were dispatched to Laclede Landing to help control the traffic congestion. As I arrived I saw cars parked bumper to bumper. Females were sitting on top of cars wearing little of nothing, guys were hanging out the window shooting their shot with the ladies, and the smell of weed was everywhere. The truth of the matter, I didn't mind none of the above. It reminded me of my hay days. Sgt. Patterson instructed us to clear the area.

"Ro, you and a few officers clear the area. I hate to do it but all these black folks are scaring the white tourists." He laughed.

I said, "You're laughing Sarge, but that's the truth."

He looked, "I know. I hate that the kids don't have nowhere to go, but too many black people make the businesses nervous. It's a fucked up thing to say, but it's reality, Ro."

I just walked away. Most of the area is cleared when we came up on a group of young brothers chilling on their car. Some of the other officers were having a difficult time with them. I walked over so things didn't get out of hand.

"Hey fellas I hate to spoil your fun, but we have to clear the area. I know you guys aren't causing trouble. We're just doing our job."

They looked at me for a second like they knew me.

"Oh snap, Big Ro, that's you. Man I grew up around the corner from you. I was a youngin when you were in high school. We good. We're about to bounce out now."

The other officers looked bitter because they couldn't get it done; I could tell they were salty.

As I prepared to walk away, one of the young guys told the other.

"That nigga used to have the whole block locked down. Ro was pushing weight."

My mouth dropped as I looked to see if the officers heard him. They did and were looking right at me. I thought to myself, *"Oh Shit! I hope this doesn't blow back in my face."*

I don't think the young cat was trying to put me out like that, but shit, he put me on front street in a bad way. I ignored his statement pretending I didn't hear it. I went on about my business. After all, it was the past.

Days went by, I heard nothing in regards to the Laclede Landing incident. I hoped it went unnoticed--which I highly doubted-- then again maybe I was just paranoid.

Driving through the district, I decided to take a route I had never driven before. All my years in the fourth, I couldn't believe I had never driven down this street. I cruised at a slow pace observing the new family flats that were neatly built. I suddenly see something that I can't believe. Joy holding Jiro was walking down the street. I nearly ran off the road, quickly swerving over to a stop.

"What the fuck! How you get my son?"

I startled her as she turned to me. It hit me. That's not Jiro, but damn he looks exactly like my son. The resemblance is astonishing.

She nervously smiled, "Roland, how you been? I want you to meet your son; his name is Jamarion."

I walked over in amazement as she said, "Jamarion this is your father."

I stood there for a minute as she handed him over to me. I backed up a bit not sure what to do-- still processing what was going on. I must have the worse luck in the entire universe.

"Joy, why didn't you tell me about this? He has to be almost two."

He is two. I didn't want to cause any confusion with you being married and all.

I snapped, "That's my fuckin son. I had the right to know regardless of how fucked up the situation is."

"You're right, but now you know. We have to sit down and discuss some things. I really don't want anything from you."

I thought, *"Yeah right. Bitch, why would you want a baby with a married man. Roland, you fucked up big time this go around."*

I gave her a ride down the street. We talked for a moment with an understanding that I had to deal with the situation like a man. Boy oh boy, how am I going to explain to Tracey that a drunken night changed my life-- possibly forever.

Bringing a child into this world should be celebrated unless you're married with a whole other family. My world turned upside down. I know it wasn't Jamarion's fault. The fault was completely on my shoulders. Nonetheless, I kept things a secret for the time being. Got to think this one out.

Funny how a wife can read through the bullshit. Tracey didn't know the specifics but she knew something wasn't right. I was mentally off for days. It was written all over my face. I knew she deserved better. For the first time in our relationship, I was frightened she might leave me.

I had a bad case of *Can't Get Right*. Knowing that I was already in deep shit, my morals were slipping deeper into darkness. I continued to have conversations with other women. I would meet them in the clubs, the tattoo shop, or just out in the district. I didn't know why I was doing so much dumb shit. I was just doing it. Maybe my days were numbered and I figured fuck it. Maybe I sought comfort from the opposite sex. Maybe I was an asshole. I always told the women interested in me, even with marital problems, I had no intentions on leaving my wife. They would say how Tracey was lucky to have a hard working man or how they would help me take the business to another level. It was all soup. They told me what I wanted to hear knowing I was a typical asshole. They rearranged my flaws to be Tracey's fault for not understanding me. A woman with ulterior motives will pamper a no good nigga with the quickness.

I pondered revealing my secret to my wife. With no easy explanation, I kept postponing the inevitable. Joy would allow me to visit Jamarion or as she calls him *"Mookie."* She was very understanding regarding our predicament. Plus, she now had a live in boyfriend who appeared to be cool. I could see the look he gave me when I came around. One of those, better you than me looks.

He did say, "Glad you got a relationship with your son, Ro."

That was solid of him to say.

Playing with Mookie, I felt guilty as hell, yet I knew he was innocent. Sometimes I stared at him in amazement at the resemblance between Jiro and him. Tracey was going to piss fire when she saw Mookie. I gave Joy money every two weeks to do my part. She encouraged me to tell Tracey about Mookie.

"Roland, you keeping Mookie from Tracey is going to make matters worse. She will forgive if you're honest but continuing the lie will end nasty. Trust me."

I thought to myself, *"Trust you? Bitch I don't trust you worth a nickel."*

I pretended to pay attention yet never did. What did I get myself into?

My boys were growing so fast. They had a strong bond with my mom. I believed they reminded her of baby me. She was honored to have named them, always boasting on their keen Japanese features. I'm glad my grandkids can carry on our Japanese legacy. Lil Loland and Jiro will have the Karasawa Page last name. They will pass it on to their kids. I'm so happy about that.

I smiled, "Why is that so important mama?"

She explained, "My children don't know their family in Japan. You don't know your father's side that well either. What family you make will carry my memory on for a long time. I want my descendants to know how we came here."

I kissed her on her forehead every time I came and went.

My attitude was critical at work. I was bitter due to existing situations. Occupational stress is a bitch!

I got a burglary assist call while working the bureau. I partnered with Will. I was comfortable with this cool ass white boy who treated people accordingly. If you gave him respect, he did the same. Never had a chip on his shoulder. One of his priorities was to stay away from drama. We arrived at the scene discovering a local jewelry store had been broken into. They entered through the front breaking a glass door. We were assisting so basically we were there as a support unit. We stayed off to the side waiting to see if they asked for our help. Rather they ignored us walking around the establishment. Will hit me on the side, gesturing me to look to my right. I noticed an officer disabling the security monitor and then put on rubber gloves rummaging through the jewelry cases. Suddenly he grabbed a handful of jewelry placing the items in his pocket. He didn't even notice us standing in the shadows. Will and I looked at each other and walked out.

We didn't see anything. Mind our own business. Drama free as we drove off.

Will once worked for Jennings Police Department, which was known for not being that friendly towards black people. It was strange to me cause quite a few black people resided there. Will told me he heard stories of the old Jennings Police, how they would call on the Fire department to spray unruly Black citizens. I asked him how did it make him feel hearing those stories? He was honest.

"Ro, it makes me feel shitty that you still got ignorant people who thought that was funny. When some told the stories, they referred to it as the *Good Ole Days*. A few still have many prejudices. They won't admit or reveal them to you, but I hear it often."

I shook my head, "It's a shame. I got prejudices regarding certain things but I'm not racist where I can't exist with a specific group. I can even consider some friends like you Will.

He sighed, "That's how society is Ro. It will eventually get better. This world is a melting pot. Us white boys like some black women." He laughed.

Man, quit pretending I see you checking out the sisters sometimes.

He replied, "Of course I'm not blind. I dated a black woman before."

"Get the fuck outta here!"

"No I have, Ro. My nephew is Black. I grew up in a diverse community. I agree everybody has prejudices--even me; however, I'm open to dialogue. You are too. That's why we get along."

I returned the respect, "Yeah you're good people Will, but you're still a square ass white boy."

We both laughed. It was quitting time. Before exiting the squad car, he asked "Ro, you ever notice during the Presidential Elections everybody draws their lines where they stand. True colors always come."

I acknowledged, "No doubt. I hear officer's talk about the section 8, welfare recipients, and ghetto black music. What's crazy is you can tell some of them come from a trailer park area and their parents were probably on welfare, but they called it government assistance. Will, racism wasn't that long ago; my parents experienced it. What upsets me is when people, especially officers, won't admit it still exists and get offended when black people complain about it. Shit man I heard many of these cops say Nigger. Not a black suspect, a nigger suspect."

Before I walked off to my car, I told Will: "I'm not sure how long I will be here but I believe in the future you may be in position to make a change for the better."

Weeks later Will tried to join the Ethical Black Police Officer Association. I guess he was trying to be a peace diplomat. I heard it didn't go over well with some of the brothers. The Police Union wasn't very supportive of the Ethical Society so the members were just suspicious of an infiltration.

I encountered so many instances where racist overtones—to put it mildly—existed. I could roll with the punches during my first few years however recently my patience was growing thin. My dissatisfaction with my career made me bitter to anyone who rubbed me the wrong way.

I responded to an assist call for an accident with injury by a school intersection. When I arrived, the reporting officer was interviewing the drivers. I asked if I could help.

"Nope, I got it."

Off to the side, I noticed a young black female holding a baby crying. I walked over to investigate.

"What's wrong ma'am?"

She was beyond emotional, "Officer that white lady made a left turn in front me and I hit her. The other officer is talking bad to me. The lady is the principal at the school my son attends. He's siding with her just because. I think he's going to try and place the blame on me."

I asked, "What makes you say that?"

"The lady told him I was eating Chinese food, which I wasn't. The impact made my box of duck and noodles spill out the container. She saw it on the car floor when she asked if my son was alright.

I had the right of way, she cut directly in front of me."

I looked over and saw the officer looking over at me talking to her.

He literally marched over and pointed at her. "I explained to you it's up to the insurance company but I see you trying to make it a race thing. You telling him on me isn't going to change shit!"

She jabbed back, "Nobody said it's about race. You talk to her civilized and look at the way you're talking to me. I'm a driver concerned about my child. You brought up race so it must be on your mind."

I step in, "Ma'am I got this. Here's my card, I already made my assessment also so don't worry. There are cameras everywhere."

I pointed them out and she immediately felt comfortable. The officer on the other hand observed what I made obvious to her.

"Dude, I told you I had this. Why are you interfering?

That lady is mad cause she got caught eating that ghetto ass Chinese food while driving."

I snapped, "How did you come to that conclusion? What I see so far is you're bias toward ghetto ass food? Tell you what, before we appear to be unprofessional in public, why don't you get the fuck out of my face before we have a problem."

As I walked away, he turned and looked, "Patterson's going to hear about this, trust me."

I then said loudly, "Tell him."

I never heard anything further about the incident.

Most officers who do suspicious shit don't want it to come out. At this point and time, I didn't give a fuck. Truth be told, Patterson would've set him straight.

I realized I was at a crossroads with my future. The problem wasn't so much just the department, it was with me also. I had mad love for the department and many people within. Maybe I was just not police material.

The home front was getting tense also. I knew sooner than later I needed to tell Tracey the truth about Mookie. It didn't settle right with me. I was afraid she would certainly leave me this time. I prayed on an answer with nothing in mind. Guess when you not living right, he doesn't hear you. Witnessing the evolution of Ro and Jiro balanced all the hysteria going on. Those dudes brought a calm to my storm.

I hadn't been able to work at the shop for two days due to decreased manpower at the department. Upon returning, Jessie seemed panicky about something.

"Ro, big bro! I need to speak with you ASAP!"

I nodded, "Let me get situated and I will come talk to you."

Whatever it was, it couldn't wait. He came to my booth.

"You got time now, bro?"

"Yeah, what's up?"

He sighed and looked down, "Dude I'm in a fucked up situation. You know ole boy Rogue from the North?"

I thought for a second, "Oh yeah! He's cool I did a few of his tats."

He shook his head yes, "I know he got mad respect for you. We were boys but we recently had a major falling out.

I replied, "How recent? I know Rogue is a true street nigga so a situation could go Deep South when it comes to him."

Jessie took a seat, "Two days ago we had a shoot-out at the gas station, Goodfellow at Natural Bridge."

I stopped what I was doing, "What! Why?"

"You going to be so upset with me big bro. Look me and him got locked up a few weeks ago. Well the Detects told him I told them everything that we were doing--basically snitching on both of us. Get this Ro. They told me the same fucking thing. Now you let me go and bond him out. What the fuck you think going to happen? Ro, I didn't say shit and I don't believe he did either. I'm not tripping but he is. However, I'm not going to let a nigga knock me without protecting my neck."

I'm silent for a few seconds, "Okay let me go see what I can do to squash this shit. Man o man bro, what you got yourself into."

On my next day off, I go to the carwash that Rogue owns.

Immediately walking in, brothers on alert checking me out. One of them recognized me. "Ro what's good homie? You did my first tat," while lifting his shirtsleeve.

"What's good fam? Where my boy, Rogue?"

"Sit tight, I will go get him."

A minute later he walked in. We slapped hands with a hug.

"Ro, I know why you here. I figured that nigga couldn't bite his tongue."

We walked outside, "Rogue, it's no secret when two of my family members are beefing. I don't want a misunderstanding to end in some dumb shit, for some hee said she said bullshit."

"That nigga said that shit bro."

I turned to him, "Rogue, how you know. Did you see or hear the conversation? Look dog, I'm coming to you as your brother not a cop. I don't approve of anything you two got going, it's none of my business. But I'm not going to let ya'll knock each other for some bullshit. That's the name of the game, to conquer and divide to see who would say what."

"Ro, you telling me he didn't say anything?"

"No, that's not what I'm saying cause I can't interfere. What I'm saying is it's not worth a life sentence. If anything happens between either of you. Don't you think the dots will be connected?"

He looked at me, "That's why I fuck with you bro, you a real nigga. Enough said."

I go back to the shop to make sure both parties understand and let the cards fall where they land.

When I arrived, Jessie's mom greets me; she's an old friend of the family.

"Hey Roland, how you been? How's the family?"

I smiled. "They're good. How about yourself?"

"Under the circumstances, I can't complain if I didn't have to worry about Jess."

I took her to my booth for some privacy. "I understand. I think I got everything under control as far as them trying to hurt one another."

"Roland, I don't condone his activities but I think having two young men gunning for each other is a crime in itself."

I rubbed her shoulder, "I'm not saying that happened. I don't know cause I don't have access to the reports nor do I know the arresting officers. Now if what they are telling me is true, then you are right, it is a crime. It's a genocidal trigger. I hope it's not true."

She started to tear up. "Is there anything I can do?"

I hesitated, "Yeah, you can go to Internal Affairs. They can get to the bottom of it. Once all parties are aware eyes are watching, they will be more afraid to do something ignorant. A drug crime doesn't warrant a loss of life."

She hugged me, "Thank you so much. I know this could bring drama to your career helping me. I didn't know who to turn to."

After she left, I sat alone in my booth. The reality is that if my name came up in this investigation, it would definitely bring me drama. Of course I'd be a hero on the streets yet a traitor among the department. I took an oath to protect and serve-- that means right what is wrong. I was not going to allow two young men to kill each other regardless of pending drug charges.

CHAPTER SIXTEEN

I DESPERATELY NEEDED SOME ADVICE so I called Manuel. We go to AJ's for a late night drink. Sitting at the bar, we discussed what I had going on.

"Que pasa, papi? I can tell you got something on your mind. You can tell your big brother anything."

"Mani, you're going to kick me up the ass."

He took a drink of his tequila, "Why, what did you do?"

I hesitated, "I had another baby outside my marriage."

He rubbed his head, "*Okay*. Well ask her to have an abortion."

"No, the baby is already here. I got a woman pregnant. She had the baby months ago and he's almost the same age as Jiro."

Signaling for the bartender, I told him: "I need a double and get him one too."

"Oh shit, papi. How in the hell did you let that happen?"

I took a sip of my tequila, "It's not like I wanted it to happen. Man, fuck a drunken night."

He asked, "Have you told Tracey?"

"Nope. I'm seriously afraid she might leave me."

He slammed the drink down his throat, "You're fucked. Who's the other mother?"

"You don't know her. Actually she's been cool. It's completely my fault. She could fuck me but she hasn't. Shit she has a whole man. I'm cool with him."

He shook his head, "Hermano, you got to tell Tracey. She deserves the truth."

I held my head down, "Yeah I know."

Mani put his arm around me, "I got your back Lil brother. There's a solution for everything."

By the time we left, we're drunk off our ass. Our cars are parked outside. I noticed Mani is driving a pearl white 1995 Mercedes S Class.

"Shit nigga! I gotta step my game up. My Toyota Supra ain't shit compared to your whip."

He laughed, "You can get this nigga. Just say the word."

I laughed, "Mani, you can't say nigga."

"I'm Boricua! A Spanish nigga. Don't tell me, I grew up in the hood just like you."

I replied, "Point taken. To the Klan we all niggas."

We laughed and drove off. About a block down, Mani flashed his high beams and pulled alongside of me. I let down my passenger side window.

"You good, bro?"

He tossed something into my car seat. "Go get one!" He drove off fast.

I picked it up noticing it's about seven thousand dollars.

"Damn Mani."

The next day I was hung over. I looked in my book bag thinking maybe I was dreaming about Mani's gift. Nope the money was there.

I caught up with Mani at the shop a day later.

"Bro, you know I can't take that. My job."

He cut me off, "A brother can't give his little brother a gift."

I put my hands up, "No, I'm not saying that but my job would trip if they knew."

He interrupted me again, "Knew what, papi? You think I would put you in harm's way. My money is good. Where you think my money comes from?"

I tossed my hands up, "I don't know. I'm not saying you're dirty bro."

"Exactly! It's good money. Show me where it says it's bad money. Have I given you any type of drugs or anything? Well lately?"

I nodded, "Naw, you been 100 bro. You're right. My brother's keeper."

We slapped hands, "Damn right."

The shop had taken off like a wild fire. My clientele was bananas. Not exaggerating my appointment book was filled one month ahead. No kidding. Tracey was there every step of the way making sure I didn't over work myself, putting up with the bullshit in the lobby, and securing my money. She even stayed out with me to pass out flyers even though she had to be at work in the mornings. I came to the realization I didn't deserve such a queen. I decided in the next day or so I would tell her the truth. Lay it out and let God determine my fate at least I would have a clear conscious.

I was starting to raise eyebrows back at the department. My financial wellbeing was 4 times what it was before. What is true is more money created more problems and financial obligations. On the other hand, more money yields power. Power brings respect. I was a St. Louis rock star no doubt. Clubs-- no problem, I walked in VIP every go around; drinks were always on the club owners, not just because of Black Pearl, but shit I kept drama down as a cop also. The hood had respect for me and I respected the hood. I would often ask individuals to hold the drama down just out of respect for me.

"Bro, you know I respect you ten folds. All I'm asking is not to pop shit off tonight. Keep the beef away from here. What you do later, I don't know and it's none of my business because I'm sure it's a reason you feel the way you do. Do this for me and there will be a time I will look out for you." Now when a street cred cop asks you to do something like that, take it. You'll need that trump card one day, believe me.

Did I forget to say I brought Tracey a new black E Class Mercedes-- didn't want to be too conspicuous? She would ask me if I wanted to drive, which I declined. I heard through the grapevine a few officers felt suspicious of my newfound source of income. I expected it from officers with no similarities but not from the brothers. So when it was brought to my attention that a certain detective didn't care for me-- felt I was too hood for the badge--I scratched my head in disbelief; I actually I thought we were cool.

Weeks later I saw him in a nightclub drunk off his ass. He tried to bully his way in, not paying admission for four of his friends. At capacity, the bouncer explained he was good but not his friends. He tried forcing his way pass the bouncer. He got popped in the mouth and was leaking all over the front of the club. Motherfucker tried to speak to me like I had his back. I laughed in his face, pounding the fist of the bouncer as I walked by. Right then and there, I knew there was a conflict in where my loyalty was. Don't get it confused, I had mad love for the badge especially for friends--black and white-- who I respected and admired for their commitment for the badge. Personally my commitment was to my family and self.

One Saturday Tracey was off and I was able to take some comp hours off. I wanted to surprise her by taking her to Red Lobster, her favorite restaurant. Walking into the bedroom, Tracey threw the Mercedes keys on the bed. She didn't appear mad so I was oblivious to what was wrong.

"You got something to tell me?"

I look in her eyes I'm certain she found out.

I exhaled, "Yes I do. I should have told you a while ago but I didn't know how to put it."

She replied, "Well here's your opportunity start talking."

"I have a son; his name is Jamarion. I'm not involved with his mother. Just an unfortunate irresponsible incident on my part. He's a few months older than Jiro."

She started to cry, "I was hoping you'd tell me it wasn't true. You not having any relationship with the mother do not make it better. It's worse. Nigga how irresponsible is that? What I should ask is how many other kids you have roaming around."

I dropped my head.

She yelled, "Answer me motherfucker!"

"Just him. I'm so sorry baby. I can imagine how disappointed you are."

She slammed her hand on the dresser, "No you can't. You only know how it felt when you stuck your dick in that bitch! You didn't think about me then!"

I felt like a 5-year-old boy being scolded by his mom.

"If you leave me, I will be heartbroken but I couldn't blame you."

"Nigga you think it's that easy? Just say fuck it? What you just leave your family here and go live your life. No! No! You're going to fix this shit. You're going to make it right for that innocent baby you brought into this world and me. Then if I decide I want to leave your ass, trust me you'll know."

Honestly I felt so relieved; it finally came to light. I was just regretting that I didn't handle it like a man.

"Whatever it takes baby. I know you don't want to hear '*Sorry,*' but I am. I'm disappointed in myself. My pops would beat my ass if he was alive."

I was scared how mama was going react to this. Completely and truly sad, she thought I had my shit together.

Tracey sat on the bed covering her face continuing to cry. I went to hug her. She pulled away almost elbowing me in the face.

"Roland, I have loved you since we were kids. You were an asshole then when I walked away from you. I knew one day we would reunite after you matured. I wondered did I make a mistake? I thought us becoming a family was what you needed to become a man."

I pulled her close hugging her even as she resists.

"Baby the truth is I'm a troubled soul. Years ago the odds were against me. God brought you to me. You are my salvation. Even with a terrific family, I was a fucked up kid. Nobody fault but my own selfish ways. You and the kids are my greatest achievement. You guys make me realize it's more than myself. You better me in every way. You're my better half and there's no other woman I rather be with. I lost focus. That's not an excuse. I hope you can forgive me. My family makes me grind harder so we can have a better life. I wasn't looking for something better because there is no better than you." Tears ran down my face as I continued. "I could be broke and busted but with you by my side, I know things going to be alright."

My heart was so heavy right about now not for getting caught because I jeopardized my relationship with Tracey and my family. I dreaded not being able to watch every moment of my kid's evolution in life. A man's job is to guide his family into prosperity and happiness.

Well Tracey found out her character only solidifies why I'm so lucky. I did discover my niece told her everything. I didn't get that upset, besides it's strictly my fault. If I had a time machine, I would go back allowing her to hear it from me. Actually I would go back further and walked my ass out that club without speaking to anyone. Lately, I hated the man in the mirror.

Back to business at the shop, Manuel brought a dozen young dudes to get tatted. They get inked from head to feet even on their eyelids. Savage!

He introduced me as his brother. "See this cat here. Give him the utmost respect. He's a heffa. Comprende?"

They all acknowledged me by shaking my hand accompanied with a shoulder hug. It was a sign of mutual respect among the kings. I noticed a few could barely speak English.

I get it in tatting all day into the night. I finished up a little after midnight. They left except Mani. He helped me wrap up until it's time to go.

"Thanks bro. How much I owe you?'

I waved him off, "We're good. You gave Tracey the down payment on the Benz."

He reached in his pocket peeling off a stack of hundreds from a fat wad of money and handed it to me. I pulled my hand back. He grabbed my hand slapping the money into it.

"You rather me give it to another tattoo shop or my brother's tattoo shop.

I agreed it made perfectly good sense. I'm glad Mani understood the concept of business. Most friends and family want shit for free instead of patronizing you. Manuel was 100, a stand-up guy who would support you till the very end. Dude had my back without question. I could be in a shoot-out on the street and he would literally pull over and go to war by my side. Wouldn't matter where or when. The reason or with who wouldn't make a difference either; true meaning of family first.

By now I'm not stupid, I know Mani is still in the game. However, we never discussed any illegal activity nor has he ever asked my assistance with any unethical act. Plus, he had legitimate businesses such as daycares, property and a vehicle transportation business. He had a heart of gold along with his success. Mani gave free daycare services to low income families or women who worked and needed child care service. All he required was they have their own lunch. The action of a true Boss is a person who guides his dynasty into peace, wisdom, and prosperity. A Boss betters those around and remains loyal even against all odds. This is something the streets taught me.

The department had elements of loyalty depending on who you were. Clicks look out for clicks, similar to the streets. If you weren't down with a certain click, then it's a strong possibility you'd get the short end of the stick. Even some police officers were more apt to go all out for a certain demographic of people than others. You know exactly what I'm saying. I tried to remain neutral though difficult at times. There comes a time when a man must take a stand. No person wants to become an intended target. I wanted to avoid it. What I didn't know was that eventually certain officers would come for me.

One evening my niece paid me a visit with her baby daddy. This is my favorite niece, I'm tremendously fond of her sweet personality and funny sense of humor. Because of her, I accepted her boyfriend, known as Gee, into my circle.

"Hey Uncle Roland. How are you doing?"

I smiled, "Hey you. You came to see your Uncle? What's up Gee?"

She still had the same voice she had as a child, "Yes sir, I was in the neighborhood and wanted to speak."

Her boyfriend entered my booth patting me on my back, "Hey Unc, you good?"

"Can't complain, nephew. How about yourself?"

My niece was browsing through the tattoo flash wall rack. Gee eased over whispering, "Unc,

I need to holler at you when you get a minute. It's something personal."

"Of course nephew. I'm almost done."

After 15 minutes I called him into my office. "What's up?"

He sat on the couch apparently very nervous.

"Unc, your niece and I are out here in a bad way. With the baby and all we're doing real bad. It's hard for me to find a job with no high school diploma and a criminal record. If you can do anything to help me out, I'm not asking for a hand out. I'll work for mine."

I leaned against my desk, "What will help you get on your feet?"

He rubbed his head, "Anything Unc. Even if you can give me some work."

I looked at him, "Work? I'm not sure how you could fit in around here nephew."

He looked me in the eyes. "Naw Unc, let me move some work for you."

I'm completely caught off guard. "Who told you I'm moving like that?"

"Unc, word on the street is your cartel connected."

I paced for a second, "Nephew, you heard wrong but I will see what I can do for you."

I gave him $300 out my pocket. He watched my pocket.

We walked out the office and Mani was in the lobby talking to my niece.

"Any niece of bro is family to me. Your grandfather was my OG."

I thought to myself, "Oh shit, bad timing."

Gee looked at Mani, then glanced at me to get me to introduce him.

I shook my head "No" to Gee.

A few customers walk in and get distracted. I was totally shook now. What the fuck was circulating on the streets. I was totally concerned about my niece but I was not going to plug Gee with something I was not directly involved in. Thus far my relationship with Mani was clean. I didn't have to ask for a kilo of white cause he would give me the money rather than allow me to get my hands dirty. Sure I knew deep down if I wanted a brick or two, he wouldn't hesitate. We were better than that. It was never discussed.

I walked up front into the barbershop. There was Gee in a deep conversation with Jessie. My conscious was going, *"This is not good at all. I feel so uncomfortable about everything."*

Before I could address them, they left. I figured I'd catch up with everyone tomorrow ASAP.

The next morning, I called Mani to meet me at IHOP for a pow-wow.

"Damn bro, it must be important for you to meet me early. The only time we talk is in the evening. I was starting to feel like your side bitch." He laughs. "You okay?"

"Yeah I just wanted to tell you if anybody in the shop ever approaches on anything, brush them off."

He sat back, "Why? What's the problem?"

I leaned forward, "I just think certain people around the shop got situations that I don't want you to get caught up in."

Mani scratched his head, "Lil bro, be specific. What you trying to tell me?"

"Bro, I just got an uneasy feeling that something ain't right."

He shook his head, "It's a bit too late for that bro. One of my guys plugged your boy Jessie."

I damn near choked, "What! When?!"

"A few weeks ago a little after I got my hair cut. You said he was fam. Plus I don't involve you in shit like that bro."

I replied, "He's fam but not like that. I don't think he's a snitch but he's hot as fire right about now. He definitely got eyes on him. I know this for a fact."

I can tell Mani is nervous, "Fam is fam bro. If you would of said he was hot, I would of backed off. I would have played him to the left."

I tried to relax, "Maybe I'm paranoid. Might be nothing."

He sat back gazing out the window, "Yeah I'm shook. Paranoia keep people safe."

I'm alarmed and all sorts of fucked up scenarios were going through my mind. I was certain Jessie wasn't cooperating with the police, but he was definitely hot. I would be able to get a better feel once I talked to him.

Later that day I pulled Jessie to the back. "Bro, I wish you would of told me that you was going to do business with my brother. With your situation, it would have been better for both of you not to connect."

He was regretful. "Naw, big bro, I would never do something to offend you, I would never involve you into my bullshit. I felt bad enough, you helped how you did with Rogue. You know your brother's not going to involve you anyway."

I agreed, "Yeah I guess you're right. By the way, what was Gee talking about? I don't want you dealing with him either."

He shook his head no, "Nothing to worry about. He was asking who was Mani and if I had a hook up on some girl (cocaine). I told him hell no. I think he might be hotter than me."

I put my hand on his shoulder, making sure he understood me. "Good, don't do shit with him, and from now on, get my opinion on people that's around me. Just because you see me rapping with them doesn't mean they're affiliated. Understand lil bro?"

Jessie pounded me up, "Without a doubt, big bro."

About a week passed and I hadn't heard from Gee. I was thinking I overreacted until he showed up again. I was doing a tat but I saw him walk in. He spoke to me from the lobby.

"Hey Unc, how you doing? I'm getting a lining up front."

I was nervous all over again but I was doing a huge tattoo. I took a break walking up front but I didn't see him. I went to finish tatting my customer. Upon completion, I walked back up and Jessie got my attention.

"Unc!" He then looked out the shop window. I looked out and there was Gee talking to one of Mani's guys that I tatted a few weeks back.

I walked outside, "Gee!"

I startled both of them. The guy knew I recognized him and he hurried to his car. Gee walked over. "What's up, Unc?"

I took him to the back knowing I disrupted something fishy.

"What were you discussing with him?"

"I was asking him where to get some good weed from Unc. I know he had that fire."

I snapped, "Look I don't need that type of activity around me. Nephew, if you're family, you don't put family in jeopardy. You know my job, they already suspicious of me and my people."

He got jumpy, "Naw Unc, I would never do anything to get you caught up. I saw him up front after your boy came to visit you. We were just talking about good smoke and that he had some. That's it. I swear on my mama."

"I hope so cause certain people shouldn't do business together. I don't want any drama around my niece and you shouldn't either."

He assured me, "I got you Unc."

Still suspicious I talked to Mani, "Bro your boy was down here yesterday. The one I tatted his eyelids and he got "*One Love*" on his back."

Mani's eyes got big, "What was he doing down here? That reckless motherfucker, we cut off recently. Who was he talking to?"

"He was talking to my nephew."

Mani stomped his foot, "Shit getting hot bro. I think the best thing for me and you is for me to bounce for a while. There won't be any dots to connect.

"I agree bro. I don't want to see you bounce but it might be the logical thing at the moment. Maybe I'm paranoid. Time will go by and you come back in a few months or weeks."

Better safe than sorry. Not to get off the topic. How Tracey like that car?

I laughed, "She loves it, and by the way I told her about Mookie."

"WHAT! How did she take it?"

I sighed, "Not well but better than I thought. She said she will learn to accept it. She actually had me go get him so he can meet the family."

He put his arm around my shoulder, "Heffa, you got a good one there. Don't fuck it up. Kiss her and the family. I'll be back soon. You got my number if you need me."

I felt like a piece of my family history was walking out of my life. Mani was part of the bodega and my father's legacy no matter the hood element. He was and always will be family to me.

About ten minutes later, Mani walked back in handed me a large heavy envelope. "My lawyer will be contacting you about this bro. I will be gone for a few months so just make sure things go smooth."

I looked baffled, "Don't worry nigga, it's nothing illegal, just some real estate shit."

He walked out. When I got home, I went through the envelope on the bed. Tracey, being noisy, opened it up, "What's this?"

"Mani wants me to give this to his lawyer or something along that line. I'm tired, I will check it out later."

She shuffled through the papers. "Baby, did you read the little post it stuck to it."

I laid down, "Nope."

"Roland, he just turned two properties over to you. These are the deeds already drawn up in your name."

I sat up and snatched the note reading it, "Lil brother, sorry for any confusion. These are yours. I only trust you. Back to NYC."

I stood up and gazed out the window. Manuel is truly my brother's keeper. People wonder why some love the streets. Even people from this environment can love from the heart.

Turns out one of the properties was where Mani laid his head, a nice condo located in West County and fully furnished. The second was I presume where he allowed a few of his guys to stay but he put them out. This one was nothing to brag about, located in Wellston. I handled the business as he wished. I called to thank him but his phone was disconnected. His attorney informed me, "Roland, Mani thought it would be better if he kept his distance from you for the time being. Young man, I agree with him. You're a policeman, right?"

I replied, "Yes, sir."

"I'm not saying your brother is a bad man. He's quite a good business man but he has a lot going on at the present time that doesn't coexist with your ethical requirements. Understand?"

I shook his hand, "Perfectly."

The bureau allowed me extra time to tattoo however I had an uneasy gut feeling that I was being watched. Couldn't put my finger on it. I confided in Tracey while lying in bed.

"Baby should anything ever happen to me, I got money set aside for you and the kids. Plus, you got the properties."

She turned to me rubbing my head. "What are you talking about? What's wrong?"

"Nothing, just saying I'm in a dangerous career."

She worried, "Yeah, but you're a good man. You treat people good. You see how many people love you, especially in the community."

I rolled over looking at her. "Nothing is certain baby. The only person you can count on is the family in our circle and that's slim to a few. Remember what I said, everybody needs a Plan B. I don't anticipate going anywhere, but just in case I want you to have a game plan."

She cuddled with me whispering, "I don't like this conversation, but I understand."

We made love like the very first time.

I never opened up to Tracey about what was going on. I had put her through enough. A man shielded his family from harm's way. Nobody could ever say that she supported anything unethical or criminal.

Once I got back to the shop, Jessie walked in the office.

"Big bro, your nephew Gee. He's hot as a firecracker. That nigga been popping up here while you're not here talking to any and every shady motherfucker. He's been meeting people up here in front."

I was heated, "Wait, can you tell me what's it about?"

"Nope, but a nigga know when something ain't right. Something definitely ain't right."

I called Gee and he avoided my calls by not picking up. I tried for a day or two until I called him from a pay phone. He picked up.

"Gee!"

"Who this?"

"This your Uncle Ro."

He paused, "Oh what's up, Unc? I was just about to hit you up. I know you wanted me to cool out from down there."

"Yeah, but you been coming down when I'm not there so what's going on?'

He's super nervous, "Naw Unc, it's just a neutral spot that everybody knows about. I be parking my car there going downtown putting in applications."

"Look Gee, if you're caught up in some type of trouble and you want to tell me. Just keep it 100, I can probably help you. The way you're moving is making motherfuckers nervous--mainly me. I got your back but if you get innocent people caught up in some bullshit, it will be hard for me to help you. The guys I know, they don't like drama. Now, I'm going to ask you this once and tell me the truth. After that, I will leave it alone."

"Unc, I swear on my mama. There's nothing up."

I replied, "Enough said, but stop moving suspect. Okay?"

"Gotcha, Unc."

A month or so rolled by and the fall season was getting a bit colder. I loved fall because I could really flex my suit wardrobe-- 3 piece suits were coming back in style. Not only was I known for being the tat man but also for getting fly when need be. I literally could wear a different suit for at least two months. I was only detached to the Central Patrol Bureau but I was hoping to get a permanent position. That would be the incentive to keep me with the department.

One evening Tracey and I went to a club on Laclede's Landing; we both had the weekend off. My mother was babysitting the boys so we said, "What the heck. Let's kick it."

We were having a great time; dancing and we had a few shots. We were standing looking at the dance floor. Suddenly the waitress brought me a bottle of Moet.

"Excuse me sir. Your family members paid for this for you." She pointed to the upper VIP.

I looked up. There's some of Mani crew toasting up champagne glasses at me. We walked up there. Tracey was flattered, "You know everybody."

They're happy to see me, "Hey heffa, que pasa?"

I hugged a few of them as they acknowledged me.

The main one said, "Family first right? One love, hermano."

I smiled, "No doubt. One love. How's Mani?"

He lit up, "Oh yeah, I got to give you his new number. I meant to stop at the shop but he told us to stand down. He's wonderful, heffa. He's back in San Juan but he'll be back in New York by spring."

"Good, I will go see him." I pulled out my phone and got his number.

Tracey tapped me on the leg and looked out the side of her eye at the back VIP booth. Oh fuck, I saw one of the professional league baseball players seated snorting a few lines. The player's guy noticed that I saw it.

"Is he cool, heffa?"

"He's a pro baller, just be careful because I guarantee eyes are everywhere. Tell that dumb fuck stop being reckless."

He looked over at his guy sitting next to the baller and signaled to cut him off. The baller got a little upset. He looked up realizing I said something. I read his lips.

"Who the fuck is he. I'm spending my money."

One of them said, "He's Five O." The player shut up avoiding eye contact with me. I got liquor in my system so I'm on ten. I mean mug him as Tracey pulled me away.

The main dude hugged me, "Mani said you was 100 bro. Thanks for looking out."

I leaned in saying, "People like that with so much to lose will snitch you out."

"No problem, heffa."

We walked away and Tracey looked at me strangely when we got to the other side of the club.

I asked, "What's wrong?"

"Roland, you just saw a guy doing coke and they reacted to you like you're their boss. What's up?"

"No bay, it's not like that. One, I'm off duty. Two, he's a baseball player and I'm not going to shit on his career. He's one of the best players we got. Three, I don't know or don't care where that shit came from. What you want me to do, arrest him or maybe call it in? None of my business, that's some Barney Fife shit."

She agreed, "Yeah, you right. It's all in the clubs anyway. I saw some girls doing it in the bathroom. They asked me if I wanted a bump." She laughed.

On the way home I wondered where my loyalty was- with the streets or the badge. The truth is every policeman knows a bad apple, a misguided person, or even an all-out hustler. Should we just lock everybody up when we don't approve of what they are doing. Shit, I've seen plenty police take shit that didn't belong to them, I've seen police try to fuck a suspect's wife in a domestic violence case, or plant contraband on a loud mouth asshole. I turned a blind eye many times; who am I to judge?

The Midwest winter was upon us. I got a slight cold so I stopped by Sprull's Lounge for a whiskey & lemon before I turned it in. I was sitting at the bar by my lonesome sniffling and sneezing.

I was not trying to spread germs. I heard a voice, "Do you need a Kleenex?"

I turned noticing a younger female handing me a tissue. I took it and smiled.

"Thanks mami, but if I was you, I would stay your distance. I had this for a few days now."

She sat next to me, "That's okay I had my flu vaccine, evidently you didn't."

I smiled continuing to look at the bar, "You're correct, I didn't. I heard stories where people reacted terribly to it. Walking backwards and shit. Scary."

She laughed, "Why are you avoiding eye contact with me. That's rude-- am I ugly or something?'

That was the problem—she wasn't and I was trying to be on my best behavior.

"Hi, I'm Stephanie."

I faced her. "I'm Roland, Stephanie."

"I know who you are. You own that tattoo shop. I actually remember you when you went to Cardinal Ritter; however, I was in elementary school."

"So you calling me old, huh?"

She giggled, "No, I'm saying I'm grown now.

There go my conscious talking to me. *That's the shit I'm talking about. You asking for trouble. Get your ass up and LEAVE!"*

We sat and talked for a few minutes. I must admit, it was a good conversation. I looked at my watch for an alibi.

"Wow, I have an early day tomorrow, Stephanie. It's been great talking to you but I have to go."

She pulled out her phone, "Since it's been great then let's exchange numbers to continue this great conversation."

I hesitated for a second, then grabbed her phone and punched in my number.

Roland, when will you learn?

You want to know if I hooked up with Stephanie or if I had enough of being a fuck up?

The answer is No! Well, no to not being a fuck up. Yes, to hooking up with her.

A few weeks in Stephanie and I were seeing each other quite often, but it was platonic. I'm not justifying the relationship directing your attention to another is still cheating. Saying it's not sexual makes me feel better about myself.

Our rendezvous consisted of late night dinners, lunch at Union Station, or watching a VHS movie. We both remained on our best behavior, however Stephanie made it known if I wasn't married, it would elevate to a sexual level.

She'd often speak on what if scenarios. *What if you weren't married... you could spend the night. What if you weren't married... we could take a trip. If you were single, I might get your name tatted on my ass. What if. What if...* but I am and that was the problem.

I didn't make the mistake of neglecting Tracey; she will always be that one. We had our date nights and family outings. Sundays at the zoo were my favorites because my kids treated it like an African safari. St. Louis has one of the best zoos in the country and it's free. I studied all information on as many animals as possible so I could answer their questions accurately. Another great place we visited often was the mall. What kid doesn't like the mall right? My kids had all the latest Jordan's. My mom complained asking why I bought expensive shoes when they grow so fast.

"Mama, this isn't the 70s; kids get bullied for having an off brand shoe. *Factual*!"

I'm sure you're wondering how my mom felt about me having a child out of wedlock. She hated it but accepted him and that's all I have to say about that besides applauding Tracey for not divorcing me.

In the bureau as a detachment, I'm low man on the totem pole so I always do drop offs to Headquarters lab, but I don't mind. I got to rub elbows with a few of the white shirts, the ones that are super cool. Our current Chief was all good; he was the type of guy who makes certain the doors of opportunities are open to all. You got some officers who believe when a black man gets promoted, it's because affirmative action not because he's better qualified than you. Most black officers know they have to work harder to advance so they don't fall under that token theory. I say fuck it if you give me a position because I'm Asian, Black, or Hispanic, I'll take it. Nepotism runs rampant in the department; you got three generations of motherfuckers with the same last name. Once you get familiar with some of them, you ask yourself how the fuck did this remedial motherfucker pass the entrance test. Let's not discuss the psychological test. So many sexual deviants and racists have slipped through the cracks. Think I'm joking? Research officers who fondle women's feet during traffic stops and see what you come up with.

One day in particular I was walking in and as I walked up the steps, I saw the guy Mani out casted walking down the steps. Yeah, the same motherfucker Gee was talking to. My stomach was in my throat. We made eye contact and he dropped his head running down the steps. He turned seeing that I was watching him in disbelief.

I immediately called my niece to see if Gee was around her. I told her to have him call me. I then called Mani; he doesn't answer. About 30 minutes later, somebody hit me back from Mani's phone, "Who is this?"

"This is Roland, is Mani there?"

They sounded a bit relieved, "Roland from St. Louis?"

"Yeah, where's Mani."

"Bro, this is Miguel, his cousin. Ro, Mani's locked up."

I dropped my head, "When and where fam?"

He told me that Mani was picked up by the feds in New York a week ago and he doesn't have bond as of yet. I panicked rushing off the phone.

"Okay, Miguel. Keep me posted if he needs anything."

Before we hung up, he said, "Mani told me to tell you to watch your back bro."

I don't go to the shop I'm nervous as hell. Gee, called me, "Unc, you called?"

"Yeah Gee. Tell me you never did business with the dude I saw you with in front of the shop. The Latino dude."

He answered quickly, "No way, Unc. I just talked about smoking good herb, that's it."

I reinforced, "Do not and I mean do not talk to him anymore about nothing. No contact, dude is bad news.

He assured me, "I promise Unc."

So many things were going through my mind yet I was avoiding the option of Gee being a snitch or an informant. I kept telling myself, "*Naw, I've known this cat for years. Took him in as my nephew. He wouldn't do anything to jeopardize the family. It has to be that outcast bitch I saw. Mani said he was a foul ass character.*"

I didn't want to be around Tracey or my kids, not now. I had to clear my head. I go to the shop. Sitting in the dark, I heard a knock from up front. I walked up there cautiously and noticed it was Stephanie. I opened the door.

"Hey you. I saw your car but the lights weren't on. I was hoping everything was alright."

I let her in looking around outside, "I'm cool just relaxing. I'm not feeling well."

"Are you sick?"

We walked to the back, "No that's not it, just stressed."

She hugged me rubbing my back, "What's wrong?"

I sat down, "I think I'm in trouble."

She looked confused, "How? At home? At work?"

I rubbed both hands through my hair, "Work sort of. "

I got two unfamiliar missed calls on my phone. So I call the number back, "Somebody called Roland?"

"Ro, this Mani people. Bro, some crazy shit just went down with some people I know. It's not us but some motherfuckers we deal with."

I got butterflies. I replied, "Go ahead."

"Man I think your nephew just set our people up. Him and that outcast motherfucker we stopped dealing with."

"It has to be ole boy. My nephew wouldn't do shit like that."

"Papi, I'm telling you it's both of them. My people are heated. They're talking about taking action. I told them to hold back till I call you."

"Fam, tell them to stand down. That would only make matters worse and my niece is around him. If something happens to her, I'm all in then."

"Don't worry, bro. I got it. I'm just telling you to watch your back. We don't rock with them like that but he looking out for you too."

I called Gee and he immediately picked up and he's breathing hard.

"Hey Unc."

I listened for a second, "Okay tell me what happened? I know, so tell me the truth."

"What you talking about, Unc? Nothing happened."

I snapped, "Bullshit Gee, stop lying. You got me in a fucked up spot. The motherfuckers you set up aren't to be fucked with."

"Honestly Unc, I don't know what you're talking about."

I yelled, "Okay then, get the fuck over here now so we can straighten this shit out."

"Okay, I'm on my way."

About an hour rolled by and Gee didn't show up. I called him and got his voicemail. I tried two more times. I got that gut feeling something definitely was not right. I told Stephanie she needed to leave.

"Go home, Steph. Something bad happened and I don't want you involved. I'll walk you to your car."

She started to tear up, "Are you going be alright? I can stay."

"No you can't, I'll call you later."

I grabbed my gun and put it in my waistband. I know now I'm no longer a policeman. I'm officially back to being a street nigga. All rules are out the door now. I'm ready for any and everything.

As I walked her to her car, I felt the chill from the cold air smack me on the neck. I opened her door for her, then closed it when she got in. I saw the concern on her face as she kissed her hand and placed it against the car door window. As soon as I stepped on the curb, I saw flashing red lights appear from every direction. I was so in a daze-- it didn't hit me what was going on. This has to be a dream. Lord, wake me up please!

CHAPTER SEVENTEEN

IT WAS SURREAL. I questioned if it was a nightmare and I was going to wake up. A loud voice command snapped me out of my daze.

"Put your hands up!"

I looked around noticing approximately four or five police and unmarked vehicles congesting the streets. I saw the silhouette of people but the lights were so bright, I was trying to process what was happening. The command became louder.

"Did you hear what the fuck I said? PUT YOUR HANDS UP NOW!"

I raised my hands, "What's going on?"

The voice returned, "Where is your weapon?"

I squinted my eyes to see where it was coming from, "It's in my waistband."

The voice said, "Retrieve it and hand it to us!"

I was really startled now. I witnessed situations like this go south many times. I started to get heated because I smelled some scandalous shit in the air.

"I'm not retrieving shit. You come get it if you want it."

I saw three silhouettes approach me and quickly grab my hands retrieving my Beretta M9 then taking me to the ground.

I yelled, "I'm a police officer."

Somebody put his knee into my back saying, "You're not a fucking cop!"

They lifted me up and I could see the street was full with police and FBI cars parked every which way. I noticed a few DEA windbreakers as they escorted me back into the shop sitting me down in the barbershop lobby. I noticed through the window Stephanie and her vehicle.

I was still in disbelief. A black lieutenant from the department approached me.

I asked, "What's going on lieutenant?"

He gave me a shit look, "You know if you would of reached for that gun, we would of blew your head off."

I snapped back, "Damn brother, it's like that?"

He yelled, "I'm not your brother!"

I replied, "You sholl right, sell out ass nigga!" I mumbled, "Blow my head off."

Now I'm heated. This whole situation was some fuck shit going on. I'm logical. I knew what I had been around, but is there a crime to be related to the game? I was trying to fathom what they

could have got me on. The property? The
affiliation? The gifts? Money payments?
Whatever it was, I was trying to figure out what
would warrant this.

The feds and police were discussing where to
interrogate me. They decided.

"Let's take him to IAD-Internal Affairs."

As I was escorted out, I noticed Stephanie was
handcuffed and being interviewed. I thought, "Go
ahead, she really don't know shit about me."

I looked to the right and my car was being
pulled onto a flatbed tow.

"Where are you taking my car?"

One of the feds politely said, "We'll let you
know all of that, once we get to our destination,
we'll talk to you Roland."

I shook my head yes.

Headquarters was merely 5 minutes away but
the drive took an eternity. I noticed every little
landmark I neglected before. I thought, *"will this
be the last time I see it in a while?"*

Once we got to IAD, they sat me down in a
room. I looked around. All my years in
headquarters, I have yet to see this room.
Maintaining a little sense of humor, I thought to
myself, *"well dumb ass, you never did shit to see
this room."* All I could think of was Tracey and
my kids. I wasn't concerned about myself, just
scared for my family.

A few people entered the room: I presumed a
federal agent, a department lieutenant (not the
cock sucker from before), and a sergeant.

The sergeant spoke, "Roland you have been part of a year-long investigation for drug trafficking. Do you understand that so far?"

"I hear you but I don't understand why but continue."

"Well you have been in contact with our CI-Confidential Informant for the past month and you have been in contact with known cartel cocaine traffickers. Do you understand that?"

I looked away, "I don't know any drug cartel and if I did, they never indicated to me they were."

"Okay Roland. Is there anything you want to tell us that will possibly help you out in the future?"

Before I answered he looked me in the eye, "However, Roland, I want you to know you don't have to say anything if you want legal representation."

The sergeant was a white guy but I got the feeling he was trying to look out for me.

"Look Sarge, I have nothing to hide. Who and what are you trying to ask me about?"

He grabbed a folder opening it, "Well, Roland do you know any known cartel figures or have you ever financially benefited from any cartel figures?"

I sighed and looked up at the ceiling, "Sarge the only people I ever benefited from has been family. With that being said, I think it's best I lawyer up. Can I have a phone call?"

He closed the folder then started reading me my Miranda rights. I didn't pay any attention; I only heard the part that stated "Roland, you are being charged with Conspiracy to Distribute Cocaine and Drug Trafficking." He ended with "Of course Ro, you can have a phone call." He signaled to an officer outside the door to come in. "Let Mr. Page have a phone call."

Deep down I believe the sergeant was throwing me a bone. I did recognize him from details around the area. He always appeared to be a solid individual.

They brought a cell phone to me. I immediately called Tracey; I needed to hear her voice.

She picked up after two rings, "Baby! What the fuck is going on?"

I spoke, "Just listen baby! I've been arrested."

She cut me off, "Roland, they're searching our house right now. They had me and the kids standing outside in the cold; a black captain told them to take us inside the living room."

I snapped and stood up, "What? Those motherfuckers!"

The sergeant signaled for me to calm down, waving for me to sit down.

He whispered, "I'll talk to you Ro."

I continued with Tracey, "Look baby I will call once I get wherever, but don't worry about me. Just make sure you and the kids are good. Don't tell my family nothing yet, okay?"

She started to cry, "Oh- Roland."

The lieutenant signaled for me to cut it short gesturing with his hand by his neck.

"Tracey, it's going be alright. Promise! Talk to you soon."

I hung up and looked at the sergeant, "They raided my home?"

He replied, "Ro, what do you think? Man this is a federal investigation, of course they had a warrant."

I understand but having my family outside in the middle of the fucking winter. Come on man!

He looked down, "Yeah that's fucked up, but they're okay now. I will check on her for you."

I looked him in the eye shaking his hand. "I might not see you again but thanks for treating me 100." He nodded.

I overheard the feds and the lieutenant discuss housing me. The lieutenant: "He has pending cases. It might be in our best interest to hold out on his bond and fly him to a different city to a federal holdover."

The federal agent replied, "Yeah we really don't like housing law enforcement in their city of residency, but…"

He looked at me, "Roland how you feel about being detained here in St. Louis?"

Man if you can please don't take me away from my family. I can jail wherever as long as I can see my family.

I was transported to the federal detainment facility in the downtown area not far from headquarters. While being processed and fingerprinted, I saw an officer I worked with at St. Charbel; she's surprised and heartbroken. We got along great back then.

"Oh gosh Roland, you're breaking my heart."

I was lying in my cell feeling like it's the end of the world. Word was the federal prosecutors wouldn't grant me a bond as of yet due to my noncooperation. A young black turnkey allowed me a phone call. I called Tracey.

"Hey baby! I'm so sorry putting you through this Tracey. Lord knows I'm trying to do right; maybe I'm just cursed."

She was crying, "No you're not cursed, you're just loyal to the wrong people Roland."

I cut her off, "Let's not speak about what's going on, not on this phone." As soon as I said that the recording came on, "This phone call is being monitored by a federal correctional facility."

Baby, okay but I can't sleep. I wish you were here."

I comforted her, "It will be alright. You're one of the strongest people I know. You got this. In the next day or so we'll know what direction to take. It's just a waiting game now. You know where the assets are so you're good. Don't tell mama."

She informed me that the kids were asleep and fine. They had no clue what was happening. Just hearing her voice gave me strength. The automated voice on the phone told me I had a minute left.

Tracey told me, "Baby, first thing tomorrow I'll call that high power attorney Rosenbaum; he's a bad boy.

I replied, "I need him. I love you and keep your head up. I'm good."

They placed me in an isolated area; because I was a law enforcement officer I couldn't be with general population. I couldn't sleep a wink. I confessed this was by far the worst moment of my life thus far. Into the morning hours I contemplated the worst-case outcome for me.

I kept telling myself, "Ro, you got this. You can handle this. There is always a solution to every problem. They can't hold you forever."

Surprisingly I didn't break down. I prayed to God and apologized for my foul ways. The notion entered my mind that maybe I deserved this after all I put Tracey through so much bullshit. For so many years I pursued an immoral path, now it was time to answer for my sins. I had taken too many bites from the forbidden apple. A man must pay for his sins.

It seemed morning would never come, but somehow I must have dozed off. I was aroused by a US Marshal,

"Mr. Page, wake up! Time for court it's your arraignment."

I rubbed my face and slipped on my shoes. Easy, I had no shoelaces. I was hoping this was a bad dream, but no such luck. I told the US Marshal, "You know what's fucked up man?"

He answered, "What's that?"

"Early yesterday I booked someone in and later that night I was booked in. Miserable feeling."

Yeah man, "I would imagine."

He handcuffed my hands and feet with shackles. Looked familiar but I never guessed I would be the prisoner. As I exit the detention sally port, there were reporters snapping pictures. I noticed some police personnel lingering around to get a glance. Motherfuckers like to see a person when he's down. I glanced over seeing a female I knew. She smiled and gestured for me to keep my head up. I smiled back. I saw a fat white asshole sergeant laughing at me.

I whispered, "You fat fuck, that's why you can barely walk. I hope diabetes gets the best of you."

The US Marshal asked, "What you say?'

I replied, "Nothing, I was talking about that fat fuck over there laughing at me."

He looked and shook his head in pity. "Yeah you know the media was going to eat this up I hate to say."

I dropped my head, "Yeah, I should've expected this. Damn!"

Arriving at federal court, the US Marshal was greeted by some guy in a cheesy suit. I can't make out what they're discussing. He nodded and walked over to me.

"Okay Mr. Page, I'm going to take you to an interview room. Your attorney wants to talk to you."

Yes, my baby came through for me.

I asked, "Do you know who's my lawyer?"

"That I don't know."

I saw Mr. Rosenbaum entering the room. I said, "Thank you Jesus."

Rosenbaum was the best attorney money could buy. I had never met him, had only seen him in the news for all the cases he had won. Surely

Tracey had to tap our bank account for this dude to be here.

I shook his hand and sat down, "Mr. Rosenbaum thank you for coming. I take it my wife retained you."

He smiled, "Yeah your wife and mom."

I shout, "What? My mom how the hell she found out?"

He laughed, "Roland, you're all over the news. What did you expect?"

"Oh Lord. I rather stay in jail."

He opened his folder, "No you don't Roland. You need all the support you can get. This judge we're preparing to see, I'm not happy about. He's a stickler and I'm sure he's not thrilled, you being a peace officer accused of a crime. You have to be ready for this. I need you to hold your head high. Evidently you know my reputation, right?"

"Yes sir, that's why I chose you."

He leaned forward folding his hands, "Good, with that being said, I don't give a fuck if you're guilty; it's my job to defend you regardless. I need you to be honest. You're accused of Conspiracy of Drug Distribution. One of the easiest crimes to prosecute so do not lie to me. I need to know everything to provide a good defense for you. For you to be here, the feds must have something on you."

I agreed, "Yes sir but I never participated with any distribution of drugs."

He cut me off, "Roland, look you're a police officer who associated with cartel members. One, that's a no- no. Secondly, you're a police officer and you knew what your so called family was doing. By law you took an oath to report any wrong doing even if it's family."

"I understand."

"Let's get the ball rolling. I'll see you in the courtroom. I want you to plead not guilty. Don't worry, follow my lead."

The Marshals escorted me to the courtroom. I'm the only defendant there. The bailiff stood. "The US district of Eastern Missouri against Roland Page for the crime of Conspiracy to Distribute Cocaine. Judge Heineke presiding."

The judge walked in, I looked at the attorney and he raised his eyebrows.

I whispered, "Yeah he looks like an asshole."

The bailiff instructed me and my legal counsel to stand.

The judge started to talk and I pretty much went blank. What he was saying sounded like the teacher from Peanuts Charlie Brown.

The judge demanded my attention.

"Mr. Page, do you understand the charges you are being accused of? I suggest you take this situation serious. If it's up to me, reviewing the evidence, I would make a recommendation of 20 years."

Wait one damn minute, did I hear him right? 20 years? WTF

"Do you understand Mr. Page. Yes or No?"

I instantly got light headed and the room started to spin. Before I knew it, my lawyer was shaking me.

"Roland! Roland you Okay!"

I heard the judge, "Mr. Rosenbaum is your client alright?"

"I believe so your honor."

I snapped out of it. "Your honor, I understand I'm not guilty."

He sharply responded, "I haven't asked you that yet but under the circumstances I accept your plea."

I looked at Rosenbaum like please save me.

He leaned over, "Don't worry, he shouldn't of said that; fuel for us to get a change in magistrate. You look pale, you okay?"

I looked up at him, "He just took the air out of me saying some crazy shit like that."

Rosenbaum smiled, "He's going through the motions.

You're a commissioned representative accused of a crime so he's saying what is to be expected."

I wiped the sweat from my forehead, "If you say so."

Rosenbaum raised his hand, "Your honor, how about a recog bond for my client?"

The judge removed his glasses, "You got jokes today Mr. Rosenbaum."

My attorney smiled, "Worth a try."

"I will review the case with the District Attorney and get back with you ASAP."

The US Marshals walked over and cuffed me.

Rosenbaum put his hand on my shoulder, "I will get you a bond, be patient. They're going to try and hold you to get you to crack. I got this."

Things weren't looking very bright for the kid. I was shipped to Marion County Federal Correctional Facility against my wishes. I was housed there until the government was required to grant me a bond.

Jail was nothing to write about. Misery, loneliness, depression and even suicidal thoughts were the emotions that flood my heart. Don't worry, I would never go out like that. The problem was the separation from my family. I wasn't concerned for my well-being but my family's. I knew so many people from my hay days that motherfuckers were calling my name when I was escorted across the yard. Luckily I had stacked quite a bit of money from tattooing. Tracey put some on my books and had more than enough to hold her over. She had an artist that hung around the shop take my place for a 60/40 cut. Her receiving a 40% income was better than nothing; it was the standard percentage for tattoo establishments. I would call Tracey daily, asking her to conference me on three-way with my attorney's office to see if a bond was instated.

Rosenbaum was so high profile that he was in and out court constantly; I could only talk to his subordinates,

"Mr. Page, I know it's frustrating, but trust us we're working diligently to get you a bond. The feds are trying to build an interstate drug case so once the dots don't connect; we can move forward with a speedy trial to get things going. You'll get a bond soon."

Honestly I wasn't new to this; I saw it many times. However, I was on the administration side, not the receiving end. I had to sit down and talk myself down twice daily.

In the rec yard, I would play handball to occupy my time. Rosenbaum made a vital suggestion to me.

"Roland, do me a favor?"

I pulled the phone away from my head thinking, Man this dude has a sense of humor but I'm not trying to hear it today. Yet I go along pulling the phone back to my ear, "What man?"

He replied, "Write a journal. Writing is great therapy. You have a story to tell. You'll never know what it might lead to."

What he said saved my sanity without a doubt. I wrote till my fingers ached. My hands were more sore from writing than they had been when tatting. I spoke with Tracey about my new endeavor, she was just as excited as I was. I talked to my baby as much as possible as well as my boys. She told my boys that I was away training.

Jiro would just say, "Hi daddy!"

Lil Ro's words would get me through the day, "Hi daddy I'm drawing just like you. I'm going to help you tattoo when I get big."

That right there fueled my quest for freedom. Weeks went by and finally I got a bond. Tracey was there like clockwork. The air outside of jail was more refreshing. In the car, I let the window down even though it was still chilly outside.

Tracey looked at me like I was crazy, "Nigga it's not summer yet let that window up!"

She took a double glance at me, "Baby I'm sorry, take it all in. Take it all in."

I closed my eyes, inhaled and pictured my entire family's face: mother, siblings, wife, and kids.

FREEDOM!

I arrived at my house and Tracey was parking; suddenly I saw a white guy dressed as a cable technician walking from my next door neighbor's gangway. The only problem the house was vacant and burnt to a crisp. Tracey said, "That's suspicious. Our cable wire is on the other side of our house. What do you think?"

I responded, "Yeah I believe my calls were being monitored."

Her voice rose, "Wire taped?"

"Yep, I got this."

Going up the steps, the guy stepped back into the gang way as if I didn't notice him.

I yelled, "Come on out man! I have no problem with you. You're doing your job, just get that shit off my house. Tell them they're not going to catch me doing shit anyway."

He walked by with no facial expression. The jig was up!

Finally, I had a good night sleep. Tracey took emergency leave for a few days. I have so much respect for St. Louis County Correctional Facility. The Administrators knew her situation and my case yet still allowed her a few days off for mental anguish. Salute!

Tracey made me a meal and tried to get me to go out. I didn't want to really show my face in public so I thought of every excuse. I got a headache and so on. It was however mandatory I go to see my mom. To my heart's comfort, she was happy to see me as tears came to her eyes, "Boy I'm glad you're okay. That's all that matters. I put the house up for your bond."

I looked in amazement to Tracey. You should know that I couldn't use Mani's property yet cause the deed hasn't completely transferred.

My mom interrupted, "That's alright. Don't worry I know you wouldn't jeopardize the house. I'm not worried, just glad you are home." She hugged me for an entire minute.

I apologize, "Mama I'm sorry for being a fuck up. I know I let you down. Daddy's turning over in his grave right this minute. I promised him I would stay on the right side of the law, but it's not what you think."

She held my face, "Roland just get yourself together so you can be there for your kids. Understand?"

I nodded yes.

Word got out that I'm home. I got a few calls from some police officers wanting the 411. Only two actually contacted me asking, "Are you alright?"

Will, my ex-partner, was one saying, "I don't care if you did or didn't do it. I just want to know are you okay?" It did a lot for my morale; at least somebody on the department still cared.

For the next few months I went into exile. The media portrayed me as a cartel drug dealer who had no heart, no family. My primary goal was to lace my pocket and greed fueled my dreams. It was said that they had been watching me for a long while now. I knew they were full of it. They hired me; if they knew my unsavory past, I would of never worn that badge. I assumed I had this coming for being a self-centered asshole.

I met with Rosenbaum on numerous occasions. He was entertaining and reassuring. He would ask me to draw all types of characters. I would say to myself laughing, *"What do this dude be on?"*

I liked his savvy way. He had a swag about himself that was untouchable. The more I talked to him, the more I felt things were going to be alright. After hiring him, I got more compliments that made me feel better.

All the OG's said, "Well if you're in a fight for your freedom, Rosenbaum is the one you want in your corner. He's a beast in that courtroom."

So the most hurtful element to this case is I discovered Gee did set me up. The sad thing about it is some of my family members refused to believe he was capable of it. It was the ones who were suckers for men. Don't get me wrong, I love them all--even Gee. That's why I felt so betrayed when anyone asked me, *are you sure you didn't do this?* What the fuck do you think?

After being released, the pieces fell in place. Rosenbaum told me that a Narcotics detective by the name of Ferguss initiated the investigation. He stated he had been suspicious of my activity for a while but didn't act on it until he gathered more evidence.

Get this: when I went back to the shop, everybody was happy to see me. They tried to make me feel better by saying, "Everything happens for a reason. You will do better with the tattoo career anyway." I appreciated the motivation; however it was not the way I wanted to end my law enforcement career. Jessie was sincerely concerned. I shared with him a bit of my case and he almost choked.

"Big bro did you say Detective Ferguss?"

"Yes why?"

"That's the motherfucker on my case, that's the one my mom went to IAD on. He's the one who told the co-defendants we told on each other."

A rage came over me. At this point I still felt a bond with the department. A small portion of my heart had love for the badge. All that changed then. I had hate for it. Love for my brothers, hate for the department. I may be guilty of my association, but I have never conspired to have two humans exterminate one another. Ruthless!

Now it made sense. The motive was clear. I wondered if I hadn't helped Jessie would I even be in this predicament. Maybe so yet my instinct told me it was not a coincidence. Talking to Rosenbaum, I got a better understanding.

"Maybe so, I heard a lot of unethical things about him… That doesn't grant you immunity for your conduct, Ro… They have all the right evidence to make a case… I can take it to trial and possibly beat it... I have won worse but I don't want them to come with a state charge of 'Police Corruption.' They might get that and that's state time. Fed time is always better if I can't win it. I have to be straight with you and lay out all the possibilities."

"I hear you man, but Police Corruption? How can they present that? When I wore that uniform, I did my job. I never used my authority to commit any crime. I never took any dope or shook down a dealer."

He dropped his pen on the table, "No, but you associated with drug dealers. They gave you money. You knew their activity. Look Ro, I'm not here to argue with you. If you want me to take it to trial and argue the fact, I will. You may be innocent, it's up to a jury to decide; but the way they have the evidence that they want to present to the jury, it may be compelling to them. You're an officer associating with drug dealers. And in some of the surveillance and phone conversations, you're calling them family."

He was right; if I was set up, that cocksucker did it beautifully. During my evidence hearing and search, I found out they had tapes upon tapes, boxes of recordings and lastly conversations between me and Gee. What amused me was that they gave Gee a recorded cell phone that he could use. This dumb fuck was using it to call other women. I let my sister hear it so she could finally go tell my niece-her daughter- the truth. I didn't get joy out of that; as I said before this niece is my favorite, and she didn't get mad; instead she was deeply hurt that Gee allowed them to use him as a weapon against me. She confronted him. He tried to deny it until she convinced him that the tapes couldn't lie. He confessed, saying that they tortured him until he agreed to do it.

My niece made him make a recording saying I didn't conspire to connect any transactions but Rosenbaum said they might interpret that as tampering with a witness. Gee didn't want me to be innocent anyway. He had copped a plea for a previous crime he committed. Serving me up would grant him leniency. He was a proud Confidential Informant aka "*Snitch*."

Gee had no intention on aiding me to avoid a conviction; he even told the US district Attorney that he heard we were conspiring to kill him. He allegedly was in the Bluemeyer Project where he got on the elevator; before the door shut, one of my co-defendants got on and just smiled at him. Rosebaum got in my shit as if it was true.

"Ro, maybe you did or didn't. I'm here to represent you. Keep you free. Intimidating a witness, especially a CI, is damaging. They could revoke your bond. It appears that's what he's trying to do."

"I haven't intimidated nor contacted anyone. I can't say I don't want him fucked up. I do, but killed-- no. That's still the father of my niece's children; I'm not that heartless. I can't control what my co-defendants do. This man has fucked over a lot of people. And no, I haven't been in contact with any of my co-defendants. I'm not stupid."

"I hope you're not."

I replied, "Never would I turn a dope case into a murder trial."

Rosenbaum was my boy; we would argue then laugh the next minute. He would switch up in an instant.

"How's the journal coming?"

I answered, "Oh yeah, I'm done."

He'd loosen up, "You're done? That's great. You know Roland, once this is over, it would make a great book. Worst-case scenario, if convicted, you will have to wait till your statute of limitation is up. Then touring, residuals, and speaking to law students, you cash in."

"If that happens bro, I got you. You really pulling me through this shit. I may be a pain at times but I appreciate you."

Returning to the shop was another therapeutic remedy for me, I tatted like a fucking maniac. This time Tracey was there as much as possible. On the weekends, I would spend time with the family. When presented with a life changing tragedy, the time one spends with the family is enjoyable. It's like eating crackers for a year, then you get an Oreo. You cherish the moment. However, I was a nervous wreck; I was suspicious about the fucking mailman. He would come in and I would say a sarcastic comment.

"Tell them motherfuckers better luck next time. They don't know shit." He would look back hurrying out like he must be crazy or something.

One of the beauticians up front, who I never really liked, tried to be funny in a sneaky way. She approached me with a newspaper containing the article about my arrest.

"Hey Ro, you a celebrity, can I get your autograph?"

Walking to the back I paused and turned around. All the workers turned away avoiding eye contact.

"My autograph? What, that supposed to be funny bitch? Trying to crack a joke off my misery? I can't put my hands on you but I would be wrong if I punched your man right in his shit. Tell you what, don't say shit to me never again. We really don't get along so that should be okay."

This is usually a loud mouth bitch but you should have seen the look on my face. I was for real and I would take my stress out on her man. A brother was pumped too. I'd been working out just in case I had to hit the yard again. Light skin niggas get tested in the joint.

I tried to loosen up but it was impossible, not knowing my fate really ate at my spirit. The only remedy seemed to be quality time with the family.

The summer of 1996 will be the most memorable year of my lifetime. We went fishing, boating at Forest Park, had a picnic at Six Flags-- all the things a father should experience with his family. Call it corny, I call it responsible. I would have traveled if I could but my pre-trial restrictions prevented me from going 50 miles outside St. Louis and I couldn't cross any state line. So I made the best of what was available to me. My focus had never been so solid. The experience I shared with my family could last a lifetime. Tracey and I had a sturdy bond but until now I hadn't recognized how unbreakable we were.

Jessie was waiting for me in the back tattoo lobby on a Saturday. He looked spooked, "Big bro I felt I had to bring this to you. I got indicted yesterday so I turned myself in. Ferguss was there to process me. He straight up brought your name up."

That name burns my soul every time I hear it, "What did he say?"

"He asked if I had spoken with you. I told him not really. He said good and told me to stay away from you. You're dangerous."

I looked at Jessie, "You're my brother. I'm no more dangerous to you as to myself. Fuck Ferguss, karma's a bitch."

The shop was booming since I could devote my all into the business. I give thanks to God for bringing a blessing in disguise. Every so often someone suspicious would come into the shop to get service. They would ask if I had the plug on work-drugs. It frightened me because after indictment, the feds will still try to bait you to see where your head is. This could result in bond revocation or additional charges to solidify the initial charges. Plus, anyone in the game can see a cornball coming from a mile away. That's why their tactics are ruthless; they will recruit a family member in desperation to infiltrate the ranks.

I became more spiritual during my ordeal. My sister Patty delivered me closer to God. I had always been a believer, but I neglected my communication with the Lord. Patty encouraged me to attend church with her. I admired my sister's devotion to God. She's the type regardless of her lows, she's high on God.

"Baby brother, God makes everything possible. Everything happens for a reason. God is calling on you. This may be his way of saving you."

I reluctantly replied, "Sis you may be right but I don't wanna be one of those people who only call on the Lord when they're in trouble. God deserves more respect than that. I'm not going to try and hustle the Lord for my freedom. When I commit, I will wholeheartedly. But I do agree with you, I know God has a plan for me."

Many label God as him; I'm not saying they are wrong but God is so forgiving-- a trait more so like a woman. In my opinion, women are more forgiving. A mother loves her child unconditionally-- right or wrong. A wife forgives her cheating husband yet a husband will never let a cheating wife forget her sins. It's a simple observation of mine.

Stephanie reached out to me after all that happened. I apologized for involving her. "I'm glad to see you're in good spirits. Never got a chance to say I'm sorry. I know that was pretty intense that night."

She pleasantly answered, "Yes indeed, regardless I'm glad to see you are alright. They said some terrible things about you."

I'm curious, "Like what? be specific?"

She continued, "How you are married and a manipulator. Have I witnessed you engaged in drug deals. You're dangerous. They were going to tell your wife you were with me... along those lines."

I shook my head, "Seemed personal huh?"

Her eyes got big, "Definitely personal. I told them you never misled me. As far as drugs, you never exposed me to none of that."

We departed by agreeing I needed to focus on following a righteous path. Before Stephanie left, she told me she would keep me in her prayers. What Stephanie said about them telling Tracey bothered me because Tracey never spoke on her experience that night. We tried to forget the entire incident.

Later that evening Tracey and I were in the kitchen cooking, having a great conversation. She was making my favorite-- pork neck bones and potatoes.

I asked, "Mami why you never asked if I was guilty? You never inquired about my case."

She continued to cook, "Well you never told me anything about it. I figured you would speak on it once you are ready. I know you don't tell me things for my safety. I love that about you."

I replied, "Yeah but are you curious if I'm guilty or not. Did the police say anything to you that night about me?"

She stopped cooking and looked at me, "Like what? That you were with another woman that night? Yeah they spoke on that and asked if there were drugs stashed anywhere-- which the dogs proved there wasn't. They were careful on what they said to me."

I got up and hugged her, "I know it sounds like a broken record but I'm sorry. That night that girl being there was a coincidence."

I told her to sit down, "The truth is I'm guilty and innocent. My actions have brought a dark cloud on this family. I'm not a dirty cop but honestly I don't have what it takes to be a cop. I'm loyal more to my fam than to the badge. Baby, my guys never exposed me directly to none of that yet I benefited financially. Deep down I knew where the money came from. I knew they liked the idea that they had a police officer in the crew. One important thing, those street cats are loyal to me. They would never leave me hanging through the good, the bad, the ugly. The streets are ruthless but there are good qualities also. Honestly, I still have mad love for the department or, should I say, some of the people there. That's why I'm bitter I guess. That Motherfucker Ferguss I dislike, but I allowed myself to get caught up. I'm more mad at myself than anybody."

She kissed me on the cheek, "You are a good man Roland and an excellent father. You got some work to do as a husband," She laughs. "But you always been honest in your indiscretions. If you cheated, you never lied and you admitted your wrong. Even with Mookie, you told me you couldn't turn your back on him regardless. I was deeply hurt but I admired your commitment as a father. I thought about leaving many times. I realize I love you deeply; we are a family and family fight together not against one another."

I hugged her so tight she grunted. I told her, "I love you. I'm so lucky."

Tracey never asked me to distance myself from Mookie only encouraging me to be there for him. To my enjoyment Mookie called Tracey mama. What a woman.

Almost a year had passed by and one would hope that maybe the US Attorney office had forgotten my case. I couldn't be so lucky. Preparation for a trial can span over a two- or three-year period; prosecutors have extensive caseloads so it a waiting game. Rosenbaum called me to his office for a meeting.

"Hey Ro, tell you what's going on. The District Attorney wants you to do time but they are offering you a deal with a light sentencing if you plea out. So basically maybe a year to 18 months depending on the point system and how they grade you."

I was quiet for a few seconds, "What do you think?"

He leaned back in the seat, "That's up to you, Ro. If you want me to take it to trial, I can and can probably win. I have faced tougher situations. The down side is if I lose, then they will try and slam you maxing you out. The charge carries a 3- to 20-year sentence. Snatching out their recommending 18 months to 2-year sentence."

I rubbed my forehead, "Man that's the only option?"

He replied, "Well you can plead no contest then leave your fate to the judge; that's an option. I can see if I can get a change for a more understanding judge. That being the case, we get character letters and hope for the best. Of course you will have to surrender your commission status as a cop, that will be a condition of the punishment."

I went to discuss it with Tracey who was waiting in the lobby. After a brief talk, I went back in his conference room.

"Let's roll with the No Contest."

He walked me through the process and all the steps to ensure I got a fair shake. Basically I was throwing myself on the mercy of the court hoping the judge had compassion. It took a few months but Rosenbaum was granted a change of judgeship. He was pleased with our assigned magistrate Honorable Judge Sheldon.

"Judge Sheldon is an excellent judge known to be extremely fair. No nonsense gentlemen and he's African American."

I did my research and found that his reputation was good. I didn't take it for granted that he is black-- after all out of all my arresting officers, a black lieutenant told me he wanted to shoot me. I prayed on it with my intuition telling me I made the right choice.

My family began getting character letters from prominent people. A few police officers wrote letters of support. I realized I still had love from the department. One of the first to write a heartfelt letter was my sister's pastor, Reverend Williams--a divine man I looked up to since I was a young boy. He had guided Patty from a life of turmoil. Reverend Williams just asked me to visit church a few times so he wouldn't lie about my spiritual counseling. No problem, Tracey and I found our visit quite rewarding. I see why people go to church; I truly felt the presence of God.

Months went by and I spend more and more quality time with my family. Though I am thankful, it only made the reality difficult—I'd have to leave them. Anxious for my sentencing date to appear, I wanted to put everything behind me.

I started making preparations for my absence; the tattooist that previously stepped in for me agreed to remain until my returned. He's a good guy by the name of Kee. I trusted him more than other individuals I interviewed. I allowed them to work a day in the shop to observe the way they operated. I dismissed many due to their lack of understanding that it's a business. Talking to them, I got an uncomfortable feeling they would jeopardize what I built. Some focused too much on women coming off somewhat as perverts. Others were too boisterous about their skills yet didn't care about the sanitation responsibilities—in other words, they were nasty as fuck. One almost tattooed a 13-year-old until Tracey intervened telling the girl she was too young. I asked him, "Didn't you card her?"

He replied, "You got to ID them?"

Duh, of course you dumb ass!

Tracey and I agreed Kee-Kee would do. He assured me, "I can handle it big bro."

The week of my sentencing approached; with each day, I get nervous and sad. I cried once or twice in the shower so no one could see me. I got to stay strong. I told Tracey if you find someone else, please just tell me so I don't be a fool. She got angry every time I mentioned it.

"Stop saying that; you must plan on having some ratchet little bitch visit you. If I find out, I'm going to be up there with you on an assault charge. We in this together baby."

As harsh as it sounds, I needed to hear shit like that. It ran through my mind to reach out to Stephanie who asked if she could visit me or insisted I keep in touch calling her collect. However, I threw out that notion realizing God was telling me to get my life in order.

"I hear you Lord. Amen."

I savored each day up until the day before my sentencing. The Sunday before the day, Tracey cried throughout the day. At moments I found myself breaking down, telling myself, "Keep it together for the family."

I went to visit my mom. She made some sushi for me like when I was a kid. She looked me in eye before I left, "You go get this over with so you can move on okay. Daddy is there with you." She hugged me telling me she'd see me in court.

At home I spent time with Lil Ro and Jiro. Jiro was too young to know what was going on, but Lil Ro had an uneasy feeling something wasn't right. "Daddy are you going on a trip?"

I put him on my lap, "Yeah daddy might have to leave just for a little bit. Don't worry I'll be back."

He leaned back yawning, "Can I go?"

I choked up, "No it's a secret mission. Daddy can't take you."

He grabbed my hand, "Like when you were in the Army or your police job."

I smiled, "Something like that. I'm going to call you almost every day so you know I'm not far. Okay. I promise."

He hugged me, "Okay."

I squeezed him tight. "Daddy needs you to be a big boy and take care of your mama. Listen to her and help her with your little brother. Can you do that for me?"

"Yes daddy." He dozed off as I kissed him on the head.

I whispered, "Be a better than me son."

While sleeping that night, I had a dream that I was at my mom's house. I saw the furniture from when I was a kid in that house. Standing in the living room, I noticed the glare of the TV in my father's room. I slowly walked back thinking this seems awfully real. Approaching the doorway, I saw my father sitting on the bed. He looked up and smiled. He patted the bed for me to sit down. I heard his voice and a warm feeling flowed through me.

"There's my baby boy."

I sat, "Hey pops. Man, I miss you."

"I miss you too."

I looked at the floor, "So I guess you know what tomorrow is for me?"

He stopped watching TV and turned to me, "Yeah I do."

"Do you think it's going to turn out okay for me?"

He put his hand on my lap, "Yes, everything is going to be fine."

I brightened up, "You don't think I will go to prison?'

He replied, "I didn't say that. What I mean is regardless of what happens, you got to make things good. You can handle whatever comes your way."

I nodded my head, "I understand."

Pops yawned, "I'm getting sleepy. You have to go."

I smiled, "Thanks pop. Can I see you tomorrow?"

He appeared puzzled, "Boy you know I'm dead. Don't worry, we'll talk again."

I woke up realizing it was merely a dream. What seemed like a few minutes was hours because it was now daylight. I carried Lil Ro to his bed kissing him and Jiro again.

The morning atmosphere was grim. We rushed to get ready so we could find a parking space. Rosenbaum called, "Be on time and make sure your family is there that's important. Ro, might not be a bad idea to have your kids there."

I cut him off, "No way, I don't want my kids to see me like that. All my adult family will be there. I'm leaving out now."

He responded, "Hopefully you won't have to surrender to the Marshals and will have a little more time with your family."

"I rather get this out the way. I don't want to prolong me coming home to my family for good."

The ride was fairly silent. Tracey was holding my hand while she drove. I was looking at the city during our travel. My stomach was rumbling. Tracey found a parking space near the front. She smiled, "We got lucky huh?"

I smiled back.

My heart was pounding; I could hear my heartbeat when I closed my eyes. I thought about just turning around and running, but I know that's not me. I was going to handle this like a man.

I checked in and sat in the defendant's chair waiting for Rosenbaum. My family gradually piled in the rear of the court seated behind the wooden gate. I wondered how many defendants had walked through this gate.

EPILOGUE

THE BAILIFF INTRODUCING THE entrance of the judge snapped me out of my trance. The life that passed so quickly in front of my eyes had opened a new chapter in my life. What's scary is I didn't know how it's going turn out.

"All rise. The court of Eastern District of Missouri is now in session, Honorable C Shelton presiding."

Honorable Judge Shelton entered the court. Everybody was silent. I still heard the women in my family sniffling. I took a good look at the judge. He's hard to read but I must admit a black judge makes me feel a whole lot better. Not saying they wouldn't do their job. I believe they understand the struggle a bit better. I even heard white convicts say they too prefer a black judge.

The judge sat instructing everyone to be seated. He fumbled through his folder. He then asked Rosenbaum if I was ready to be sentence. Not much of nothing was said, I don't think it even computed. I was ready to get this over with.

He then looked at me.

"Mr. Page, do you feel that you were properly represented by Mr. Rosenbaum?"

I replied, "Yes, your honor."

He continued to look at me, "Are you ready to accept your sentencing?"

"Yes, I am your honor."

"Is there anything you wish to say before I impose your sentence; if so the platform is yours."

I think for a second, "Yes there is your honor."

I had no speech rehearsed, merely a load of guilt that I wanted to confess. I took a deep breath and opened my heart to speak.

"Your honor, I would like to start off by apologizing to my family and peers that I let down. I do not want this situation to have any negative reflection on my upbringing. My family was excellent role models who impacted my life in a positive manner. The unethical crime that I have committed is strictly my fault. I take full responsibility. I contribute it to pure ignorance. With that being said, I'm ready to put this behind me so I can build a better foundation that's stable for my family. I know what I have been charged with, your honor, but I don't want the court to think I used the badge to commit any crime. When I put that uniform on, I did my job to the best of my ability. I am not a corrupt police officer however I do admit that I don't have what it takes to wear the badge. I can't turn my back on family that's been there for me through thick and thin. This is not the way I wanted my law enforcement career to end but I have no option except to make the best out of this. I hear God makes things happen for a reason however I feel so disappointed in myself. For years I have taken things for granted, promising the next day to change for the better. It was a matter of time that my sins caught up with me. I will pray and ask for forgiveness from the Lord Almighty. I know you have a job to do; I hope I am worthy of leniency in your eyes. Regardless of the outcome, I promise you I will rebound as a better than man."

He closed the folder and took off his glasses. "Mr. Page, I got a lot of phone calls on you and you're correct I have a job to do. Mr. Page, after reviewing your case I am not comfortable with imposing a prison term for you. Yet you cannot go unscathed, therefore I sentence you to three years' probation and 200 hours of community service to help people with drug addiction."

The court erupted with cheers. I hugged Rosenbaum and looked him in his eyes. "You're the man. Thanks brother for saving me." I knew Rosenbaum fought tooth and nail to negotiate a fair deal for me. His reputation and relationship with the court helped without a doubt. I looked over at the opposition and they had sour faces. Check this, surprisingly before walking out, the US District Attorney shook my hand.

"Roland, good luck."

He was cool about it, better than I assume the DEA agents were.

I walk over to my family and hugged my mom and wife. I looked up to the ceiling. "Pops, I'm going to be alright."

One month later I find myself sitting in a support group for people fighting drug addiction. The group consisted of maybe twenty people, mostly women. I listened to sad stories of how drugs affected their lives. Some of the stories were horrific, especially the women confessing how their boyfriends sold them sexually for drugs. One said that she allowed her man to hide dope in her baby's diaper to avoid being searched but the narcotic dog detected it and she got popped for it. The boyfriend denied it was his. I felt ashamed to speak yet it was my turn.

"Hello, everyone, my name is Roland Page. I'm here for not drug abuse but my affiliation with people who promoted drugs. I want to apologize to each and every one of you. I'm truly sorry. I did have an addiction though. My addiction was greed and I forgot what it was to be a true man. I gave in to temptation. I ate the forbidden apple one too many times. Eating the forbidden fruit almost cost me everything."

~THE END~

ABOUT THE AUTHOR

Author Roland Sato Page was born in Brooklyn New York in a military household with a mother from Osaka Japan and a combat trainer father with three war tours under his belt. He grew up in a well-disciplined home with five other siblings. As he got older his family relocated to St. Louis where the author planted his roots and also pursued a military life in the Army Reserves.

Roland married his high school sweetheart and started a family of four. Roland joined the St. Louis police department were his career was cut short when he was convicted of federal crimes due to his childhood affiliation.

After enduring his demise he rebounded becoming a famed a tattoo artist opening *Pearl Gallery Tattoos* in downtown St. Louis Mo. The company grew into a family business yet another unfortunate incident tested his fate. He was diagnosed with Lupus which halted his body art career. However, with tragedy comes blessings. Roland's sons took over the business and propelled the shop to a higher level. Roland consumed with depression began writing to occupy the time. With a newfound passion, he traded visual art for literary art.

LINKS:

Twitter https://twitter.com/reppin_bpent
Website http://www.authorrolandpage.com
Facebook
http://www.facebook.com/RolanSatoPage
Instagram
http://www.instagram.com/thepearl_tattz
YouTube
https://www.youtube.com/watch?v=ZqyiWV
vhSlE